A Dubious Alliance

Jacky Hutchins

Prose Venture Ltd

First edition published in Great Britain by Prose Venture Ltd, 2023

Cover Design by James Hutchins and DALL·E, Human & AI

Prose Venture Ltd
82A James Carter Road
Bury St. Edmunds, Suffolk IP28 7DE
United Kingdom

www.proseventure.com

ISBN: 978-1-7395260-0-9

For my Family

CHAPTER ONE
Portugal 1808

"Heavens! How much longer are we to wait? The sergeant at the gate said he would send for his officer a quarter hour since."

Tossing her muff onto the carriage seat, Antonia Cabral jerked aside the leather blind at the window, to be only slightly mollified by the approach of a tall young man with the red sash of a British officer. "At last. Perhaps now we shall be allowed entrance to the town."

From the seat opposite her elderly companion stretched out to pat her hand. "Don't be too harsh with them, my dear. They only do their duty."

With a smile of tired apology, Antonia sank back on the cushions. She had not intended such an autocratic air but it seemed to her - increasingly over the last few days - that only by doing so had they made any progress at all - And progress they must make. . .

Still, it was a just and timely admonishment. "Indeed, I don't mean to be harsh, cousin," she sighed, "but you know, we have come so far, and been stopped so very often — and now we are to be questioned anew by this young man. I suppose he is what passes for authority in this place."

The carriage door opened as she spoke. The scarlet-coated guard had straightened to a salute, and framed in the opening was the young captain she had just disparaged. He offered one hand to help her down. In his other was a sheaf of papers.

"Senhor Sergio Tavares?" He gave a curt nod as Antonia, gathering the folds of her gown, stepped down without his assistance to the cobbles. "And Senhora Dona Cabral."

She tilted her face to him. "Indeed, sir. Are we to be detained much longer? We have travelled a good many miles today, and are understandably anxious to find accommodation."

The officer frowned. "There may be some difficulty there, Senhora. The town is full, and I doubt your finding suitable lodgings." His glance took in Tavares, the two serving men, and Antonia's abigail. He touched his hat but was still frowning when he turned back to Antonia. "I do not know what brings you to Celerico, ma'am," he said, "but you would have been better advised to remain at home, wherever that might be. If there should be fighting you may find yourselves caught up in it, and the Army needs to move easily along these roads."

"Thank you, Captain," Antonia replied, "we are well aware of the situation. Nevertheless our business is urgent, and we shall be going on to Guarda. As soon," she added, with a lift of her chin, "as we are rested." She noted that his fingers had now begun to drum on his sword hilt, and the sergeant who had earlier halted their progress winced as if in pain.

"I am trying to make plain, ma'am," the officer said, "that you would do better to turn back."

"And I am trying to make plain, sir, that I have reason and authority to go on."

"And that reason is . . . ?"

"None of your business, I believe, Captain. Please instruct your men to let us pass into the town."

She heard the sergeant draw a sharp breath at her tone, but the young officer continued in a low, precise voice: "I am not sure that I recognise your authority, ma'am - but in view of the fact that it is almost dusk you may, if you insist, attempt to find a billet for tonight." He handed back her papers. "And you will kindly see Captain Walter tomorrow before you make arrangements to depart."

"Captain Walter?"

"He has charge of the town's security." The young man paused. "He will also want to know your business before you proceed, so you had better be prepared to speak to *him*."

"I believe I should prefer to speak to your commanding officer . . . " But the officer was already walking away. He jerked his head at the sergeant.

"Let them pass, but bring me word of where they lodge, if you please."

"Sir." The man saluted, and turned to offer Antonia assistance into the carriage, but she was staring after the captain as he strode away, tall and straight, to pass under the arch of the gate. "Ma'am?"

"Who is that gentleman?"

"That would be Captain Hurst, ma'am. Captain Walter's busy with a deputation just now."

"I see." And blinking back swelling tears of frustration and exhaustion, Antonia accepted the soldier's arm as she remounted into the carriage. "Thank you, Sergeant. Go on, Felipe."

The door closed behind her, and the coach jerked away to roll under the arch after the unhelpful officer. In another moment it had overtaken him. He glanced up as it passed, giving Antonia another sight of ice-blue eyes and thick fair hair, and then he was gone, disappearing into the shadows of a doorway, leaving her with the image of a stern profile and a distinct impression of frostiness.

"We have done well to get so far today." Sergio Tavares interrupted her thoughts. "God willing, by this time tomorrow we shall have further news."

He sounded so optimistic that Antonia managed a smile in response. "Indeed we may." The coach had rocked to a halt yet again, this time at the entrance to a shabby hostelry, and as it swayed, creaking in the sudden silence, she added in an undertone: "But what if Duarte cannot be persuaded?" She smudged away a tear with her gloves.

"If you cannot persuade him, my dear, then he cannot *be* persuaded. What is it, Felipe?"

The coachman touched his whip to his hat. "Senhor, the innkeeper here can offer supper and a private parlour while João and Pedro commandeer beds for the night?" - and receiving a nod of assent Felipe jumped down to lower the steps for his passengers, and the bags were thrown from the carriage roof. Antonia exchanged a weary glance with her kinsman.

"Well, we shall at least be spared the jolt of carriage springs for a few hours," she said, and led the way into the inn.

*

From across the square William Hurst watched them from his window. "God help them if that hovel's where they're lodging," he muttered. "The place has the hungriest fleas this side of the border."

The travellers were indeed alighting. The old gentleman was first down, his profile that perfect image of a Portuguese nobleman. Was he the young woman's father? Hurst wondered. And decided he was not. He was reminded briefly of his own sire and, conscious of a sudden heartache, recalled the angry recriminations of their last meeting. Automatically he bent to rub at the scar in his thigh. And now there was Madame. She stood in the road while the bags were tossed down. Hurst guessed at her age: two-and- twenty perhaps? Married? Her title gave no clue. 'Senhora Dona' could mean Miss or Mistress, and a pair of kid gloves and a muff concealed any rings she might be wearing. Hurst's lips tightened. It would seem Dona

Cabral was rather used to having things her own way, he thought. Her bearing was as proud as her companion's, and a firm mouth matched the steady blue gaze she had fixed on him earlier. She was tall too. Her bonnet had all but poked him in the eye, and he stood over six foot in his stockinged feet. Black, her bonnet. Madame Cabral was dressed head to toe in mourning.

Sombre colours suited someone so fair, William mused. And it had been some time since he'd encountered someone both well-bred *and* easy on the eye . . .

He collected himself. *The last thing we need here*, he reminded himself irritably, *is damned civilians clogging up whatever few roads are passable in winter. Common sense ought to keep travellers clear of the frontier when God alone knows what the French will take into their heads to do next . . .*

And he was damned if he liked the manner in which he'd been addressed.

He jerked the shutter across the window. The civilians were none of his business and after tomorrow Celerico would be behind him. He took out his watch and frowned. Four o'clock. He wondered if Frederick Walter had finished his meeting. Well, there was supper to find, and if Walter was still busy, he could wait till morning for news of the civilians. Hurst snapped his watch shut.

Bloody civilians. He threw his half-packed haversacks into the corner and went out.

CHAPTER TWO

Next morning, however, Hurst found himself regretting not having supplied Frederick Walter with exact details of the new arrivals, for much to his surprise and annoyance he had been summoned to attend the interrogation of the Senhora and her companion. Now, from a window embrasure cut deep in the castle walls, he bent to scan the old granite bridge below the castle that took the road out of Celerico towards Guarda –

Which was where, he muttered, *he should be!* That damned sabre slash had been the devil to heal, and he was still not as fit as he might have hoped to be by now. *By God*, he thought, massaging his aching thigh, *Walter takes a lot on himself for someone with only ten months seniority.*

"Captain Hurst tells me your intention is to proceed to Guarda."

"That is our intention, yes." The young woman seemed hesitant. "We understand the reluctance to let us travel further east . . . "

"I do not expect you to travel at all, senhora," Walter snapped. "East or otherwise, unless it be to your home again." It was clear that the interview was trying his patience. Plump and short sighted, the older officer was no fighting man, and recent reports that the French were less than fifty miles away had clearly unsettled him. Hurst was not much amused, however, to hear the Senhora responding to Walter in a rather different tone to that used in *his* conversation the previous evening. "So I ask again," Walter was saying, "what brings you from Coimbra at this time of year?"

"A personal matter."

Hurst turned from the window, wondering what Walter would make of this.

"Yes?" prompted Walter.

"I am," the Senhora said stiffly, "in search of my husband, whom I understand to have joined the Loyal Militia. He may be serving even now with your Army."

"Your *husband*, Senhora?"

She seemed to flinch at Hurst's incredulous query and turned on him with flashing eyes. "My husband, sir. Who is missing from his estate and his home."

Walter quickly intervened, waving a hand to silence Hurst. "For a personal matter, ma'am, I am less inclined to offer assistance. In any case, how do you imagine you will find him?"

"I need not trouble you with details. With your permission, we might leave at once. You need think no more of it."

"My dear young lady, you do not perfectly seem to comprehend the situation. You may travel nowhere without an escort."

From her expression, it seemed the lady had been told this several times already. She drew herself up and fixed Walter with a stare. "Then sir, if you will kindly provide such an escort. . ."

"I cannot spare the men, Senhora. Still less an officer to command them."

"An officer is not necessary. One of your sergeants would do as well."

Hurst turned his back, disgusted. *Damned right a sergeant would do! British sergeants were good enough to be commissioned in Portugal's army . . .*

"I daresay we should not detain anyone above a week." The lady's tone was more conciliatory now. "We had word that my husband may be in Guarda, and if it were not for the threat of the French . . ."

"If it were not for the threat of the French, madam, you should not find us here ourselves." Hurst spun round to face her. "Do you think we serve no purpose here but to assist every wife that comes chasing after an errant husband?"

"Captain Hurst!" Walter's reprimand was sharp, but before the Senhora could respond her companion broke his long silence.

"I should not like to think your efforts are limited to insults, Captain," Tavares interrupted, in heavily accented English. "You are no doubt aware that the gentleman of whom we speak, Alvaro Duarte Felipe Gonçalves Cabral, is the younger son of Dom Luis? Dom Luis of Lisbon and Coimbra? One of the few nobles to remain in Portugal after the departure last year of the Royal Family and the Court?" Hurst and Walter exchanged a frown of incomprehension. "As you must also realise," the old man continued, wheezing now and clearly tired by the effort, "that my young cousin here, Senhora Dona Cabral, has a close connection to your Secretary for War. Her concern for her husband's safety is not unreasonable, I think?"

Again the British officers exchanged a glance. They were unfamiliar with the name of Dom Luis, but that of Lord Castlereagh, Secretary of War, was another matter.

"Cousin, I'm obliged to you," the lady broke in. "But I am sure these officers are gentlemen enough to ensure our anxieties are not left unresolved."

Hurst felt her gaze on him. Narrowing his eyes in response, he stared over her head. The suggestion that she was somehow connected to the statesman influencing the entire war effort only served to sharpen his antagonism - but he noted that the hint was not wasted on Walter, who was now nervously clearing his throat and shuffling papers. Glancing at him, Hurst knew exactly what would happen next. The interference was intolerable.

"Well, you may proceed to Guarda, ma'am," conceded Walter, just as Hurst had predicted, "and you shall have an escort. Mind, I have few men to spare."

"Let alone a *sergeant*," Hurst added, and felt the older officer's glare fall on him yet again as Walter rose and, with a bow, indicated the door.

"If you will wait in the outer office, sir, ma'am," Walter said, "I will see to the necessary orders. Captain Hurst will attend you directly. I shan't keep you long."

Senhor Tavares bowed too. "I am obliged, Captain Walter."

"We are indeed most grateful, sir."

Her thanks seemed wholehearted at least, Hurst acknowledged as the Senhora gave her hand to Walter, but *he* got no more than a cool look as she swept from the room followed more slowly by her kinsman.

The moment the door closed behind them Walter exploded.

"You go too far, Hurst! One of these days your confounded lack of tact is going to land you in hotter water than you can handle."

Hurst stiffened. "I apologise, Walter. I imagined our resources far too thinly stretched for nurse-maiding civilians."

Walter winced. "Well, what else am I to do? If the feller's related to the Court, as the old man says, and the girl to Castlereagh? And Portugal one of Britain's oldest allies? Fine story it'll be if the husband is in difficulties, and it gets known I've refused assistance. You must make an immediate apology."

"Damned if I'll do any such thing. What do you imagine has occurred to take Senhor Cabral from home if he'd join the militia without telling his own wife? She can chase all over Spain for him but she's not likely to get him back. I daresay he knew well enough what he was about when he left home."

"If the French should take him," Walter ventured, "I daresay he would prove a useful hostage."

"We don't know that he's anywhere near the French."

"Well – Well, his wife shall have an escort as far as Guarda at least, and if he is still there, Colonel Ashe can make any further decisions."

Hurst gave an exasperated sigh. "Then whom do you intend to send? Sergeant Logan is not yet fit . . . " He broke off, for Walter's face wore an odd expression.

"Since our visitors are important, I had thought to send an officer with them," Walter said.

"But Sheldon and Martin are on their way south . . . " Hurst felt the stir of disbelief and with it a touch of anger. "You do not intend I should accompany them?"

"As you have just said, man, who else am I to send? Since you are already bound in that direction, it seems only sensible that you should escort them. You have said yourself you are anxious to rejoin your regiment."

"My regiment," Hurst reminded him, "is part of Sir John Hope's force escorting the artillery into Spain, as well you know, by Talavera and the southern route - but yes," he conceded ungraciously, "I am expecting to meet other regimental remnants in Guarda." The main body of British infantry bound for Spain had passed through the area some weeks earlier. *And if I had set out immediately,* Hurst thought, impatiently, *I might have met up with them before they reached Valladolid. That's damned unlikely now.*

"As I say, then, who better to escort our civilians? And before you refuse to do so," he added, for Hurst's expression was mutinous, "you might remember who is senior here. Until you reach Guarda you are nominally under my authority. Perhaps you will learn another time," he went on, taking a seat at the desk, "to mind your tongue. I'll write your orders." He bent his head, then looked up. "You're dismissed, Captain Hurst."

Hurst glared. "Thank you, Captain Walter. I'm obliged," he managed, and snapped a salute that would not have disgraced the Guards before striding to the door, jerking it open, and shutting it with a bang behind him.

*

In the outer office the civilians heard the raised voices if not the angry words. With an uneasy glance at her kinsman, Antonia blinked as the door flashed open and shut and the young captain strode out. On seeing them, he halted, his mouth thin with anger, then took a deep breath, jerked his head in a barely civil nod, and passed out of the further door without a word.

Antonia had not slept well enough to be rested, and it irked her to have been obliged today to divulge what she had refused to explain to the younger officer the previous evening. "I'm afraid that gentleman is much put out at our wish to proceed," she murmured. "I wish I had not been quite so short with him yesterday. He has evidently not forgiven me, and his support would have been helpful. I was very tired, I confess, but he seemed quite as short-tempered as I was myself."

"It was most unlike you to be quite so imperious, my dear, but perhaps there is a reason for his short temper. I notice he is limping." Sergio Tavares gave his young companion a wry smile. "However, since we need the assistance of these officers in order to proceed, we must bear with the young man's temporary displeasure." He patted her mittened hand. "They are here to assist Portugal, and you can take some pride in that. I am bound to say, however," he added, with a shake of his head, "that I take it very ill of your husband to make life so difficult for his family, with New Year upon us and his going off without good reason as far as I can see."

His indignation had winded him. He began to wheeze again, and any protest Antonia might have voiced was stifled. She bent over him. "Let me pull this muffler round. Shall I send for João? It's not right to have kept you waiting so long in this - this great barn of a place." Her glance encompassed the chamber, all too similar to the one they had just quitted in its scanty furnishings, its poor fire and its bleak views. Antonia experienced a sudden brief sympathy for the troops obliged to serve in this ancient northern stronghold. In the warmer southern garrisons there was comfort and gaiety - and in Lisbon, Bonaparte and his generals seemed far away. Here, danger seemed suddenly more immediate and real.

It had been foolish to set out after Duarte, she appreciated that now – but it had been three months since his departure, since he had bent, smiling, from his horse to kiss her and promise a speedy return. Antonia bit her lip. Captain Hurst's astonishingly uncivil comment concerning errant husbands had shocked her. Duarte had not *vanished* . . .

Her thoughts scattered as Captain Walter came through from his room, papers in his fist. He handed over several sheets. "These will ensure safe conduct, and I have orders here for Captain Hurst." He looked them over. "You will be in good hands, I assure you," he promised, but he cleared his throat, and his fingers came up to fidget with his stock. "Captain Hurst may seem a trifle – abrupt, at times, but he is an excellent soldier. You could not be in better hands."

Antonia stared. "Is Captain Hurst to be our escort then? I understood you had no officer to spare?"

She was answered from the doorway.

"There is no officer but myself to spare, madam. Unfortunately. And Captain Walter feels your importance warrants my escort. I am at your service." He swept Antonia a bow but not smoothly enough to conceal a glance that seemed to convey a deal of sarcasm.

What an insolent, humourless creature the man is, Antonia thought, studying him. The bowed head with its crown of thick hair seemed only to emphasise the impression. Cool and straight, with a pale gleam where the light fell on it, his hair was no warm curling gold, but a shade most often matched to colourless brows and lashes – But his were darkly visible as he raised his head again, and Antonia found she was staring now into a narrowed blue stare which he did not alter until she glanced away, flushed and mortified. Oh, she did not think she could bear to have this man escort her to Guarda. She squared her shoulders. "I am sure if the captain has other duties, we would not wish to keep him from them."

And if looks had the power to kill, she thought, *she would surely be dead*, but the officer merely reminded her, curtly, that an escort was required and he was the escort she was getting. His resentment communicated itself well enough; Antonia felt his antagonism an almost tangible barrier between them. If this man persisted in regarding her with such dislike, the journey would be intolerable; having to spar with him all the way was a difficulty they could do without. She must make amends, she thought, and held out her hand. "In that event, I'm greatly obliged to you, Captain Hurst. Thank you for agreeing to accompany us."

He seemed to hesitate before taking her hand, dropping it at once. "Agreeing, ma'am," he began, with a cold glance at Walter, "was not quite the way of it – "

Walter intervened. "You will do well to be advised by Captain Hurst in every respect, ma'am. In return he will do all he can to assist you. You must consider yourselves under his orders, or I cannot be responsible for your safety."

"I understand," Antonia said steadily. "At what hour is the coach to be ready, Captain Hurst?"

The light eyes flared. "Coach?" he echoed. "There will be no coach, Madam. How do you suppose we are to make any progress in a lumbering coach? I understood you to be in some haste."

Shocked, Antonia turned to Walter but it was clear the senior officer would involve himself no further. "You will make better time without a coach, ma'am," he said, "and Captain Hurst is anxious to rejoin his regiment."

"I see." Antonia swallowed. "I suppose it was naïve to imagine that we might – but then how . . . ?"

"Mules, probably." Her escort seemed to relish the words.

"Mules!"

Walter hastily touched hand to hat. "You'll excuse me, ma'am? I have other business to attend," he said, and made good his escape.

"Mules?" Antonia repeated. She turned to see what her companion made of this, but found he had heard little. Sergio Tavares sat white-faced in the chair, eyes closed, one limp hand upon his chest.

"Sergio!" Antonia flew to him, dropping on her knees beside his chair.

The old man's lids fluttered, and he managed a smile as Antonia chafed at his hands. "I'm all right, my dear," he gasped. "Only a little tired."

"Of course you are. I've been so inconsiderate. We must get you to bed, and send for a physician."

"No need, no need," he whispered, but Captain Hurst was at his side.

"I agree with the Senhora, sir," he said brusquely, "and I will assist you, if you will permit?" Gently, he helped the old man to his feet but almost immediately Tavares sagged against him, eyes closed. The captain grasped him. "Open the door, if you please." Antonia hurried to obey, astonished to see her cousin scooped up in strong arms and carried past her out of the room. "Where are your rooms?"

Gesturing, Antonia led the way, her maid and the servants flying after them, out and across the street, to the hostelry where clean beds had finally been found.

"Never mind all these people," the captain snapped, laying the old man gently on his bed. "Your kinsman needs a doctor." He hushed the old man's protests, holding a glass of wine to his blue lips.

"A doctor has been summoned," Antonia promised, relieved to see colour returning to Sergio's ashen cheeks, and his eyes open.

"Your cousin will need a good long rest, I imagine."

Antonia glanced at the officer. She had not imagined him capable of any such humanity.

"But you must go on to Guarda, Antonia," Tavares insisted hoarsely. "Take Pedro and go on with the captain."

"I could not leave you here alone, dear."

"Leave me João and Felipe, and I shall do very well. You must continue, now Guarda is so close."

"I will stay with you."

"When you have quite finished discussing who is to stay and who to go," the captain interrupted with icy calm, "You will perhaps let *me* know whether I am expected to serve as escort under the circumstances?"

Antonia was saved from a reply by the appearance of the physician, who advanced upon his patient with an air of competence, and his arrival evidently persuaded the officer he was no longer required, for when Antonia turned a moment later to thank him for his help he had disappeared.

*

Hurst imagined he was now free to leave. The old gentleman was clearly in no condition to travel, and unlikely to be so for some time, and in spite of his words to her, Hurst had not seriously expected the Senhora would do other than remain in Celerico until such time as her cousin was fit to return South. He imagined he had now heard the last of his escort duty.

He was taken aback therefore to have the girl appear at his side, breathless and distraught, in the few minutes before his departure for Guarda. Attired still in shades of mourning, she wore a travelling dress of charcoal wool under a fur-lined cloak fastened carelessly around her throat and thrown back over her shoulders. Her cheeks were pink from hurrying, and her breath condensed in the cold air. Wisps of fair hair straggled out from the hood of the cloak, and she looked impossibly fragile and helpless.

"Captain Hurst, you cannot be leaving? Our preparations are not yet complete."

"Preparations?"

"To travel. My cousin's ill health has put us at sixes and sevens. My apologies. I know you are anxious to leave, but you must please allow us a little more time."

Hurst's hands dropped from the saddlebags. "You are not seriously intending to continue?"

The eagerness in her eyes seemed to fade. "But of course," she replied. "I'm afraid you don't perfectly understand. I *must* find my husband."

Hurst took a deep breath. "Quite right, ma'am," he began, quietly. "I do not understand. I do not understand how you can leave an elderly relative of whom you appear to be fond, and a gentleman in so obvious need of your attention, to chase after a man who, however much you care for him, is undoubtedly more able to look after himself than your kinsman. A man who feels, furthermore, that his present duty is to his country. I sympathise with your husband, madam. I too desire to serve my country, and you are preventing my doing so." His voice had gradually risen with each word, and the lady took a step backward, but it seemed she was not to be intimidated.

"Do you, or do you not, Captain Hurst, have orders to escort me to Guarda?" she exclaimed, her voice shaking.

For a moment Hurst was unable to answer, and when he did it was through gritted teeth. "I have orders to escort you to Guarda, yes."

"Then if you will wait one further half hour, you may escort me there."

Turning on her heel, she stalked away.

"Senhora," he shouted after her, bringing her to an abrupt halt in the middle of the square.

"What is it?" She would not turn around, but Hurst could tell from her voice that she was furious. He should not have shouted at her in public, but he was not done yet.

"One half hour," he warned. "I shall wait one half hour, and then I shall leave. With you or without you."

"It will be *with* me, Captain Hurst," she retorted, and hurried away.

And half an hour later William Hurst found himself outside his lodgings with the Senhora Dona Cabral, attracting all the attention he would gladly have foregone. With the lady came her maid, Maria Josefina, the manservant, Pedro Teles, and two mules beside, laden with baggage that apparently could not be left behind. Already irritated by the delay, he also found a small crowd gathered to witness the Senhora's efforts to persuade her maid to mount the horse provided but, muttering his dissatisfaction, he was nevertheless conscious of a certain grim pleasure. He had never intended the mules other than as pack animals, but his comment had evidently caused the Senhora some anxious moments. "Senhora Cabral."

He saw her stiffen. "Captain?"

"It appears we are, after all, obliged to spend some time together. I would be grateful if you would bear in mind that this will be no summer picnic." He observed the flicker of anger in her eyes but she said nothing. "So, when you are quite ready?"

He glanced round, noted that a considerable amount of baggage had quickly been abandoned, and nodded, satisfied. He had made his point. "Guarda, then," he said, and climbing into the saddle, urged the mare to a trot.

CHAPTER THREE

Within an hour of their departure a pale sun had struggled through the clouds, and with its appearance Hurst's spirits began to rise. His scar had started to throb, a reminder of the grief the wound had caused, but even this could not depress him. Healthy and almost healed after a lengthy convalescence, he was on his way at last and, God willing, would soon be with friends again.

He had always believed himself generally easy-going and sunny-natured, and though he was conscious that weeks of constant pain and the fear of losing his leg had rather shortened what had once been a sweeter temper, today though, with the sun glinting on the gold embellishments of his scarlet coat, he found he was tempted to smile. What if he *had* been saddled with this escort duty? It was to end at Guarda, no more than twenty miles away on the ridge commanding the valleys of the Mondego and Zezere, and though the climb ahead would be slow, the journey would hardly take much longer than if he were alone.

He eyed his fellow travellers. He had already warmed to the manservant, Pedro, who gave every impression of good sense and good humour. He knew nothing of the maid except her name and that she was, unsurprisingly, no horsewoman. She had said little, had hardly raised her black eyes to him since witnessing the exchange with her mistress outside the inn - and Senhora Cabral too had held her tongue since their departure. William hoped she had learned he would not be disregarded. He studied her now with a horseman's eye as he moved his mare up past the maid. The Senhora had a good seat and light hands, he conceded, and she rode well, better than might be expected of a grand lady who must prefer the comfort of a carriage, but no doubt he would soon hear the first complaints: of the road, the length of the journey, the inadequacies of facilities en route . . .

To the Devil with them all! His involvement ended at Guarda, though he doubted the Senhora would find her husband there. Any of the Portuguese serving with the British would almost certainly have crossed into Spain weeks before, and those with the Royal Lusitanians, he understood to be further northwest. Hurst shook his head. Why waste time in speculating? It was hard enough to comprehend how any woman could harry a man set on serving his country, and expect him to return home . . .

He had been glad enough to escape his own home. From early childhood he had wanted nothing but the life of a soldier – only to find his father completely set against it. It was the clear duty of his only son, Sir John said, to concern himself with the Bartonhurst estate; to marry and raise heirs, not to risk life and limb in foreign lands. And as a result, relations between them had come perilously close to severance . . . William might never have got away if it had not been for the intervention of his aunt who financed the purchase of her nephew's commission.

His aunt was nothing like his mother, William remembered, and was probably the only woman for whom he had any real affection and respect . . . Women in general, it seemed to him, were nothing but trouble, and especially so for the army. If not trailing the troops in the raggle-taggle horde of wives and camp followers, they were, in William's experience, likely to be ladies of doubtful virtue, who found excitement in bright uniforms and were all too ready to help a young officer spend his pay. And though they might keep far enough off to avoid the sickening sights and sounds of war, they were eager enough to watch from a distance. He had even known them try to outdo each other to ensure their carriages were best placed to view a battle . . .

Ugh! Hurst dug his spurs into his mare and moved up to head the small party east across the northern slopes of the Serra da Estrela.

*

The journey was uneventful for some hours, and he was still in thoughtful mood when he signalled a halt in the lee of a ruin that might once have been a farm, sited by a rocky stream and surrounded by olive trees. By now the sun had hidden itself and there was a chill in the air, but one of the panniers strapped to the mule was, William knew, well stocked with food and drink. With the long climb ahead, it seemed only right to lighten the load. When the baskets were unpacked however, he could only stare at what came out of them. Not only food. There was a feast there, to be sure: an abundance of cold fowl, smoked pork, ewe's milk cheese, breads, and fruits, ham, slivers of dried salt cod, little cakes, bottles of wine in straw-lined boxes . . . He observed the accompanying ceremony in mounting disbelief. A fine cloth was spread, silverware laid out, glasses unwrapped, delicate china displayed . . .

It seemed the Senhora did not, however, mean to feast alone. She heaped plates of food for the servants, who took them away to sit upon nearby rocks. She looked up at Hurst, indicating the banquet. Her hands were gloveless now, and he saw that she wore no more than a single ring on her slender fingers, a plain gold band.

"Are you not hungry, Captain Hurst?"

William thought of the coarse bread, and cheese and sausage in his saddlebag. "Share your food, Senhora?" he asked. "Are you quite sure you have enough?"

She glanced up at him, but he had made his face a study of innocence.

"I would be very glad if you would share what we have," she said. "My cousin ordered this vast quantity. I'm afraid it has taken up a good deal of space."

"Almost as much as the linen and crystal," he agreed, biting into some cold pork. He glanced down to find her frowning at the ground between her elegantly booted feet. He frowned too, aware that it was unlike him to be quite so determinedly boorish. "It was a kind offer," he conceded, and she jerked up her head with what seemed to be a blink of surprise and suspicion before lowering her gaze without replying. "You're not eating, Senhora? I commend the smoked fillet." She shook her head, and Hurst was horrified to see the large blue eyes had filled with tears.

Tears! he observed bitterly – a favoured weapon with his mother, with that ability to make him guilty and uncomfortable whether or not he was at fault. His incivility had been undeserved and unwarranted certainly, but surely no cause for tears. Still chewing, he retreated, glancing back over his shoulder. She was still looking out over the valley but had not, so far, given way to a full flood. By God, William thought, you never knew what a woman would do next. Yesterday she would have bitten off his head for his comments; yet today it was tears . . .

A sudden screech from the maid, a shout, the crash of shattered china, pandemonium from the mules whirled Hurst round from his reverie, and he flung away what was left of his meal. The maid was scrambling into the rocks; the mules were bucketing around on their tethers; Pedro was running about in circles, frantically shaking his jacket and shouting at the top of his voice, and overlaying every other sound was a fierce squealing. Lord! Hurst observed, trying not to grin. Wild pigs, a whole tribe, were milling out from under the trees as if they intended a share in the picnic. They had trampled the fine cloth underfoot, smashed china and glassware, flattened what was left of the picnic. It would be comic were it not equally dangerous. Behind the gnarled trunk of a small olive-tree, twenty yards off to his left, the Senhora stood very still, very white, with the hem of her gown muddied and torn, while immediately in front of her danced a large boar on tiny feet, grunting as it rooted at her discarded cloak, its wicked tusks ripping at the fur-lined fabric.

Recognising it for a futile gesture Hurst drew his sword. He did not know whether the lady could not or dared not move, but he could, and did. He sprinted for the pistols in his saddle holster as Pedro came roaring back across the hillside, and the boar raised its head to examine this new threat. It was the target William wanted and his shot dropped it where it stood.

A hurried survey showed no further threat. The discharge of the pistol and Pedro's shouts had dispersed the remaining pigs, and they were scurrying back through the olive grove. He let his arm drop. He would suffer later no doubt for his intemperate haste. He limped across to the Senhora. "Are you hurt?"

*

Antonia Cabral had never been so frightened. Her blood ran like ice; she was shivering and felt sick, but she was not hurt.

"No, Captain, I am not hurt." How steady her voice sounded to her ears. She looked down at the boar. The captain's shot had felled the brute just in time. She had distracted it briefly by tossing her cloak over its head, but it had shaken free before she could run. Its little red eyes had half-hypnotised her, and her legs had turned to water.

She watched, sickened, as the officer pushed the beast off the trampled cloak. The garment was shredded, matted with blood and hair. Pedro ran up to help. He had been first to flee, and his face was creased with guilt and anxiety.

"Lady, are you hurt?"

"I am not hurt, Pedro."

"Your cloak is beyond repair, I think." The captain was holding it at arm's length.

"It's ruined," she agreed, and was aware that he eyed her oddly as he said,

"I hope you will accept the use of mine. Can you walk to the horses?"

"Of course."

"Will you take my arm?"

Shaking her head, Antonia walked stiffly to where the horses were tethered. His steady arm would have been welcome, but she would not have the captain think her weak; his opinion of her was quite low enough. If she'd been more alert, she told herself, and not so deep in gloom, she might have reacted more quickly when the pigs appeared. At least no one had been injured.

Antonia bit her lip. Perhaps she should not have considered continuing this search, when there was still so far to go, and when the hills ahead were so high and so bleak, and when it was more than likely that there would be no news of Duarte when they arrived at Guarda. He would have moved on and was now where she would never reach him. The officers had been right . . .

But this Captain Hurst was the coolest, the most unsympathetic, the most uncivil individual she'd yet had the misfortune to meet. Antonia wished he had choked on the pork he had accepted so ungraciously.

The pig however had choked on him.

Surprising herself at finding any humour in the situation Antonia stooped to hide a weak smile in the horse's flank, and then drawing a deep breath she put her foot into the stirrup and mounted, her chin high.

Below her, Pedro and Maria Josefina were salvaging what they could. Her maid worked in fits and starts, exclaiming over the chaos, glancing over her shoulder every few minutes in case the pigs returned. Nearby, the captain had unfastened his cape from its saddle roll. He brought it to Antonia.

"It compares poorly with your own, but it may serve," he said. He turned to indicate the dark clouds that now rested on the rounded peaks above them. "It seems we shall have a soaking."

Antonia studied him. That was a good shot, she knew, to drop the boar like that. What a provoking character the man was. He was evidently well used to taking charge. A strong face, a strong profile, blonde stubble just showing in the jaw line, his hair very fair, lighter than hers, but dark brows, dark lashes. What, Antonia wondered, had drawn those fine lines beneath the ice blue eyes?

"Are you going to be much longer?" he shouted suddenly at the servants, and Antonia started.

"Pedro! Josefina! Leave everything not already packed. Captain Hurst thinks we have brought too much already." She turned to find him frowning. "This is, after all, no summer picnic, Captain," she reminded him, and slapping her horse with her reins, she cantered away up the road, leaving him to stare after her.

CHAPTER FOUR

The sun that had shone so encouragingly in the morning now hid itself behind wintry clouds scudding across the empty hills. There was snow already on the highest peaks but the travellers were, as yet, far below the Torre, and even Guarda, the highest town in Portugal and distinguished for its cold situation, lay some hours before them.

Snow did not come. Rain did, an icy wetness, blown in gusts that found its way into every seam. Having offered his cloak to the Senhora, Hurst declined its return and was now chilled, wet, and miserable. Rain dripped off his shako, ran down his neck and under his collar, oozed down his tunic and into his boots. He smudged an elbow over his face, consoled only by the knowledge that the lady could be no drier. The entire party was soaked through, the maid looking the most wretched of all, a tiny figure hunched on her horse. Hurst thought it unlikely she cared very much for the fate of her lady's husband. No doubt, just like him, she would have chosen to be elsewhere.

Anywhere but here, he thought.

He might, had he been alone, have plodded on in spite of the appalling conditions, but he was convinced that at any moment the Senhora would demand a halt and complain of his inhumanity in forcing them on. She did not do so however, and eventually even Hurst, with thigh aching, had had enough. In the rain-misted distance he had seen the outline of a small village. Holding back his mare until the Senhora came up, he gestured in the direction.

"There," he said, screwing up his face against the rain. "We'll make a stop there."

She turned to look. Raindrops slid down her face and, under the hood of the cloak and the ruin of the silk bonnet, her fair curls were draggled and misted with moisture. Her appearance should have been laughable yet there was something about her - and Hurst was not tempted to laugh. Soaked to the skin or not, she was still quite lovely. And her husband had deserted her?

"Where are we?" She raised her voice slightly to be heard.

"Other than 'on our way' I've not the least idea. And if I had a map, which I do not, I would perhaps be foolish to study it in this weather." Maps were useless anyway - roads indicated where there were none, towns left off entirely.

"Not Guarda then?"

"Lord, no. That's up there." He pointed into the cloud-covered heights. The Senhora turned to stare where he pointed, her dismay evident. She was not the only one depressed by their lack of progress, Hurst thought. He had hoped to reach Guarda by nightfall, and it was still miles away. They were all going to be disappointed.

The afternoon was almost over as the travellers trudged up the village street. There was only one miserable tavern, and on seeing the officer and his companions its hostess protested she had no accommodation for such fine company. Eyeing the interior, William could only agree, but with the rain still teeming down and a tantalising aroma rising from a pot bubbling on the hearth, nothing now would induce him to shift, and he took off his hat and tunic and shook them, making the fire spit and steam. The Senhora had followed him in and was looking around her with curious eyes, wrinkling her nose at the smell and the smoke that clouded the low-ceilinged room. William limped across to her.

"It's very plain here. Basic. Not what you're used to at all," he told her. "Give me your cloak if you please, and I'll have the woman dry it before we set out again. I daresay we can get a meal. And very likely a bed too."

Antonia raised doubtful eyes as she took off the cloak and untied her limp bonnet. She had never been in so poor a dwelling, and felt some anxiety at spending any time in its shabby rooms, let alone a night in whatever doubtful bed was allotted her. Sergio would be horror struck to see her in this squalid lodging, and it was clear the Captain expected some protest, for hands on hips he was regarding her with tight-lipped impatience. Dye from his tunic had streaked his shirt scarlet wherever his waistcoat had not protected it. "Your shirt is quite ruined, Captain," she observed, handing him the cloak and bonnet.

"Never mind my shirt." He glanced down at it. "Will you stop here or not?"

Antonia raised an eyebrow. "Did you not just inform me that we might have a meal here and a bed?"

"That was not to say that you would agree to it."

"Oh?" She walked across to the fire. "I understood by your tone that the choice was not mine to make."

There was a moment's silence. "Quite right," he said, and turned away to speak to the tavern keeper's wife.

Pedro and Josefina had come in behind her, and after a rapid exchange of words, they hung their outer garments to dry, and disappeared into a back room. Tempted, like the officer, by the contents of the cauldron, Antonia gave the pot a stir and listened to the Captain speaking to their hostess, his voice surprisingly deep and resonant.

He spoke Portuguese well for an Englishman, she realised. Many of his rank and station did not trouble to learn more than a few words and phrases: enough to get their needs satisfied in haste. The officer's vocabulary seemed extensive, and he had an ear for the pronunciation. It was not so difficult to learn Portuguese, Antonia knew, with a background of Latin and French such as any gentleman might have, but she was impressed all the same by his competence, and by the service he had managed to coax from these simple folk; she had heard these villages near the border were intolerant of foreigners in any guise. Portugal had just been liberated from the French, but now it was the British taking all the decisions affecting the country, and many Portuguese felt forced into a situation of Britain's making. Many too were convinced that, ultimately, they would be betrayed and abandoned. It seemed a dubious alliance - yet there were cheerful smiles all round as a table was prepared for their meal, and Antonia wondered how handsomely the officer had had to pay for such service; bribes were a soldier's usual answer. Head tilted, she regarded him. His hair was slick with rain; the blonde straight locks smoothed gleaming back from his face, raindrops clinging to his brow. She'd had his cloak, and now, she thought guiltily, he was soaked through. Well, she'd offered to return it.

He turned, and seemed surprised to find her examining him. His expression, animated and businesslike only a moment before, was now guarded and shuttered.

"If you have drier garments," he suggested, "you might consider changing into them. I will have what you are wearing dried. I understand accommodation is being prepared. You won't object, I hope, to sharing a room with your maid?"

"Thank you for your concern, Captain Hurst," Antonia said. "Josefina and I have often shared accommodation. Where shall you sleep?"

"Here." He shrugged. "Pedro and I are not so particular that we expect a bed. Shall you change before we eat? I would advise it."

Antonia inclined her head. "Then I shall change at once." She went to the kitchen door for directions.

To William's astonishment, she returned shortly afterwards in a gown of black silk, high waisted, long sleeved and trimmed with velvet ribbon - and in the extravagance of tiny tucks and pleats he recognised an expensive creation, and whistled under his breath. The Senhora evidently had the services of a fine dressmaker and money to pay her. Did she wear black, he wondered wryly, in the expectation of finding herself a widow, or because she knew how well it suited her? He cleared his throat.

"I trust the meal will do justice to your gown, Senhora, but frankly, I doubt it."

She frowned as if she guessed the comment was more criticism than compliment but before she could respond, their host, trailed by Josefina and Pedro, was hurrying in with earthenware platters. His wife bustled after them armed with a huge ladle and a loaf of new bread, and everything else was forgotten as they settled at benches round the rough scrubbed table and heaped plates with the stew. For some time after that there was no sound but the soft crunch of bread and the scrape of spoons on the bottom of bowls, followed in due course by sighs of satisfaction.

William spoke for them all when he finally laid down his spoon. "That was very good."

Their hostess beamed. Beans, she told him, with potato, and a little pork knuckle. It was all she could offer. Had their honours satisfied their hunger? Would they care for more?

William glanced round the table, and shook his head, aware that the pot had still to feed their hosts. He smiled at the cook. *"Bastante, Muito obrigado."*

"De nada!" All smiles, the woman curtsied, cleared the table, and disappeared with the servants into the back room.

"You speak Portuguese very well, sir," the Senhora commented. "How have you come to do so?"

William paused in the act of extracting a small, battered silver case from a pocket. "I had good opportunity after Roliça to do so, ma'am. A period of - inactivity and - confinement led me to learn something useful." He held out the case. "May I smoke?"

She nodded. "Roliça? There was a skirmish, some months ago . . . ?"

He eyed her. She had heard of the British forces' first attempt to drive the French from her native land. He lit a cigarillo, inhaled, and blew a cloud of bluish smoke at the low ceiling.

"Were you at Roliça, Captain?"

"Unfortunately." His hand strayed involuntarily to his thigh.

"And wounded," she said. "I suppose that is how you come to be separated from your regiment."

He nodded, but had no desire to dwell on the incident. "You speak *English* very well, Senhora. How have *you* come to do so?"

Her blue eyes opened wide. "But I am English!" she said. "Did you not know?"

William blinked. He had assumed from the first that Dona Cabral was Portuguese. He drew again on the cigarillo, and exhaled before answering. "Naturally not, or I should not have asked - but then how does an Englishwoman come to be in Portugal in the middle of a war?" Another foolish question. She had married into a Portuguese family. He already knew that.   But it seemed she was ready to answer him.

"I was with my husband's family last year when the Court left for Brazil to escape the French," she replied. "We were unable to sail with them, and therefore obliged to remain behind."

"That *was* unfortunate."

"It was. My mother-in-law had taken a fever, and just as she recovered, I fell ill. We hardly dared stir." She shrugged. "However, by remaining in seclusion we were lucky enough not to suffer too much from the French. Apart from being obliged to pay their taxes, that is. They were fearsome enough."

It was the longest speech William had ever heard her make, but he was now feeling a fool for having entertained the notion that somewhere in her Portuguese heritage there had been northern blood. Considering her complexion and colouring, it must be obvious to anyone that the Senhora was not native born.

"So - you have - lived in Portugal for some time now?" he managed.

"Something over a year."

"Only that?" He made an effort to sympathise. "I daresay you would prefer just now to be in England with your own family?"

He was taken aback when she responded almost sharply. "Not at all, Captain, the Cabrals treat me as their own. How close are you to your own kin?"

"I am not a woman, Senhora," William returned, "and a soldier does not expect to see much of his family." Even to his ears he sounded disapproving.

"Do you tell me, sir?"

He should have been warned by the clipped response that the Senhora did not care for his tone nor his remarks, but he persisted. "Surely your husband's family would have done better to send some male relative after him, rather than exposing you to danger?"

"I cannot see that it is any concern of yours, Captain. Obliged though I am to you for it."

William ground the cigar stub out in a series of fierce jabs. "I cannot believe," he insisted, "that you think it right to continue to pursue your husband in this way, when he apparently feels it his duty to serve his country."

She drew a quick breath. "I suggest you kindly mind your own business, sir. You know nothing of the situation."

"And I suggest you can know nothing about men, madam."

Her face flamed. Her hand flashed out, but William saw it coming, and forestalled her by catching her wrist. "I would *not* advise that," he warned in an intense murmur. "I do however apologise for my interest in your affairs. You are quite right, and I should mind my own business." He dropped her hand.

Glaring at him, she rubbed furiously at her wrist. "How dare you insult me in this fashion. I am sure your commander cannot begin to know what kind of officer he sees fit to send as escort."

He glared back, angry at the unspoken threat but even angrier at his own lack of civility and common sense. What was it about this young woman that made him behave as if he had been born in a barn? He rubbed at his temple, on the verge of making an apology, but she had turned away.

"Good*night*, sir!" he heard her say, and without waiting for a response, she disappeared into the darkness.

"Goodnight, *minha Senhora!*" William muttered automatically, adding in an even lower tone: "And I hope to God you wake up sweeter tempered in the morning."

"As I do you!" he heard from the darkness at the top of the steps.

*

In the candlelit space under the sloping roof, Antonia sat on the edge of a rough cot and stared at the door. She was trembling from her outburst and rubbed again at the marks on her wrist, half-frightened, half-maddened by the cavalier treatment meted out to her. No man had ever laid hands on her in anger. Captain Hurst was a barbarian! He was supposed to be a British officer! A gentleman! Duarte would defend her honour. He would be outraged to hear how this man had behaved. Duarte could never have done what this - this *wretched* officer had done! And she had been attempting some gesture of civility, some friendly overture to smoothe over their past misunderstandings. Antonia lifted her wrist to her mouth to soothe the smart from the captain's iron grip. She could still feel the circle of his fingers around her. Lord, he was strong! She would be in no hurry to cross him again however much he deserved it. He was not to know though, that the last place she would ever wish to be was in England again with her father. She had only managed to achieve some kind of independence from him through her marriage, and she had no wish to return.

'Nonetheless, the wretch is right,' she told herself, and for a brief moment felt almost crushed with longing for her husband. 'I should not have begun this pursuit.' She buried her face in the coarse blanket. "Oh, Duarte, why did you leave?" she whispered, her voice muffled by the pillow. "Why did you leave us with barely a word?"

Lengthy self-pity, however, had never been one of Antonia's faults. Very soon she sat up, dried her tears and telling herself that it was no help to give way to despair, she struggled out of the black silk to hang it carefully on a nail in the rafters. She frowned as she smoothed her fingers over the gown. The captain seemed determined to find fault with everything apparently, even finding it necessary to criticise her clothes. The truth was, she thought, shaking out the black skirt, that it *was* a fine gown, and she had not intended to wear it until the reunion with her husband, but after all, at the officer's own prompting, she had brought little enough else to wear. . . She lay down once more, pulled the blanket across her, and glanced around the shadowed, ramshackle room. How different everything was from what she had imagined when she had set out all those weeks before, she thought. And there was not much hope of a better tomorrow.

She propped herself on her elbow to blow out the candle beside her bed, sank back and let her eyelids droop. She must sleep. She was desperate to sleep.

But when Josefina crept in much later, her mistress was lying pensive and still awake.

*

On the floor below, William Hurst was also awake and, staring into the embers of the dying fire, he was thinking of Antonia Cabral.

It seemed barely credible that this girl should travel the length of Portugal to beg her man to return from defending his homeland. William was sure the Senhora was not so helpless she could not cope without her husband. She might be wealthy, and beautiful, but William did not believe she was helpless - and he wondered what the real reason was for the husband's disappearance and her efforts to find him. However, the glowing coals held no clue to such vague speculation and eventually he closed his eyes and with a sigh rolled over to sleep.

With a disposition like the Senhora's perhaps it was not so very surprising that Cabral had disappeared without warning and could not be found.

CHAPTER FIVE

Overnight the rain had ceased, but with the wind the temperature had dropped, and a rim of ice whitened the puddles on the road. The Senhora insisted however on returning Hurst's cloak, so Pedro shrugged, pressed his own into service for his mistress, exchanged a few coins with their host and obtained a replacement.

The sun did not shine for William Hurst. He should have been cheered by the thought that he would soon reach his own destination, but he felt morose and uncommunicative. With the Senhora showing a similar disinclination to speak, their communication was limited to cool nods, and they were on their way as soon as they had breakfasted. Only Pedro was cheerful enough to attempt a tuneless whistle as they went along, and they slowly climbed the ridge by a series of bends that took them higher and higher, through the bare trees and rock-strewn pastures. They passed no one on the road but a shepherd boy with the very last of his woolly flock on their way down to the valleys, and by then even Pedro had given up his tune.

A clatter of stones on the path ahead; no more than a shower of pebbles and earth; a low rumble that grew in intensity - and a small boulder bounced across the road, and flew into the valley below, followed swiftly by two or three more.

"Rock fall!" William wrenched at the mules, but he'd shouted in English. Only the Senhora seemed to grasp the situation. She grabbed at the nearest bridle, but Josefina was still urging her horse forward. Stones and rocks began to crash around them. Josefina panicked. Her horse reared. She screamed, trying to cling on. Her mistress kneed her own horse closer, but Josefina was beyond reasoning or reassurance. Terrified, she let the reins drop, and clapping her hands to her mouth, swayed crazily from side to side in the saddle. Before she could tumble, William was there. He reached out, grabbed her round the waist, and swung her across to his own mount as Josefina's horse bolted down the mountain road, leaving the maid wailing with fright. The fall of rocks gradually tailed away, leaving the path strewn with stones and boulders and the air full of dust.

The whole incident had lasted no more than a minute.

"Hush, Josefina, hush, we're safe now." Antonia, quite as shaken as her maid, tried to soothe the girl, who despite finding security in the Captain's encircling arms was making her misery all too obvious. "No one is hurt after all, you see. It's only the horse that is gone, and he appears to be in no danger now. Dry your tears. The path is still clear, and we shall be in Guarda directly where you shall be comfortable again."

But Josefina was not to be soothed. She had never liked this journey, she wailed, ever since they had left Viseu, and she wished she had not asked to come with the Senhora all the way from Lisbon. And she wept and complained until it seemed the Captain could take no more. He thrust the mules' reins into Pedro's hands.

"Come now, miss," he said firmly, in the maid's own tongue, "this is an unpleasant venture, but we shall be in Guarda shortly, and the Senhora has promised you shall be made comfortable. Meantime I have you safe before me, so sit still, there's a good girl, and let's have no more tears." Josefina sniffed and sobbed a little longer but did as she was bid. "That's better," he said, jogging his mare into a walk, and the maid looked up into his face with a watery smile, and nestled comfortably against him.

Antonia was astonished at the girl's altered manner, but it seemed to afford Pedro some amusement, and the Captain gave him a tight smile.

"Don't laugh so hard, my friend," he warned. "Bad luck seems to favour our company, and the next casualty may be you."

*

There were no more incidents however, and Guarda loomed ever closer, its grey granite cathedral dominating the town like a fortress above the town walls and high gates. There was a steep climb as they came up from the west but the stupendous views were behind them, and the valleys were indistinct in the mist that had lingered on into the forenoon.

William had no fancy to ride into a town full of troops with a girl on his saddle and swung Josefina to the ground. "Go to Pedro. He'll carry you now."

Rather sulkily the maid obeyed, but her mistress sat unmoving, head bowed. For a moment William imagined she was making an act of thanksgiving for their safe arrival, but as he came up he saw she was shivering. The rock fall, he realised, would doubtless have shocked her almost as much as her giddy maidservant, and there had been that unpleasantness of the previous evening. Perhaps she had not slept well, and it had been a trying day.

"Are you unwell, Senhora?"

"No."

William was disturbed to see that she swayed as she straightened in the saddle. Her face was ashen. "Can you continue?" He frowned. "We are almost there."

She seemed almost to force herself upright. "I know." She kicked her heels, and her horse walked on. William moved alongside her. He glanced at her uneasily.

"I am under orders as soon as we arrive," he reminded her, "to report with you to Colonel Ashe. You may then, with his permission of course, make whatever arrangements you wish for accommodation."

She nodded, curtly. She was still very pale.

"Are you sure . . . Let me assist - " He was reaching for her reins when to his astonishment they were jerked out of his hands. The Senhora had touched heels to her horse, and William was left in the road outside the old gateway of the Porta da Rei. Tight lipped, he sat staring after her, and then with an oath he slapped his reins on the mare's rump and followed.

He was simmering by the time they were shown into the chamber where they were asked to wait, and they sat in tense and total silence while a clock on the mantelshelf solemnly ticked away the minutes. Finally, a young lieutenant with his arm in a sling came out of an inner office to invite the lady's attendance.

The moment she had disappeared William sprang up, to limp to and fro until the gentleman in the room below came up to complain about the noise and was sent away with a flea in his ear. William was in no doubt that Colonel Ashe would be hearing a litany of complaints. Each detail of every impolite speech he had uttered, every unfortunate example of his behaviour, not to mention the Senhora's opinion of his complete unsuitability for his post, all these would already have been rehearsed and trotted out. No doubt Senhora Cabral had already hinted at her kinship to Castlereagh, and her husband's relationship to whomever, and was blinking those extraordinary blue eyes at the Colonel! William sat down again on the hard wooden chair and glowered into the middle distance, his right hand moving impatiently on his thigh. He was not sure how long he did sit there, waiting to be called or dismissed, but at length the door opened and the lieutenant came out and shut the door behind him.

"This way, sir." The young lieutenant smiled, and to William's surprise indicated a second door opening into another room, where he was further surprised to find his erstwhile commander. A big man, with a shock of white hair and cheeks veined with red, Bertram Ashe towered over his desk as he got his feet, and acknowledged William's salute. He leaned towards him, hand outstretched. "How are you, lad? How's the leg?" He shook William's hand vigorously.

"Well, sir, thank you," William lied and cast an uncertain glance towards the young lieutenant. "I'm hoping to rejoin the regiment as soon as I can."

"Of course." Seating himself on the desktop. Ashe indicated a nearby chair, and as William took a seat, the Colonel leaned forward. "Now then, sir," he growled. "What's all this? I find you've brought company with you." He straightened to study William from under thick white brows. "So, what have you got to tell me about the lady?"

William blinked. "Might I first enquire, sir, where exactly Dona Cabral might be at present?"

Ashe jerked his chin. "In the anteroom."

William took a breath and squared his shoulders. "My orders were to accompany the lady here from Celerico, sir."

"And you were told why she wanted to make this journey?"

William swallowed. Here came the bawling out, much as he had anticipated. "The Senhora appears to believe her husband must be with our Army or the Loyal Militia attached," he replied, "and for some reason she is anxious that he should return home with her. I believe she expects to find him here."

"You're acquainted with the lady's husband?"

"Not at all, sir." William blinked again. "I believe his name is Alvaro Cabral. I'm told he is the younger son of Dom Luis Cabral of Lisbon."

"Is he?"

William frowned. "Is there some suspicion that this is not so?" He turned to the lieutenant, but the younger officer merely shrugged.

"This is his portrait." Ashe held out an oval case, some five inches high and fashioned from mother-of-pearl. William opened it to find, inside the brown-velvet-lined case, a miniature portrait, beautifully detailed. He looked towards the door. "I have it from her hand," Ashe explained.

William studied the miniature: a head and shoulders study of a young man, dark, handsome with a poised, easy air. Senhor Cabral had a wealth of dark brown hair. His face was long, with a firm chin, clean-shaven, olive skinned. Brown eyes looked out from under dark eyebrows drawn in the faintest of frowns, and the full mouth was slightly pursed giving the impression that the sitter knew he honoured the portraitist in sitting for the study. William raised an eyebrow. A good-looking man, Alvaro Duarte Cabral. A foil for the fair beauty of his wife.

"You've not seen this? The lady has not shewn it to you?"

"She has not, sir." William hesitated. "It is doubtful the Senhora would have done so. She and I have not been on the - warmest of terms."

Ashe smiled faintly. "Oh?"

"My fault, I daresay," William admitted. "I expressed certain views - perhaps a trifle tactlessly. I felt, I *do* feel very strongly, that here, near to the frontier, civilians ought positively to be discouraged from making unnecessary journeys - and I - I believe I acquainted the Senhora with those views."

"Oh?" repeated the Colonel.

"Frankly, sir, it seems to me," William went on, "this search serves no useful purpose. The husband joins the army, the wife thinks he should stay at home." He frowned. "Senhora Cabral should be proud that her husband's conscience provokes him to serve his country. Few feel the same. Most think they can leave the fighting to the British.

"Come through, William. You don't seem to have heard the whole story. You can tell me what you think," Ashe murmured, "but privately, later." He nodded at the lieutenant, who left the room, and the two officers walked into the adjoining chamber where the Colonel seated himself behind a table, leaving William, even more confused, to take up a position by the fireplace.

CHAPTER SIX

"I do know some part of the story, sir," William confessed as they waited. "You're of course aware that the lady has some connection with our own Secretary for War?"

When Ashe nodded, William sighed, but almost immediately the senior officer added, "Her father came over in '06, you know: Henry Davenport, part of the British mission, with Admiral Lord St Vincent. Apparently, he met the Cabrals at Court and was sufficiently impressed to invite the sons to England on his return home. The younger Miss Davenport – Dona Antonia there – was said to have been swept off her feet by the younger son. You can see why," he added dryly, gesturing at the portrait. "They married, and she came back with him to Lisbon. Daresay she wishes they had stayed in England now."

"Then the gentleman is who he says is. Or rather," William corrected himself, "who the lady says he is."

"He may be *who* she says he is, but perhaps not *what* she says he is," said Ashe mysteriously, but just then the outer door opened, Antonia Cabral was ushered through, and the door closed behind her. She seemed startled to see William but said nothing and took the seat offered. He was not surprised to see she had been weeping; tears would doubtless have been produced for Ashe's benefit. Rank and fortune, he thought sourly, are probably enough as a rule to get her what she wants. I suppose she imagined a hint to Ashe would produce this husband and has just learned it can't be done.

"Dona Antonia," Ashe was saying, "Would you repeat what you have just told me?" She seemed to hesitate, glancing up at Hurst. "It would certainly help *me* to hear your story again, so that we may decide the best course of action." Ashe's tone was persuasive, and after a moment during which the girl struggled visibly to compose herself, she began.

"Several months ago, my husband - he is the Cabral's younger son - began to feel someone should check on the estates in the north. The Cabrals own a considerable amount of land near Coimbra, and the French had of course been recently in occupation.

"My father-in-law, Dom Luis, eventually agreed, so it was settled that Duarte – that my husband should make the journey, see what damage had been done, and take any necessary steps to put the estate in order." Her hands which had been lying in her lap, twisted now in the silken scarf she carried. "My husband sent word that he had arrived. And then – then Emilio met with a terrible accident."

William looked at Ashe, mouthing, 'Emilio?'

"The eldest brother," the Colonel murmured, gesturing apologetically for Dona Cabral to continue.

"Yes, the brother. There is one sister, Beatriz." She swallowed. "But Emilio was always the favourite. A daring horseman, renowned even, but – perhaps he was overconfident - he put his horse at a wall – everyone told him - but he just laughed, and – "She shrugged, helplessly. "He broke his neck, and the horse was shot. Naturally. My husband's family was devastated, of course, stricken with grief. We realised my husband must come home, and he was sent for. But as you will be aware communications have been notoriously unreliable ever since the French were driven out. There was no reply, and he did not come. So it was decided he must be fetched."

"*You* were to fetch him? That seems unreasonable. A male member of the family, a servant even, might go."

"It was my decision. I could not let such news be broken by a mere servant. I felt one of the family must tell him. Dona Beatriz' husband, Senhor da Fonte, is crippled, and could not be expected to travel such a distance." She looked at William then. "Senhor Tavares - to whom you were so kind - is uncle to Senhor da Fonte, and since we expected to find my husband in Coimbra, and Senhor Tavares was returning there, it seemed a good plan that he should accompany me."

William was still puzzled. "So you found your husband in Coimbra, but he would not return with you?"

She sank back in her chair. "He was not in Coimbra. The servants said he had left for Viseu before Christmas and they'd no further news of him. We assumed he must be on his way home, but – but when we got to Viseu ourselves, we discovered that – that he apparently intended joining the Militia. He does not yet know of his brother's death, and you cannot imagine how badly he is needed at home." She brushed a hand across her forehead. "Dona Isabel is - Well, Emilio was her darling - but Dom Luis…." The quiet voice paused as if to steady itself. "It has aged my father-in-law beyond recognition. The simplest decisions seem beyond him. I can depend on you, I hope," she added, her voice low, "to ensure that what I have told you goes no further. There are some who envy the Cabrals and might use this news to their advantage."

"It does not however explain, ma'am, how you came to be in Celerico," William observed. She glanced at him, and her chin came up.

"We need my husband at home. I know if I can reach him and explain how much he is needed, he would return with me. It would seem he is following the army, but no one can tell us where he is serving. In Viseu we were told someone in Guarda would know. I believe there are not so many gentlemen of my husband's quality and rank in the Portuguese forces that he should remain unknown."

A flicker of something William did not quite understand unsettled him. He could understand Cabral wanting to serve his country, but what would have persuaded the man to leave his beautiful young wife without warning when they had not been married so very long? He had no great regard, personally, for the married state, recalling with some distaste his own parents' marriage; love had played no part in that, nor did it appear to have strengthened the union between Dona Antonia and her handsome nobleman. Nor had it apparently been enough to keep Senhor Cabral from following the dictates of his conscience - and surely this was as it should be.

"May I have the portrait, Colonel Ashe?"

"Of course." Closing the case, Ashe handed it to her. "I took the liberty," he said to William, "of showing this to those officers presently to hand. I generally dine out any gentlemen passing through Guarda, you know, but none can recall this young man." He glanced at the girl, but her head was bent over the miniature. "However, it is just possible that your husband might be with the troops further south, Dona Antonia."

Her head came up at once. "Oh! this is what I had hoped to hear! Thank you, Colonel, thank you."

William stared. If Ashe had such information, why had he not told her earlier? Why mention it now? His gaze shifted. The girl looked positively radiant! And she was - no, not smiling, even now. There was an incredulous brilliance in her eyes that lit her face, but even as he marvelled the more familiar clouds darkened her expression.

"But you cannot be sure it was he?"

Ashe seems to be weighing her up, William thought, perplexed. It seemed there was more to this interview than he had imagined.

The Colonel had crossed to a large map pinned to the wall. He studied it for a few moments.

"Dona Antonia," he said finally, "I'm aware that you've come a great distance and endured a great many difficulties. While I sympathise with you in this respect, and while I feel in honour bound to offer some assistance, I have however to tell you that I cannot myself provide a search party, nor permit your continuing further unless" - He held up his hand - "unless there is an understanding that this search is not unduly prolonged. I must warn you furthermore that between here and the border there are armed men - deserters, brigands, not to mention the ever-present possibility of enemy patrols, and I, of course, owe it to your family to ensure your safety.

"I can however provide an escort, for a limited time only, after which I must insist you return and present yourself here before proceeding south again." He indicated an area with a small circle of his forefinger. "Within five days, therefore, whether or not you are able to locate Senhor Cabral, you will return to report to me. Should you find this gentleman, and should he prove to be your husband, you will give him your news, and permit *him* to make the decision to remain or to return with you, in which latter case you become his responsibility. I trust he will agree to return, but your escort will report his decision to me. Do you understand?"

She nodded doubtfully.

"What I propose then," continued Ashe, "is that Captain Hurst here, with whom I imagine you are now well-acquainted, serves as your escort. He will assist you in your enquiries and provide necessary protection. Further, should this gentleman prove indeed to be Senhor Cabral, Captain Hurst can lend weight to your argument that he return home as soon as is practical."

Antonia's glance flew to the captain. She had seen him colour violently as he apprehended what was required of him, and with one angry look in her direction he stood up abruptly and went to the window. But she was equally dismayed. She thought over all that had happened since her arrival. What had the officers been discussing while she waited in the anteroom? And why must the Colonel now put forward this officer of all people to accompany her? Had Captain Hurst given his superior no indication of how bitterly he would resent such a duty? It seemed hardly just that he should vent his frustration on her. Did the Colonel not appreciate how impatient the young man was to rejoin his regiment?

Her heart sank as she realised that from now on, she could expect yet more of the Captain's sarcastic tongue and black looks, and the joy she had felt a moment earlier in the renewed possibility of finding Duarte was suddenly overlaid with gloom and apprehension. Yet if Captain Hurst, she told herself, was the price she must pay to find Duarte, then she would pay. Gladly.

"Sir!" The man had turned to his superior with what sounded like desperation, but he was ignored as the Colonel took Antonia's hand, and raised her to her feet.

"Well, my dear, we shall do our best to find this missing husband of yours, shan't we, William?" He appeared not to notice the gritted teeth he was shown in reply. "Make your requirements known to that young man outside, Dona Antonia, and we shall try to get you comfortable quarters for the night."

Before she knew it, Antonia, startled at the smoothness and speed of her dismissal, was outside the door.

William had turned back to stare, unseeing, out of the window. His ears were on fire, he was sure they were crimson, hot with anger. What was Ashe thinking of to put him forward as escort? Had the Senhora not managed to convince the Colonel that he was quite unsuited to the task? She'd had time enough to try. He rubbed angrily at his thigh. Of course she had complained about him. Indeed, Ashe had seemed amused by his account of their acquaintance so far.

William rounded on his senior the moment the door had closed. "Sir! You cannot seriously intend me to continue this chase after the lady's husband."

Ashe glanced at the closed door. "Lower your voice if you please, William. I am indeed in earnest. You will not believe how serious I am that you accompany Senhora Cabral."

"But - my Regiment - "

"Must wait. Just now this search is more important."

"More important than my rejoining my men? To whom?"

"Captain Hurst," Ashe said, sharply. "Your impatience to rejoin your men does you credit, but the manner in which you put your case does none." His expression softened. "I'll allow you've had a wretched time these last few months, and no doubt you're worn from your journey, but do me the honour of listening without further interruption."

Shamed by the reprimand and humiliated by the excuses Ashe had made for him, William stiffened. "I beg your pardon, sir. I forgot myself. I apologise."

Ashe nodded. "So let me tell you," he said gravely, "that at this moment I consider the Senhora's search for her husband every bit as important as your rejoining your regiment. Your being here is fortuitous. Let me explain." He waited until William had dropped reluctantly into the indicated chair. "You saw the portrait? Not a man you'd mistake in a crowd?"

William muttered a reply.

"Then I can tell you that this gentleman, William, has been seen in action against our troops. Now perhaps you can understand why I should want to hear that there is someone who can identify him and is looking for him too?"

William sat straighter in his chair.

"Senhora Cabral says her husband left to join the Portuguese militia and has had reports of his movements this way. So where is he? He's not passed through here with the army on its way to Spain, nor in the rearguard either. I make a point of meeting our allied officers. A man of his breeding would hardly go unnoticed in the common herd. And there you see, when I showed that portrait to the few officers I have left here, no one recognised him. No one, that is, except young Foster out there, who arrived a week ago with messages from Sir John Hope. I'll call him in."

It seemed that young Foster had been with the infantry crossing the frontier with Moore in the previous October when they became aware that their movements were being observed from the hills. It was assumed they must be French scouts, and the young officer was amongst those detailed to pursue them. It soon became clear that they were not French, but Portuguese. The features of one man particular had impressed itself upon Foster's memory. "It was a gentleman's face," Foster elaborated.

"Cabral."

Ashe smiled. "They never did catch up with them, but some time later our young lieutenant here returns with despatches for Hope's artillery in the South. Hope sends back, and young Foster finds himself in this same part of the world once again."

"I realised quite soon that I was once again observed by this group of horsemen with this same gentleman still amongst them. This time though they opened fire, and I got a ball in the arm. Not a bad wound luckily." Foster grinned. "But there was a prolonged chase until at last we ran into one of our patrols, at which time my pursuers turned back. Innocent observers? I take leave to doubt it."

Ashe interrupted. "So, William, when I learn that this gentleman of Foster's appears to be the mislaid Senhor Cabral, and that his wife believes him with the British Army, you can understand why I'd like some questions answered."

William let out a breath. "But the Senhora is English. You said yourself her father approved the family. Surely her husband must be above suspicion?"

"That is something I should very much like to know."

"You don't imagine *she* knows what game he is playing? Her expression - When you told her - She was genuinely astonished. I cannot believe that look was contrived."

"No - o," said the Colonel.

"She wouldn't come here with such a complicated tale of dead brothers, and inspecting estates, and Portuguese militia."

"You think not?"

"I am sure of it."

"Well, then," replied the Colonel, "no-one better than you to help her find our missing gentleman and prove her honest."

William sprang to his feet. "But Good God, sir, why me? Why should I be of more help than one of your own men? Some must know this country better than I ever will."

"Firstly, William, you are at present unattached. Secondly you have already acted as her escort. She must see now that an escort is essential and cannot object to your continuing as such."

Can she not though! "Surely, sir, she has made her dislike of me abundantly clear? No doubt you've been enlightened as to each and every sin of mine on the journey so far?" William hesitated. "Or is that perhaps why . . . ?"

"I cannot imagine what the lady is supposed to have said..."

"Believe me, sir, when she has a moment to collect herself, she will refuse to countenance my continuing as escort."

The Colonel laughed. "Come now! If she feels so strongly, why has she said nothing? She has said nothing, I assure you."

"She has made no complaint?"

"Now then, sir," said Ashe, "what are you supposed to have done?"

William realised he had dug a pit for himself. "I - I simply made it very clear, sir, that I deeply resent this escort duty when - when I am needed elsewhere."

“As you have to me! And?”

“Well – ” William swallowed. “I deserved it, perhaps. I angered the lady sufficiently to have her come near to striking me…”

The Colonel choked. “What?”

“ – And I was obliged to restrain her.”

“Good Grief! I should never have thought it. Of either of you.”

William's lips tightened. “She vowed I should hear more of it.”

“I can imagine she might.” The Colonel seemed to be struggling with himself. “William, ever since I have known you, I have been made aware of your deficiencies in tact and patience. A pity, since you will never rise to any great height as a commander, no matter how brilliant a soldier, without acquiring the ability, if necessary, to smile and say nothing when provoked. However,” Ashe was serious now, “you are to accompany the lady to the area in which we last heard something of these 'observers'. If we spread the word that the wife is in search of her husband, it might provoke some action. We cannot tolerate a band of spies and snipers hampering our troop movements.” He looked grim. “Confidentially, I may not be long here myself. As I said, your being here is fortuitous. A sortie against them is already in hand, but a thorough search will tie down too many for too long. You may attract less suspicion, and perhaps achieve the desired result in shorter time. If you can learn something – who these men are, where they are based, what they intend, I believe we should find it very helpful.”

“But – what if this man is not Cabral? I shall be riding out with two women, into rough country where we are already agreed there is some danger from armed ruffians. If this man has no connection with the Senhora she is not safe. I doubt that her manservant and I are force enough to guarantee protection.”

“That cannot be helped, William. For the present, there *is* no one else, and I am convinced this man is Cabral.”

“And my plans, sir?” William asked, voice low.

“Will have to wait, lad, as I said before.”

Optimism faded now, along with his hopes of a speedy return to the fighting, and William's anger flared. “I cannot see why *I* must go.”

“My men have duties of their own, Captain Hurst. But as it happens, you will escort Senhora Cabral because I say you shall.” Ashe rose to his feet. “Well done, lad,” he said tolerantly. “I see you can keep your temper when you try.” He clapped William on the shoulder. “Do as you think fit to find this Cabral, but make an effort that shows, please. And discover whatever you can before you return. We can barely spare even you just now," he added with a twinkle that William refused to acknowledge, "so be sure to find our missing nobleman as soon as you can. Get along now and get some rest. I'll make your orders as brief as I can. They'll show you act as the lady's escort as far as the area I indicated, following which you are to return here before proceeding to your regiment. Your actual orders will be unwritten and given to you tomorrow morning. Report then, at eight, and I'll see you have those, together with all the information we have on our mysterious horsemen."

William picked up his shako and replaced it in one abrupt movement.

Ashe acknowledged his precise salute, and sighed as William strode to the door. "William."

He turned sharply. "Sir."

"Take care. And take care of the Senhora too."

Ashe waited until the door closed again behind the young officer, then re-seated himself and took up his pen. The Senhora might not appreciate immediately how fortunate she was to be in the charge of William Hurst, but she would come to do so in time.

He smiled ruefully as he read over what he had written. It might prove no more than the means of reuniting the Cabrals - at least that would see an end to that business - Better still, William might bring information that would rid the area of a threat to their forces. In either case, the young officer's report would be useful.

Ashe studied the papers a moment longer, then - satisfied - added his signature with a flourish.

CHAPTER SEVEN

Much against her will, Antonia recognised that she must accept the Colonel's conditions together with Captain Hurst's unwanted company or relinquish the search for her husband.

She remembered with a heavy heart the letter that she had summarised to the two British officers, the letter that had come to her in Viseu and had led her here to Guarda. She had been in a state of shock at the time, and it had all to be read several times over before she could take in its meaning. Now every word was imprinted on her memory.

'My dear, forgive me,' the letter had begun. *'Affairs at Coimbra are well in hand, and no longer need my time or attention. Others can now deal with these matters. Meantime, I cannot stay here when I see so much elsewhere that must be done. Nor can I return to my life of idleness in Lisbon. My father has no real need of me; Emilio sees to all that is necessary. I cannot be idle when I see how much my country needs my help. Friends are seeking my assistance. I plan to offer my services.*

'I fear I should be obliged to stay if I return to announce my resolve, and this is why, regretfully, I leave this news to be announced in this manner. Forgive me, Antonia, I shall write again when I know better what is to happen in the North, but do not be anxious if you hear no more of me for some time - "

The letter ended with expressions of affection and messages for his family, but Antonia had hardly registered these. She could not bring herself to believe that her husband could leave so abruptly without some discussion on such a momentous decision. Admittedly, in the two years since their marriage there had been some misunderstandings and, at times, an odd distance but that was perhaps only to be expected considering their differing cultures and upbringing. She was aware too that Duarte felt to some extent disregarded by his father. Emilio was to inherit and, though Duarte tried to hide his jealousy, Antonia had always suspected how deeply it ran in him. But she was sure that Duarte still cared for her. And he could not know how desperately he was needed now. With his help, Dom Luis might find his grief less of a burden. Now Duarte could show his father his worth. But the fact remained that her husband had deserted his family for the Portuguese rebel army. He had left to join the fight against the French with nothing more for her than a note. So she must, after all, accept the Colonel's conditions and endure Captain Hurst's company if she ever wanted to see her husband again.

Unexpectedly, the first difficulty was with Maria Josefina. It appeared that the maid believed that in reaching Guarda she had reached safety, and ever fearful by nature she now dreaded what lay ahead. She wept when she learned they were to go on.

"The mountains are cold and dangerous, lady. I cannot manage a brute of a horse up those difficult paths. You saw how it was yesterday."

"But there can be no question of you remaining, Josefina," Antonia began. "Who knows what may happen to you here alone, with the town full of troops. Perhaps the Captain . . . " She pressed at her temples, sighing at the uselessness of wondering if the officer might help. "There is no question of your staying, Maria Josefina. You have come so far, surely these last few miles can make no difference?" But she saw from her maid's pressed lips and downcast eyes that an appeal was useless. Then could she perhaps manage without the girl? She had been little help on the journey so far and as an unwilling attendant would likely prove even worse. But how could she abandon the maid?

Maria Josefina was fiddling with her bracelets. "Oh, but Dona Antonia," she volunteered unexpectedly, "while you waited on the British officers this morning, a woman across the square came to talk to me. She says she is in need of a servant. I could remain there with her until you return with Senhor Alvaro? She would give me bed and board in return for work."

Antonia stared at her in disbelief, and her maid began to wail.

"Leave me here, mistress," she sobbed. "These northern mountains frighten me. I cannot help it. I will find work in Guarda, I swear it, until your return with the Senhor, and then I will return with you to Lisbon." She caught at her mistress's hand. "Please, do not make me go with you."

Antonia pulled away, imagining Captain Hurst's reaction if Josefina were to throw hysterics en route. Although now that she remembered the officer had been quite remarkably patient with the girl, and the minx had even appeared to enjoy the experience. "Listen to me, the English captain comes as our escort. He will see no harm comes to us. He looked after you, remember, when your horse took fright."

"He frightens me too," hiccupped Maria Josefina. "He is very fierce when he is angry, and he does not care that you are a Cabral and related to Dom Luis."

That was true, Antonia thought. And he certainly did not see this escort as any part of his plan. He was eager to catch up with his men. She had a sudden, brief, mental picture of William Hurst in the thick of battle. He must have been badly wounded at Roliça; only that could have delayed him so long behind the army he longed to rejoin . . . But now why was she feeling sorry for *him?* She was in much the worse position.

Antonia was exasperated at the ease with which her thoughts had been distracted. *Well, miss,* she said under her breath, *much as I sympathise with your reluctance to share our journey, I shan't forget this defection when we reach Lisbon and home again!* But if this woman across the square proved to be genuine, and the girl could be left in safe hands, that at least was one problem solved.

The next difficulty was with Pedro. He seemed quite prepared to continue the search but made it very clear that he disapproved of his mistress's proposal to travel with no other servant but himself, and told Antonia that he was certain Senhor Tavares would not have permitted it. It was not proper, he told her, that a daughter - albeit by marriage - of a Cabral of Coimbra and Lisbon should ride alone with a foreigner into the mountains, and without a woman to attend her.

"I have been able to care for myself since I was five years old, Pedro, and I am quite capable of managing to dress without a maidservant." He seemed shocked at her frankness, but she went on, "You must see it could be wiser to leave Josefina behind? You are worth twice as much to me as a companion."

"You must have a woman, *minha Senhora.* We'll hire another girl."

"I cannot be doing with any more hysterics," she insisted.

"But, Dona Antonia, what will the Senhor say when he learns you have followed him unattended?"

Antonia ran a hand through her curls. "That is the least of my concerns at the moment, Pedro."

"But the Captain does not care that you are a Cabral and related to Dom Luis!" he muttered.

"No, so I understand! But he is my one hope at present of finding my husband, and I cannot help his attitude." She stooped to look into Pedro's face. "Things are hard enough as they are. Don't make further difficulties. You know how much the Senhor is needed at home, and the sooner he is found the sooner we can all return. I take full responsibility for leaving Maria Josefina here."

So Pedro let himself be persuaded that all would be well, and agreed to tell the officer they would be ready to depart as suggested.

*

If Antonia had hoped to astonish William Hurst with her efforts to reduce her baggage she was disappointed, for he merely raised an eyebrow at the sight of the leather satchel she strapped to her saddle next morning, and did not ask what had become of the remaining items. He took rather more notice of the shirt and breeches she now wore under her jacket and cloak, and silently commended her good sense. His only reservation was that any distant observer might find it hard to identify her as the bait necessary to attract her husband. In that respect, he thought grimly, the breeches were a mixed blessing. On the other hand, if the Senhora let her hair blow about her face in a great fair cloud as it did now there would be no mistaking her sex - And should there be no Senhor Cabral in the mountains it might attract quite the wrong kind of attention.

His resentment had continued to smoulder. The journey might prove as dangerous as it was difficult, and no one must suspect the reason behind his presence as an escort. Furthermore, a man who had once deserted his wife for whatever reason might hardly be enthralled to see her so soon afterwards. And if Cabral had been in action against British troops he would hardly be delighted to find his wife in the company of a uniformed British officer.

Not all Portugal welcomes us, William reminded himself. Yet here he was, with his regiment somewhere across the border, encumbered by a Portuguese noblewoman and her servants, embarking upon an expedition into unfamiliar territory to effect the capture of a Portuguese gentleman - and with orders to trap a man with his own wife, a wife whom he imagined safe somewhere else entirely.

William Hurst did not look forward to this expedition in the slightest.

CHAPTER EIGHT

Before nightfall on their second day on the road William was forced to concede that in spite of his resentment and misgivings things had not gone badly. Pedro continued to merit his confidence, and it had become evident that Pedro's mistress was not one to quail at a little hardship.

Perhaps, William thought grudgingly, it was a blessing that the maid had stayed behind. He could not envisage her displaying as much equanimity as her mistress as she scrambled over the path hauling a skittish horse after her. Well, horses and Josefina did not suit, and the maid after all had none of her mistress's reasons for pressing on. The Senhora did try at least. That apparent frailty was deceptive; she was made of sterner stuff than he'd imagined. She did not say much, but her responses were civil enough. He had offered neither encouragement nor assistance, yet where he led, she followed without discussion or argument, only, sometimes, showing a flicker of uncertainty in the eyes she raised to him.

William was disappointed only in his failure to make contact with Cabral, and was aware the girl felt the same disappointment as she paused on the road to shade her eyes and survey the summits. It was not often that the mountaintops were visible, and why she might imagine there was someone on the heights to see, William did not know; he had said nothing of Foster's account. There was nothing to be seen, yet he too sensed they were being observed, a distinct unease, enough to make him shift his shoulders under his red coat; an idea that someone might have a musket sighted in the middle of his back.

He had suggested their destination should be the village closest to the last sighting of the mysterious stranger, and though the Senhora wondered aloud whether her husband might still be there a week or more later, she appeared to take reassurance from the explanation that someone would know where the militia had passed. She seemed convinced her husband would be found.

She has changed, William thought.

He studied her with narrowed eyes as, without a word, she knelt beside him to feed the small brushwood fire. She seemed not to mind that the ground beneath her knees was hard and cold, nor that their camp that night was in the open. There had been no word of complaint, something he would not have imagined possible a few days earlier. He had judged the Senhora haughty and spoilt. Had he misjudged her? Could Ashe have given her a lecture? William snorted. Unlikely!

He got to his feet and went to speak to Pedro.

Antonia looked up as the captain walked into the darkness, and stared after him curiously till a spurt of flame from the fire made her jerk back her hand. The officer had shown remarkable restraint since leaving Guarda, she thought, sucking her fingers. He'd said nothing of her maid's defection, nor of going on without the girl. He'd said very little, and what had been said had at least been civil, with no trace of the sarcasm that had so irritated her before. She added more fuel to the wood burning in its ring of stones. Well, Captain Hurst might be as rude as he liked, provided he found Duarte for her, she thought, and he would do that soon.

Much later Pedro came to shake the captain awake for his turn on watch, and pronounced all in order. Crouching over the fire he rubbed his hands in its warmth.

"I think we shall have snow." He looked up into the sky, then across the fire at his mistress sleeping soundly under a pile of blankets.

William stood up, covering a yawn, and tugged his cape closer. "Let's hope we find Senhor Cabral before the weather closes in entirely." He grimaced, and rubbed his thigh. "I'd forgotten how uncomfortable it can be to bivouac - "

"Hush!" Pedro nodded at his sleeping mistress. Their low voices had penetrated her dreams and she turned, murmuring in her sleep, her outspread hair glinting in the firelight.

"Duarte." The name was just audible. William frowned at Pedro.

"The Senhora dreams of her husband," Pedro whispered, with an awkward smile. He crossed the fire and pulled a blanket closer around the fair head so that she should not feel the cold and waken.

Duarte? William had understood that Cabral's given name was Alvaro - but in this part of the world he had found that forenames and surnames were many and complicated. He glanced briefly at Pedro, then at the girl dreaming in the firelight, and with a scowl went to inspect the horses.

They found what passed for civilisation late the next afternoon and then only by chance. It was snowing at last and visibility was poor, but William had spotted the small houses, grey in the greyness, huddled on a crag. The path leading to the village was badly marked and they were obliged to dismount and climb, leading the animals behind them as they struggled through the thickening flakes of snow.

"What will you say?" The Senhora caught his sleeve as they approached the tumbledown dwellings. She was breathless from the climb.

"I'll think of something," William returned grimly. Attention must focus on the wife in search of her husband; but it was as important to stress that his presence was at the lady's request; that as soon as she could be resigned to her family's protection his part was done. If Cabral was one of Foster's horsemen, he would want nothing to do with a British officer, unless to take him prisoner, and William suspected he was in rather more danger than Ashe would admit. All very well to say he had only to discover where the riders were based, and how to direct a force against them. William imagined he could consider himself lucky if he rode away from Senhora Dona Cabral with nothing more than a farewell wave; it was more likely to be a musket ball in the back.

He gave her a sideways glance as she climbed the village street beside him, and wondered if she had any idea what her search might cost him. And as she matched stride for stride, her cheeks rosy with the effort, breath coming in clouds through half-open lips and her eyes alight with hope, it occurred to William for the first time to wonder what the search might cost Antonia Cabral. 'By God, madam,' he muttered, 'that husband of yours may break your heart yet.' And wondered, almost savagely, why he should care.

The accommodation offered here was even more basic than before. Ground floors were taken up with storerooms, with space not only for wine and grain but for animals too. The human inhabitants occupied the floor above, where access was by an outer stone staircase. There were no chimneys to speak of, and smoke from fires that were necessary because of the cold filled the rooms and seeped slowly out of gaps in the door and windows.

"I wonder if we should not do better outside in the snow," spluttered Pedro, beating at his chest.

They had been offered room in the largest house, but even here they were totally without privacy, and it was so smoky and noisy that Antonia had opted for the warmth of the stable below. Pedro was horrified at the idea of a Cabral sleeping in the straw, and after a sharp discussion with the farmer a small room was found and miraculously emptied for her. To endorse their story she must of course be seen so, much to the astonishment of the inhabitants, she was seated at one of the rickety tables to pick at a greasy chicken stew while Pedro and the captain questioned the few villagers present. Antonia had wanted to put her own questions, but Pedro insisted it was beneath the dignity of a Cabral to address peasants, with their strange dialect and rough tongue, and with William's agreement, did most of the talking. The exercise seemed pointless. Heads were shaken. Cackles of disbelief rose. No one had seen anyone to resemble the gentleman in the mother-of-pearl portrait.

"Are there patrols?" William asked casually. The head shaking grew more doubtful, and his audience lost interest and edged away. William wondered if the unwillingness indicated something more sinister. He glanced at the Senhora, pushing distractedly at the remains of her food. Her face showed her disappointment all too clearly, and William was suddenly exasperated. What else were they to do? They could hope that word of their search would spread, but the weather was not likely to make that easy or soon. "What a completely hare-brained idea this is," he muttered yet again, and wished to heaven that he had never set eyes on any of the Cabrals.

They held a council of war the next morning over a wretched breakfast which was saved from disaster by scalding cups of coffee, courtesy of the captain's own supplies.

Hands curved gratefully around the hot bowl, Antonia sat and gazed over the rim, past her companions and out of the open door at the hills beyond.

"We'll go on to the next village," she heard. "Make enquiries there."

All attention now, she interrupted. "You don't think it advisable to delay here a little longer?" She saw the answer in his face, and averted her gaze before he answered with what was for him unusual patience.

"Folk know our business. We'll be the topic of discussion for some time yet. Word will spread, don't worry about that." He regarded her. "You don't care to spend a second night here, surely?"

Antonia shook her head, thinking of her bed in the Cabral's great mansion outside Lisbon. It had been a wretched night, tossing, turning – and bugs in the questionable bedcovers. She had slept better the night before, under the clouded stars. "If you think it better to move, then of course we should."

If she noted the small grimace of surprise William aimed in Pedro's direction, she was too preoccupied to take exception to it, and in a half hour, having paid more than generously for their lodging, they were on their way.

The snow had settled but the wind blew still, and little flurries swirled around them as they continued across the slopes of the Serra in the fitful sunlight. In the late afternoon they neared another hamlet, where irregular lights from the huddled houses gleamed out over the path as they approached in the gathering dusk. This was welcome enough, but pleasure was intensified in discovering a good solid alehouse at the edge of the village, with polished tiles, and shining windows, and a welcoming fire that crackled cheerfully in the hearth, and the smoke of which went up a proper chimney. The place had few patrons, but the woman of the house bustled about and made them welcome, and in no time at all they were sitting down to hot bowls of soup, vegetable omelettes, and fresh bread.

Pedro rolled his eyes at the food. "We have died and come to Heaven," he enthused, before hurriedly crossing himself. Looking up with a smile for his enthusiasm, Antonia met the captain's eyes and, much to her surprise, before she could lower her glance again they had exchanged a diminutive glance of amusement.

William was even more astonished. It was amazing what a hot meal could do, he reflected, wiping away his own smile with a rough napkin. He stretched his long legs more comfortably under the table, then gathered himself up.

"I'll see the animals have been tended." He nodded at Antonia. "Make sure the Senhora's accommodation is secure, will you, Pedro?" He left the table, pushing his way through the small crowd that was beginning to fill the room, and went outside. Pedro excused himself and disappeared.

Left alone, Antonia too stretched discreetly. The comfortable glow of a good meal and warm surroundings after a winter's day on horseback had made her drowsy, and she blinked tiredly as she looked around the tavern's now crowded interior. Although the room was full, she had seen from the first that Duarte could not be there. She wondered when the Captain would begin his enquiries. He had already spoken to the tavern keeper. Presumably the man was now discussing their errand with his customers. Antonia studied the faces of the men as they talked, laughed occasionally. Many returned her glance, wondering who she could be, scandalised by her breeches, but aware that her attire, the suede, the silk, the velvet was of the finest quality. They took care to avoid her eyes, knowing their place where aristocracy was concerned.

Antonia ceased her idle surveillance. Rubbing the tiredness from her eyes, she focussed on a man who stood just inside the door, thirty yards or more away. His features were nothing out of the ordinary; he was just a man, average height, brown eyes, black hair, round nose. She did not know who he was, but his face was familiar. He dropped his gaze and turned away as if conscious of her observation. Antonia knew him, she was sure of it. But where, who. . ? She searched the room for sight of Pedro before glancing at the man again. This time he looked at her askance, surreptitiously. She half rose. There was something about him. He looked startled, shook his head. Just then the outer door opened, letting in a flurry of snow, and William Hurst stepped inside, shutting the door behind him with a bang, and rubbing his arms with every evidence of being frozen. He shared a joke with some of the men standing near the door before returning to the table, and Antonia realised the stranger had disappeared. She looked up at the captain, shocked.

"What is it?" he said, sharply.

"There was a man . . . "

"What did he do?" Hurst jerked his head to look behind him.

She shook her head. "Nothing. He . . . "

"What's the matter?" Pedro had just returned to the table. He stared from one face to the other. "What's happened?"

"Who was it?" Hurst asked. "Did you know him? Not your husband?"

"Of course not!" Antonia shook her head once more. "No. He seemed – " She shrugged. "He seemed familiar, but I did not know him. He looked . . ."

"What?"

"I thought perhaps - that he knew me. He was looking at me, and he shook his head."

Hurst and Pedro exchanged glances "What did he look like?"

"Nothing out of the ordinary. Dark. Not tall."

"Like most Portuguese, then," Hurst observed dryly. "Like Pedro."

Both men turned to look. "He is gone now," Antonia reminded them.

"Are you sure it was you he was watching?"

"I - I think so."

"But you didn't know him?"

She shook her head for the third time. Hurst went to speak to the tavern keeper, and Antonia was aware of gestures in her direction and the landlord's solemn denials. In a moment Hurst returned.

"No help. We'll ask the others." He took Pedro by the arm. "Come, my friend, I have a use for your tongue." As he moved away he turned to frown at Antonia, sitting anxiously alone. "If you see him again call me," he ordered. She nodded half-heartedly and watched the two men disappear into the throng.

Glancing down at her hands, Antonia saw they were shaking. Hardly surprising perhaps, when she thought of the hopes that had been raised in her so briefly. The man *was* familiar, she was sure of it, but from where? Might Pedro have seen him before? He was not from the Lisbon estate . . .

Antonia became aware of a lad standing respectfully beside her chair. He had a rough tray in his hand, and on the tray was a folded piece of paper. He held it out.

"*Desculpe, minha Senhora,* the note? I am asked to bring you this note."

"Thank you," Antonia said, her throat dry. "But where is the man who gave you this?" Her eyes searched the room.

The lad shrugged. "Gone, *minha Senhora.* He left almost at once and told me I must wait until you were alone. He gave me this, see?" He held up a coin, pleased.

"I see." Antonia wondered if the Captain or Pedro were watching, but they were some yards off, their backs to her table. "Have you seen him before? The man who gave you the coin?"

"Perhaps. He comes to the inn once, maybe twice, before."

Antonia fumbled in her satchel for the velvet lined portrait case before recalling that it was being shown around the inn. She cursed softly. "Have you seen the gentleman in the portrait? The one that officer is showing to everyone? It is my husband," she added, embarrassed.

"I have seen the picture, lady, but not the gentleman, I regret."

Antonia let her shoulders sag. She unfolded the paper and frowning over the almost illegible script, read a few words - then flushed and hastily refolded the note. She searched for a coin to reward the boy and pressed it into his hand. "No need to speak of this again," she murmured.

The lad bowed, and backed away. *"Minha Senhora."*

Antonia waited until her heart had stopped its erratic thumping, and then, holding the paper below the level of the tabletop, slowly unfolded it and read again.

'Sei vosso marido, Senhora Dona Cabral,' it began. *'I know your husband, Madam Cabral. Say nothing to your friends, if you please, but if you wish news of the Senhor I may have something to tell you. Meet me at the stable entrance. As soon as you can.'*

One hand to her mouth, Antonia studied the note. *Who might admit to knowing her husband? and why did he not address her openly? Why must she say nothing of the note?* She glanced at the untidy scrawl. That such a man could write at all was remarkable. He knew something, but was it genuine? Or had he heard of their search and hoped to cheat money out of her with false information? Or was he telling the truth, and she was to have news of Duarte at last?

Antonia refolded the note, pressing the creases. *The stables as soon as possible.* Her nails pressed into her palms. *Say nothing to your friends.*

What was she to do? How could she be sure that if she went to meet him, alone out there in the darkness and cold, this man would tell her what she wanted to know? Perhaps he was not alone. Anyone could be with him. They would know she had money; it might be no more than a ruse to rob her. *Say nothing.*

But she must go just the same. She must. Antonia swallowed, feeling sick with apprehension.

"Is something the matter, Dona Antonia?" Captain Hurst was leaning on the table, frowning down at her. "You've seen that man again?"

Antonia crumpled the paper into a ball. "I have not seen him a second time," she said, with a shake of the head. "I should have called you if I had." She tried out an unsteady smile. "I must confess to being desperately tired."

"As are we all," he agreed, gravely. "Will you retire? Pedro assures me a bed is prepared."

"Thank you, I believe I will." She rose slowly from the table. "I might take a breath of air first, before I shut myself up in that room."

"I'd feel happier if you remained inside. It's black as pitch out there, and bitterly cold beside."

"I appreciate your concern but I shall be no more than a moment."

"Then if you'll permit, I will come with you. I'm not entirely happy about this mysterious man of yours."

"There's no need – "

"It's no trouble, I assure you."

"Oh!" Antonia was defeated. "How obliging. But I would not disturb you to go outside again. I'll go to my room directly. Goodnight, Captain."

"Goodnight, *minha Senhora*. I shall see you at breakfast?"

"Indeed," Antonia murmured, and hoped she would come to no harm before then.

Ten minutes later, having scrambled down the stairs behind the inn to make her way across the yard at the back of the straggling buildings, Antonia found herself beside the stable. It *was* dark, but some light from the inn windows threw odd patches of brightness on the snowy ground, which reassured her a little, but there was no one to be seen. She waited a minute or two, shivering in the cold in spite of her cloak. "Is anyone there?" she whispered, and gasped as a grey figure detached itself from the shadows and joined her. It was the man she had expected; he wore a cloak now and his hat was pulled down over his face but Antonia knew it was the same man.

He glanced about him. "You said nothing to your friends?"

"They are not friends," Antonia tried to disguise her nervousness. "One is my servant, the other the escort I am obliged to accept. But if I am outside any length of time, I shall be missed and they will come looking for me. Why did you forbid me to speak to them?"

"I cannot explain now, but you want news, I think, of your husband, *minha Senhora?*"

"What news do you have?"

"The Senhor is well, and not far from here."

"Not far?" Her whisper betrayed her excitement. "How far?"

The man hesitated. "You are a wealthy woman, *minha Senhora*. Wealthy enough, no doubt, to spare a gold piece or two for what I can tell you?"

Antonia swallowed. "If you think I might pay for such insignificant information, you are mistaken - and if you imagine I have come out into the night carrying a purse, you are doubly mistaken!" she retorted.

"My information is honest. I left your husband only two days ago."

"Two days?" faltered Antonia. "How do I know this is true? Who are you?"

"I have served Senhor Alvaro most of my life, Dona Antonia. For many years I worked for the Cabrals on the estate at Coimbra. You will not remember me, but I saw you once in the stables long ago. My name is Pereira, Afonso Pereira."

Coimbra? Was that where she had seen him? "You serve my husband?"

"I came with him from Coimbra into the mountains."

"Then you know - " Antonia bit her tongue. "You'll take me to my husband then? Tomorrow?"

"I think that would not be sensible, *minha Senhora*. But I can take a message perhaps? For a consideration."

"Do you take me for a fool?" She lifted her chin. "How can I be sure you would deliver any message? Let me tell you I have come a considerable distance in search of my husband, and I have no intention of turning back now. Especially now! But," she continued, eyeing him, "if you do take me to my husband, it will be worth your while."

The man muttered his uncertainty. At last he conceded. "I *could* take you to him."

"Will you do so then?"

"You must say nothing to the officer."

"He is my escort," Antonia declared, "with orders to assist me. Why may I not tell him I have news of my husband?"

"No doubt your husband will explain, Senhora, but if you speak of me to the Englishman I cannot stay." He turned to go.

"No! Wait." Antonia was startled. "A moment. I must think." She paced the yard hurriedly, and returned to confront Pereira. "I will come with you, but my servant must accompany me."

"And the Englishman?"

She hesitated. "I will say nothing, if you insist."

Pereira studied her. "Tomorrow evening, then."

"In the dark? Is that safe?"

"I shall not feel safe until the Englishman has departed."

"But I cannot promise that he will go."

Pereira shrugged. "Then it must be at night."

"What if the captain decides we leave tomorrow morning? How am I to leave without his knowing?"

"You must decide how best to remain until the evening, *minha Senhora*, then you can slip away after dark."

"You ask the impossible. What is there to fear? When I have found my husband that officer has orders to return but I may not be able to persuade him to leave me here. What difference can it make to you? Have you something to hide?"

The man drew himself up. "I have nothing to hide from you, Senhora, but I tell you that the Englishman must not know that you have seen me, or that you come with me."

"I will not come without my servant Pedro."

"Your servant comes, if you wish."

It was wrong. Very wrong. Antonia knew it was wrong. She should tell the Captain - but he was sure to forbid her to leave without him. Pereira could take her to Duarte, but would not do so if the officer had anything to do with it. *Why* must she say nothing to the Englishman? Why the secrecy? What should she do?

If Pedro was with her . . .

She could not come to much harm if Pedro were to go with her, could she? Antonia's head had begun to ache. "Very well," she sighed. "Tomorrow evening. At what hour?"

"You shall know all tomorrow. Be patient, *minha Senhora*, and I too will be patient." Pereira's smile gleamed in the darkness. "For the reward you have promised." He bowed. "*Amanha*, Senhora."

"Tomorrow," Antonia agreed. She waited a few moments, then returned without much difficulty to her room, and sent a servant to request that Pedro attend her at once. Five minutes later, Pedro tapped at the door. Antonia pulled him into the room, shushing his exclamation. She peeped into the passage, and satisfied that he had not been seen, closed the door. "Where is the Captain? Does he know I sent for you?"

"He heard the servant give me your message. He is talking, downstairs."

Antonia bit her lip. "You can tell him I wanted to know what had become of my husband's portrait - "

"He has it still, *minha Senhora*. Shall I fetch it?"

"No, never mind that - "

"Then why - ?"

"Hush!" Antonia shook his arm. "Pedro, that man I saw before, I saw again just now. I spoke to him."

"Lady, why did you not say so at once? The Captain would have come. I'll tell him now. We'll go after him." Pedro put his hand on the latch.

"Wait. He spoke of my husband. He knows where he is, and will take us to him."

Pedro's look of relief was quickly replaced by doubt, and hastily Antonia recounted the substance of her meeting.

"You believe this Pereira?"

"Yes."

"And would go with him?"

"Of course. You're to come with me. You will, won't you?"

"That goes without saying, Dona Antonia, but the Captain will insist on joining us."

"He is to know nothing of this," said Antonia earnestly. "Pereira has forbidden me to speak of it to him. He refuses to take me if the Captain knows of the plan."

Pedro threw up his hands. "Then he is most certainly not to be trusted. You don't imagine he is to be trusted, do you? If we are not to tell the Captain? The man means mischief! Why else would he swear you to secrecy?"

"I don't know, Pedro." Her voice was steady. "All I know is that I believe he can take us to my husband."

"What are you saying? How have you managed to convince yourself that this man is honest?"

Antonia covered her ears and walked away. "I am convinced that he knows where my husband is!"

"If so, then we must tell the Captain."

Antonia was conscious now of deep desperation. She knew Pedro was right; there could be no reason not to tell the Captain, only that Afonso Pereira had forbidden her to do so. "Say nothing tonight, I beg you," she pleaded. "Let me think on this further. Perhaps - perhaps in the morning -?" She gazed into her servant's honest, troubled face. "Promise me, Pedro, you won't speak of this to Captain Hurst tonight."

Pedro studied his boots.

"Pedro!"

He raised his eyes. "As you wish." He heaved a sigh. "I will not speak to the Captain of this." But under his breath, he added: "Not tonight, anyway."

Full of guilt, and hope, and anxiety, Antonia eventually retired to bed. Pedro was right. She knew he was, and it would be the height of folly to consider leaving with Pereira. Yet she must go with him if she were to hear any more of her husband!

In the morning perhaps, she would confess all to Captain Hurst, and see if he could suggest some way that he might persuade Pereira to reveal what he knew, or perhaps even some way that she might manage to accompany the man in safety. For a while she tossed and turned, and eventually fell into a troubled sleep in which she dreamed that Duarte appeared to her in the scarlet uniform of a British officer. Smiling, he held out his arms, but as she hurried towards him, hampered by the skirts that dragged at her legs, his smile vanished to be replaced by a furious scowl, and he began to shout - words that she could not understand - of betrayal and anger. They hammered in her head until she awoke with a start and discovered that there was a banging at her door, and that it was Captain Hurst who was shouting.

CHAPTER NINE

"Madam Cabral! Wake up, Madam Cabral, I want to talk to you! Can you hear me? Get dressed at once, if you please!"

William Hurst hammered on the wooden panels, returning with a glare of his own the looks of disgust from two strangers in the narrow passage. He was about to shout and hammer again when the door opened and showed him Antonia Cabral, barefoot, her shift covered by a hastily thrown on cloak, and with one arm up to shade her eyes. She blinked at him in the early morning light. William blinked a little himself. "I want to talk to you," he said shortly. "Get yourself dressed."

He saw at once that she knew exactly why he had come, but the guilt in her eyes was quickly replaced by a flash of contempt. "I will get dressed when I please, Captain Hurst. How dare you hammer on my door as if I were a tardy menial? Who do you think you are?"

"I am your escort, Madam!" retorted William, "and you and I have some words to exchange on that matter. I shall expect you downstairs in ten minutes." He turned to go.

"Captain Hurst . . ."

He turned back, his face grim. "Madam?"

"If we - we are not to have privacy downstairs, I should prefer that our − discussion - should be here."

William's eyes narrowed as he regarded her. How defiant the chin, even if her mouth trembled. He knew his appearance had shaken her, but she seemed determined not to yield an inch and there was some sense in what she suggested. "Ten minutes then, ma'am." Malevolently he added: "You'll not object to your servant being present, I take it?"

"If you insist," she answered, stiffly.

"I do, Madam. Believe me, I do!" William glowered at her for a brief second before finding he was again facing a closed door, and was drawn into giving vent to a few choice oaths before descending to the taproom to locate Pedro, and to order his presence above stairs.

"You don't suppose Madam has slipped away already, Captain?" Pedro sounded uneasy as they arrived at her door.

"She could well have done," William responded with weary disgust. Nothing the Senhora did would surprise him now, and if it were not for the fact that he had still to report to Colonel Ashe, William would have regarded it as a blessing if the lady *had* run off. Changed, he had thought her, two days earlier! That was as much of a deception as that air of fragility. Changed? She had not changed at all. William banged on the door, and raised an eyebrow at Pedro as her voice bade them enter.

The two men found her standing by the low window. She gave Pedro a look of reproach bitter enough to shame him into retreating into a corner where he stood, eyes downcast to the floor. Giving him a sour glance, William confronted the girl.

"Well, Dona Antonia, not to beat about the bush," he began, hands on hips, "I find you have been contacted by a man called Pereira, and that he has persuaded you to say nothing to me of his proposal to take you to your husband. Is this so?"

"Have you not had the whole story from Pedro already?" She flashed the servant a further glance, and Pedro fidgeted and shuffled his feet.

"Don't you dare blame him, Senhora," William snapped. "He was doing his duty, and it's a great pity you never thought to tell me yourself. I asked you last evening if you had seen that man again. You denied it. Now I hear you had contact with him after all." He stared her out, his eyes blue ice. "You *lied* to me."

"I did not - *lie* to you, Captain," she said. "I had not seen him when you asked me."

"Don't play games with me, miss. You know damned well you should have let me know at once that you had been given a note. You're my responsibility. You heard Colonel Ashe say my orders are to keep you under escort until you find your husband and then, and only then, is my duty discharged."

"Well, I have found my husband, Captain Hurst," she declared. "Or as good as." She drew herself up to her full height. "No thanks to you, I believe. Your enquiries have brought no result, while I have found someone who knows my husband and is prepared to take me to him."

Over my dead body! William wanted to retort, but instead he reminded the Senhora sharply that he was instructed to remain with her until she had found her husband in person, not proxy.

"Senhor Pereira insisted you were not to accompany us," she pointed out, defiantly.

"And did *Senhor* Pereira say why?" He dared not sow the suspicion that it was her husband who had something to hide; better to suggest Pereira was suspect.

"What has he to hide, I wonder? If he is acting within the law, why should he object to my company?"

She hesitated. "I know you disapprove of the purpose of my journey, Captain Hurst," she replied unsteadily. "I know you find it intolerable that my husband's family needs him more than his country does just now, but if my husband had only known what was to happen, he would not have left us as he did. Why must your ridiculous suspicions prevent me from finding him?"

Wake up, William wanted to shout, *don't you wonder what your husband is doing here?* "You don't ask yourself, Senhora," he said, through gritted teeth, "what this man means by such secrecy? Does it not occur to you that he has something to hide? Don't you want to know why his plans for you demand secrecy? If nothing else, how can you be sure he is not one of the deserters Colonel Ashe spoke of? A bandit?"

"That suggestion is preposterous, Captain."

"Then what difference can it make," William demanded, "if I escort you to your husband?"

"I never wanted your escort, Captain Hurst," she answered, her voice low.

He glowered at her. "So you have given me to understand," he said bitterly. "Don't think I'm unaware of *that*. However, I *am* your escort, and you will just have to bear with me. When are you to meet this man again?"

"I have nothing more to say to you, sir."

"Pedro? When did he say?"

Pedro grimaced. "He said he would contact the Senhora during the day. Another note perhaps?"

"Keep watch then, and let me know if any note arrives."

"Captain Hurst," she burst in, "I will not have my servants used against me."

He rounded on her. "I thought you had nothing more to say to me, madam."

She stared at him, looking appalled, before turning away to dash her hand across her cheek.

"Your remorse is heart-rending," William said, and saw her stiffen.

"Captain!" Pedro protested.

William glared. "Oh, for God's sake, not you as well." But even as he cursed, William knew the servant was right. He would gain nothing by angry recriminations, and unless he made amends he might lose this opportunity to locate Cabral. He clenched his fists. It seemed only an apology would do. Again! and he had never cared for apologies!

He was taken aback when the girl swung round to him, her eyes downcast.

"I'm sorry," she murmured. "I was wrong to act as I did. I apologise."

William frowned, suspicious. "You *were* wrong not to let me know about the note, Dona Antonia, but I can understand the anxiety that persuaded you into this situation. Perhaps I should have made allowances too. If you will give me your word to keep me fully informed at all times, I am sure we can make some arrangement to have you escorted to your husband."

"You intend to accompany me then?"

"As I have explained . . . "

"And as I have explained, Captain, I assured Pereira that you would not come."

William's foot began a small tattoo of irritation, but he said with studied politeness, "If you will allow me to continue? I do not insist on accompanying you, if you will swear that when you reach your husband, and if he is willing and able to return to Lisbon, you will both return here to meet with me. If for any reason he is unable to return, you must promise that *you* at least will meet me here so that I may fulfil my duty and escort you back to Colonel Ashe in Guarda."

He heard her gasp, but to his surprise her first words were, "Wh - what of your orders?"

"I am interpreting my orders as I see fit. Personally, I had far rather come with you, but if this Pereira refuses to co-operate I see I must remain behind. Pedro tells me he is to accompany you, and apparently Senhor Cabral is not so very far away. I suppose he can be relied upon to protect his wife from whatever dangers there may be?" He gave her a sidelong glance. "I should be deeply unhappy to think that a further day in my company might deprive you of your husband."

"Your attitude seems vastly altered, sir."

"I was angered by your refusal to acknowledge my authority, Dona Antonia. Your apology changed that."

The strong face was suddenly so bland. It was hard to believe, Antonia thought, with a deep unease, that her apology had done that. "You'll let me go then? With Pereira and Pedro?"

"Since you insist, yes."

"I told Pereira I would slip away tonight. Without you noticing."

He eyed her. "He appears to have scant respect for me. I suppose you will have to pretend to do so then."

He must take me for a fool, Antonia thought, uneasier than ever. She had been appalled at his vehemence, and at the turn of events just as she was about to confide in him. There was no point in explaining now. Pedro had forestalled her confession, and her tears had been tears of frustration as she suddenly realised she was dicing with her one chance of reaching her husband. Everything seemed to be going wrong.

"You'll let me know then when Pereira contacts you again, Dona Antonia. It's part of our bargain." The strange, light eyes threatened all kinds of trouble if she neglected to do so, and Antonia felt again the frisson of fear he had induced in her earlier.

"I will let you know."

"I'm obliged," he said, with the same dangerous gravity. "You have only to wait then until he contacts you. Come, Pedro, I've done here. Your servant, *minha Senhora.*"

As he bowed and left, Antonia found herself thinking that she was more afraid of him when he spoke like this than when he shouted. Would he follow her? Was that what he intended? But why should he do so? He would not care so very much, she felt sure, if she were to come to any harm, only that he would be blamed for his neglect. Antonia sat down suddenly and dropped her head in her hands. Oh, she was tired of this pursuit, and even more tired of Captain Hurst. And if she did not find Duarte soon, she said out loud to the room, she would give it all up, and return to Lisbon.

Slowly she got to her feet, thinking how foolish she had grown of late, but at least she would be ready when the order to leave came at last.

*

It came in late afternoon, after what seemed the longest day that had ever idled itself away, and it came in the form of another note as Pedro had foreseen. Antonia seized it, ripped it open, and having absorbed the message within took the note down to the room the Captain shared with Pedro.

Forewarned, Pedro bade her enter, and William swung his booted feet down from a small table, and unfolded himself from his chair.

"Just the note?"

"The boy brought it as before." She held it out.

William scanned the single page. "He must be very sure of his way if he can take you there in the dark." He walked over to the window and looked out. The sun was going down but the skies were brilliantly clear, and a full moon promised. It would be bitterly cold, and icy. Slippery on the mountain paths. In spite of himself William felt a stab of anxiety. The bastard was probably out there at this very minute watching to see what preparations were in hand. William lit a cigar, opened the casement and leaned out over the sill into the cold air. He blew a thoughtful puff of smoke, and in a moment closed the window again, fairly satisfied that there was no one in the yard below.

"Follow instructions then, if you please. Pedro will look after you." He eyed the girl coolly. "I trust this will prove to be the end of your search - I wish you joy of your reunion, if so it proves." He held out his hand. "I shall expect you. Remember your promise."

Antonia laid her hand in his, alarmed to discover that she desperately wanted the Englishman's escort after all. She understood, now that it was too late, that ever since the captain had felled the boar with a single shot and then rescued Maria Josefina, she had been finding strength and security in his infuriatingly cool confidence, from his aura of competence - even when he was angry. Who could tell if she would ever see him again?

She felt his fingers close very briefly over hers. "Thank you for your co-operation, Captain Hurst," she faltered. "I hope to see you again very soon. With my husband."

"With your husband," he agreed, leaving Antonia more disturbed than ever by the expression in the cool depths of his eyes.

CHAPTER TEN

"Up there!" said Pereira, and his weary companions turned to peer into unilluminated darkness. Twenty hours or more had passed since they had slipped away from the tavern, and Pereira had reined in his horse and was pointing to the dark peaks above them.

"What's up there?" Pedro groaned.

"Senhor Cabral is up there," Pereira replied, observing that Cabral's wife leant forward eagerly in her saddle. He grinned. She would see nothing even in the brightest day. The old monastery was invisible from the paths across the hills, its ruined walls merging so perfectly with the surrounding rocks and crags that only those who knew it well could find it, and Afonso Pereira was not yet ready to reveal the mountain' secrets. In his imagination he had almost begun to feel the cold hard edges of the promised reward. He was not entirely certain that the Senhor's reaction would be one of unqualified delight if his wife were suddenly to appear out of nowhere, yet he and all the men had heard Cabral in his cups regretting her loss, and there might yet be a further reward from him too.

"How soon shall we be there?" The Senhora edged her horse closer.

"An hour or so." Pereira shifted in his saddle to scan what he could see of the deserted landscape behind them. He had been troubled all day by the idea that the English officer might have tracked them, in spite of the circuitous route and in spite of the Senhora's assurances that the officer had drunk heavily after supper and cards the previous evening and had been put to bed by Pedro. 'It will be broad daylight by the time he wakes,' Pedro had said, 'and by then we shall be long gone!' Pereira devoutly hoped so. He had been looking for some sign all day and was almost satisfied. "The path is difficult," he said. "We shall sometimes have to walk."

Antonia suppressed a shiver as she imagined Duarte at his post in the forbidding crags. They must be very close to the border if he and his men patrolled the frontier from this place, and she wondered anxiously what danger he courted. If his task here was of such value, perhaps he could not return with her however much he might wish to do so. These were anxious times for England - but the

Portuguese meanwhile had suffered the indignities of invasion, and Antonia could understand now just how desperately men like her husband were needed to protect Portugal from further incursions. She had sometimes thought Duarte almost too dashing for his only concerns to be those of managing his father's estates and business; he must now be using his talents in a capacity far more suited to his temperament. Captain Hurst's arguments did not now seem so unreasonable. Yet she had promised Dona Isabel she would find her son, and when she recalled the scenes as she took leave of the distressed family – folk who had done their best to make an English bride welcome in a strange land - Antonia knew she owed them at least the obligation to try.

"Let us make haste if we still have so far to go," she urged, and Pereira nodded and turned his mount towards the hidden track.

William might have missed them there if he had not observed from the way his mare picked her path amongst the scattered rocky debris that travellers before him had turned uphill. He was not far behind now, and well aware of Pereira's anxieties. They must be close to Cabral, and the five days Colonel Ashe had given Dona Antonia were almost over, but for the life of him William could not see where it was Pereira led. The mountains appeared too empty to hide the number of men that Foster had described.

Gazing at the climb still before him, William took off his shako to rake his fingers through his hair, then took a breath of the cold thin air, replaced his hat, and kicked the mare gently upward.

*

Antonia had begun to think that she could go no further when there was a sudden shout from above, 'Pare!' and the three travellers came to an abrupt halt. They had been walking the last half hour, and Antonia, arm, hooked over her saddle, stumbled with weariness. The shouted order revived her flagging spirits and she looked up to see, at the end of a rocky defile, a half concealed gateway set in what appeared to be a ruined stone wall.

Taking a deep breath, Antonia brushed her hair back from her face with a glove muddied from constant contact with the boulders that had lined their upward path. Was this it? Was she to see Duarte at last? Would he forgive her? Would her unexpected arrival please or dismay him? She knew she must look bedraggled and worn, and she was so tired, and thirsty . . . Her heart began to thud. What would her husband think to see her?

Pereira had disappeared, and Antonia was disconcerted to find him now on the rocks above her in apparent disagreement with their challenger. Her heart sank. This then was not where Duarte was to be found; her journey was not yet done, and she was not sure her strength was equal to going on. A moment later however Pereira reappeared to report glumly that they must wait until the Senhor had been informed of their unlooked-for arrival.

"He is here?"

"Did I not say?" Pereira looked aggrieved. He jerked his chin at her. "You have not forgotten your promise, Dona Antonia?"

"When we see the Senhor, my friend," Pedro broke in. "Not before." But Antonia was already untying the neck of a leather pouch and tipping out coins.

"You have done well to bring us this far, Senhor Pereira, and when I have spoken to my husband you shall have as much again."

The man snatched the coins with an appreciative nod, and Pedro growled at him. "What now? How long must we wait?"

"I shall be admitted shortly. You must wait until my return. Be patient."

Even as Pereira spoke, someone emerged from a wicket gate set in the massive doors to beckon impatiently, and with a doubtful glance at his companions Pereira advanced with the supply-laden mules and disappeared inside.

"How long do they plan to keep us out here in the dark and cold?" Pedro complained, shivering beside his mistress's horse. "I tell you, lady, I cannot commend your decision. Nor can I think it wise to have rewarded that fellow so promptly. It might prove our undoing." He slapped his arms around him. "By my faith I could murder for a hot meal!"

From his vantage point some two hundred yards off, William settled more comfortably among the concealing rocks and drew out a slender eyeglass. Before him lay the high grey walls of what looked like an old fortified monastery, some parts in poor repair but where sound there were windows, narrow and barred. Set high above the path a fretted tower topped with a large cross was silhouetted squatly against the darker rocks, and inside the tower hung a bell. The place was certainly well hidden; if its former occupants were monks they had shut themselves away from the world right enough; an army might search for weeks and never find this retreat, but the Senhora, bless her, had led him to the very place.

William scanned what he could see of the ruins by moonlight, jotting observations in a scarcely visible notebook, taking note of the setting, and judging what cover might be useful. He saw Pereira disappear into the darkness shadowing the old gates and wondered how long the others would be kept outside. The Senhora would not be best pleased at the delay.

He focussed on the figures below, easing the snug uniform overalls over his thigh. It would be useful to know how many the monastery concealed, but that would have to wait until the Senhora returned to the village. He did not foresee Cabral returning with her.

Would *she* return? That question had bothered him ever since he'd ridden out of Guarda; it was one even Ashe could not answer. Why should the Senhora not remain here if Cabral thought he could keep her? Perhaps he had been too impatient to consider it before, but what *was* Antonia Cabral going to do when she had seen her husband, told him of the tragedy and asked him to return? How would she react when her husband explained his position, as William was sure he must do? When she had learned what his business was in these mountains, and discovered he'd set himself against forces loyal to Portugal, would she stay? A woman's emotions were not always influenced by reason, he told himself, and if Antonia Cabral loved her husband, politics and patriotism might count for nothing. Where would her loyalties lie then?

Would Cabral allow her to leave once she'd discovered the truth? Would he trust her enough to let her go? Knowing his secrets and intentions? What if Cabral decided his secrets were more important than his lovely young wife? William's frown deepened. Senhora Dona Cabral might be in more danger than he'd suspected, certainly more than *she* could ever have imagined. His hand moved automatically to his leg. Would she return?

He focussed on the slim figure waiting outside the gates. Pedro was evidently chilled, beating his arms to keep warm, but now he moved closer to his mistress. His arms had gone round her. She was under strain, of course, tired from their bizarre expedition. Distressed.

William drew a quick breath. Or had she learned this refuge did not conceal her husband after all? Damnation! He began to fidget with the focus on the glass.

CHAPTER ELEVEN

Deep inside the monastery walls, in a chamber hung round with tapestries and bright with the light of many candles, Afonso Pereira stood and sweated over his most recent indiscretion. It had been an acrimonious interview; Dom Alvaro had barely paused for breath - and the insults had been so bitter that even Pereira's wit could appreciate that there was no reward forthcoming, no reward, that is, that he would welcome.

"In the name of all the Saints," the Senhor was shouting. "What *possessed* you to bring my wife *here*?"

"But lord," croaked Pereira, " - your wife, surely . . . ?"

"Especially not my wife!" Alvaro Cabral took a deep breath. "So, whether or not this is the most ill-considered thing you have ever done, Pereira, my wife is here. Tell me again, without excuses, and without bragging, how you came upon her."

Pereira winced. "The Senhora and Pedro Teles came from Lisbon to find you, my lord. I met them by chance in the tavern at Cerchoso. They followed you east from Viseu."

"Who told you this?"

"The servant, Pedro. He told me how it was." Pereira smudged a hand across his face, aware that he must not on any account mention the English officer.

"You believed him? Why would my wife make such a journey?"

"The Senhora brings a message, I think. Teles said she expected to find you with the British Army."

Cabral snorted. "I expected her to think so, but I did not know she would follow it to find me. What is this message?"

Pereira had no idea. His master flashed him a look of disgust. "You are a fool, Pereira. You'll bring the British Army up here next, I dare say."

"But Senhor," moaned Pereira, "to see your wife after all this time. I thought to please you . . ."

Cabral planted his hands on the table. "You thought? You do not think! You obey orders. I suppose you were promised a full purse." He waved away Pereira's protestations. "There are more important things now than wives and families. If I'd wanted to see my wife, I'd have returned to Lisbon." Into his mind, however, slid the memory of the morning of his departure: Antonia at his stirrup in a white muslin gown, the cloud of her hair bound with a pretty ribbon; Antonia looking up at him with the wide blue eyes that had bewitched him at their first meeting. There was indeed far more to consider now than wives and families, but Alvaro Cabral had found it hard to forget his English wife. God's truth! He had never meant to marry, and certainly not with an Englishwoman. He thumped the table, causing a candlestick to lurch and Pereira to flinch. Lunacy to have his wife here; even worse to permit her entrance. He had misled her so completely he wasn't sure he could explain the truth even if he wished to do so. Did she harbour any suspicions? If he revealed his reasons for being here, how would she react? She was English after all. How strong was her loyalty to him? Cabral was suddenly no longer sure. He sank his hands into his hair. Antonia was outside the gates . . .

Cabral knew what he should do. He had his responsibilities and he had his men to consider. He must have word passed that, regrettably, the Senhora's journey was wasted. Senhor Cabral had departed, so she must return the way she had come.

The way she had come, and might remember?

Cabral cursed Pereira yet again. All this while he had successfully pushed thoughts of his wife to the back of his mind. If necessary, he could forget her again, but if he sent her away. . . He dropped into a nearby chair and stared into the darkness beyond the candles. If Antonia were allowed entry, she must remain in the monastery until he could be certain her loyalty to him was beyond question. . . He raised his head, his brown eyes glittering. "Send word then to the gate, and have my wife admitted. Thanks to you, you son of a misbegotten jackass, she now knows where we are, and I'm obliged to welcome her." He got to his feet, and Pereira backed away. "But I tell you now, Pereira. You step not one foot outside this place alone again. Get out of my sight."

Pereira fumbled for the latch, and went.

Cabral sank into his chair, his fingers clenching and unclenching around its carved oaken arms while his brain tested and rejected a hundred ways of accounting for his presence in the mountains. Finally, his patience exhausted, he sprang up and went to meet his wife.

In his rocky observation post William tried to ease the cramp in his long limbs. God in Heaven, how much longer were they to keep the woman waiting? He squinted at the ground separating him from the entrance, aware that at this distance he could do little but observe if any threat arose - then flashed the glass to the flurry of movement at the gates. Was that Cabral? Grinning with satisfaction, William brought the focus back to the Senhora for her reaction. Pedro had touched her arm, and she raised her head and was looking where he pointed; Cabral stepped forward...

In a flash the girl was running towards the gate, hair flying, cloak streaming behind her, and though William could not see her face, every line of her lithe figure, every movement expressed joy and relief. Cabral opened his arms wide. Another step, and she was in them with such force, such passion that William flinched as if he had caught her himself. He gasped and let the glass drop, then cursed and put it to his eye again.

She was welcome then, received with every indication of satisfaction, an obvious and deep affection between the two of them. Cabral was hugging his wife, kissing her . . . William swore. Did they have nothing to *say* to each other? He withdrew into the shelter of the boulders, realising he and Ashe might have jumped to all the wrong conclusions. Antonia Cabral *must* know what her husband was. How could it be otherwise? And if she did know, she was in the same league, as dangerous as the handsome nobleman who held her. What if they had all been misled by her story? What if the Senhora had merely used them to make contact with her husband? Cabral was expecting her. He was leading her toward the gates -

Of course, the way to discover how deeply the girl was committed was to see if she kept her promise to return. Back in Cerchoso William could question her. Meanwhile he would wait. If she had not reappeared by midday at the very latest, he must assume she had no intention of keeping her promise, and he would know how to proceed. Cautiously he pulled a smooth, flat watch from his waistcoat pocket, and by the fitful light of moonbeams tried to gauge the position of its delicate hands. Presently he tucked it away, dispirited. Ten minutes past eight o'clock. He had a long wait ahead. Hell's teeth, he would be frozen to these damned rocks by morning.

CHAPTER TWELVE

As they walked side by side into the monastery's vast entrance, Antonia rested thankfully against her husband. "I have so much to tell you, Duarte," she murmured into the hollow of his shoulder. "It is not good news, and I have so many questions."

He tightened his grip around her waist. "You're exhausted and hungry, my love," he said. "When we are alone you shall tell me how it is I suddenly find you here in these mountains. But is that Pedro Teles, looking as if he doubts his welcome? What? To come all this way with my wife only to be neglected?" He waited for Pedro to catch up, clapped the servant on the shoulder and shook his hand. "You'll be wanting food, and a bed too no doubt."

He shouted an order, and a surly looking man hurried up, short and bulky, with a scarlet kerchief round a thick neck. "Silva, take Teles here to the refectory. See he gets a good meal and a bed. I'll speak with him in the morning." He grasped Silva by the arm as his man moved to escort Pedro away, and murmured something to him before releasing the man with a little push in Pedro's direction. Antonia regarded him with anxious eyes.

"You are not sorry to see me, Duarte?" she faltered. He was slow to answer. "Duarte?" she repeated, uncertainly. "Did I do wrong to come?"

Cabral pulled her towards him. "Of course I am glad to see you. How can you think otherwise? But you must forgive my being out of countenance at this sudden appearance. Look at you! Is this the most elegant lady in Lisbon, dressed like a boy?" Antonia managed a faint smile at the humour in his voice as he continued, "My quarters first. They will bring food and wine, then we shall talk. Then after, hot water, towels, and you shall have a bath." He tucked a muddy curl into place behind Antonia's ear, and gripped her by the shoulders. His voice took on a soft, strange intensity. "And then bed, wife."

Antonia smiled again, feeling unaccountably nervous, but she took the hand Duarte held out to her, and followed him as he led her through another vast hall, up a broad curving flight of stone steps to an upper storey, and along another corridor to the chambers he presented as his quarters. In this warm privacy, Cabral unfastened Antonia's cloak, and helped her out of her leather jacket, but the almost immediate appearance of two men bearing in platters of hot food, goblets, plates and flagons of wine, was timely. For a quarter of an hour or more there was no peace while covers were set, and dishes were laid for Antonia's approval. The noise and bustle after the strain of the last few days was almost too much for her. "Duarte, I must explain what brings me here . . . "

"Eat first, my love. The food will spoil, and I know you must be hungry."

"But what I have to say . . . "

"Antonia, not another word until you have eaten and drunk. When the platters are cleared, sweetheart, you shall have my undivided attention." He picked up a skewer of lamb and offered it with such a persuasive smile that Antonia, who had been twelve hours without food, took it without further protest, and tried to chew. A glass of sweet red wine was offered and accepted gratefully. Her throat was dry, and under the heady bouquet the wine was velvet-textured. The Dão Valley of course. Her husband refilled her glass and topped up his own.

"No more, please," she said at last, and tried to smile. "When I recollect my errand, it seems quite wrong to be merry."

"Heavens, Antonia. So tragic!" Duarte laughed. "Has my sainted father died? Nor my mother either? Then there is no one else to concern me if you are in health, and you appear to be so." His expression changed. "You are not with child?"

"I would hardly have risked this journey if that had been so, but Duarte - Duarte, there has been a terrible accident. Emilio – you see, Emilio - his horse jumped a wall badly." Antonia reached out a hand. "He - he was killed, Duarte."

"Emilio?" He shook her off. "Emilio is dead?" He had paled, but now the colour came flooding back into his face. "Then - then I am heir."

"Why, yes," Antonia stammered, startled at the bald statement. "But forgive me, I have not managed this at all well..."

"You've come from Lisbon to tell me Emilio is dead?"

She flinched at the edge in her husband's voice. Grief, she realized, affected people differently. "We thought - I thought it better that you should learn the news from family rather than through the offices of a stranger . . . " but her husband seemed more astounded than saddened by his brother's death. True, he had never shown an obvious affection for Emilio, but whatever jealousy might have existed regarding their inheritance surely could not affect the pain Duarte must feel at the loss. Antonia regarded him uneasily. She supposed it would rankle that the elder son would inherit all the wealth while the younger depended on a mere allowance. She'd heard Pedro speak of the old peasant tradition that allowed only the eldest son to marry, while the younger sons remained on the land, unwed. But that had been years ago. There was a large enough inheritance for both of Dom Luis' sons; Duarte would never be poor and his marriage appeared to have been welcomed by his parents.

Realising now that his reaction to her request to return home with her was equally uncertain, Antonia faltered, "For the sake of your family - and I would not ask but for them, Duarte - I beg you will return with me. Your parents need you badly."

Her husband stood stiff and unyielding, his mouth a thin hard line. "Do they indeed?"

"Yes," she said, "they do. And I need you too, Duarte. Will you not come back to Lisbon with me?" She held out her hands to him.

He stared over her head. "I cannot. Nor will I."

Antonia let her hands drop. "You cannot have had time to reflect - I - I have broken the news badly - "

"I've no need to reflect. I have different obligations now."

"But your place is surely with your family at a time like this?"

"My place?" he echoed, his voice rising. "My place is here. I do not recall my father considering 'my place' when responsibilities for the estates were allotted. It was all Emilio then. Emilio to make decisions. Emilio to inherit - I have always taken second place to my brother. My father, I assure you, will not thank me for returning. He will tell me, no doubt, that I should have died before Emilio!"

"No!" Antonia cried. "Don't say that. Your father loves you, needs you. You're upset - I cannot believe - "

Her husband held up a hand. "My dear Antonia," he sighed, "I'm afraid you know very little about me, but I would like you to understand, if you can. I cannot explain tonight but I will try and make you see my point of view." In the silence that followed he stroked Antonia's hair back from her flushed face. "I have shocked you," he said. "A poor welcome, is it not?"

"Then – then it is quite impossible for you to return?" Antonia's heart sank.

Her husband dropped a kiss on her brow. "We'll not discuss it tonight. Tomorrow perhaps, when I've had time to think over what you have told me. But no more talk tonight." He tilted her face to him. "Does that seem fair?" She twisted away without answering. "Antonia." He made her look at him. "Does that seem fair?"

Antonia gazed into his eyes, the eyes of this man she had married and did not seem to know at all. "Yes," she whispered, and buried her face in his coat.

He tightened his arms around her. "I have missed you more than you know, Antonia."

She bit her lip, wanting to cry, *'Then how can you refuse me?'*, but Duarte must have his reasons, and he had promised to explain them. She buried her face deeper in his chest. "I've missed *you*."

"I can still hardly believe you are here." He drew her to a stool close by, pulled up its twin and sat down, holding her hands in his own. "How have you managed to come so far, with no one but faithful Teles to escort you? Could no one else be spared?" His voice was gentle again.

Antonia gave an unsteady laugh. "I started out with quite an entourage, Duarte, but they all fell by the wayside. Baltasar's uncle Tavares insisted on coming from Lisbon with me in spite of his age, but he was taken ill in Celerico. He insisted he would be well enough without me to fuss over him, so I left him to return to Coimbra, with his valet and Felipe - the coachman you know. I had a maid myself then. You remember Josefina? We left *her* behind in Guarda! Her temperament was ill-suited to the journey, I fear, and the Captain alarmed her."

"I hope she got the whipping she deserves. But who was it frightened her? A captain, you say?"

"A British officer," Antonia said slowly. "I had almost forgotten him. He was our escort for a while."

"You had a military escort? A British escort?" His tone was suddenly sharp. "How many men, with this captain?"

"Oh, he had no men," she sighed. "He alone was our escort." Antonia gave her husband a rueful glance. "And it was not a duty to his liking, I can assure you."

"Where did he leave you? At Guarda?"

Antonia wondered what she should say of her promise to William Hurst.

"No - o," she answered at last, "he came with us from Celerico to Guarda, and was to have left us there to continue north, I believe, but his superior at Guarda ordered him to continue with us."

"How far, Antonia? How far did he bring you?"

"To the village where Pereira spoke to me. Cerchoso, I think - "

“Does he know where you are now?”

“I don't believe so . . . ”

Cabral dropped her hands. He strode to the door, only to turn back before lifting the heavy iron latch. “You don't believe so?”

“Pereira insisted he was not to come with us, so he remained behind to await my return.” Duarte was evidently troubled by the idea of the English officer, and Antonia did not know what to say to reassure him. He had opened the door, and was giving brief orders to someone, but what he said was beyond hearing.

“I should have hung Pereira long ago.” Her husband gave the door an angry push. “He said nothing of this.” Antonia saw his colour had risen, and his hands were clenched. She began to be afraid for Pereira. Duarte must have ordered him fetched.

“He meant no harm, I'm sure, Duarte. He saw how anxious I was to find you, and as it happened, he was all the escort we needed. No doubt he thought to be very well rewarded for his trouble.” Antonia tried to smile. “I should never have found you without him. No one seemed to know where you might be.”

Cabral took her suddenly in his arms. “Are the British anxious to know where I am?”

“The British? I don't believe they have any interest in you! They are far more concerned that Dom Luis's daughter-in-law and, I might remind you, someone with a vague connection to one of their own statesmen, should be seen to have their assistance.” Antonia looked up. “They will be heartily glad to see the last of me, Duarte. I have been thoroughly troublesome in my anxiety to find you.” Her expression altered. “If you only knew how afraid I was that I should not find you after all. When I had your letter at Viseu, I wondered what I should do.” She rubbed her cheek against his shoulder. “It was cruel of you,” she scolded, and despite herself her voice broke. “To leave without any explanation.”

“I did not mean you to fret, sweet,” her husband said eventually. “My letter said it all. But how did you come by it at Viseu?”

Antonia explained how she had received the letter.

“So it has taken you until now to find me?”

Antonia smiled wearily. “We were sure you must be with the British.”

“I never thought,” said Duarte, his face grave, “that you would dream of following me.”

“I confess I might not have done so had I been in Lisbon when your letter came, but someone had to find you.” She touched his cheek. "I wanted it to be me. I know you must do your duty, Duarte. I would expect no less of you." She added softly, "I am so proud of what you are doing here."

Her husband was silent for a moment. "You will be, Antonia, when you understand." He gave a light laugh. "But here you are, still travel worn and muddy. You shall have the luxury of that bath I promised. That water will be hot by now."

Antonia said awkwardly, "I did bring one dress with me." She gestured at her breeches. "I intended to be seen in my finery, not like this. But I should imagine it's not fit to wear, being stuffed in a bag since we left Guarda." It was the dress William Hurst had criticised. She swallowed. "It's - it's black, of course. For Emilio."

"Black has always suited you, love," Cabral told her. "But we will not talk of Emilio again tonight. Unpack your gown," he said presently. "Hang it in the steam, and its looks may be restored, though to be frank," he added softly, with a look that brought heat to Antonia's cheeks, "I should be happy to discover you consider *nothing* you have with you is fit to wear." He went to the door and shouted again.

In two minutes, a hipbath, placed in front of the fire and screened from the door, had been filled with hot water brought up in steaming buckets from the kitchens. Duarte returned with an armful of thick white sheets, which he proceeded to put to warm before the blazing logs in the vast hearth. Hands in her lap, Antonia sat watching her husband order the proceedings: pointing, waving, dismissing all at once. She was half-afraid that it was a dream, that she would wake on a cold mountainside to find he had vanished, leaving her comfortless with only Pedro and the impatient looks of Captain Hurst for company. Idly, she wondered if Pedro was satisfied, now that his master had finally been found, and smiled to think of the servant, warm and well fed at last, and perhaps without a grumble for the first time in days.

And William Hurst?

Firmly, Antonia dismissed the thought that he might have been right in his insistence that no man would thank his wife for chasing after him. She put out a hand to her husband. She had found him, had she not, in spite of Captain Hurst? Duarte was glad to see her. How could she think otherwise when he was smiling at her now, his brown eyes aglow?

He took her hand, kissed it and let it fall, to clap his own hands in dismissal. "Leave us. Out!" and when the last soul had disappeared he closed the door, locked it and turned to study his wife. "I have you to myself again," he said. The words and the smile made Antonia tingle to the tips of her fingers. She turned towards him on the stool as he crossed the room towards her.

"They will know why you have locked the door," she breathed, but her smile was unsteady. Duarte had never been quite so obvious in his need of her before, and Antonia felt an unexpected awkwardness. She was muddy, she told herself, and she had meant to meet him in a new gown. "I should bathe," she whispered. He was beside her, very close. She could feel the heat of his body.

"Bathe," he repeated softly.

"The water will cool . . . " Antonia indicated the tub, and her husband took her arm and began to kiss it, pushing back the ruffles at her wrist, baring her arm, beginning at her palm, her wrist, the soft skin inside her elbow . . .

"Duarte - " she whispered.

"Antonia?"

"Let me bathe."

He moved his lips from her skin, and smiled lazily. "Bathe?" he repeated, and trailed his fingers up her arms to her shoulders to caress her neck and chin.

She wriggled. "I want to wash," she whispered, half-laughing. "I'm filthy, you told me so yourself."

His hands came up to hold her face, and his eyes were dark, glittering. "I don't think I care," he whispered, and bent his head to kiss her with an intensity that at first alarmed and then inflamed her. She clung to him, blood pounding in her veins, throbbing in her head, and then he let her go, so suddenly that she almost fell and she heard him cursing furiously under his breath. It was then that she realised the pounding seemed all around her. Someone was hammering on the door.

"I'll have someone's head for this," she heard Duarte storm. "I gave orders not to be disturbed." He shouted at the door. The knocking persisted. A voice was shouting back through the door's oaken thickness. In the next moment her husband had turned the key in the lock and had flung open the door. There was a hurried murmur of voices, and her husband's exclamation and a further oath. Shaken, Antonia could see no more than shadowy figures outlined against the walls by the distant flare from torchères in the corridor, and all she could hear was the agitation in the deep murmuring voices at the door, and the odd disjointed word. *'Taken - discovery - officer'* -

Presently Duarte turned from the doorway, and it was clear he was disturbed and angry. "You must excuse me, wife," he said, "I am called away. I must leave you for the present."

"What is it?" Only a moment before he had been tender, loving.

"Nothing to concern you," he said, "I trust." His voice lost its edge. "Forgive me, Antonia." He shrugged, and gave a short laugh. "I suggest in my absence you make use of that hot water. I shan't be long."

"But Duarte . . . "

"I must go," he said firmly, and disappeared, shutting the door with a bang behind him.

Antonia regarded the closed door in some dismay, then shook herself and stood up, wondering what had happened. Something serious, evidently. Nothing less would have called her husband away. How long would he be gone? She stooped to dip a hand in the clouded water steaming in the tub and glanced once again at the closed door. Fragments of the overheard conversation ran through her head, and she tried to seize on something that would make sense, give her a clue as to what had called her husband away, but the words had become confused with other, earlier conversations. Much of what had been said, some of the attitudes her husband appeared to have adopted, troubled Antonia. They were new in her experience of him. It bothered her that she appeared not to know her husband as well as she had imagined and she felt guilty at her ignorance. When had she missed the clues that might have told her how he had altered?

Depression slid over her as she saw how unlikely it was now that Duarte would return with her. Her journey had been a wasted one. Her husband seemed to feel nothing but irritation at the news of his brother's death, and he had expressed no emotion at the idea of his parents' grief or their needs. He had wondered more at her own arrival, and his most immediate questions had been of her escort and where it was the British officer had left her. Anyone would think, Antonia sighed dispiritedly, that Duarte was more concerned with *him* than with his family.

The thought seemed to reverberate in her tired brain with a strange clarity. *Duarte was more concerned with the officer.* Antonia straightened in one sharp movement. What had the men at the door said? "Taken – Officer –?" Abruptly she sat down and dipped the end of a sheet in the water, wiping it over a forehead grown pale under the dirt. She must be mad to think there could be a connection between the overheard words and Duarte's questions. There was no reason to believe either man would concern himself with the other. Why *should* either care about the other? It was mad to think so. And yet despite agreeing to remain in Cerchoso the Captain had been clearly frustrated at being forced to do so. He was not beyond making some effort to discover where she had gone. Would he have followed her here? Why would he have followed her here? Antonia dampened the sheet again, telling herself she was agitating herself over nothing. If Captain Hurst had followed her why should it matter? It was too fanciful. By the time she had bathed and dressed Duarte would have returned and she could ask him for an explanation.

Her fingers fumbled at the buttons of her shirt, but her eyes were drawn again to the door. She swallowed. Her hands reached for her jacket. She slipped her arms into it, pulled it around her, and fastened it. Hesitantly, she walked to the door and tried the latch. It was unlocked. With an indrawn breath Antonia pulled at the door, and it swung open with a gentle creak to show her a darkened, deserted corridor, lit by the flare of distant torches. Even more distant was the muffled sound of voices.

Antonia stepped into the corridor, and with a last regretful glance at the brimming tub behind her in the candlelit room she closed the door and walked quietly towards the sound of voices.

CHAPTER THIRTEEN

The darkened corridors were chilly after the bedchamber and Antonia shivered, regretting her cloak. With one hand to the wall on her left to guide her, she made her way along the passage. The light grew stronger and the voices louder, and Antonia realised she was near the head of the wide staircase that led to the hall below. She moved on tiptoe now, and at the top of the stairs halted in the shadows and peered downwards.

Her husband was in the hall. She could hear him, even angrier than before. He would be furious, Antonia told herself, if he thought she was spying on him. Other voices were audible. None that Antonia recognised. She began to feel reassured, rather foolish. Her imagination had run away with her; there was no connection; some other matter had provoked Duarte's anger: Afonso Pereira. But if that were so, Antonia thought uneasily, then indirectly the fault was hers. Pereira shouldn't suffer the entire weight of her husband's displeasure.

She sidled down the first few steps, wondering who was with her husband in the leaping shadows at the foot of the stairs. There were several figures grouped below her. Then someone spoke, the words thick and indistinct as if there were a speech impediment. The words were English.

Startled, Antonia took another two steps. A man in the hall was struggling with the others. Antonia craned her neck for a better view.

The voice rose again, slurred and undefined. "D'you take French money to spy on your British allies? Or does your kind of patriotism come free?"

There was a flash of a fist, a sickening thud that made Antonia gasp, and the captive's head jerked back. Fair hair flopped over a bruised forehead, and fell into light-coloured eyes.

"No!" Antonia took an involuntary step back up the stair, hand to her mouth. She had spoken aloud, but went unheard as the hostage spoke again, this time through gritted teeth.

"You can go to Hell."

Another blow followed the first. "Stop, stop!" Antonia cried, "What are you doing?"

Her husband spun round as she started down the stairs, his expression thunderous. "This is no concern of yours, madam," he barked. "Get back to my room, now – and stay there!"

His men gawped at each other. William Hurst raised his head to stare at Antonia with exhausted eyes.

Breathless from her descent, Antonia saw that the captain had somehow lost his scarlet coat. "Duarte, you don't understand. This is a British officer. Captain Hurst. I spoke of him earlier. He was our escort to Cerchoso . . . "

"I believe they know that already, Senhora . . . " The captain's voice was no more than a derisive croak, but it was enough for Cabral to order quickly in Portuguese: "Keep him quiet!" and Antonia heard the indrawn hiss as Hurst tried to avert his face. Only a small sound, but it was enough to rouse Antonia to fury. She darted in front of Hurst, arms outflung.

"Stop it! Duarte. Stop them."

Her husband seized an arm. "Be silent. You do not understand . . ."

"How could I possibly understand this?" Antonia shook off his hand. "I cannot believe you capable of such barbarity . . ."

 The slap silenced her. Antonia stumbled, ears ringing, her hand to her stinging cheek.

"God in Heaven!" Hurst was struggling even more violently.

"Get him out of here." Cabral jerked his head. "Take him down to the Abbot's Room. Lock him in! And make sure there's a guard on the door. You!" he said to one of the men. "Escort my wife to my quarters."

Antonia retreated in alarm from the ruffian who bore down on her, just as the man who had challenged Pereira outside the monastery pushed forward.

"Kill the Englishman now," Silva advised. "He is a threat while he lives."

A rumble of assent rose from the other men, and their prisoner grew still.

Cabral's eyes blazed. "Be silent."

Silva said nothing, but his expression remained mutinous.

"Take the Englishman away," Cabral repeated, staring Silva down, and now the men obeyed him. They hustled Hurst through the nearest doorway while Antonia turned in confusion from one to the other.

"Get my wife upstairs. I will not be defied. Keep her locked in my quarters." Cabral glared at Antonia. "You try my patience, madam. Do wives talk thus to their husbands in England? If so, you had better learn who commands here. Go back to the room. Now." His tone made Antonia flinch and, with a last glance at this suddenly dreadful stranger, she allowed herself to be led, unresisting, back to the upper floor.

*

When her husband finally unlocked the door, Antonia was sitting frozen in shock by the hearth. She recoiled at the sight of him in the doorway.

"I do not permit interference in my affairs," he began, gripping the half open door. "Is that understood?" Antonia's hand crept to her reddened cheek. "You owe me your duty, Antonia, and I will have your respect and your obedience. Is that quite clear?" She could not answer, and went on staring at him. "Is that *clear*, Madam?" he roared, slamming the door behind him and making Antonia jump with fright. "Do you understand me? I will have your obedience! Is that clear?"

"Yes," she whispered. She told herself that she had been stupid to provoke Duarte's displeasure. This was not England, after all, and she might have learned by now that a wife deferred to her man even more reverentially than at home. To argue with her husband, and in front of his men, was in his eyes unforgiveable, it has been ill advised to challenge him . . . but his slap had shattered her world. The Duarte of old would never have raised a finger against her, and the pain in her head and the ache in her heart only confused her. This was a man she had loved, the husband she had come so far to find - and he was a stranger she could not recognise.

"Yes," she repeated dully. Nothing now made sense. What she had over-heard was beyond understanding, and the image of the captain's battered face would not leave her. "But it cannot be true, Duarte," she breathed. "You cannot be working for the French."

He crossed the room in two strides. Antonia flinched, but instead of the expected blow he snatched her to him, clamping his hand over her mouth. Antonia struggled but his grip was strong. He shook his head at her.

"Hush. *Hush!*" He unclamped his hand to place a warning finger on his own lips. "Listen only." He was altered once again. Antonia could only stare in fright as she strained to free herself. "Antonia," he soothed. "Antonia. Don't fight me. Be still!" His urgency penetrated. She was still. He nodded, laid his finger to his lips once more, pointed to the chair, and gestured for Antonia to sit. More confused than ever she did so, and her husband crossed to the door, pulled it open and crisply dismissed Carlos, waiting outside the door, to his duties. He watched as his man disappeared from sight, then came back into the room, closed the door and locked it.

"Listen to me, *querida*. Ah, don't look at me as if I were a monster. Listen! You will see I have a reason to act as I did." He made as if to touch her bruises, and seemed mortified when Antonia flinched away from his hand. "You must know I would not willingly hurt you. And when you understand what I am about to tell you, you will see why I acted as I did. Hear me out. I'd no wish to hurt you, Antonia but I had no choice. I must act a part." He smoothed her hair. "You must believe that I would never use you so unless it were absolutely necessary."

This odd declaration succeeded in penetrating Antonia's jangled mind. "I don't understand," she whispered. Her husband glanced at the door.

"Listen, Antonia. After what you witnessed downstairs you will have realised all the company here swear loyalty to France. Wait, I'm not done. While it's true I command here, I act in complete secrecy. Under British orders. My real role, I trust, is unknown." His eyes locked on hers. "The British placed me here. I am not what you think me, my love."

She stared at him "You - you're working for the *British*?"

"You find it so much easier to believe I would help the French win Portugal?" Duarte wondered. He looked saddened. "Ah, Antonia, such faith you have in me."

"You are working for the *British*?" Antonia repeated. She gave a tremendous sob and flung her arms around her husband. "Oh, Duarte, Duarte! You cannot believe what I thought…."

"Oh, I think I can, *cara*. But hush now. Keep your voice low. If anyone suspects, I'm finished, believe me."

She clutched him, appalled at the risks he was taking. "Why did you not warn me? I could not guess. We assumed you were with the Militia, guarding the frontier – but then to suspect you were in league with the French . . . I never would have followed you if I had thought for a minute my doing so would place you in danger."

"How could I tell you? I never expected to have to explain. I tell you, *querida*, my position here is so confidential that only the very highest command has been told of it. Even the nearest British force has no idea I am here, and your English Captain clearly views me as a - a traitor. So it must appear to him but, but believe me, Antonia, I ensure our activities are of no benefit to our enemies." He smiled, but was immediately serious once more. "Just what *is* the officer doing here, Antonia? Your appearance during his interrogation was very unfortunate."

Antonia drew a breath. "Unfortunate! What was done to him was - was vile, cowardly. Ah, this is too much to comprehend. How could you allow such treatment?" Her voice failed. The search for her husband had placed the English officer in more danger than she had ever imagined, and although she and William Hurst had formed no more than a dubious alliance, she was appalled to think that through her he had come to harm. "You won't let them kill him," she choked. "You must not."

"Hush! I know how it must seem to you, but I shan't let it happen, believe me. But Antonia, did he follow you? You said he meant to remain in Cerchoso?"

"He must have followed me." Antonia shook her head. "His orders were to remain with me until I had found you, and I - I know he was not pleased when Pereira insisted he should stay behind."

"Ah," said her husband softly.

"This duty was not to his liking." Antonia stared into the fire. "But I think he would insist on it all the same. He is that kind of man."

"Don't fret, *querida*." Her husband took out a watch and glanced at it. "I shall take care of the captain, I promise you."

"Are you in very great danger, Duarte?" Antonia whispered. "I cannot bear to think of your risking your life every moment like this. And perhaps because of me."

"So long as no one suspects I am not what I seem, I am safe, Antonia, but I must have you returned to safety at once. It frightens me to think that you're unwittingly involved in my secret."

"Why did you say nothing when I arrived? I would have turned back, gone away at once, had I but known!"

Her husband's mouth twisted. "How could I send you away, without a word of explanation or welcome?"

"But later?" she persisted. "Later, when we were alone…"

"I hoped there would be no need for an explanation. Clearly the least known the better, my dear. I intended to tell you as much as was safe in my own time, but unfortunately, as you see, circumstances have overtaken me. My men discovered your captain spying on us and brought him in. I cannot be seen to shield him in any way." His voice dropped. "These are dangerous men, Antonia."

"Is there no one you can trust?"

Cabral bent to kiss her. "There is one, and he will soon prove useful, my love, but meantime I entrust *you* with my secret." His expression was grave. "You must leave here without speaking of what you have seen. You will forget the route by which you came, and tell no one that you have seen me here. Do you understand?"

"Yes, oh yes!" Quiet desperation.

"Then all will be well. But now," he said, pulling out the watch once more, "I must arrange the business of the captain."

"Wh - what will you do?"

"Don't trouble yourself about him. I shall have him smuggled away by the one man I do trust here. The others will hear he has been executed, but you and I will know the truth."

Antonia shivered at the word 'executed'. "Will he not speak of what he has seen? How can you make sure of him? He will not find his treatment here easy to understand, or forgive."

"Don't fret!" Her husband smiled again. "I'll make sure of him. He shall take away some sign to prove all is well. No further incursions will follow, and I shall remain safe."

Antonia buried her face in his chest. "Oh, I pray you will."

He gently disengaged himself. "I must go, Antonia."

"But you'll return?"

"I think not, tonight. My plans are set awry, and I must see to the captain before the men get out of hand." *Out of hand?* The thought chilled her blood. "There has been excitement enough for one day, I think." Her husband tilted her face to him and kissed her lightly "Rest now while you can, I must see you safely away tomorrow."

"As you say, Duarte," she murmured, but her eyes filled with tears of disappointment as she stood on tiptoe to kiss him. "You'll come tomorrow?"

"I'll come tomorrow. Early. Till then, my love, try and sleep. I shall be thinking of you. Goodnight." He kissed her forehead, and put her from him, and went to the door. When he had unlocked it, he stood looking back at her. "Goodnight, *querida*."

Antonia gazed at him steadily. "Goodnight, Duarte."

CHAPTER FOURTEEN

"Is that you, Hugo?" Cabral closed the door on his wife and stepped quietly into the corridor.

"You sent for me, Senhor?"

Cabral glanced up and down the shadowed length of corridor and drew Mendoza away from the door. "I need you to attend to a delicate matter, Hugo." Cabral's voice dropped. "Quietly, at once, and with all discretion. Take the English officer from the Abbot's room. No need for further interrogation - his arrival appears coincidental. He has come alone, apparently following my wife from no more than a misplaced sense of duty. She however has begged me to save him." His tone changed. "Finish him, Mendoza. What he knows is a threat to us all, so ensure there is no opportunity for him to escape. There must be an end to this." He jabbed a forefinger into the man's chest. "I don't care how you dispatch him but make sure you leave no evidence. My wife believes I'm arranging for his safe departure, and I'll not have her know otherwise. Is that understood?"

"Understood, Senhor." With a nod the man turned to go.

Cabral detained him. "My wife is to know nothing of this. I have been at pains to convince her that I work here for the British and I will have no one persuade her otherwise. If any man breathes a word of this in her hearing, it will be the last thing he ever does."

"It shall be as you wish, Senhor."

"Good." Cabral turned away.

"Senhor - What of the other? The Senhora's servant?"

"Pedro Teles! Of course. I told Silva to ensure he saw nothing to arouse suspicion and that I would satisfy his curiosity in the morning. Where is he?"

"Secured in the sleeping quarters."

"Finish the officer, then dispatch the servant." Cabral reflected. "If my wife should enquire, I can persuade her that Teles desires to remain here with me. She might take some reassurance from that. He has no family to make trouble."

Mendoza disappeared to do his master's bidding, and Cabral strode off in the other direction.

The two men had been no more than three yards from Pedro in his hiding place in a niche behind a statue of the Virgin in the same corridor, and he had heard everything, his chest growing tight with terror. In spite of the chilled air, sweat dewed his forehead. He told himself he should never have volunteered to accompany the Senhora in her search. Hadn't he had his suspicions all along? Yet this was not what he had expected of the journey . . .

Upon his arrival at the monastery, Pedro had been surprised to find himself casually imprisoned, and infuriated at this unnecessary and unjust treatment he had, after a moment's thought, determined to free himself and complain to his mistress. It had only been the work of a minute to pick the lock with the long handled bone knife he always carried, but now . . . how was he to avoid being missed when Mendoza went down to his cell?

Never in his life had Pedro imagined hearing plans for his own murder – and that of the Captain – discussed with such calm treachery. Was this the Cabral who had ridden off to Coimbra only a few weeks before, the son to whom he had cheerfully given the respect due to Dom Luis of Lisbon? If Pedro had not heard him with his very own ears he would not have believed such treachery possible - So now, how was he to prevent the Captain's murder? And if they ever managed to get free how could anyone convince the Senhora of her husband's betrayal?

Still, after her own brutal treatment, perhaps even poor Dona Antonia might now accept the truth.

Alone in the gloom Pedro was racked with indecision. He had been on his way to find the Senhora, and she was the closest in a room along the corridor. He might get to her now; the sound of footsteps had faded . . . But the Captain was in the most immediate danger. And with the officer freed, they might all stand a better chance of escape. It seemed Pedro would have to follow Mendoza, since the villain knew where William Hurst was held. Pedro swallowed. He could not count on finding hiding places everywhere. He was not a brave man. He knew it; even his tricks with a knife were a skill more to impress than for any deadly purpose, but now it seemed lives depended on him. It was up to him to save them.

Accordingly, he crept out from behind the Virgin, and started quietly down the hall.

*

Hugo Mendoza gestured at the ironbound door of the abbot's room. "The Englishman comes with me. Hurry."

"Senhor Alvaro is to question him again?" The man searched the ring of keys he carried, produced one, turned the heavy metal in the lock and pulled the door half-open. "Watch him," he advised.

Mendoza held out a length of rope. "Bind him then. Tightly as you can. I take no chances."

William Hurst, sick and furious with himself for being discovered and captured so quickly, was slumped on the edge of the stone seat that ran the length of the wall. He had earned additional bruises by now, and looked up at the two men without moving his head when the gaoler growled at him.

"I need another pistol," said Mendoza.

"In the armoury. When this one is secured." The gaoler lashed the rope around his prisoner's wrists, knotted it fast, then pulled the long end through a ring high in the wall and gave the rope end to Mendoza before departing.

With a vicious tug, Mendoza hauled William to his feet, wrenching up his arms to half cover his face. William swore under his breath. His captor had a look that boded ill, and it was clear no assistance would be forthcoming from either Antonia Cabral or her servant. He wondered what had happened to the Senhora and Pedro; their welcome must have been very short lived. He deserved no pity, he knew, but he winced as his gaoler returned. The other man took the second pistol from him, and thrust it into the sash around his waist.

"Take care, Mendoza."

The other snorted. "You had far better warn the Englishman. He's finished as soon as I have him outside."

William struggled to remain expressionless. He had not expected much, but to meet death quite so soon and to learn his fate so casually tested his self-control. He was certain neither man knew he understood their language.

"So you are to kill him?" The pair glanced at William, who glared back. "If the English hear of it they will avenge him."

"They've no forces to spare for just one man."

"I hear the most part of their force is gone into Spain, and that Soult is advancing from Burgos to meet them." Again, William fought to keep his expression neutral. "The Marshall had a great victory, they say, at Burgos over the Spanish rebels."

"I heard." Mendoza scowled. He pointed the pistol at his prisoner. "Well, I've this business to attend. Remember, the lady's to know nothing. Out, you!" He pulled the rope from the ring and gestured that his captive move ahead of him out of the dark cell into the hall.

*

It seemed to William that he had limped the length of a score of corridors, and stumbled down innumerable stone steps at the rope's end, before he sensed he and Mendoza were as alone as they were ever likely to be. He was edgy, irritated from being prodded with the pistol at any hesitation, and finding it harder by the minute to remain passive. He gripped the rope linking him to his guard.

"Down here!" Mendoza commanded suddenly. They had come to an arch beyond which steps spiralled up and down into equal blackness. William felt air cool on his bruised face. One end of the staircase must be open to the outside, the end of this expedition then, with his executioner? Every fibre in his body tautened. Could he jerk on the rope? Pull Mendoza off balance down the stairs past him? And if they hadn't broken their necks falling after each other, could he beat Mendoza senseless in the dark? Or when the man went to prod him again, could he jab back with enough force? Perhaps snatch one of the pistols? And fire it? With his hands trussed tight enough to cut off all feeling to his fingers? Very clever if he could manage that! But something must be tried, now - before he was forced into unhelpful darkness. William's hands tightened on his tether. He swung round. Jerked the rope. Mendoza gasped. William swung more fiercely, describing an arc with the taut rope. The other man lurched forward, amazingly fast, slammed into the arch, fell in a heap.

Astonishingly he did not rise again.

William stared, panting. He propped himself against the arch to look down at the body still linked to him by the rope. Incredible luck!

Or perhaps it was the knife in the man's back that had killed him.

"Mother of God!" Pedro's face was a study of terrified triumph as he hurried forward. "What possessed you to pull him like that? I might have missed."

William bent double, catching his breath. "Thank God you did not." He was shaking, on the verge of mirth. "By the Saints, Pedro, I thought it was my trick that had done for him." He regarded the hilt of the knife protruding from between the shoulders. "Hurry! Take back your knife. These knots have made my fingers numb." He chafed at his swollen wrists and tingling fingers. "I was never so glad to see anyone in my whole life," he whispered, wincing as restored circulation shot needles of discomfort into his hands. "Where in heaven have you come from?"

"They had me locked in some sort of cell. I picked the lock, and went exploring." Pedro slid his knife back into his boot, and hastily explained what he had overheard.

"So Dona Antonia is to believe I have been returned to safety," Hurst muttered grimly. "Where have you left her?"

"In a room upstairs."

"I'd better fetch her," William sighed, stooping to retrieve the two pistols. "Hurry. Help me dispose of this brute."

"I know where she is. It would be better if I brought her to you." Pedro panted, as they struggled to roll the body into the darkness. "But you - I imagined you still in Cerchoso."

William straightened, wiping his hands. "Did you?" He saw from Pedro's grin that his arrival had not been wholly unexpected. He kicked the rope after Mendoza.

Pedro's grin vanished "But my lady knows nothing of any of this, I swear. But did you find another way in?"

"I was brought in by the front door," William admitted. "They found me outside." He'd make no excuses. He'd been tormented into stretching the pain out of his scars and the cramped movements had been detected. "Listen, Pedro, you must escape however you can. Return to Guarda. Tell Colonel Ashe what has happened, how to find this place."

"If I can remember. But you forget my duty to my mistress, Captain."

"You're dressed warmer than I for the journey." He indicated his shirt and breeches. "And you must go now. When Cabral discovers this, he'll want the place emptied. We may lose him again. You must go." He was relieved when Pedro reluctantly agreed. "I fancy that staircase leads outside." He nodded at the archway. "You might try that first. Mind the body." He checked one of the pistols and held it out, but Pedro refused it, patting the boot that once again concealed his knife. "Right, tell me again exactly where to find the Senhora." Pedro told him. "Good enough. Off with you then, and Pedro - " He flashed him a grin of desperation. "Find Colonel Ashe as soon as possible, won't you."

"How will you get away, Captain?"

William grimaced. "By the skin of my teeth, if I'm lucky."

CHAPTER FIFTEEN

Turning the key in the lock, William creaked the door open. Seeing no one but the Senhora curled in her cloak and dozing in front of the fire, he slipped into the room, closing the door after him. Glancing about, his attention was caught by clothing strewn on a half open chest. His expression brightened, and quietly he crossed the room to sort over the chest's contents. Dumping an armful of warm clothing on the bed, he proceeded to pick out and put on various items, then turned back to the sleeping girl.

The occasional spurt of flame from the dying fire lit the tousled hair and the planes of her fine boned face, and showed him a cheek still discoloured from her husband's blow.

"Senhora." His voice was urgent but not ungentle. He gripped her shoulder. "Wake up, Senhora." The girl stirred but did not waken. "Antonia!" The sound of her name roused her, and she opened her eyes and gazed frowning into the fire. "Senhora. Quietly now."

With a gasp, she twisted round. "You?" She blinked at him and pushed back her hair. "You!" she said again, "What are you doing here? Your face – Are you all right?"

In the cracked note of concern, William took a degree of reassurance. "No questions now." He glanced at the door. "We have to leave. Are you ready?"

She followed his glance. "Leave?" Her voice shook. "Weren't you to go back with one of my husband's men? What has happened? Duarte said tomorrow. Is it tomorrow already?" She stumbled to her feet, her cloak falling to the floor.

"Quietly," William warned again. "There's no time to explain. We have to leave." He dropped clothing at her feet, and picked her jacket from the pile. "Put this on quickly – "

She did not move. "I don't understand . . . "

"Put it *on!* Quickly now." When she still made no move, he took the jacket, stuffing her arms untidily into its sleeves. "Put it *on!*" His urgency penetrated at last, and like a child, she lifted her arms as bidden, raising her chin for him to fasten her cloak. She seemed to be trying to read the expression in his eyes.

"What has happened?"

"A change of plan."

"You've seen my husband? He explained?"

"I know we have to go."

"But Pedro . . . ?"

"Has gone ahead. Quietly now." He took her hand and drew her to the door. Putting a warning finger to his lips, he pulled out one of the pistols and with his free hand unlocked the door, waited one moment, then pulled it open, and stood to one side.

Antonia was wholly confused. She watched Hurst as he peered into the corridor, wondering if she was not to bid her husband a last farewell, but when the captain reached back for her hand, she gave it to him without demur and followed him out.

They had gone only a few yards when Hurst stopped so suddenly that Antonia bumped into him. "Back," he murmured, and pushing her behind him, regained the room. Shutting the door, he leaned against it, and Antonia saw there were fine beads of perspiration under the fall of fair hair. "Your husband is coming," he said.

"He doesn't know you are free!" Antonia realised that Hurst could not know Duarte had ordered his release. He had escaped somehow and imagined her husband his enemy still. Before she could reassure him, he had taken her hand, gripping it with an intensity that matched his words.

"You are going to have to trust me as you have never trusted me before, Senhora," he began, and his attention wavered briefly from her to the door.

"I do trust you, Captain," she murmured, "even though you've deceived me in promising not to follow, but you have no need to be anxious – "

"Senhora," he interrupted, "your husband is nothing more than a traitor."

"So it must seem – " How was she to explain when she was not to speak of Duarte's real purpose? "But you must understand . . ."

"Understand he's convinced you that he's helping the British?" Hurst's eyes were on the door.

"You know?"

"Pedro heard him bragging of it. As he also overheard your husband's plans to have the pair of us killed. And you were to believe . . ." He stopped abruptly as there was a tap at the door, and pushed Antonia behind him.

"Antonia? Are you awake?" The door opened, and her husband edged into the room. Staring at the empty bed, the muddle of clothing on the floor, he halted, swore, and turned to leave. But the captain had swung the door shut.

Cabral's hand went to his sword hilt, and Antonia gasped.

Ignoring her, he challenged Hurst. "What, are you still here? I thought you gone by now."

"Save your breath, Senhor," Hurst replied coldly. "Your wife knows the truth."

Her husband did not waver. "Antonia, go outside," he commanded, "and call the guard!"

She looked from him to Hurst, and back again, wholly bewildered.

"Antonia!"

"I - I don't understand," she whispered.

Hurst had shot out a hand as if to prevent her leaving, but now he let it drop. "She knows your plans, Cabral. How you planned to have me murdered once you'd convinced her I was to be freed."

"You believed this nonsense, Antonia? When I explained everything not an hour since?" Pushing his sword back into its scabbard, her husband shook his head. "Call the guard."

Antonia did not know what to do, or whom to believe. "Please understand," she pleaded, "I - I cannot . . . "

"Your wife comes with me, Senhor." Hurst sounded almost exultant. "And so do you."

Antonia looked up at that, shocked.

Hurst nodded. "My superiors have a consuming interest in your husband and his activities, Senhora," he said grimly. "And I plan to return with him."

"You must not . . ."

"The fool doesn't understand what he's walked into, Antonia! I told you how it would be."

She covered her ears. "Stop! Do not speak." Turning to Hurst, she knew she had to explain. "He does not want me to tell you, but my husband is here as a British agent. He must remain undiscovered. And only one other man knows the truth . . . "

"So why did Pedro overhear him giving orders to have us both killed after promising you I should be freed?" Hurst gripped her arm. "Don't let him fool you again, for God's sake!"

"K - killed? No! You surely must have misunderstood. Wh - where is Pedro?"

"I told you," Hurst reminded her, his voice low. "I sent him off. He's gone. Didn't I say you must trust me?"

"You must be mistaken." Antonia looked uncertainly from him to her husband. "I am sorry. I don't - I hardly know what to believe any more."

"In that case," Hurst retorted, "I'll not trust you to help me!" He gave her a baleful look. "Damn it! What more proof do you want? Didn't I say from the beginning there was something odd in all this?"

"Antonia," interrupted Cabral, "Listen to me. As your husband . . ."

"You are a traitor!" Hurst exploded. "Could you command her loyalty if she knew the truth?" He turned to Antonia. "He has never worked here for the British, nor should I imagine," he added contemptuously, "for the good of Portugal either."

"What do you know of loyalty or of the good of Portugal, Englishman?" Cabral snarled unexpectedly, and his eyes were suddenly wild. "You and your complacent insufferable countrymen! How is it you always assume you know what is best for Portugal? You know nothing of her needs, her ways, her real friends! Your country has involved mine in a war not of our choosing, and for the good of England, not Portugal. Your admirals and your statesmen have forced our leaders to desert their kingdom so that Englishmen can decide policies for Portugal. Ah, we must throw France out for trying to order our lives, but England rules us now! Well, I promise you, you won't be here long!"

Antonia gasped. Blood was pounding in her ears, and she felt almost sick. She pressed against Hurst, but in an instant she had stiffened, to stand apart.

"What *is* this, Duarte? Junot would have seized the Queen and Prince João as hostages. Portugal would have been helpless."

"Is Portugal any stronger for having its Royal Family in Brazil? Did it stop Junot from occupying Lisbon?"

"Junot is not in Lisbon," Hurst reminded him. "The British have driven him out."

"Great leaders indeed! The Signatories of the Convention of Sintra! I don't doubt you are another example of that breed. Complacent and careless!"

"But England has always been Portugal's strongest ally," Antonia protested, with a glance at Hurst, who had paled at the insult.

"Much good such an alliance has done Portugal," her husband swore. "Hamstrung by the threat to blockade our ports unless we agreed to resist French entreaties. A blockade? It would have ruined us entirely. Trade built up over centuries gone forever! We were *forced* to assist England! Portugal might have come through this situation a deal better without such a pressure. The Emperor would never have sent his forces down upon us."

"You blame England for that?" Hurst demanded. "How can you possibly know what Napoleon's plans were for Portugal?"

"How?" Cabral shot back. "Junot himself told me . . ."

"Junot?" echoed Antonia. She stared at her husband with stricken eyes. Duarte had been in conversation with the French general? His outburst had betrayed him more surely than Hurst's accusations. And by his expression, her husband seemed to know it too. He backed away from them, drawing his sword.

"There you have it," William said grimly. He threw his cloak back from his arm to move Antonia out of harm's way. "*Now* will you help me, Senhora?"

She ignored him, repeating her husband's name as if bewitched, and William saw he could count on no immediate assistance from her. "Drop the sword, Cabral."

"If you fire, Captain," sneered the young nobleman, still edging away, "you lose whatever advantage you now possess."

William wasn't sure if he could cope with two reluctant prisoners. It had never been part of his original plan to capture Cabral - and he could see that the girl was not to be trusted but now neither of them could be abandoned. He pulled back the hammer on the pistol. In the hush the click seemed deafening. "Drop the sword, Cabral," he repeated. "And stand still."

"Captain!"

He threw the girl off as she clutched at his arm. "Not *now*!" But it was distraction enough for Cabral to lunge at the head of the bed, and seize a pistol apparently concealed in the pillows. As he moved, William fired automatically, and the ball tore through the silk hangings beside Cabral's head, missing him as he straightened with weapon in hand, by fractions of an inch.

"Stalemate," William said calmly, pulling out the second pistol as the girl stifled a scream, but inwardly he was cursing, knowing the noise would bring assistance. He pushed Antonia to the door. "Go. Dammit!" She stumbled ahead of him as he backed away from

Cabral but it seemed her numbed fingers could not cope with the latch and he elbowed her out of the way. "Stand aside, then! Let me!"

Cabral raised the pistol.

William snatched the girl back to his side as the door came free. "Your wife comes with me," he warned again. He stepped into the open doorway - and with a sense of detached horror detected the intent in Cabral's narrowed eyes in the second before he fired. "Jesus Christ!" In one rapid movement he jerked the girl out of the line of fire. Felt the ball graze his shoulder. Fired back – and Cabral, clutching at his chest, staggered. Thudded first to the bed, then the floor. William stared where he had fallen. He loosed his grip on the girl, flew to scoop up her husband's discarded sword, and hurried back to the door. He glanced at the now useless firearms, stuffed them in his belt, grabbed the stunned and frozen girl, and dragged her away.

The door clicked shut behind them - and on the far side of the bed, a hand showed itself, grasping desperately at the coverlet. Slowly Cabral climbed painfully to his feet.

CHAPTER SIXTEEN

If William had ever imagined that with the Senhora's assistance he might bluff his way out of the monastery it was now abundantly clear he must think again. Not only had the shots attracted attention, distant shouts and running feet but, by the girl's blank face and reluctant steps as he pulled her along, William could see Antonia Cabral would be no help at all.

Struggling back down the length of the same corridors along which, not long before, he had hurried in search of her, William, panting and out of breath, was soon forced to stop. He must try to instil some sense of urgency. Pulling the girl into the shadows he saw he would be wasting his time. Her eyes were glazed and uncomprehending, and he realised in despair that if she could not be brought to her senses she would hamper his efforts to get them away. He had been twenty-four hours without food or sleep and battered from all he had endured since his capture. And his shoulder burned like fire. Impatiently, he shook her.

"Senhora. Antonia!"

She raised her face to him like one waking from a dream, and he saw realisation dawn in her eyes. "No," he said, as her head turned back the way they had come. "You cannot go back."

"But he's hurt," she breathed. "You shot him!" She twisted out of his arms. "I must go back."

"Don't be a damned fool," William hissed. "He's dead. You can't help him. But you can help *me!* Now be quiet, for God's sake, and just follow me." He took her arm. "But hurry!"

"You killed him!"

"He would have killed us."

"No!" she protested, struggling so hard that William was hard pressed to hold her. "No. I must go back." Cursing, he flashed a desperate glance up and down the corridor. They would soon be pursued in earnest; he prayed the route Pedro had taken had proved successful. The girl was in no condition to be reasoned with; he would do better to abandon her. "You killed him," she repeated despairingly.

William felt a shaft of remorse. Of course he could not abandon her. She had been shamefully used. She had tried to defend *him* not long before; was, Heaven knew, in just as much danger, being

English herself - and he had just robbed her of the one man who might have protected her.

"Yes, I killed him," he agreed, wearily, "and it won't help to say I am sorry for it. Even if I am. So hurry! Your husband's men are after us, and I have no intention of being taken by them again. Do you understand?"

"I won't come with you," she said weakly. "Leave me here." She pushed at his hand.

"God in Heaven give me patience! What do you imagine they'll do if I leave you here?" But she only shook her head. William glared at her. If he had to carry her out unconscious, he would do just that. By God, she could be no less trouble that way. "You got us into this mess, madam, but I'll be damned if you'll prevent me from getting us out of it," he promised. "To think I was on the point of feeling sorry for you."

The furious mutter seemed to have an effect. She stared up at him. Very slowly her chin lifted, and when he took her arm again William was relieved to encounter only the slightest opposition. "Down this way, then," he said, pointing. "Keep very close, and very quiet."

*

They emerged suddenly from the cold darkness of a tunnel into a world of thinly whirling white flakes, and he heard the girl gasp at the shock of cold air. Hurriedly he plunged the sputtering torch he was carrying into a puddle where it hissed and puttered out. They must go on. They had been lucky so far in avoiding their pursuers, but they hadn't a chance on foot; flight was hopeless without horses or mules, even if they would need to be led some distance. He'd concealed the mare, but his captors would certainly have made a search for it.

William wondered if he dared leave the Senhora long enough to make a brief reconnaissance. She'd made no audible protest as he hustled her down the winding stairs and through the interminable dank tunnels lit eerily by the hastily made torch, but in reality she was not with him. Not in her mind. Stung into action once, and startled briefly now by the snow, she had relapsed into shocked self-absorption as soon as he stopped pushing her on. He drew her back under the shelter. "I must leave you here, and find mounts," he said. He might have been speaking to a child, a simpleton, for all the response he got. He repeated his words more slowly. "Wait for me here. Do you understand?"

She blinked listlessly. "Wait?"

"Yes." He pulled the cloak around her. "Wait here." It was pointless to tell her what she must do if he failed to return. He must get back; she would freeze to death, probably without making the least shift to help herself. He pressed her gently to the ground. "Wait for me here," he said again, and with a last uneasy glance behind him bent his head against the falling snow and walked away.

He was gone some time. In the tunnel mouth, Antonia sat chilled and helpless while her thoughts blundered about in her aching head. There was some truth she could cling to and draw comfort from, if only she could find it out. But the remembrance of her husband dying, lurching, falling to the bed, hands clutched to his chest, hampered her reasoning. Duarte dead? Was she supposed to believe him a traitor? The Captain said he was, had sworn Duarte had betrayed them all. Antonia tried not to remember the argument that had raged about her.

"Your insufferable countrymen!" her husband had shouted. *"You always assume you know what is best for Portugal! What do you know of her real friends?"*

Antonia covered her eyes. She would not think about it.

Duarte's expression had grown so ugly as he stood there cursing them. When challenged, he'd drawn a sword. Fired a pistol! To stop them leaving! Was this innocence? What could it be but an admission of guilt? And her husband's aim, a small voice reminded her, had come perilously close to killing her.

No! Antonia rocked back and forth in silent misery. It could not have been deliberate. How many times had he assured her of his love? And why, why, should she believe a man she had known such a little while when she had known and cared for Duarte for - oh, so much longer? The Captain *must* be wrong. Hadn't Duarte said no one would understand? She must have faith in her husband, she must. And yet every instinct insisted William Hurst told the truth. That was disloyalty of the worst kind. Pedro would know. Pedro could confirm the Captain's story if it were true. But where was he?

She gave a despairing little moan. William Hurst had killed her husband. He had aimed the pistol. Shot him. How could she forget that? But Duarte had fired too - and only the Captain's quick action had saved them. Again, the little voice reminded Antonia that she had so nearly been her husband's target. Could he love her and risk her safety so carelessly? Was that what a man who loved her would do? Was he so desperate that any opposition must be suppressed? She put a hand to her hot and aching throat. William Hurst must be right. Duarte had never worked for the English, only the French. Her husband was a traitor. And he could not love her. Antonia began to sob with a wild desperation.

A shadow fell across her. She jerked up her head, barely able to focus through her tears, and was aware of a figure standing awkwardly in the mouth of the tunnel. He held out an impatient hand. William Hurst. Antonia smothered her sobs, not wanting to hear what he had to say. She wanted to be alone, shut away in the dark with her bewilderment and pain, but it seemed the officer had no mind to help her.

"It must carry us both," he was saying, "but we're lucky to get it." He put his hand under her elbow, and lifted her, exhausted and unresisting, to her feet. "Quickly now." Antonia knew he was pulling the cloak's hood forward over her head, and then he was leading her out of the tunnel and into the snow.

Not only had William found a mount; he'd recovered his saddlebags which, besides an item or two of spare clothing, contained a canteen of water and the food he'd brought with him days before, together with a silver flask of rum, his spyglass, and a precious compass. The bags were already strapped in place.

It took several attempts to put the girl into the saddle. He was trembling with exhaustion, and would dearly have liked to ride, but it was too dark and too dangerous to do other than lead the horse and stay alert. "Cling tight, Senhora," he advised quietly, and taking the bridle led the horse from the monastery and down the mountainside.

The journey in the dark was a nightmare. Months afterwards William would wake, sweating and breathless, imagining he was still on the steep path, the Senhora barely conscious, and the horse skittering over stones, and threatening to plunge them all over the edge at any moment . . . There was ice, frost on the path. He skidded and stumbled, his progress unsteadier by the minute, his ears strained for sounds of pursuit. Luck had got them out of the fortress, but there was still the descent of a bare and snow-swept mountain, and all the hidden dangers of darkness. It had been hell coming up. What would it be like coming down? In haste? He wondered if the men above knew better, and would leave any pursuit until daylight. . .

In an instant the bridle was torn from his grip as the horse, with a whinny of terror, went down. William grabbed at the reins, had his arm nearly wrenched from its socket. The girl was catapulted from the saddle into the darkness, and though William heard the gasp as she hit the ground, she was now nowhere to be seen. Badly shaken, he soothed the animal, which had found its footing and stood blowing and trembling beside him, to peer into the snow filled darkness. "Where are you?" he hissed. "Senhora! Speak out if you can. I cannot see you. Are you hurt?"

There was no sound but the wind sighing around him. "Senhora!"

A groan rose from some way below the path. William dropped to his knees.

"Take care," came a faint voice. "The edge h-has crumbled . . ." The rest was cut off in a little sob.

"Are you badly hurt? I am coming down."

"Not b-badly." William thought she was biting her lip. "Only my leg, my ankle." She drew a breath. "I see you now, against the sky. Be careful."

He thought he saw her too. He let the reins drop and stretched across the rocks. Reaching down, his fingers brushed her jacket. He struggled for a hold, but she was further off than he could easily reach. He swore, stretched further, got a purchase on her sleeve. "Can you hold on to me?" he gasped, half-distracted by the thought that if the horse wandered off they stood no chance at all. There was no reply. He tugged at the sleeve he held so precariously. "Can you take my hand? Seize my arm, Senhora, quickly. I cannot hold much longer."

There was a stifled sound. He felt her dragging her arm away, pulling him further over the edge. William felt a lurch of panic as his head moved another foot lower than his heels. He heard her telling him to go, to leave her there. Anger gave him strength. He hauled her towards him, how he never knew, until he could seize her with both hands. He dragged her unceremoniously up the rocky slope, leaving her sprawled on the cold, rough path. His shoulder was on fire and he was trembling with exertion and fury. For a week - longer! - he'd been taking risks of every kind for Antonia Cabral. Risking his life for this ungrateful, *useless* woman, and she was giving in without a fight. Dear God, when he got her back to safety, he would be more than thankful to have nothing further to do with the creature. William steadied the horse with shaking hands, checked and straightened the saddle and stirrups. When he had done, he turned around. The girl was still huddled on the path. "Get up," he said, through gritted teeth.

He made no effort to help her as she slowly climbed to her feet. "Come! Get up into the saddle." She seemed to stumble the few steps that separated them, and William recalled that she was hurt. Not so very badly, he thought bitterly. He stooped, hands held out for a stirrup, and would not ask her how she was. "Up!"

Placing her foot in his hand, she rested one hand on his shoulder, and was thrown into the saddle. Every movement seemed shot through with hopelessness. He turned away in disgust.

"Y- you are hurt, I think, Captain," she whispered. "Your sh- shoulder – "

"I wonder at your noticing it, Senhora. I don't doubt your little drama made it rather worse than it was before." Even to his ears the words sounded quite as bitter as he intended, but infuriatingly he found he could take no satisfaction in her indrawn breath.

"I am s - sorry," came the faint voice, "I - I had not . . ."

He interrupted: "I am sorry too, I assure you. But we had better keep silent now, do you not think."

Antonia wanted to hate him. She had, she thought dully, every reason in the world to hate William Hurst. She sat above him, her hands on a level with his blood-soaked shoulder, and thought of hating him, of hurting him as he hurt her. But she was too exhausted to do anything but struggle to remain in the saddle. She was shocked from the fall, every inch bruised and grazed from being pulled so roughly back onto the path. Inside her boot her ankle had begun to throb. But she was not a child, she told herself. She would not give way to the tears that swelled in her aching throat. The Captain would only use such a show of weakness to insult her again. But he had saved her life on the path. Clinging to a scrubby plant on that sudden slope, Antonia had realised that beneath her heels there was nothing but space, a sheer drop, but after the first panic, that first instinct to survive, she had abruptly given up caring whether she lived or died. Why go on? What had she to live for? The sorrow of explaining that Duarte was dead? That he had been shot as a traitor by an Englishman that she herself - so stupidly unsuspecting - had led to her husband? Duarte was dead. Killed. She would never see him again. She no longer wanted to live . . .

and William Hurst had kept her from dying. She had not meant to endanger him. He had already suffered because of her: the beating, his battered face, the shot fired at almost point blank range when . . . Oh, God, when Duarte had tried to shoot them both. Antonia bowed her head, wishing for the hundredth time that the Captain had not been quite so quick, nor so strong.

But she would not give way to tears now. Or she might weep for ever.

CHAPTER SEVENTEEN

The fall proved to be only one of many shocks to William's taut nerves on the nightmare descent, and he soon became oblivious to every thought but one; he must sleep or he would stumble from the path and kill them all. It was no good hoping they might soon see the way more clearly. In midwinter dawn came late. Without the thinner covering of snow that brightened the path they would have made little headway, but as night wore on the snowfall ceased and the wind dropped away, so that a thick mist crept up the mountain in a freezing cloud. William realised he must halt and find shelter.

He could not bring himself to speak again, and when he halted and pushed his way into the darkness of a crevice in the rock walls beside them, he did not explain why. He led the animal in behind him, and without a word held up his arms to the girl. She half slid, half fell from the horse and when he pointed, limped wordlessly to the spot he indicated. He pulled off a blanket and tossed it in her direction before attending to their mount. In the dark he could barely see what he was doing. Had she the sense, he wondered dully, to wrap herself in the blanket, or was she in a daze once more? Exhausted, he dropped to his knees and crawled the few yards between them. His hands encountered the rough wool of the blanket, the rigid form beneath its cover. There was an indrawn breath.

"Go to sleep," he said with a cold weariness, and tugged his own blanket around him only seconds before he fell asleep himself.

In spite of his exhaustion he endured an uncomfortable and restless night, awake long before dawn came grey into the eastern horizon. He got to his feet, rubbing his unshaven face with tired fingers. His shoulder felt hot but less painful.

The horse whickered softly as he replaced the saddle and tightened the girth, but there was no fodder, and nothing but stale bread and cheese for their own breakfast. William forced himself to eat some of the food, then took a mouthful of brackish water from the canteen, grimaced, wiped his mouth, and replaced the stopper. He cast a glance at the still form curled in the blanket and stepped cautiously outside.

Mist lay deep in the clouded valley, leaving the world above a dull grey, with outlines of ridges and distant mountains dimly seen.

What William could make out however was enough to show their direction, and he verified it with the compass, before deciding to examine his shoulder. Despite the poor light, he judged the wound could be left without further attention and shrugged back into his jacket, wrapped the cloak about him, and crept reluctantly back to waken the Senhora.

In another two hours they had progressed far enough to have the path widen, and with a groan of gratitude, William climbed into the saddle. Pereira had taken them up to the monastery by a truly circuitous route, but their return might prove less tedious despite the ridges left to negotiate. William wondered what luck Pedro had had. There was no way of knowing what outposts they might encounter. He must just hope their inhabitants owed no allegiance to the fortress above them. It was too much to hope that no one would follow. There was little cover, and although the landscape seemed deserted, he and the Senhora were not likely to remain undiscovered long. Their tracks were clear enough. The horse, picking its way down the snow-covered slopes, seemed well able to cope with its double burden, but then the girl was no more than a featherweight. He had her on the saddle before him, but he did not speak, and neither did she.

It was late afternoon before William first became convinced they were being followed. He stood in the stirrups, scanning the country above and behind them at frequent intervals, but it was only as dusk drew on that he became aware of a blot in the distance, travelling fast. How many men he could not say but they were Cabral's, for sure, and with the slush beginning to freeze again he found himself wondering if their pursuers would come on through the dark.

His unease gradually impressed itself on Antonia, but as he said nothing she did not question him. He was clearly preoccupied, still angry. Antonia, weary and dispirited, had no desire to provoke his contempt. The cloak he had pulled about her made a little cocoon of warmth, and with the fur close under her chin, and his chest at her back she was conscious of feeling shielded from a world grown hateful and empty - even if a man she hardly cared to address provided her haven. She began to drift into an uncomfortable doze.

A sudden jerk on the reins woke her, and she opened her eyes to find it was almost dark.

"You're awake, are you?" His voice was curt. His arms dropped from her sides and in another moment he had dismounted. "Off with you." Cramped and stiff, Antonia slid from the saddle, wincing as her ankle took her weight.

The Captain nodded at rocks ahead. "Up there." His voice brooked no argument, and Antonia scrambled awkwardly over the stones, conscious that he followed close behind. "Hurry!" came the low, impatient voice below her, and in a moment she felt a hand grip her boot. "Far enough."

She was thankful to stop. Every step required an effort, and she was gritting her teeth against the pain, but upon seeing the Captain's face she forgot her own distress. He was grey with exhaustion, his fair hair lank, his mouth cut and swollen, bruised jaw stubbled with three day's growth. He smelt of blood and sweat, and leather, and under the clear blue eyes - red-rimmed now from lack of sleep - the fine lines were even more pronounced. Looking at him, Antonia felt a huge, and unexpected, rush of emotion: pity, sorrow, anxiety - and an overwhelming desire to comfort this uncomfortable man who had turned her life to chaos. For a second, she and William Hurst regarded each other in the silence of what seemed like understanding.

He was the first to look away. "Rest while you can," he said harshly, and thrust the blanket at her.

William neither trusted nor expected the Senhora to keep watch and, reviewing their situation over hurried puffs at a clandestine cigar, he spent most of the night in a state of uneasy sleep similar to the night before. Each time he lifted his head to scan the pass below he was intensely aware of the curled shape beside him, so that it was with a start of alarm that he opened his eyes to moonlight, to find the Senhora's discarded blanket by his side. A glance showed him the girl huddled by the cliff edge, and with an exclamation of annoyance he scrambled to his feet.

What the Devil -?

He stared for a moment, puzzled, then crept forward. She was shredding paper in some agitation and letting the pieces drift on the wind to float down into the pass. She was making some signal, some trail for her husband's men to follow! He lunged at her. Seizing her wrist with one hand, he jerked her to her feet, wrenching away the paper with the other. "What in God's name are you about?"

In his fear and anger he used more force than he knew, and the girl cannoned into the rocks, hitting her head with a crack that must have brought tears to her eyes, but as he smoothed out a crumpled page she came at him with a smothered cry. He evaded her easily, pushed her back against the rock, pinning her to it with a forearm across her throat, opened the paper and began to read.

It was the remains of a letter. He read a few lines, turned over a torn page, read a few lines there, and looked up at the girl in shock. "What *is* this?"

"You have read it, have you not?" the girl choked, and gasped as his other arm tightened about her, and cut off her breath. Her feet had been lifted off the ground. His next question was almost a shout.

"Then why are you throwing the damned thing all over the mountain?" He gave her a rough shake. It was a letter from Cabral. A love letter, for God's sake! He'd been so sure the pages held a signal of some kind . . . and now he'd lost his temper. Raised his voice. Anyone might have heard it in the still night air. He glared down at her only to be taken aback at the blaze in her blue eyes. He had hardly expected such fire.

"Why?" he repeated.

She did not answer. She jerked her face away and left him looking at her profile. Their faces were no more than six inches apart. The moonlight highlighted the fine down on her temples, the dark sweep of lashes on the curve of alabaster cheek, a pulse throbbing under the taut skin. A fair curl fluttered, stirred by his angry breath. Under his outstretched arm William was conscious of the quick rise and fall of her breast, the curve of his arm round her waist matching the curve of the warm body. Breathing faster, he was aware that she had aroused him more than he cared to know. The furious thudding of his heart had become a pulse pounding deep in his head and, abruptly, he let her go. "Get back over there."

Her head came round at that. The fire in her eyes had died. "Leave me here," she murmured. "Please. Just — just go on without me."

"That's what you'd like?" he retorted. He bit his lip. "Don't think I haven't thought of it! You've been a thorn in my side since the day I set eyes on you. Don't think I *haven't* thought of it," he repeated. "Now, get back over there, where I can see you."

She moved unsteadily away. After a moment, he forced himself to join her.

"I hope for your sake that this is the last foolishness of yours that I shall have to endure," he warned. "If I cannot close my eyes for half an hour without your - your - going off somewhere - I shall have to stay awake, and if I am forced to stay awake, we shall both be sorry, Senhora. Do I make myself clear?" She frowned and bent her head.

"Is that *clear?*" he snapped.

"Yes," she answered in a strangled whisper, and lay down, hiding her face.

William regarded the quivering shoulders, and cursed under his breath, dismayed to find her distress had the power to hurt him, that he was on the point of muttering an apology. He hardened his heart. It would do her good to weep. He frowned at the crumpled papers still in his hand, then screwed them into a ball, and hurled them to one side with an oath. Getting to his feet, he stood looking out over the pass for some long minutes. Under the calmly sailing moon, all was still. Sighing, William picked up his blanket, wrapped it round him, then lit a last cigar, and sat down to watch through another long night.

Shaken by unfamiliar emotions, and unable to suppress the hot tears that coursed down her cheeks, Antonia heard him cursing. Pinned to the rock with an arm like an iron bar, with the aroma of cigar smoke in her nostrils, and the roughness of a sleeve harsh against her face, she had scarcely been able to answer his questions – That letter carried so long against her heart, every word engraved on her memory, had been a talisman in her quest to find her husband. When no one else had seemed to know or care where he was, it had given her strength and faith to go on.

And then tonight she had lain awake, feeling the familiar pages pressed against her breast, and Duarte's words had shrivelled and burned in her thoughts. Everything she had trusted, and loved, and cared for was false. Her husband, his loyalty, his love - everything that had meant anything at all had turned to ashes in the space of a few short hours. The letter was a lie from start to finish. She would carry it no longer, end its power to hurt her . . .

Captain Hurst had surprised her, forced her to watch as he riffled through the pages of Duarte's last letter, read words intended for her alone, knowing as well as she did now that while her husband wrote of love he deceived and betrayed her. Antonia was humiliated and bitterly wounded. Why, of all men, must this ruthless Englishman be the one to uncover the truth of her foolish delusions? He had even used Duarte's angry words.

Swallowing a sob, Antonia remembered she had sworn once before to repudiate any further weakness. This then, she promised herself, this was the very last time she would weep for herself or for Duarte Cabral.

A small spark glowed in the darkness, and the scent of cigar smoke drifted across the distance between them to wreath itself around her. She could see William Hurst's silhouette as he sat looking out over the valley. Antonia closed her eyes and drew a long breath that ended in a shuddering sob. The aroma was oddly comforting, a reminder of when life had been carefree, and normal, and safe. Had it truly ever been so?

CHAPTER EIGHTEEN

The clouds next morning wore the threatening colours of a storm, and it was still as bitterly cold but at least, William thought, their pursuers appeared to have approached no nearer during the night. Desperate now to be done with the whole business, he had already decided to leave the Senhora with some respectable family at the first hospitable village they came across before proceeding with all haste to Guarda. Unencumbered by the girl and with fresh horses he would make better time. Speed was essential if an attack on the fortress was to be successful - and responsibilities he wanted no part of weighed too heavily for his liking. Taken aback by the shock of desire he had experienced on the cliff edge, he had only been able to address the Senhora once since their meagre breakfast, with a gruff suggestion that she fill the canteen with the icy water that bubbled up from beneath a snow covered bank. She had held out her hand for the bottle without a word.

Meanwhile the patient horse had found some bruised blades of grass beneath the trampled snow and was pulling them up in eager snorts. William checked their provisions again: a quarter of a flat brown loaf, stale; a heel of cheese, and three inches of the unpalatable sausage he hadn't wanted when it was fresh. There was water -

The Senhora was holding out the filled canteen. He took it with an irritable glance at her lowered eyes, her averted face. "Thank you. Have you drunk?" She nodded. "Up with you then."

Antonia regained the saddle with a sense of relief. Her ankle was hurting badly, and a moment earlier she'd struggled to pull off her boot, disturbed to find the joint swollen and discoloured. She'd soaked a cloth in the icy rill, and though she'd flinched at its pressure, the compress eased the pain. While she rode, it was possible to push *this* hurt to the back of her mind; other aches insisted on precedence, and not all were physical. Once or twice earlier, on the road between Guarda and Cerchoso, she had felt that she and the Captain had approached some kind of understanding and now, now that every waking thought was painful, Antonia ached for a confidant - but that person was not, and was never likely to be, William Hurst.

They rode all afternoon under a sky blanketed with clouds smeared yellow and grey. Pulling up his collar, William muttered imprecations. He lifted himself in the saddle for a look behind, then bumped down, and pressed the horse into a canter.

"What is it?"

He pretended not to hear her; he would save his breath, but there were four horsemen in sight, catching up alarmingly fast. He had two pistols, but no ammunition. Unless . . . He recollected a small wrapped box in a pouch and a bag of powder too. The balls might fit the pistols. Wounds and exhaustion were no excuse. Why hadn't he thought of reloading the day before? Could he spare time now? The tree line was below them, but there were rocky outcrops within reach. William stirred the horse to a gallop.

The girl clung gasping to the saddle and to his arm, but in a moment the horse had reached a spur and William pulled it to a quivering halt.

"Down! Quickly!" he urged, already out of the saddle and dragging off the saddlebags. "Get over there behind those rocks. Take the horse." He hauled out the pistols and rummaged in the bags, pulling out, with grim relief, a sand-coloured pouch. He could not outrun their pursuers and this place was as good as any to stop them. But that left him two men to deal with - if his first two shots were perfect. If he missed those . . . He yanked at the drawstring with his teeth and began loading the second pistol. The girl meanwhile had hobbled back. He jerked up his head. "I told you to stay over there."

"I can reload when you have fired. Guard your back."

William bit back a retort. She'd be no use in the flurry he'd be in. Two shots, then a third and fourth, but it was more than he could manage himself if matters grew desperate . . . He'd toss the pistols aside, trust to his sword to finish the fight. Perhaps she *could* help. He glanced over the parapet of rock. "You can load this?" He held out a pistol and glanced again over the rock.

Smoothing the weapon, she nodded. "My – husband has – *had* – a pair very like. I would sometimes load them for him."

William frowned. Was he mad to trust her with a weapon? She was hardly in a state to be relied upon. He sighed. She was all the help he had. "You won't lose your head with all the noise." He made it an order, not a question, and did not look at her again.

"I think not."

"I hope not!" He turned to face her. "More lives than ours depend on us getting safely back to Guarda." Her gaze dropped before his stare. "Then, if you will listen, and do exactly as you're bid -" She peered over the rock as he had done and he felt himself warm almost imperceptibly to the gesture, " - I daresay I shall be glad of your assistance." The warmth was quite gone when she looked up once more. "Put the reload close to my right hand when you have it ready. Can you do that?"

"Yes."

"Right." He glanced once more at the fair curls, disordered and blowing about her head. "We wait. And not too long, I fancy."

There were four of them. Rough, dark men with dark, determined faces, wrapped round in rough, fur-trimmed garments. Riding close together they came on towards the rocks, and William had a good sight of them between the thick, leafless branches of a stunted bush that grew in a crack. He eyed them as they spurred onward, not much surprised to see that one was Silva - Silva, who had been so anxious to have him killed. Silva should be his first target, he decided, and waited until he was certain they were in range.

Bracing himself, he sprang to his feet. He fired once, dropped the pistol. Saw Silva fall forward before the horse bore him out of sight. Impossible to know whether he was dead or not. William was steadier now. He fired again. Spun a second man off his horse. He swung round. The two survivors were circling, had not yet had the sense to dismount. He stooped for the reload. Found it thrust, still warm, into his hand. Stood. Took aim for the third time. The ball found its mark. Knocked the man backwards off his saddle. A spur tangled as he fell, dragged him behind the panicked horse before he dropped heavily to the ground. The fourth man was off his horse. The second-fired pistol was again in William's hand - but his quarry had vanished. He would run for the rocks . . .

Breathless, William pushed the girl towards the horse. "Mount up!"

Antonia scrabbled for the pouch, thrust the first pistol into her cloak, got to her feet - and felt the world swirl around her. For a moment she could not move. Biting back a cry of pain, she reached for the nearest boulder, then limped to the horse only to be swept by another wave of giddiness as she fumbled with its reins. Even as she swayed she was dimly aware of the fourth man as he sprang suddenly out from the rocks.

He launched himself at Hurst who stepped backward, fired, and missed. The two of them sprawled on the ground in a flurry of fists and faces. Antonia dragged out the pistol with shaking hands. Holding it at arm's length, she aimed it at the figures rolling grunting and cursing not ten feet away. She could not fire with safety, nor was her aim as sure as the Captain's. The barrel sight wavered and Antonia, faint and helpless, was forced to let the muzzle droop. In another moment Hurst had staggered to his feet, dragging the other up with a hand clenched in the man's shirtfront. One mighty punch cracked into the man's jaw. His head snapped back leaving Hurst taking his whole weight. He let the man drop, stood half tottering over him, chest heaving with the effort, and blinking sweat out of his eyes.

Panting, William raised his head – and froze. The pistol was aimed directly at him. He tried not to flinch. God knew she had reason enough to want him dead – but then the muzzle dropped to cover the man on the ground, and William breathed again. Dropping to his knees he took the man's jaw in ungentle hands. No more bother for an hour or more, he thought grimly, and let the head drop.

"It's Carlos," faltered the voice at his elbow. "I – I think it's the one that Du – that my husband called Carlos."

"Your husband's man, at any rate." He got to his feet. Three bodies on the ground. He trusted he'd made sure of Silva too, but that first shot had been a little too unnerving. The Senhora had done well though, he thought wryly, scrambling onto a boulder to spy the horses; she should have her own mount now.

Disbelieving, he swung round, to search again. The mountainside was empty; not one beast to be seen. "I don't believe it." He searched again, up and down the slopes stretching away into the misty distance. There were no horses. Anywhere. "I don't believe it," he repeated. "The damned animals have run off." He spun back to the girl. "Wait here, I'll round them up. Where have you tied the mare?"

The girl turned with an effort. "Why, h-here. . ." Her voice tailed away as she regarded the void where their mount had been tethered, and her face paled.

"What have you done? Did you not secure it? Jesus Christ, woman! What have you done?" He almost choked. He strode to and fro. Halted, appalled and helpless. Looked round once more. They were stranded, halfway up a mountain, with a storm about to break. They had no food, no blankets, no water. And no bloody horse! Fists clenched, William took several deep breaths, and turned on the girl beside him. And as he glared at her, thick flakes of snow began very softly to fall.

Antonia was utterly dismayed. Too stunned even to begin to apologise, in too much pain to argue, she stared white-faced at Hurst as his eyes poured contempt on her.

He was so patently furious that Antonia dared not speak. And when he strode away down the slope, with a curt order to keep up or they should be caught without fire or shelter in a snowstorm, Antonia was so sure he was more than ready to abandon her among the bodies of her husband's men that she had started after him.

The effort of descending the steep slope put even more stress on her ankle. Her first few steps were agony, and Antonia limped several more paces before halting, fists clenched by her sides. Her vision seemed to blur. Below her, moving further away by the minute, the Captain took deep, ranging steps, his long legs moving steadily down the slope. He seemed not to have noticed that she had stopped, and for a moment Antonia was tempted to call out. Her mouth opened - and closed on a weak cry of despair. There was nothing for it. She must go on. To show any further weakness was unthinkable.

She drew a ragged breath, lifted her chin and started out once more. One foot, then the other, she told herself as pain lanced up her leg and sweat dampened her forehead. One foot, then the other. By sheer effort of will, hesitantly at first then more evenly as though she were an automaton, her feet took her down the mountainside after William Hurst. After a time, the effort of measuring her progress - one foot after the other, one rock after another, one stunted shrub after another - began to act like a drug, and Antonia found she was using pain to remind her when the next foot should bend, lift, drag forward . . . Soon the intervals between the sharpest pains became blurred, and her mind began to wander. Against her will, her thoughts would dwell on all that had happened since she had first encountered Alvaro Duarte Cabral, making physical hurt a welcome distraction. She concentrated on it. An uneven step, a misplaced footing, became a jolting relief, and soon she was stumbling along in a stupor, half blinded by pain yet hardly aware of it.

She did not see that the Captain had reached the tree line at last, that he was turning at last to check her progress. She was vaguely aware of him as she trudged unsteadily downwards through the ever-deepening snow, but he had no place in her thoughts as she overtook him - and as she passed him Hurst caught at her arm, and jerked her to a halt. With a muffled cry, Antonia Cabral fell face down into the soft, white, welcoming earth.

She came to a moment later, to find her face being rubbed vigorously with a handful of snow. For a second she felt nothing, then the pain returned with such ferocity that she was pitched, groaning, into darkness once more.

William was stunned. He had been watching her catch up, taken aback to have her stumble past without a look or word. He had only caught at her arm - and suddenly she was measuring her length on the cold hillside. He tried to bring her round with another handful of snow, alarmed, when she opened her eyes, by her vacant stare.

"What is it? Are you hurt?" On his knees beside her, he shook her gently.

Her lips moved soundlessly. William pushed a hand through his hair. She could hardly have fallen; she had followed him down the mountain. Had she been hit by a stray shot? There was no obvious wound. His glance came to rest on the twisted leg. "Oh, God!" She'd been limping earlier, but he hadn't paid attention. He was thinking of other things, the tinderbox, matches, and half the food still in his possession, and now they were free of their pursuers and with the timberline closer by the minute the prospect of a fire was no longer an impossibility. He laid his hand gently on the ankle, and at the first touch she cried out.

"Hush!" He sat back on his heels, regretting now the small phial of opiate that six months earlier he would have had on him. He'd forsworn its use, and all he had now was the flask of rum. He took it out, uncorked it, and stared at it. Useless to think that would help. He took a deep swallow of its contents, re-corked the top, and stuffed it back in his jacket. They needed help. It would soon be dark, and he had not the vaguest notion where the nearest village was, even if by remotest chance there might be someone skilled in bone setting there.

The Senhora was moaning quietly. Massaging his own leg, William looked around. Nothing could be done here. If he shifted her into the trees, found firewood, made a fire . . . ? He stooped and ignoring the weak cry of protest, scooped Antonia Cabral up into his arms.

Outside the crude shelter of branches, the fire in its ring of stones crackled and spat. And remembering other times and other campfires, William knew he had never felt quite as isolated as he did now. It was a while before he could steel himself to remove her boot for once it was off it couldn't be replaced. Pulling out the rum flask, he uncorked it and raised the Senhora's head. Her lids fluttered but did not open. Gritting his teeth, William forced the spirit between her lips. She choked a little, but he made her swallow a second mouthful before laying her down again. She would not be used to spirits, he hoped, and with luck . . . He waited a few moments more, drew out a knife, and seizing the soft leather slit the boot from top to bottom.

She jerked upright and fell back, and William pulled the boot away. There was a cloth around the ankle, and as he unwrapped it the foot swelled again: tight, hot, shiny skin, blotched with purple and red. There was no open break, but above the ankle the bone seemed to push out at an angle. This was no new injury, he realised. She'd wrapped this, and there'd been no opportunity for that since early morning. He'd had her reloading pistols. He hadn't known. She'd said not a word. He took fresh cloths soaking in melted snow and re-wrapped the ankle to lay the foot on the saddlebag. He added his own cloak to hers, draped that over her, then got to his feet, rubbed the stiffness from his limbs, and crawled out from the shelter.

He eyed the scurrying flakes, wondering why he'd even considered bringing Antonia Cabral when she could have remained under her husband's protection in the fortress. Pedro and he could have made their escape without involving her. Why hadn't he just left her there? His fists clenched and unclenched against his thighs. He hadn't known. Why hadn't she said something? Why had she let him to go on when she must have known she could not follow? He cursed, and turned wearily back, stamping his feet in the settling snow. Damn it! If only she'd said something!

He rubbed a tired hand over his face. Tomorrow he must find a village, horses. Tomorrow they must have better luck.

Snow fell all night, but his efforts with the fire meant there were embers enough in the morning. Wondering for a moment where he was, Hurst opened his eyes on the cold dawn, relieved to find the snow-laden shelter had kept out the worst of the weather. He rolled on his side and drew his cloak back. She was conscious, lying with eyes open, quite still. What a little thing she seemed, he thought once again in surprise. Her glance flicked to his face. Yesterday's tears had dried on her cheeks, and strain had dulled the blue eyes and deepened the hollows of her face. She seemed too exhausted to answer any questions.

He spent the next hour painstakingly constructing a litter from branches, and wondering if he would have the strength to pull it. He'd already filled the small cup to the brim with snow once again, and by the time he'd finished working, the snow had melted. He carried the warmed cup carefully to the shelter and, fighting the temptation to bawl her out for concealing the injury, insisted she drink. "Can you eat something?" She moved her head, and closed her eyes. "I've made a litter. You lie on the thing, and I drag it. We'll get down the mountain a little further, find some houses, a village soon." He hoped he sounded more optimistic than he felt.

She opened her eyes. "If you will lend me your arm," she whispered, "I may be able to walk."

"You've broken your bloody foot. It's the litter or you don't move at all." He had not meant to snap and was shamed even further by her tired gaze and the quiet way in which she murmured that she understood.

"I'm glad you do," he replied, and got up to kick snow over the fire.

The litter, not as helpful as he hoped it would be, was incredibly hard work. Despite the cold he was soon perspiring as he manoeuvred the load down through the trees, the makeshift harness catching at his wounded shoulder and pulling him up short. After what seemed some painfully long hours, he halted and cast an eye at the leaden sky. It must be nearly noon though there was no sun to confirm it. With a sigh he took up the weight, and without warning the harness snapped for the fourth time that morning, jolting them to a halt yet again. This time William could see the harness was beyond repair. Swearing under his breath, he hurled it aside. The girl's pinched white face gave him a stab of alarm, but when he bent and spoke her name she opened her eyes, albeit with an obvious effort.

"I'm no good at this," he said. "And making you suffer more than I imagined when I suggested it. I think it's time to abandon it."

"Yes." Her lips barely formed the word.

"I must carry you. It can hardly be more difficult."

He did not know how wrong he was. She was not heavy; he knew that already. A dead weight would have been easier, but guarding her against knocks and jars was damned near impossible. Every few minutes he'd to swing aside to avoid a branch; every ten minutes he'd to set her down, to rest himself. He began to dread the tensing of the light body; knowing she was struggling not to protest seemed to make him clumsier than ever.

"This is useless," he panted after an hour of backbreaking progress. His thigh hurt like blazes, his shoulder was on fire, and he was light-headed from exertion and hunger. He halted, swung the girl to the ground, and sank down beside her, exhausted. They'd seen nothing all day. No tracks, no animals, so sign of human habitation. Only rocks and trees and snow covered slopes. He raised his head, gulping in the cold air, marginally cheered to see the skies were clearing. Clouds banked in scarlet-lined mourning hid the sun but there were already patches of deepest turquoise overhead. In another hour the stars might be visible. Wearily, William scanned the horizon. He had hoped by now to be close to civilization but there had been nothing to see.

His tired eyes were caught by a twinkle above the far off hills. The stars had begun to appear. It must be later than he imagined. Tomorrow, he thought, I shall have to carry her a different way.

The stars continued to twinkle. In the gathering twilight William blinked at them. He got slowly to his feet and found the tiny pinpricks of light no longer on the horizon but below it. He rubbed at stinging eyes, stared again, and muttered a little prayer of relief. It seemed civilization was not so very far away after all.

CHAPTER NINETEEN

It was too late to consider travelling the remaining miles in the gathering twilight. There was nothing for it but to make another shelter, another fire, and though William had intended saying nothing to the Senhora about the lights, one look at the closed wan face under the wrapped hood, told him some encouragement was needed.

"There are lights over the next hill," he said, crouching down to pull the cloak more securely. "It's difficult to know how far but I don't doubt we shall reach help tomorrow. You can be brave till then, can't you?" He patted her shoulder awkwardly. "You've done well. Bear up a little longer. I'll have you safe as soon as I can." She did not reply. "Senhora?" He put his hand to her cheek. She was very warm. He laid his chilled palm against her forehead, and flinched when she cried out.

"Senhora." Slowly the dark lashes lifted. "Senhora?" he repeated. "Antonia."

Her hand crept out of the cloak to rest on his wrist. How hot and dry it felt. She blinked at him, licked dry lips.

"Duarte," she croaked.

"Antonia, it's William Hurst. Can you understand?"

She frowned again, and William saw she was trying out his name in her mind.

"No," she murmured at long last. "Wh - where is Duarte? I - I feel - unwell . . ."

"You are not well. You had an accident, but you'll be safe very soon."

"Where is D - Duarte?"

"He's not here. I am here. William Hurst - Captain Hurst. You remember me."

Her eyes closed. Tears squeezed under the lids to slide down her hot face. "No," she said huskily. "No."

He would not fuss her. Should he check her foot again? It would need another compress. As would her poor fevered head. He tugged out the tail of his shirt, still red-streaked from the rain a week before, and wincing with the effort, ripped off the lower half. Heaping snow into it, he twisted the ends - then held it briefly to his own face, wishing tiredly that someone would look after the pair of them. He could sleep for a week himself.

In the dark, he sat with eyes half-closed, and listened to the girl as she tossed and groaned through the night, her words no more than a murmur, disjointed and confused. The only word pronounced with any clarity was a name, and William heard it over and over till he was sick to death of both the man and his name. What had Cabral done to deserve such attachment to his memory!

William clamped his hands over his ears. He was sick to death of Cabrals.

With a sigh, he lowered his hands, felt her forehead, lifted away the compress and freshened it yet again. It must be the twentieth time that night, he thought, and she was no better. "Drink this," he murmured. He raised her gently, holding the cup to her lips. She tried to push it away but he insisted. "Drink!" and having got her to swallow, lowered her again and studied her in despair. What should he do? What could he do? She could be from another world as far as he was concerned. If it had been one of his men, he would have known better how to act. What was he *doing* here? He should be with his regiment in Spain, not perched on a hillside in Beria Alta with a sick and helpless woman!

He bent to give the smoothing of the compress his gravest attention.

Antonia Cabral ceased her muttering, uttered a heavy sigh, and as William tensed, she seemed to slip into a more comfortable sleep. His mouth curved into the faintest of weary smiles. His shoulders eased. He wriggled himself into a more comfortable position and was asleep before he had even closed his eyes.

The morning's first task was to check the settlement he had marked the night before, and a long increasingly anxious search was finally rewarded with the sight of a cluster of roofs in the furthest distance, betrayed by the merest wisps of smoke rising in the still air. It was further off than he had imagined. He could reach it by midday. But not with the injured girl. He could not reach the settlement carrying her. It was beyond what little strength he had left. He limped back and eased himself down beside her. She seemed asleep, her breath coming without distress. The compress was still warm, and as William lifted it away as he had done so many times during the night, Antonia Cabral opened her eyes.

"Good morning," he said quietly.

Her lips moved eventually. "G'morning."

He felt washed with relief. "You feel a little better."

She shook her head feebly. "Have I been ill?"

"Feverish. You still are. You must drink." He set the cup down hurriedly. "Don't try to sit up!"

Too late. With a groan she toppled backwards. William grabbed at her and felt something tear in his shoulder like the burn of a knife, the hot wetness of blood trickling down his chest. Clutching the limp body to him, he swore. "I said 'Don't move'!" Stiffly, he laid her down again, hearing her teeth chattering with cold and shock. "Oh Jesus!" Gasping, he put his head between his knees, and the spinning black spots in front of his eyes faded. He raised his head, and with a hand to his shoulder began very weakly to laugh. He'd imagined last night that they would soon reach safety, and they were as far from it as ever! But the girl's teeth went on chattering, and laughter died on his lips. He reached for the cloak. "I'm going for help," he whispered. "All is well."

He made every preparation. Remembering the wild pigs, he even placed one of the pistols loaded and ready to fire beside her, though he doubted if she could fire it. What if she could not even manage the cup? William put a hand to his aching head. He ought not to leave her. What guarantee was there that *he* would reach the settlement, let alone bring someone back? And could he find her again? Perhaps the villagers would be hostile; perhaps there would be nothing to ride. But they could not remain on the mountain, and alone he could not get Antonia Cabral to the village. Help must come to her. For her sake, he must reach the village and return with help. Soon.

Thankful that she was awake and lucid, he crouched beside her, explained that he was leaving, detailed the preparations he had made, what he had left with her, what she should do. Her eyes never left his face.

"You understand?" Guilt and anxiety made him sharp. "I'll be back as soon as I can, but until then you'll be on your own." She nodded. "Try not to be anxious." There was a lengthy silence. "So," he said, finally, "I must be gone.", and flinched as she laid her hand on his sleeve. *Don't beg me to stay*, he prayed. *I don't think I can deal with that.* "What?" he asked, and had to strain to catch her answer.

"T- take care, Captain," she whispered.

William could not speak. He turned and squeezed out into the cold air.

Heaven must have been watching over him. Just after noon he came staggering up to the first of the shabby houses in the town he had seen from so far away, aware that he was being stared at and avoided as if he were a madman. Limping, dull-eyed, bearded, and - worse - in an unfamiliar grubby uniform, he *looke*d like a madman, with the bloodstained shirt torn and loose. Men passed by on the other side of the street.

He sagged against the corner of a building, thankful to find himself among people again; he did not think he could manage another step unaided. He raised a weary hand to the curious watchers.

"*Ola!* I need help," he gasped in Portuguese.

A man brandished a stick. "Away! We want no deserters here."

Hurst pushed himself off the wall. "I'm no deserter, dammit," he panted. "There is a lady needs your help. Up there." He waved unsteadily in the direction of the mountain slope. "Get me horses. I can pay." He fumbled in his breeches, produced two gold pieces. "Hurry! She is hurt and alone." He bent, hand to the wall, coughing with the effort of speech. There was a conference among the gathered crowd.

"A lady?" The man who had spoken first approached a little nearer. "What of her? What would a lady be doing in the mountains with the likes of you?"

"There's no time for this," Hurst began. "Her name is Cabral. Senhora Dona Cabral. I am a British officer. Her escort. But we have lost our horses, and she is hurt." He appealed to the others. "I must get back to her. It will soon be dark, and I cannot be sure of the way."

"A British *officer?*" someone repeated scornfully. But the name meant something after all. "Cabral, did he say? A Cabral from Belmonte?"

Hurst tensed. Had he jumped from the frying pan only to land in the fire? Struggling to stay upright, he thrust his hand, half frozen with cold, inside his jacket for the concealed pistol. But there was no danger.

"Get horses," he heard someone say.

They were the sweetest words he had heard in a long time. He slid slowly to the ground. "Not before b-bloody time!"

CHAPTER TWENTY

To William's dismay, with still some way to go and before it was quite dark, the men began to talk of stopping to rest the horses. He urged them on, aware that the fire he had left burning would have died. They must keep going while they could. They followed him, grumbling, but as they climbed higher and William began to recognise certain landmarks, their enthusiasm returned. Night drew on by the minute however, and their shouts and calls went unanswered. Finally, after a heated debate, the men declared they could go no further in the dark and stopped to make a fire. His appeals had no effect, and eventually William seized a flaming branch, and limped angrily away.

"Let him go," one of the men said. "The horse will not let him mount while he carries the brand."

It was as well William was on foot, or he might not have recognised the mysterious line in the snow for what it was. It crossed his line of march, uphill in one direction and down the other. He thought them animal tracks at first except they were too dark and too deep, and when he knelt to examine them he got up hurriedly.

Footprints! Climbing the hill.

Who had been here? Had Antonia Cabral already been rescued? Was that why they had heard nothing? Hurst looked up the slope and down again to the campfire and his companions. This ground was so familiar. She must be close if she were here at all. William gave a shout and began to climb as fast as he could.

He was not expecting to stumble almost at once over a heaped figure, crumpled in the snow twenty yards further on. Falling headlong, he had the breath knocked out of him, the brand leapt from his hand, and he lay for a second, dazed, before regaining his feet. He had fallen over a body. A cold, stiff corpse of a man, face down, arms spread.

Silva. Full of foreboding, William rolled the body over.

His gut contracted. It was not Silva.

It was Alvaro Cabral!

And there, inches from his outstretched fingers, lay his pistol, the pan blackened and empty. It had been fired even as he had fallen.

William sprang to his feet. Dear God, no! He snatched up the half-extinguished brand. Broke into a run that covered fifty yards of hillside. Stopped short at the circle of rocks surrounding the cold ashes of a fire.

He was just about to shout her name when he saw her, lying a few yards off, face down, as stiff as the man on the hill. He sprinted the last few yards, flung down the torch, and dropped to his knees. He had not finished Cabral after all! The man had followed them and found only his wife. The fair hair lay spread half-frozen to the snow by a glistening darkness.

"Damn you," he said savagely as he rolled the limp body over and found the snow splotched with stains. "Damn you! Damn you!" he repeated through gritted teeth. "I was coming as fast as I could." He brushed snow from her waxen face, freed the sticky hair. "I was coming, dammit!" He seized the bloodied head in his cold hands, and gripped it hard, as if he could make the dead girl hear.

The breath caught in his chest. There was movement under his hands. The lashes, so dark against white cheeks, lifted. Slowly Antonia Cabral opened her eyes. William's hands tightened around her face, and he lifted her closer. "The horses are here," he croaked. She frowned tiredly. He willed her to understand. "The horses. We have you safe." His speech was firm and clear now, and he saw her struggle to comprehend, the blue eyes fast on his. "Can you hear me? You're safe."

Her lips moved. He bent closer.

"You came back?"

"I said I would."

"I —I did not b-believe you." Her eyes closed and her head lolled to one side. William clutched the limp body to him. Over his shoulder he yelled. "Up here! Hurry!"

*

There was a convent in the town. William had been told she would be as well looked after there as anywhere in Portugal, and he was only too glad to hand responsibility to the black robed nuns. He stayed long enough to see Antonia Cabral carried into one of the long rooms and placed in one of the cots before the nuns, shaking their wide starched caps over the girl, shooed him away. There was nothing more he could do.

William was glad to get away. The Senhora's life was in other hands now, whether she lived or . . . In any case his duty was to report to Colonel Ashe. Reluctantly, he allowed the nuns to dress his shoulder, begged a clean shirt and angry and depressed, headed back to Guarda. Five miles outside the town, he encountered Colonel Ashe with the vanguard of the hurriedly organised expedition. Pedro had arrived safely, and they had been wondering where he was. He was besieged with questions – on the fortress, his escape, and Cabral's fate. Pedro was horror-stricken to hear his mistress was hurt, and demanded to know every detail. William gave them what information he had.

"The ball grazed her head. She lost blood – it seemed an alarming amount at the time, but I'm told she may not suffer too much from that. Her leg is broken, at the ankle - and then, of course, she'd been lying hurt and chilled far too long." Why did his thoughts pin themselves to that last memory? He'd felt quite sick with relief, but then to hear she had never believed he would return – William was shocked to find how much that hurt. "I don't know if she realised it was her husband she'd shot. She may have thought him Silva, as I did. Silva might possibly have escaped the ambush, but I imagined I'd taken care of Cabral at the monastery. Dear God, it was a hell of a shock to fall over him. Worse to realise he'd already fired!" It was hard to credit how quickly he'd covered those last few uphill yards. He fell silent. Then with a shrug, and a glance at the Colonel, he said at last, "Cabral's death will have altered your plans, sir."

"No matter." Ashe frowned. "You look in bad shape. Better get back to Guarda and get some rest."

"I was coming with you, Colonel."

"No, you weren't," Ashe growled. "I've got Pedro here, and we've been over the details often enough. You've only confirmed what he's been able to tell me. You've done enough. Off with you now, before you find yourself in need of those nuns' ministrations."

William tried to smile. "A happy thought."

"I'll want to talk to Senhora Cabral when - if - she recovers. Ride down in a day or two. We'll rendezvous there."

"Very good, sir." William did his best to hide his lack of enthusiasm; he had hoped to have seen the last of the Cabrals.

"I should also like to visit Dona Antonia if it is permitted, Senhor." Pedro was clearly upset.

"Of course you shall, sir. But we have a job to do first. Farewell for the present, William. Wish us luck."

"I do, sir. Take care of the Colonel, Pedro. Good luck to you both."

"Look after my lady, Captain," Pedro implored, and with a last anxious glance hurried away.

They were soon gone. William waved the expedition on its way, and when the last man had passed, he drooped in the saddle. Good luck indeed! Duarte Cabral was no longer in his bolthole, and it was unlikely there was a soul left in the place. He looked at the troops trotting into the distance, sighed and turned his face once more towards Guarda.

CHAPTER TWENTY ONE

At the convent gates, William battered at the faded paintwork for admission. For three days he'd slept the clock round, but it had been hard to summon energy and enthusiasm enough to return. He knew he should feel relief at the successful outcome of the whole miserable adventure, but though Cabral's wife was no longer his responsibility her last words continued to haunt him. He'd sweated blood to find her, he thought bitterly. Had given his word to return. It felt as if his promise, and the effort he'd made, meant nothing. And why should he give a damn for her opinion anyway? He yanked at the bell rope once again.

Through the grille he saw a small plump figure being blown across the courtyard towards him, her hands to the stiff white sail of her coif. Opening the gate, and learning his business, the little nun escorted him past a dilapidated statue of the Virgin to the white and orange-washed infirmary and left him at the door with a warning not to stay long.

William had no intention of staying. The smell greeting his nostrils was all too familiar and he grimaced at the odour of sickness and decay, remembering his own experiences. It was clear the nuns worked hard to keep the place scrubbed and the sick cared for, but William pitied anyone unfortunate enough to be confined here. Anxious to have the ordeal over, he entered the gallery where he had seen Dona Cabral admitted, then hesitated. It was the wrong place. He paused at the empty cot.

At the top of the great hall, a harassed young novice appeared to be coping alone. William steeled himself to approach her. "Forgive me, Sister," he began, "There - there was a sick lady here – " He pointed.

"The lady died, Senhor. Just this morning."

His voice seemed to come from a great distance. "She – she died?"

"Are you quite well, Captain?" A warm voice at his shoulder turned him round to face a middle-aged woman garbed unlike the other in white.

"Perfectly - well," he answered faintly. "Merely - dismayed to learn - " He cleared his throat. "Senhora Dona Cabral." he said. "I - I saw her brought in only three days ago."

"I remember," the nun said briskly. "I was here when you brought the poor child in. I am Sister Jerome." She seemed to study him intently.

"She — she - died?"

"Not at all," the nun replied. "She was moved to a private room upstairs. She is after all a Cabral." She nodded in response to William's suddenly outraged expression, and laid a roughened hand on his sleeve. "Don't look quite so relieved, Captain, the creature is still very sick." She nodded again. "There, you can reassure yourself if you wish. The staircase at the end of the hall, second door. Sister Matthias is with her." As William, with a dazed murmur of thanks, turned to go she added soberly, "The child seems to have little will to live."

He averted his face. "Hardly surprising," he said eventually. "Her faith in a great many things has been badly shaken. She saw her husband shot if any other reason were needed. And as it happens," he muttered as he climbed the stairs, the nun's startled face in his memory, "she thinks I killed him."

Upstairs he found the door he was seeking. Taking a deep breath, he knocked twice. A nun peeped out. "Sister Matthias? I'm told I may see your charge."

The door opened to reveal an airy whitewashed room, unadorned and sparsely furnished. Opposite the door stood a massively carved chest, above which hung a tortured crucifix of black wood. A high bed, mysteriously heaped with mounds and cushions took up most of another wall and in the bed lay a still, sheeted form, propped on a heap of pillows. The nun held a finger to her lips. "She sleeps. Do not stay long."

William had no desire to stay at all. He nodded impatiently.

"A small moment then." The nun walked to the window and with creaking joints knelt to resume her prayers. With an uncertain glance in her direction William crossed to the bedside - and was shocked to a halt. He knew it must be her from the colour of the hair on the pillow, but - but was this Antonia Cabral? She seemed even more frail than Hurst remembered, the hollows of cheeks and eyes more like bruises than facial contours, the fragile beauty almost extinguished. A rough barely healed wound scored through her hairline, and the hands lying on the sheets were almost transparent.

Unprepared in spite of Sister Jerome's warning, William felt as if he'd been thumped in the chest. He sat down abruptly on the edge of the bed, wondering if the nuns knew what they were about. He had expected some signs of recovery. Had all that effort had been for nothing? A sudden anger swelled in him. Had Antonia Cabral lost the will to live merely because of that bastard of a husband? She couldn't give up. Not because of Cabral!

But wasn't *he* himself as much to blame, for provoking Cabral, and for exposing his lies – and for making her party to all of it?

He found to his horror that he had captured one thin hand and was gripping it fiercely. He let it drop as if he had been scalded, and stared about him. Silence filled the room, broken only by the girl's light, rapid breathing, and the gentle click of rosary beads. In another moment Sister Matthias would tell him to leave, William thought. He should leave. It had been a mistake to come, and it would be a relief to go. There was nothing he could do. He glanced again at the pallid face, the hair layered in damp curls, and jumped to his feet to take several steps about the room only to return, helplessly, to the bedside. He should leave, he told himself again, gripping the high, carved headboard. But even as his fingers unclenched, Antonia Cabral opened her eyes - and suddenly he was back on the mountain, crouched in the snow, desperately cradling her face in his hands. Behind him he could hear the other men labouring to catch up, and as he swore at her, Antonia Cabral opened her eyes - as she did now - and struggled to speak. How could he have read accusation in her words? William wondered now, when her expression had held nothing but a profound gratitude.

He stooped over the pillows. Once again his fingers reached for hers and held them. *I am here,* he assured her silently. *Show me that you know I am here.*

But she had lapsed once more into sleep.

*

Returning to his lodgings feeling utterly drained, William went to the room he had taken on the first floor, threw his hat on the bed, picked up a bottle of brandy, and poured a great beakerful before throwing himself into the nearest chair. His head ached, and he felt as battered as a ship that had come through a storm. He took a long swallow of brandy. Had he been wholly complacent in assuming Antonia Cabral was safe with the nuns? Swallowing another mouthful, he dropped his head back against the chair. He had never expected the brief visit to affect him. Why *had* it affected him? He knew he felt guilty - and he was angry because he felt guilty. He'd done his best, he told himself. He'd done his best, and he was damned if he should feel guilty. Yes, he might admit to feeling pity - and to feeling anxious for her recovery; and yes, all right, he would admit to guilt and this oddly unsettling anger. But Antonia Cabral was no more to him than an unwelcome interruption, a troublesome duty that was now, thank God, discharged. Tentatively, his thoughts touched on another emotion, and flickered hastily away. He was painfully aware that when he'd fought her for Cabral's letter, when he'd had the slim, struggling body warm in his grasp, with her lips no more than a breath from his own, he'd felt something uncomfortably close to desire. He'd been appalled at the sudden intense longing, the unexpected urge to possess her.

Possess Antonia Cabral! William gave a bitter laugh. He'd as soon deal with the Devil!

He poured another drink. He *must* be tired. The creature was desperately ill, wasn't she? Her husband killed not a week before? How could he think of her like this? God, he was sick to death of thinking about Antonia Cabral. She'd been a thorn in his flesh from the moment he'd set eyes on her! Hadn't he told her so? William drained the glass, set it down with a thud, then swore and rubbed at his forehead.

There was a rap at the door. "Who is it?" He swung his feet down from the windowsill.

"A message, Senhor Captain."

From the convent? William wrenched open the door. The servant held out a piece of paper. He took it and tore it open.

His shoulders slumped. Colonel Ashe had arrived, his mission achieved, and he and Pedro would be glad to speak with Captain Hurst at the earliest opportunity.

William tried without success to persuade them that Antonia Cabral was in no fit state for visitors. Unwilling to accompany them, he waited on the floor below, unsurprised to see them descend shortly afterward, their faces pale and shocked. The three men stood at the bottom of the stairs and murmured together. The Senhora was no worse, the nuns had told Ashe; she was holding her own. Recovery was expected to be slow. Ashe could only shake his head. "A tragedy," he said.

"It is not right!" Pedro choked. "I should never have agreed to her following Pereira. You should never have agreed to her going, Captain. I thought you would take care of her. "

"Steady!" said Ashe. "Captain Hurst did his best. He's hardly escaped undamaged himself, as well you know."

"Pedro's right though," Hurst confessed.

And flinched as Pedro wailed, "How am I to break this news to the Cabrals?"

Until he knew what the family wanted done, Pedro was to stay on; his duty was to Dona Antonia. His brown eyes seemed full of reproach now, and for the hundredth time William wished himself elsewhere. Pedro would do all that was necessary. He and the Colonel had duties to which they must both return.

"Will you pass through Celerico, Captain?" asked Pedro, diffidently. "My lady's cousin, - Senhor Tavares, you remember? - may be there yet. You could perhaps - explain - the situation to him?"

William looked uneasily at Ashe. "I had not intended returning that way, but if you would have me take a letter - "

"No matter."

"Dammit Pedro, I'll do what I can." William laid a hand on the servant's arm, and Pedro sighed.

"You'll want to rejoin your regiment, William," Ashe broke in. "Return to Guarda, and we'll see what can be done."

"Thank you, sir. I should be glad to get back to - to some kind of normality." His jaw tightened. "She's in good hands, Pedro. We can do no more here."

There was a silence, and finally Pedro nodded. "You'd best be on your way."

CHAPTER TWENTY TWO
1809

William meant to keep his promise to Pedro, but the reports that had arrived thick and fast from Spain and awaited the two English officers on their return, were such that all other matters were driven from their thoughts.

The British troops had been forced to retreat to Corunna in the bitterest winter in living memory. Morale had collapsed, and the discipline of all but the best regiments had disintegrated as the men learned they were not to make a stand. There had been disgraceful, brutal scenes among the retreating troops: men had thrown away their rifles; stragglers froze to death where they lay, unable to march on bleeding, rag-wrapped feet, and giving up the struggle against hunger and the cold.

The remainder had rallied to make a stand at Corunna, but during the final French assault, Moore had been mortally wounded, Sir John Hope had taken command, the British forces had embarked virtually unmolested, and had sailed for England on 17 January.

William studied the reports, aghast. What had happened to his regiment? How many men were lost? How many friends? What of John Cunningham? Edward Fairburn?

"Where the Devil does that leave *us*?" he asked, looking up at Colonel Ashe who was stuffing dispatches into a valise. "The French will be across the border amongst us shortly. How can we pull back? Another retreat will give them Portugal."

Ashe shrugged. He wore a perpetual frown nowadays. "We are hardly in a position to halt them."

William swore, crossing restlessly to the window. "I should have been with them," he said, banging his palm against the stonework. "Not chasing about in the mountains!"

"You've seen the reports, William. Think yourself fortunate! Men froze on that march. Drunken looters half of them. Defying their officers."

"Not every regiment." It was not pleasant to think one's men might break ranks, or lose all sense of discipline.

Ashe flashed him a bleak look. "Not yours, you mean."

The Colonel seized on his orders to return south. There was no time to waste if the small force he commanded was to avoid capture or annihilation, and William was once more pressed into service. Perhaps later, Ashe promised, he might sail for England and rejoin his regiment, but he was marching for Lisbon, and William Hurst was to accompany him.

In the midst of their hurried preparations to leave William recalled Antonia Cabral. For more than a week he had given no thought to her or Pedro, isolated as they were near Belmonte. He stood in the cobbled, rain-slicked courtyard where he'd been overseeing the loading of supplies, and cursed the oversight. Pedro's letter had gone off to Celerico three weeks before — but, with the chaos and confusion since, there had been little opportunity to consider much else. Had Dona Antonia made progress, he wondered, sufficient progress to allow her to travel south with her servant? No word had reached him from the convent. They might come to no harm - but if the French re-occupied Portugal . . .

Cabral had worked for the French. If the worse came to the worst, William supposed, pacing the cobbles, Cabral's wife - widow - could always demand recognition of her husband's service . . . He swore again.

Belmonte, of course, was on the route that Colonel Ashe had drawn up for the march via Abrantes towards Lisbon. They would be leaving soon. Perhaps Ashe would allow him to detour and explain the situation to Pedro.

*

The last thing William wanted was to re-visit the convent. He certainly did not plan on seeing Antonia Cabral again; his previous visits had been too unsettling, and when he found no sign of Pedro at the inn where he lodged, he decided a note for Pedro's attention would do.

In the taproom, he took up his pen to stare at the blank sheet on the table before him. What could he say that would not cause panic should the note go astray? He would be gone by the time Pedro came to read it. How could he be sure it came to the right hands? Biting on the quill-end, William struggled to concentrate. He scribbled a few words and read them over. The note would need to be left with someone completely trustworthy, and who did he know apart from Pedro? Sister Jerome? Ah, no! William shook his head, but the letter could be entrusted to one of the nuns. Pedro would pass in and out of the convent often enough. He finished the note, sealed it, then sat studying the inscription before jumping up and hurrying into the street.

At the convent, the Sisters told him that they had not seen Senhor Pedro since the previous evening when he had returned after several days' absence. They did not know where he was presently to be found. And of course, they would be happy to see that the note reached him. The Captain might be pleased to hear that Dona Antonia was a little stronger. Would he wish to call on her?

William smiled grimly. The Senhora was made of sterner stuff after all, and had not given up on life, in spite of Sister Jerome's fears. He made his excuses.

One foot already in the stirrup, he stiffened as a voice hailed him, and recognised in the surprised tones the very person he had thought to avoid. Dismounting, he turned to greet her with a salute. "Sister Jerome."

"I am astonished to see you again, Captain. Have you come from visiting Senhora Cabral? She is recovering well, is she not?"

"I am told so, ma'am." William smiled awkwardly. "I did not come to see her, however. Only Pedro Teles."

"Not come to see her? But she is so much better! And I am sure she would wish to see you."

This was embarrassing. "In truth, ma'am," William insisted, "I must be elsewhere. I am only here very briefly - "

"I am sure you can spare a moment." She laid a hand on his arm. "She would be glad to see a fellow countryman just now when every day we hear such unsettling news. You can give her reassurance."

William opened his mouth to argue, and closed it again.

"Strange that I should speak of you so recently," the nun went on. "How shocked you were the first time you visited! Do go up and cheer her a little."

"Sister," he sighed, "I assure you the sight of me is not likely to - "

"Come, come, sir," she interrupted, and William knew further argument would be awkward and embarrassing. Disguising his impatience, he returned with Sister Jerome to the convent, deeply relieved when she left him at the foot of the stairs. He knew, whatever she said, that he could not be a welcome visitor, and remembering what he had done, and what he had said, he told himself he must be the last person the girl would want to see.

He climbed the stairs with leaden feet, muttering that he'd be hanged if he'd submit to bullying, and outside the door could not immediately bring himself to knock. He lit a cigar and limped to and fro for some minutes, taking fierce, fretful puffs . . . But he was wasting precious time, and he knew it. He ground the butt under the heel of his boot and banged on the door. He cocked his ear for a reply. There was no response. Sleeping then, no need to disturb her.

William found himself lifting the latch.

The bed was unoccupied. He was unpleasantly reminded of an earlier visit, and when someone spoke from the other side of the room, he started.

"Is that you, Sister?"

William recognised the voice, weak though it was. He stepped towards the chair that faced the window with its view of distant hills.

"William Hurst, Senhora."

"C-Captain Hurst?" There was a rustle as she stirred in the chair, then a smothered exclamation. "Come closer if you please, sir," he heard her say breathlessly, "I cannot rise."

He came to stand before her. He had not expected much, but it was plain that the Senhora was still far from well. There were hollows still beneath the exhausted blue eyes, and if she were not as skeletal as when William had last seen her, she hardly appeared to have gained weight under the loose muslin gown she wore. Her lower limbs, supported on a footstool, were exposed - the left leg slim and smooth as marble, the right - What had they done to the right? He stared. Her ankle was imprisoned in a strange frame, but the flesh above and below was so discoloured and swollen that the extremities were the only recognisable feature. Whatever it was, it looked cruel - and painful. William winced.

The girl struggled to re-arrange the muslin. "I beg your pardon, this must appear most unpleasant to a stranger's eyes."

What a knack she had for finding the exact phrase to wound, William thought. "Hardly a stranger, Dona Antonia," he got out at last, and tried to smile. He had known how it would be. He had seen her face alter. She was thinking that before her stood the man who had killed her husband and left her hurt and alone on the mountain. It was stupid of him to have come. He would make his apologies and leave. But his mouth was dry and for a moment no words would come. "I had not intended to intrude, ma'am, thinking only to speak to Pedro," he said stiffly. "The last time I was here, you were so - so very unwell . . . "

"I - it was - kind of you to come again."

Kind? "It was the least I could do," he returned. He remembered his own recovery. "Are you in much pain?"

She lifted her chin. "Not — not so very much, now," she faltered, "The nuns take care to give me a draught . . . "

"Before it becomes unbearable?" His voice grew harsher than ever. "You'll get better. You must not be discouraged by what may seem slow progress."

Her eyes met his. "I am not yet — discouraged." He winced at the tone of apprehension. "The Sisters think I - I may be fit to travel in a few weeks."

"Then I hope you will be, Senhora." His voice dropped. "To be frank, you and Pedro would do well to return to Lisbon as soon as possible."

"We hope we may, now that my cousin Tavares is here."

"Here?"

"Since yesterday. He is in the town with Pedro."

"Then he is quite well again?"

"I suspect he will never be completely well."

"But you will soon be away?" William hoped the old gentleman would not prove more a liability than help. And these questions he could leave with Pedro.

"We hear the British have — have suffered a defeat, and are leaving Portugal." Her voice was a whisper.

He frowned. "There was a retreat," he agreed, "but it seems the Army has embarked safely, and will reform in England."

"You remain?" she ventured. "Y - you were so eager to rejoin your regiment."

She remembered that? "I have no news of my regiment," William said, and thoughts of the mutiny and of the bitter retreat in the snow filled passes of Galicia darkened his eyes.

"I am so very sorry."

"Sorry?"

"Sorry that you have no news - of those for whom you evidently care a great deal."

Was she in earnest? "Some will have been lost, but I am sure most are safely embarked. Though no doubt," he added grimly, "any stragglers were picked off by the French." His lips tightened. "The honour of protecting the Army as it retreats is a duty that often falls to the regiment. We have done a deal too much of it in this campaign." He glanced at the pale, lovely face, at the dark-shadowed eyes with their pinpoint of feverish blue brilliance, and felt again the dreadful weight of guilt. "But I did not come to talk to you of fighting, Senhora."

Now she looked away. "I - I did not expect to see you again, Captain."

"Nor I you, Senhora," he admitted, equally quietly.

"The Sisters told me of your earlier visit . . . "

"They despaired of you," William said awkwardly, "for a while."

"So they tell me."

"I am – much relieved to find you on the path to recovery. I hope you will find yourself in Lisbon again very soon." He hesitated. "I shall speak to Pedro. Meanwhile, I must apologise for disturbing your rest, Dona Antonia." He bowed, stiffly. "Your - your servant, ma'am."

But at the door, hand on latch, he could only turn back. "I wish to God," he breathed, "that I had known how badly you were hurt. Why did you say nothing?"

She said nothing now, but Hurst caught the unhappy glance she threw in his direction and was cut to the quick. He stepped back into the room. "You imagine me heartless? You do me an injustice, Senhora. You must realise I would have given anything to prevent this happening?"

"I realise," she responded faintly, "how beholden to you I am. What I have not - been able to recall myself, Pedro has spoken of in detail. I - I am aware that I have a great deal to thank you for -"

"Thank me for?" Glancing at the footstool, William gave a sharp laugh. *For this? For leaving her in the snow? For betraying her husband, and for helping to make her a widow?* He gritted his teeth. "You have no reason in the world to be grateful to *me*, Dona Antonia."

In the silence, Antonia stared up at him, nonplussed by the raw emotion in his voice. She had been jolted to have the Englishman appear. She had never thought to see him again, and her heart had been thudding at the unexpected sound of his voice. The memories of those few dreadful days on the mountain were never far from her mind. She shivered.

How angry she always seemed to make him. Must they always quarrel? She had only wanted to make him see how grateful she was.

"I am a fool," he said tersely, surprising her by catching up a nearby shawl, "to forget how very ill you have been." He stooped to drape the fine wool about her shoulders. "You are tired. Chilled and exhausted."

"I - I am tired -" Antonia confessed, astonished.

He shook his head "And I - I am thoughtless, and inconsiderate." His fingers tightened in the shawl. "Forgive me, I should not have come," he added in an even lower voice. "Nor spoken as I have done." He paused, his hands still resting lightly on her shoulders, and made her look at him. "Dona Antonia, whatever differences there have been between us, I hope you can believe that I would not willingly have had any of this happen."

Antonia could not respond. The Captain's eyes were level with her own, and she was astonished at the depth of apparently genuine regret in his voice and his expression. She stared at him, all the while conscious of an urge to reach out and touch his tired and troubled face . . .

There was a sudden hubbub of voices outside the door, a knock, and Pedro peered around the door. "Captain Hurst! Sister Jerome said you would be here." He came into the room, followed by the thin figure of Sergio Tavares.

Hurst straightened. He was barely up to greeting either man, and the Senhora seemed to recover first from the shock.

"Captain Hurst is - is here to see you, Pedro. Cousin Sergio, you remember the captain, I am sure."

In control now, Hurst managed a smile. He nodded at Pedro, shook the hand Tavares offered.

"I am *delighted* to see you again, Captain," the older man smiled. "How fortunate that I should be in a position to thank you once again, not only for your attention to me in Celerico, but for ensuring the safety of Dona Antonia. I understand that without your help she might not be here today." Wondering what the old man had been told, Hurst glanced from Pedro to Antonia Cabral, but Pedro was murmuring something to his lady. "You suffered yourself, I understand," Tavares was saying. "I am grieved to hear it. Are you quite recovered from your hurts?"

"Nothing to speak of, sir." Hurst shifted his still tender shoulder, guessing that Pedro was to blame for this extra embarrassment. "I am glad to see you looking so much recovered yourself, Senhor."

"Ah, yes." Tavares lowered his voice, glancing anxiously at his young relative. "If only there could have been a happier outcome to our search. It was a tragedy that her husband proved a casualty in the encounter that spared her."

Hurst was not much surprised to find the girl's apprehensive gaze upon him. He must find out what had been said. Did Dona Antonia still believe he had killed her husband? She had no need to fear what *he* would say. He would support whatever story she wanted to tell, having no great reason to be proud of the truth. Giving her a nod, he turned back to Tavares. "You must forgive me, Senhor, I am expected elsewhere and must take my leave. I would however appreciate a word with Pedro before I return to my duties. Downstairs, Pedro?"

"Of course, Captain. I will walk with you to the gate."

"I will leave," Tavares offered. "I have some sad correspondence to attend to - I am hoping my young nephew Baltasar can be entrusted to break the news of this tragedy to his parents-in-law rather than waiting for our arrival — but I hope to see you again, Captain, before you ride out?" And before Hurst could protest, Tavares had kissed the girl's hand, bowed and left the room. Hurst smiled tersely at Pedro. "A moment, then. Downstairs. Wait for me by the church door."

When Pedro too had gone, Hurst returned to stand before the chair. "I cannot hope," he said, struggling for the right words, "that we should ever be - friends, Senhora. Too much has happened, I think, for you to regard me with any liking, but I confess I find it hard to leave knowing that - you regard me as - as an adversary."

"I do not do so," she faltered. "You must know how grateful - "

"I have never deserved your gratitude," Hurst insisted, his eyes holding hers. "But - I should like to think that you - understood, that had there been any other way, I would not have done what I did."

She turned away. "It is hard for me to know what I should feel under the circumstances — but I too should not like to think we - we parted now as - " She straightened her shoulders, and looked up at him then, holding out her hand, her chin tilted in the way Hurst remembered. "Goodbye, Captain. I shall not f- forget you."

He took her chilled fingers between his own warm palms, feeling a weight lifting from his shoulders. "No, ma'am," he murmured. "I doubt that you will. I hope the remembrance might not always be with anger and sorrow." He pressed her hand. "Adieu, Senhora."

"Goodbye, Captain Hurst."

And meeting the steadfast gaze, Antonia could only marvel that she had once thought the blue eyes cold. She contemplated the door through which the captain had disappeared, feeling stupidly weak and emotional. This William Hurst was not someone she could come to terms with so easily. The abrupt and angry officer she had first encountered in Celerico, and the heartless escort who had been with her in the mountains, the harsh and contemptuous man who had pushed her on, refusing to let her die when he had just killed her husband –

Antonia bit her lip. The harsh words had not always matched the expression in his eyes, and even in her delirium she had been conscious of gentle hands and a concerned and anxious face. This was a difficult man to understand, she thought wearily. And she had known for some time that she could not bring herself to hate him, no matter what he had said, or what he had done.

Well, William Hurst was out of her life now – they were not likely to meet again. But she would find it hard to forget him.

*

Within a week Antonia was considered well enough to be carried from the convent and installed in the carriage that was to take the little party back to Lisbon. She was touched to find that many of the nuns had come to bid her farewell; they lined the path to the convent gates, and it gave her inexpressible pleasure to confide that Senhor Tavares had found workmen to restore the once lovely statue of the Virgin to whom the convent was dedicated.

Sister Jerome pronounced blessings on their journey. "I don't envy you the times that lie ahead, child," she said, patting Antonia's cheek, "and one could wish you had a sturdier escort." She eyed Sergio Tavares with misgiving. "But your man will serve you well. A pity the Englishman could not see you safe home. Shall you meet him again?"

"Oh, oh, no. He is to rejoin the army as soon as possible."

"The army is likely to be in Lisbon."

"N – nevertheless I doubt that we shall meet again."

"He was greatly concerned for you, child."

"Concerned?" Antonia gave an uneasy laugh, but Sister Jerome smiled gravely.

"I once heard it said that Englishmen are renowned for their lack of emotion, but yes, I believe he was concerned."

"They are certainly quite unlike the Portuguese," Antonia admitted, trying to smile, and remembered passionate avowals that had once swept her off her feet. Hastily she put out her hand. "Bless you for all you have done," she murmured, and was still looking into Sister Jerome's face as the carriage gave a sudden lurch and pulled away. "Goodbye," she cried, as the coach gathered speed, and her last view of the convent was pale walls merging into a hazy distance.

*

The parting stirred many emotions. Antonia was aware that her reluctance to return to Lisbon was cowardly, but it had been a matter of secret relief that the sisters had considered her unfit to travel until now. She was glad to be well enough to leave, but she did not look forward in the slightest to returning to the Casa Cabral, where she would have to face her husband's parents and answer questions better left unasked. She was returning furthermore without their son, and she had promised to bring him home. Sergio would lend his support. Indeed he had, in an attempt to dissipate the first shock, already written to warn his nephew, but he knew nothing of the true circumstances of Duarte's demise. Beside herself, only Pedro and the two British officers knew the truth, and Pedro was as torn as she was between his loyalty to the Cabrals and regard for William Hurst. How could she tell the Cabrals that their younger son was not only dead but a traitor? To both their countries?

It would be necessary to keep a great many things secret from now on. Antonia prayed she would find the strength to do so.

CHAPTER TWENTY THREE

It was very much as she feared when after days of travel on the long journey south, the carriage bowled up the drive to the Casa Cabral. Her return with Sergio Tavares brought grief back into sharp relief, and it was clear that her in-laws blamed them for not reaching their son in time. Since nothing had been said either of how Duarte had died, these were the first questions that faced the weary travellers. All that Antonia could say was that there had been fighting close to the border, and in the course of that Duarte Cabral had been killed.

Dona Isabel pressed Antonia for details she could not give, and would not be satisfied with what she was told. "A hero! Our best and noblest of sons!" she sobbed, apparently forgetting that Emilio had always been the favourite. "Our boy, dead in the service of his country! He has sacrificed himself for Portugal! But how has it come to this? Surely you might have made more effort? If you had only reached him sooner, he would have returned to us."

Though Antonia could understand the mother's grief, it was hard to hold her tongue and pretend it was all just as she said. With every day that passed it became more and more impossible for Antonia to confess the truth, and she grew truly uneasy at the parade of semi-lies, yet she could never reveal how and why their son had died. The presence of Baltasar da Fonte and his wife, Beatriz, was all that sustained her, for by this time Dom Luis seemed to be losing his grip on reality, almost out of his mind with sorrow with one death following so soon upon the other.

"Now, of course," Beatriz confided, when Sergio had finally departed northwards, taking Pedro Teles with him, "it is even worse than when we lost Emilio." Night had fallen, candles had been lit, and her parents had withdrawn to their private chambers, leaving their daughter, son-in-law, and Antonia nursing glasses of wine in front of the large open fireplace. "We have tried so hard to bring Papa back to his old self, but it seems quite hopeless. He has lost all interest in the estate, seems not to care anything for business. Baltasar does what he can but – "

Her husband sighed. "Sometimes nothing he does or says makes sense. But time is a healer, and please God, all this will pass." He moved his wheeled chair across to where his wife sat, looking dejectedly into the flames. "We'll get through this, my love."

His wife shook her head. "Thank goodness you, at least, have come back to us, Antonia."

Antonia studied them as the firelight played on their kind, concerned faces.

She had met Baltasar da Fonte no more than three or four times before Emilio Cabral's death, but from the beginning she had found him a charming and sympathetic personality, without a trace of bitterness for his fate. Dark and slender, with expressive brown eyes, he had, like her, married into the family against the Cabrals' wishes, and it had made them allies of a sort. Now, though their disabilities differed vastly, they would often laugh together over their struggles as, since being badly hurt in his youth at a bull run, Baltasar da Fonte was confined to his chair. He could hobble with assistance from chair to bed, or from chair to carriage, and when he wanted to move about the house, his devoted manservant would carry him upstairs and down, but no one in their right mind, Antonia reflected, would ever consider him a cripple. He was constantly to be found making the essential rounds of farm and village, and had managed his own estate for many years, so Beatriz said, with flair *and* profit. Dom Luis however seemed to regard him as only half a man, and had done everything he could to oppose the marriage his daughter desired.

Beatriz, smiling back at her husband, was no beauty. The looks of the family had gone to her brothers, but in spite of homely features and a quiet personality she'd been made many offers by men attracted to her father's position, and the promise of a generous dowry. Duarte had often boasted of the connections his sister might have made, but Beatriz had wanted da Fonte. He was a neighbour and an old friend with wealth of his own, and with Baltasar, Beatriz told Antonia, she felt easy and relaxed. She had confided early on that it was she who forced the match.

Six years of marriage seemed to have endeared them to each other.

Antonia eyed them, envying them their calm happiness. It had not been so long before that she had contrasted their staid relationship with the passionate commitment she shared with her own young husband, and had wondered rather cruelly then if Beatriz had ever known what it was to be swept off her feet by emotion. Now she knew better.

Baltasar leant forward to take his wife's hand. "We shall manage, I believe, if Dona Isabel can bring herself to trust me to help her until Dom Luis is himself again. It concerns me that she is as stricken as he is, though her grief shows itself in a different way. She is frightened for the future, and for her husband's sanity, and perhaps that is why she seems to be so angry much of the time." He smiled ruefully. "I must confess that I seem to anger her with my advice, no matter how tactfully I try to offer it."

"Your estate is a model of all that it should be," Beatriz told him. "Mama has only to look at that." But Dona Isabel, Antonia thought, no longer seemed to be the woman she had once been, and perhaps that was indirectly her fault.

Dom Luis grew worse. He seemed to spend the whole day in fits of weeping. "Like a great, sad, helpless baby, "Antonia thought, and he was certainly in no fit state to manage his estates which, since Emilio's accident, had fallen into difficulties. As Baltasar said, they might have managed – if Dona Isabel had allowed him to help - but she was now consulting soothsayers and fortune-tellers, contradicted Baltasar's decisions and took bad ones of her own. No one was safe from her hysterical tirades, and in no time every enterprise began to founder. The Cabrals had always engaged clever managers, but very soon they were completely alienated along with the best and ablest of the workers. And being closest, Antonia bore the brunt of the unpleasantness.

"Where are *my* grandchildren?" the matriarch shrieked suddenly one spring day. Some youngsters had run laughing into the great kitchen while she and Antonia were overseeing stocktaking in the storerooms, but now they took fright and fled as she screamed at Antonia, "Two years you were married to my son, and have nothing to show for it. Are you barren? Why have I no grandchildren?"

Antonia had faced this enquiry several times before, but the venom in the question shocked her. She stopped writing, gripping the slate hard to keep control.

"My Duarte is dead!" her mother-in-law wailed. "There are no sons to bear the name of Cabral. Why could you not have borne him children? What use have you been as a wife without children? My beautiful boy, my brave beautiful boy. He could have had any woman, but no! He chose you, a barren Englishwoman."

She does not really hate me, Antonia reminded herself. She is striking out in her grief. I must try and remember how kind she was to me when I first came to Lisbon. But it had grown harder to remember those days as time went by.

CHAPTER TWENTY FOUR
May 1809

William Hurst came into the firelight from the darkness, pulling his cloak about him. It was mid-May, but nights were chill especially close to water, and William, glad of company and the fire's warmth held out his hands to the flames, nodding a response to the murmur of greetings. He sat down and a plate was passed to him. He inspected it without enthusiasm, wrinkling his nose at the smell. "What is it? Rabbit?"

Amusement rippled about the fire. "Don't ask!" someone advised. "But it doesn't taste as bad as it looks."

"Or smells?" William pulled a face, and picked out the hunk of bread floating on the greasy mess to chew on it.

"All quiet along the river?"

Mouth full, William nodded. There was no reason it should not be so. The French were streaming away to the northwest in disarray, and no one round the fire had even seen a Frenchman since the day before when the two armies had faced each other across the Douro. Just that morning indeed, almost before it was light Sir Arthur Wellesley had taken his 17,000 troops over the river, and before the enemy had even realised the British were on the move, had established a bridgehead within a mile of the French Headquarters.

"A good day's work, don't you think?" John Cunningham sat down beside William. "We'll be chasing the buggers all the way to the frontier with a bit of luck."

His optimism drew a faint smile. Affairs certainly seemed to be improving. Moore had said Portugal could not be defended but while its frontiers might be indefensible, its all- weather port at Lisbon was not. Wellesley had landed there in April and had immediately marched north to deal with the French Maréchal Soult, dallying in Oporto in an intrigue to make himself king.

Soult was dallying no longer, William reflected. He was hurrying back to Spain, with his men throwing away arms and knapsacks in their hurry to keep up with him. He and his regiment might not yet be reunited, but William was quite content now, to be here where the British were facing up to the French instead of retreating yet again. In the space of three months, he had marched the length of Portugal to the South and back again, but that was no matter even in the mud and rain of the last week. This after all, he thought with some satisfaction, is what he had come for.

But perhaps not *this*! He poked at the stew with the spoon, closed his eyes and took a mouthful.

"Bates' rabbit," Cunningham informed him. "Not as bad as it looks, is it."

William gave him a sideways look. "That would be impossible, John, my friend." But he finished the meal and wiped the plate with his crust. "You've been in Oporto before?"

"Not I," returned Cunningham. "Don't know any more than the country we've passed through on the way here, 'part from Lisbon. How well do you know Lisbon?"

"Hardly at all. You forget I arrived after you, and only just after Sir Arthur. I *was* kept pretty busy in the interval!"

"Wonderful city. Knocked about, you know, by an earthquake fifty years ago. Rebuilt."

"I remember hearing that." William nodded. "Wide avenues in one part of the town, with the oldest part behind the castle more like a labyrinth."

"That's it." Cunningham settled himself more comfortably, and there was silence for a moment. William cleared his throat, and without looking at his friend asked casually, "Did you go much into Society?"

"A fair amount. One could go to a Ball, or a different theatre every night of the week. Some of these people hardly know there's a war on."

William could imagine that. "You enjoyed yourself?"

Cunningham smiled. "What else were we to do? We were waiting to know whether we were to stay or be shipped home!"

"Quite." William fidgeted with his plate, and finally laid it on the grass beside him. "Did you ever hear of a family called Cabral? When you were in Lisbon?"

"Don't recall the name. Pretty daughter in the family, was there?" Cunningham raised an eyebrow.

William ignored the hint. "The father was well known, I believe. Dom Luis? You never heard of him?"

"Dom Luis? Cabral you said?" He frowned. "No, unless - Unless, there was a landowner, a nobleman, I think. There had been some tragedy in the family. Lost two sons in the same year, and lost his wits after. That's what people said. Is that the fellow you mean?"

William was taken aback. "I had not heard that he was so affected."

"Was it that fellow though? Did you know him well?"

"I never met him."

The curt answer surprised his friend. "Then why -?"

"I'd heard of him, that's all." William got abruptly to his feet, and scooped up the plate. "How long did Bates say he had that rabbit in his knapsack?"

"Four days." Cunningham blinked at the change of subject.

"He's a liar then, or it died of something horrible before he caught it!"

The other grinned. "Well, he had it in his pack four days. But I did hear it had been dead a week by then."

"That would explain a great deal," William replied. "In that case, I'll take myself and my delicate digestion away to rest while we can still do so." He handed back the plate, and nodding to the others round the fire, walked out of the circle of light into the enveloping darkness, leaving John Cunningham to stare after him with a curious and thoughtful air.

CHAPTER TWENTY FIVE
1811

Wellesley had retreated slowly before the French as they marched once more into Portugal, but he had not been idle in the preceding winter, and the French advance found its way to Lisbon barred by the British Lines at Torres Vedras well to the north of the city. By the spring the French general Massena had been forced to acknowledge the impossibility of further advance, and his army retreated through a countryside laid waste, committing atrocities in the towns and villages through which their forces passed.

At the Casa Cabral however, though food was sometimes scarce, life seemed to go on much the same, with Antonia believing she could bear the spite of her mother-in-law despite having every day to listen to the insults and blackening of her character and an increasingly extravagant praise of a man she knew to be wholly false. The da Fontes continued to be her lifeline. Baltasar retained his calm, ever polite manner in spite of the bewildering and infuriating parents-in-law, which spoke volumes for his self-control. His sense of humour sustained them all, and Antonia felt sometimes that she depended on him almost as much as Beatriz did. Beatriz she loved for her gentle determined strength and her unwavering support, and did her best to conceal the friction caused by her mother in law. The da Fontes now had both southern estates to manage, more difficult than ever with more than half the workforce conscripted, like most other able bodied Portuguese men, by Wellington for the defence of their country. They found time however to help Antonia understand how it was done, and over the course of the year she had learned how to judge when the vines should be harvested, how much cork the *tiradors* could strip from the great oaks without damage, and when the barley was ready to mow. Her injuries were almost healed, and she could ride out daily to inspect the land, usually accompanied by Baltasar in his carriage if he was available, and by Beatriz if he was not, grateful to be away from the house and Dona Isabel's hysterics.

Inevitably however, news of Dom Luis's decline spread abroad. Many of his other affairs faltered.

"We have no choice." Beatriz was pacing the floor in the salon. "The farms may just keep us from starvation but we should sell what we have no need of here. That way we may yet hold on to the land, and keep afloat until this war is over."

Her husband protested. "There are my estates to support us too, Beatriz. There is no need for you to lose your inheritance."

"What need have we of an inheritance, my dear, when there are no children to follow us. Forgive me Antonia, for being so blunt, but this is the situation, is it not?"

Antonia had sadly to agree.

Months passed, and the Cabrals' misfortunes, together with rumours of fresh fighting, made the entire estate uncertain and jittery. A start had been made on some kind of inventory of items in the house that still held some value, but it was a project that could not be left to the staff, and soon attracted Dona Isabel's voluble protests. Since Beatriz was now the only one who could manage her mother and Baltasar was already occupied, it fell to Antonia to proceed with the task. She found herself day after day, moving from room to room, ledger in hand making notes of what could be spared. There were many rooms and many items, and it was a dismal undertaking in spite of the fact that many of the things she listed were quite lovely.

By now summer was at its height, and in some of the seldom-used apartments the heat was intense. Up on the second floor Antonia, feeling her mind almost as stifled as her breath, found herself longing to fling the windows wide for the chance of a breath of air. But this was Portugal not England. When she folded back the shutters sunlight flooded in but there was no stirring of wind, and the languor of the afternoon lay like a dusty veil over the vista before her. Somewhere below there was the sound of Dom Luis weeping, and further away Dona Isabel was screaming at someone. It felt as if the world had somehow turned into a lunatic asylum. And now there was this scene below.

The click of the latch behind her turned Antonia to the door, and she was surprised to see Baltasar wheeling himself into the room. Acknowledging him with a terse smile, she turned back to the window.

"What now?" he said, manoeuvring the chair across to the window.

Antonia nodded at the knot of estate workers assembling in the garden, men and boys, milling about on the gravel between the once neat box hedging. Some carried pitchforks, and others had picked up stones and seemed to be weighing them in their hands. Their voices were loud, and reached the observers on the second floor.

"Hmm. They seem to doubt there is money to sustain the estate further. What have they heard now, I wonder?" Baltasar leaned forward in the chair. "Open the window, Antonia, if you will."

The men looked up, but still they muttered and made no move to disperse as they once would have done, and Antonia felt a frisson of alarm.

"Call Fernando."

Antonia smiled faintly, and lost some of her fear. It was like Baltasar to know their names. He would have known the names of their children, and family histories too, she thought.

"Call Fernando. Ask him for flowers."

With a glance at her brother in law, Antonia complied. "Fernando, would you be so good as to cut some of the lilies in the west courtyard for me to use in the chapel?"

There was a moment's hesitation before the young man nodded. He spoke to his companions and left, and after another few moments, much to Antonia's relief, the group dispersed, though they muttered still.

"Thank you, Antonia, that was well done," Baltasar said quietly. "I will speak again to the men tonight, when it is cool and they have been fed. They need reassurance."

"What can you say?" she responded, almost bitterly. "I'm sorry. I shouldn't snap when your patience seems inexhaustible. I should be able by now to cope better . . ."

"You have been very sick, Antonia," he reminded her gently. "I wish I could do more, but I fear Dona Isabel has no mind to pay me much heed." He smiled. "I suppose I cannot blame her when neither she nor Dom Luis wanted me for a son-in-law!" His tone was humorous, but Antonia knew it had never been easy for him. "Have you much more to do on this floor?"

"This is the last." Antonia gestured. Many of the rooms were stuffed with all styles of furniture, some dating back a century or more.

"My grandfather once owned a desk, very like that one there," Baltasar said, wheeling the chair across. "Have you noted it in that ledger of yours? His own was very curious. He showed me once. It had a secret compartment. There was some kind of lever concealed in the inkpot well." Baltasar peered into it. "Look here - rather like this. When you grasped the edge - so - and pulled it up - " He pulled at the wood, and laughed. "That would be too much to expect, would it not?" His smile died. "I think it moved."

"Don't jest!" But all at once there was a distinct click from inside the desk. Baltasar and Antonia looked at each other, Baltasar raised the lid, and before their astonished eyes lay a polished section of wood - a false back which had sprung out to reveal a line of small drawers behind it.

Antonia gasped. "We could not be so fortunate? Could we?" Her fingers trembled as she opened the first drawer. It was empty. The second? Empty too. The third slid out with a rattle - and showed her a mound of gold coins. Baltasar gave a whoop of delight, but when they had counted them out, there were no more than fifty.

"Hardly enough to save us from bankruptcy!" he commented ruefully, then laughed. "I suppose it was foolish to expect more."

Antonia tried to hide her disappointment. "But we did find something."

"And here it is, my dear." Baltasar tipped the coins into her hand. "Don't spend it all at once!"

At dinner that evening, making a joke of it, they told the family of the discovery but though Dona Isabel expressed little interest other than to demand the coins, Beatriz had grown very thoughtful, and when her mother had gone to bed, mentioned rather shyly, that she believed there had been a twin to the desk somewhere. Baltasar's brown eyes sparkled.

"We shall be saved yet," he declared. "But you, my dear Antonia, have a long search ahead, I think."

It was some weeks before the second desk came to light, in a study that had been used only by Duarte Cabral, and treated since as a shrine by his mother. Antonia waited till Baltasar was home from overseeing the harvesting, and drew him aside.

"I have located the twin of that desk with the secret drawer," she murmured. "Will you see if it will open as before?"

He seemed delighted, and after supper they ascended to the previously locked study, and studied the desk.

"Well, now! Are we to make our fortune, or are we to be disappointed? Will it just be a few coins as before, or will those drawers hold nothing?"

"We have yet to discover if it has any secret drawers, you know."

"But it does appear to be just the same. Allow me." Baltasar leaned across and pulled at the edge of the inkwell. There was no movement. He pulled at one side after another, with similar lack of success. "The da Fontes do not give up easily," he said, grunting with the effort.

"Let me." Antonia was standing beside him, almost jumping from one foot to the other in her impatience. Just as she laid her hand on his, there was the click, and a muffled thump from inside the desk.

They stared at each other. "Quickly!" Baltasar lifted the lid.

There were no drawers this time. The panel had come free, however, and now, lying spilled in the bottom of the desk interior, were a bundle of folded papers.

"Bills? Banknotes?" Antonia did not know whether to be delighted or downcast. She lifted out the bundle, and looked at the pages more closely. "Some papers of my husband's only," she sighed, handing them to her brother in law.

"Why hidden, though?"

Baltasar, Antonia remembered, knew no more of Duarte Cabral's treachery than the rest of the family. Something in that wrapped bundle might yet betray him. "Do not bother with them now," she said, trying to laugh. "If we are not to find a fortune – " But Baltasar evaded her attempt to remove the papers from his hands.

"Ah, ah, do not be so dismissive. Such a find surely demands further study." He began to fold over the papers. "No, you are right, only bills and letters. I am sorry to raise your hopes, my dear. Letters, letters – but what -?" Da Fonte had paused half way through his inspection. "These are in French. Who is writing to your husband in French – this signature - ? And this? Antonia, these are letters from – No, how can this be? Junot, Murat, Soult, Lapisse!" He held them out to her in disbelief. "The generals of France?"

Feeling quite faint, Antonia made no move to take the papers, and Baltasar shook his head, re-examining the bundle. "Look here! This one details what rewards there will be for his help – So much? Really? This one then, congratulating Alvaro on his decision . . . ? How can this be? Antonia, do you know anything of this?" He looked up, questioning, when she remained silent, not knowing what to say. "Antonia?"

"No," she whispered at last, "I had no notion that Duarte was in correspondence with these men." Something in her tone must have betrayed her.

"But - " He waited for her to speak, a frown darkening his face. "This is not complete news to you, I think?"

There was no longer any reason to keep the truth from him. Antonia could not lie to Baltasar. She told him all she knew of the expedition to the monastery, and its outcome.

He fell back in his chair, stunned. "All this time? Why?"

"I thought I could protect the family."

"But he hurt you, betrayed you, betrayed his country! He was a traitor!"

"He paid for it." Antonia laid her hand on the arm of his chair. "Baltasar, would you cause any further pain to the Cabrals, to his mother and father, to Beatriz?" she pleaded.

"But you have had to bear all his mother's reproaches! When you knew what her precious son really was! How could you remain silent, Antonia? Could you not have confided in me?"

"Have you not had enough to concern yourself with already?"

"My dear girl . . . " He covered her hand with his own. "I confess, I do not know what to do for the best." He fluttered the papers. "I cannot keep this from Beatriz."

"Can you not?" Antonia was close to tears now. "Can we not just burn these cursed papers, and be done with it?"

"Or put them back in this damned desk? Even so, Antonia, the truth must eventually come out."

"Let us consider then for a while what must be done. Please."

"Ah, I do not know what we should do!" Baltasar shook the bundle angrily, and several thin sheets slipped from the bundle and floated to the floor. "Do not let them escape," he warned, and hastily Antonia stooped to collect them. She glanced at the last, straightened up, and examined it more closely.

"No," she whispered. "No, not that too."

CHAPTER TWENTY SIX
England - Autumn 1813

From her shadowed vantage point above the brilliantly lit ballroom, Antonia looked down at the ranks aligned for the next dance, relieved to observe the portly figure of Sir Henry Davenport circling the ballroom fringe. Nodding, smiling, chatting affably enough to the guests that were not dancing, her father had evidently not spotted her here in the balcony.

"My dear Mrs Davenport!" A pleasant voice just above her head startled Antonia out of her seat, and she dropped a curtsey to the tall, elderly lady who had addressed her.

"You have found me out, Lady Margaret," Antonia confessed. "I had thought to avoid attention."

"Don't concern yourself, my dear. I am not here to be a nuisance," the older woman assured her. "Though it seems a pity that you do not appear to be enjoying your own party as much as the rest of your guests. I am myself in search of a little quiet. Now, won't you seat yourself again, if you please - and I shall sit here - so - and we shan't speak again if you don't wish it."

Antonia eyed the older lady, who was comfortably upholstered in an old fashioned gown of taupe and rose. Margaret Spenlow opened a very large fan and, with a sidelong glance, asked: "But how does it come about that you don't wish to be dancing yourself?"

"I - I always did love to dance." Antonia turned her head to the lights and the music and the couples paired for the quadrille, "But I have not danced for so long now - and to tell the truth I am not in spirits enough to believe I would enjoy it."

"Your father will be disappointed, I think."

Lady Margaret nodded at the figure below, and Sir Henry's daughter following the glance, sighed. "Yes".

There was a brief pause. "I loved to dance," confessed the older woman, "and not only when I was younger." Her face softened. "My dear husband could always persuade me to stand up with him - He was such a handsome figure I was always proud to join him. You would never have met him, I think. He died in '88. Well of course you would not have met him!" She laughed. "And you never met me before our introduction this evening, I think?"

"I don't believe so, ma'am," Antonia responded. "I never met your late husband; I was only two years old in 1788 – But you were evidently very fond of each other?"

"Ah, we were, we were - He was devoted to me, and I to him." She shook her head. "But that was long ago . . . far too long ago. I knew your mother of course," she added inconsequentially.

"Did you, ma'am?"

"Indeed, though not at all intimately, and she was - " Margaret Spenlow glanced at her young hostess. "Your mother was - um - "

"Unusual." suggested Antonia gravely.

"The very word!" agreed the other, and suddenly they were both laughing.

"Oh, dear, I did not know my mother very well either," Antonia said ruefully, "but I'm afraid she *was* 'unusual'. She led my father a merry dance. I believe it was a marvel to him that he got on in the world as well as he did, considering -" She broke off, conscious of several indiscretions, but the older woman seemed to understand at once, leaning forward to pat her arm.

"You've nothing to fear from me, I assure you, my dear." And without quite knowing why, Antonia understood that it was the truth.

"Lady Margaret, - " she began.

"Molly, please!" interrupted her new acquaintance. "Everyone I like calls me Molly - "

"Lady Molly, then, forgive me - I see my father coming this way - "

"To bully you back into the hall, I daresay?"

Her father did look extremely irritated, thought Antonia, and he probably did intend to chivvy her out of her seclusion. How was it that, after all these years and all that had happened, he made her feel like a child under his control?

"Has he seen you yet, do you suppose?"

"I don't believe so."

"Then move further back, into the curtains, and I shall head him off." Lady Spenlow stood up as she spoke, and glided towards her host like a ship in full sail. "Now, Sir Henry!" his daughter heard her say as his guest took his arm and bore him away, "I'm so glad you've arrived in time to partner me for this next dance - " and the conversation that followed was lost to her ears as the startled Sir Henry returned with his partner the way he had come.

"Your father was enquiring as to your whereabouts," Molly Spenlow continued when she returned to the balcony a half hour later. "I was not sure whether I ought to continue to deceive him or not, but I sent him back to the salon again, in any case."

Antonia could not help but smile as she made room for Lady Spenlow on the sofa beside her. "You're very obliging, ma'am."

"But in return," said the other, nodding, "you must tell me why you are set on avoiding a father who is so kind as to give you this splendid evening. I will not say *no* expense had been spared," she added dryly, glancing about, "but this affair will have cost him a pretty penny, and you do not seem quite grateful enough!"

Antonia agreed. "I am ungrateful, there is no doubt about it." Her lips tightened. "But I do not care to be *managed*, and my father insists upon it."

"Managed? You are a married woman, and as such surely independent of a parent, if not of a spouse. Were you not married — not so long ago — to a foreign gentleman? Why do you use a different name now?"

"I was indeed married. Briefly. He - he was killed in - fighting on the Spanish border. I am therefore no longer Miss Davenport - but I cannot bear to use his name."

"Oh my dear, I am so sorry. A casualty of the war in Spain?"

"Some time since. I - I don't care to speak of it."

"Of course not." Lady Spenlow's sidelong glance betrayed her longing to know more, but her breeding and kind heart would not allow her to pry further. "Dear Mrs Davenport, don't let me grieve you. I don't mean to speak out of turn, but you are not the only young woman in England widowed by this war, and you are young - You think perhaps you will never love again, and perhaps you will not - Not in the same way - But you will marry again. You must. But this is what your father is trying to do, I suppose, when you accuse him of trying to manage you?"

Antonia Davenport raised her eyes, and regarded the older woman for some moments as the latter continued to smile sympathetically. Eventually she said: "My father tells me I must have another husband - and he thinks he can find me one at an occasion like this."

"It does happen."

"I do not intend to marry again."

"Why ever not, my dear? As I said before, you are still young. Too young to sink into widowhood for the rest of your life. We widows are very boring, you know. We talk too much to anyone who will listen, and get all our amusement from other people's lives." Her eyes twinkled so delightfully as she spoke that despite her earlier reticence, Antonia could not help laughing. "I like to see you laugh," Molly said. "You are so very pretty when you laugh! and I think you have not been laughing nearly enough lately."

"I think you are probably right," Antonia smiled, but her eyes filled with sudden tears.

"Now then, miss! - Lady Spenlow, ma'am - " Henry Davenport had loomed up in front of them, and this time there was no escape. "Is this where you're hiding? I expect you, Antonia, to be downstairs, greeting those I have invited to meet you, not gossiping – excuse me, ma'am, - up here. I paid out a goodly sum to make sure you was noticed tonight, and I find - " He suddenly noticed his daughter's brimming eyes. "What have you been saying to my daughter, ma'am?"

"I have been telling her," Molly Spenlow retorted, "that she is quite lovely when she laughs, and she does not seem to laugh often enough."

"Well, that's true enough, but why does that pipe your eye, miss?"

"Your daughter is a widow, Sir Henry. I believe she may cry when she wishes without people being surprised at it."

Henry Davenport stiffened, but his guest went on: "Did she ask for this soirée this evening? You can't bully her into marrying again, you know, Sir Henry."

It was hard to tell who was more amazed at the words tripping off Lady Spenlow's tongue. Sir Henry's mouth opened and closed without a sound as he turned and stared at his daughter. "I don't know what I have done to deserve this!" he said at last. "My daughter returns from the Peninsula, refusing to live with her husband's family as she should, and expects a welcome! She married well. I saw to that, even if he was a Johnny foreigner. She could be comfortably off by now. Instead, she's back here in England. And without two farthings to rub together."

Lady Spenlow interrupted Antonia's indignant protest.

"We're fighting a war in the Peninsula, Sir Henry. How can you desire your daughter to be exposed to any further danger there?"

"With our army driving the French back through the Pyrenees, what can be the problem? My contacts in Porto, in the wine business, assure me life goes on much as usual. She'd be safe enough in the south."

"We'd all like to think so!"

"Lady Spenlow, please," broke in the appalled daughter of the house. "I appreciate your defence of my position – but I believe I can defend myself. Please do not upset yourself on my behalf."

Molly Spenlow quickly closed her lips on what she had been about to say. She turned to Antonia. "You're quite right, my dear. Of course this is none of my business - It's just that I can't abide a bully. Good evening to you, Sir Henry. My gratitude for your hospitality. I am delighted to have met your charming daughter." To Antonia's astonishment, Molly patted her cheek with her mittened hand as she walked away. "Call on me any time you want to talk, Mrs Davenport. I hope we shall meet again soon. Goodbye, dear."

*

Antonia was not much surprised the next day to be summoned before dinner to her father's presence. She had expected to be upbraided once again for her failure to participate as required the previous evening, but not to be asked what she meant by conspiring against him with Margaret Spenlow.

"Conspiring? Come, Father, that's ridiculous. I never met the lady till last evening, and we had no more than a half hour's conversation."

"That woman is subversive. I cannot think how I came to invite her, except that your mother would do so in the old days." Henry Davenport tucked his hands up under his tailcoat and strode back and forth on the turkey carpet in front of the drawing room fire. Bright afternoon sunshine twinkled on the shining fire dogs and gleaming fender but there was no brightness in his expression as he grumbled: "I thought she would add some *gravitas* to the proceedings – someone of her age – with her family background. And fortune. Hoped she might offer," he mused, "to introduce one of her nephews too, but they're still at sea, she says. Eldest just made Commodore."

Antonia could see that he was once again deep in consideration of her remarriage.

"I should not much care," she said, evenly, "to marry a sailor at present, Father. I should almost certainly find myself a widow again, and back home with you in no time."

Her father glared. "I do not care for your flippancy, Antonia. And while you are under my roof, you will remember that my wishes take precedence over yours. It was insulting to have you hiding in the gallery when there were so many people to introduce."

"I believe you introduced me to everyone at the beginning of the evening, sir."

"Pah! Any worthwhile acquaintance requires a certain amount of hard work in making conversation. It was quite obvious that you had no intention of making that small effort. What do you imagine I can do for you if you will not make a push to engage yourself in company? When I think of the trouble and expense I gave to ensure there were several eligible suitors..."

"There was not one person there under forty," Antonia exclaimed. But her father had not finished.

"I don't know what you expect, madam. Your history is not calculated to attract a younger beau."

"I do not want a younger beau," she declared. "And I particularly do not want an old one! Please, Father, can you not understand? I have no desire to marry again."

"Well, please will *you* understand that I am not going to keep you indefinitely under my roof."

"I do not ask you to keep me . . . "

But this was a conversation that had taken place almost daily since Antonia's arrival three weeks earlier, and she compressed her lips and stared up at the portrait above the fireplace while her father continued to upbraid her. The portrait, painted by Romney twenty years earlier, showed her pretty mother Charlotte – who had proved so vain and giddy – the eldest son, Charles, standing at his mother's shoulder, supercilious even as a youth - and the two daughters, Henrietta and Antonia, the little girls in blue-sashed white dresses, leaning on their mother's knee and smiling up into her face. Antonia could almost remember those sittings. Charles had been eleven. She had been four, Henrietta eight. Before everything had started to unravel.

Her father was still talking. "I cannot conceive why you should take it into your head to leave Portugal and return at a moment's notice to impose yourself on me. I'd suggest you write to Yorkshire for an invitation, but you needn't think you'll be any more welcome there than I was made last year. Unpleasant fellow that husband of Henrietta's."

"Your choice of suitor again, sir, as I recollect."

Her father scowled. "Cabral was good enough for you at the time, miss, and Hetherington was good enough for Henrietta. At least my elder daughter don't run off and leave her in-laws at the first little difficulty. I must say, daughter, you quite shame the name of Davenport by running home when the Cabral's have such need of you. Your return smacks of selfishness."

For a moment there was silence in the elegant drawing room but for the faint cry of a herb seller in the street below. Antonia smoothed the grey gauze of her skirt with great concentration.

"I had hoped you knew me better than that, Papa," she said at last. "Forgive me, but I had always thought of *you* as family, and I had not appreciated that my arrival here would cause an upset." She had never expected a triumphant homecoming – but she had hoped her father would show some warmth; it had after all been more than five years since they had seen each other. She should have known better. Why imagine that he would have changed in the years she had been away?

Henry Davenport studied his daughter. She'd grown pale and thin since he had seen her off to Portugal, he thought. Her brief marriage, it seemed, had done her few favours, but she was still a fine looking girl - took after her silly mother in that respect - and when, he mused, she was properly over that unfortunate accident and the unexpected loss of the husband which she should be after all this time, she should marry again. To be sure, a second match was unlikely to command the fortune of the first. He imagined he'd done well in putting Antonia in the way of the Cabrals all those years ago - if only she'd stay in Portugal! He had thought that in settling her abroad, with so wealthy a family, his responsibilities as far as his daughters were concerned were at an end. Henrietta had her estate in the North, and Antonia had had her prize too. He couldn't have done better than with the younger Cabral - except for his untimely death. Wrong place at the wrong time. Damned careless of him. But Antonia was no longer a Davenport concern. His life should be his own.

"Wife or widow, Antonia, your place is with the Cabral's," he said. "But, no. You return to England the minute Dom Luis is buried. Indeed he can scarce be cold in his grave." He flicked his coat tails, and got up to pace the carpet. "Dona Isabel must expect to depend on you in these troubled times."

"Dom Luis has been dead and buried these ten months now, Father, and I imagine Dona Isabel can only find life less stressful without me to be constantly about her, a continual reminder of the loss of her sons. I assure you Beatriz made no reproach when I told her I intended leaving."

"Beatriz? Who the devil – Oh, yes, I recollect, the sister, but child, this is not your home now."

"You make that perfectly clear, sir. Pray forgive the lapse. For so many years I called it by that name."

"You must see, Antonia, that when you took Alvaro Cabral, you took yourself a new life and a new home. You will not tell me now that you are dissatisfied with what your marriage provided. Certainly the Cabrals have every advantage of wealth, charm, connection - I cannot imagine you are dissatisfied with that part of your settlement, whether you are widowed now, or not?"

"'Satisfaction' had nothing to do with my decision to return. It had simply become - impossible for me to continue at the Casa Cabral - "

"But consider! You give up your rights when you abandon that family as you have done. You must realise what you forfeit by being absent when the old lady goes off at last. You will find the da Fontes not slow to influence matters when she is dead. To their advantage, no doubt."

Antonia stood up at that, hands clenched. "This discussion is achieving nothing," she said. "Frankly, the da Fontes deserve every advantage, and Beatriz and Baltasar will cope better in my absence." Without her to be used, Antonia thought, by a mother-in-law who seemed intent on setting each of them against the other. But her father exclaimed at her last remark.

"Poor blighted Beatriz. Hasn't she troubles enough? Childless, married to a cripple, with all the cares of the two estates on her shoulders. And now her father dead, with both of her brothers, and her mother prostrate with grief."

"Do not pity Beatriz, Father." Antonia found herself trembling. "She has many blessings, and deserves them too. And Senhor da Fonte may be unable to walk but he is more than capable of managing all the estates in the south, and it is solely due to him that the Cabrals have retained the Casa Cabral and all its land. Don't you dare pity Beatriz."

Her father stared. "There is no call to fly down my throat, young lady! I do not know how your marriage agreed with young

Alvaro, but he must have found you as trying as I do when you are in this mood."

"Then I will take myself away," Antonia exclaimed. She limped towards the drawing room door, but her father hurried to stand in her way.

"Come, come, this won't do. Don't go off in a huff now. We've not settled affairs between us. I have said I will make you a small allowance, nothing more, but now you must look about you, and make another match as soon as is decent."

Antonia lifted her chin, her blue eyes suddenly brilliant. "I will not marry again!" Had not her father long before made it clear that he considered his own marriage a boyhood folly? Yet he would wish on her a second, unwanted, marriage! It seemed to Antonia that the more she had to do with men the less attractive the prospect of being involved with another seemed to be. Every close relationship – with her father, her husband, her brother, even Baltasar – each one had disappointed, fallen short of her expectations. As for Baltasar, though he was goodness itself Antonia despaired of whatever she had done to provoke that sad declaration on the terrace, that little scene that had finally led her to abandon all hope of continuing her life at the Casa Cabral. As for Duarte – No, she would not think of him now. To think of him was to probe a still raw wound. What had kept her blind for so long? She would never use the name Cabral again. Never. Antonia locked her fingers together.

And after all this time, a sudden remembrance of William Hurst's bruised face came into her mind; the tired ice blue eyes, that lock of blonde hair falling. . . Antonia brought herself up short. Captain Hurst had not been what she had thought him either so it was evidently some failing in her, some defect that made her unable to recognise people for what they really were. She suddenly felt desperate. She could not stay here, where she was very clearly not welcome.

"Please excuse me, father," she said abruptly. And without waiting for an answer, she limped into the hall, closing the door behind her.

CHAPTER TWENTY SEVEN

Seizing a jacket, and hastily tying on a bonnet, Antonia left the house and headed out into a fine September afternoon. The trees were already golden, and the nearby river Thames glittered in the sunshine but Antonia hardly noticed her surroundings, or the discreet presence of the usual manservant walking some paces behind her for her protection. She could not continue to live with her father, and she would certainly never submit to his conditions.

Antonia hardly knew what to do. She had left Portugal with little in the way of funds and, but for a small income from her mother's legacy, had little money of her own, but somehow she must find somewhere to live. Perhaps she could advertise herself as a governess or a housekeeper? The thought was not attractive, but she needed a breathing space where she could consider her options.

Though she had not disclosed it, Antonia had in fact, only a day or so earlier, received that invitation to spend a month or two near York, but had so far hesitated to accept, wondering if she could bear to witness yet another wretched union? Having last seen Henrietta on her wedding day seven years before, Antonia heard infrequently from her sister, but she very much suspected from her letters that the marriage was not a happy one. Perhaps Hen too had been as eager to escape her life in London with their father, but it had always surprised Antonia that her sister had accepted Richard Hetherington, who seemed a difficult man to like, overbearing and hypercritical. The subject had never been discussed between them. The invitation, however, had indicated Lord Hetherington would be absent for the greater part of the stay, and Henrietta had added that the children looked forward to meeting an aunt they hardly knew. It *would* be good to see her sister again, Antonia thought, and it would give her the opportunity to talk over her own situation. Her father's carriage might take her as far as Peterborough, a hired coach would get her to Doncaster, and if her brother-in-law's carriage would meet her there – Perhaps she should consider the visit.

Antonia had just made up her mind to accept the invitation, when a carriage drew up nearby and a voice hailed her.

"Lady Molly!"

"My dear, I have just left my card at your father's, and heard you were not at home. May I offer to take you wherever it was you wanted?"

"You're very kind. I was only walking to clear my head. My father's man is with me."

"Oh send him home, dear, and do climb into the carriage. You don't mind dogs, do you? He's only small, and never bites. Move over, Samson. Yes, John will take you wherever you want to go, and we will take you home directly afterward, if you wish, but I would far prefer it if you were to come and drink a dish of tea with me. I was so hoping I might not miss you."

"Well – if you are quite sure? Thomas, thank you, I shan't need you now." And with an uncertain smile at him and at her new acquaintance Antonia accepted Lady Molly's hand and climbed into the carriage. A very small spaniel, with large friendly brown eyes, held out a paw, and Antonia shook it solemnly.

Molly patted the little dog proudly. "Isn't he a love? You see, I am leaving for Hampshire at the end of the week, and was anxious to see you again before I left. I might not be in London again for some time now, and I am having a little dinner before I go for all my friends. Will you come?"

"But Lady Margaret – "

"Molly, dear Mrs Davenport."

"Molly, we only met a week ago. You cannot know me sufficiently well to wish to include me in your party?"

"I liked you the minute we met, my dear, and should like to get to know you a great deal better. Let us drive on a little to enjoy the sunshine, and then you shall come back to Henrietta Place, and we shall have tea and bread and butter, if you like. Now, where is it we're going?"

Bemused, but vastly entertained by the speed of the interchange, Antonia made a suggestion and the carriage bowled off.

Over tea, Molly Spenlow talked of her intended journey. She was to leave for her house near Winchester the day after her dinner and expected to be gone for at least a month. "I have a pretty little house in the country, Mrs Davenport, and should love you to see it. Samson loves to go down there, don't you, my sweet? – But spring will be an even better time for a visit, when the garden is at its best. You say you plan to visit your sister though. It will do you good.

You look forward to seeing her again, I am sure. You have an elder brother, I believe. Shall you be seeing him at the same time?"

"We are not close. Have never been so, I am sorry to say, and I do not expect to see Charles before the New Year."

"But you have seen him since your return?"

"No." Antonia gave Molly Spenlow a wry smile. "He will not have considered my return of sufficient interest to disturb himself. He has not made any invitation."

"You don't get on?"

"There is no antipathy. Rather that we have no particular feeling for each other. Neither Henrietta nor I had much to do with him as children. He is somewhat older, as you probably know, and always considered us a perfect nuisance."

"My brother was older than I but we were dearest playmates. It is a great pity that we are no longer so close." Lady Spenlow heaved a sigh. "Of course, it will be Christmas and the New Year before we know it. You will not leave it too late to travel back south, I suppose. The weather will be rather fiercer in the Ridings than here. Will your family return to London with you for the winter?"

"Gracious no, ma'am. My brother-in-law barely moves from his estate, and observes no season but the hunting. My sister has a quiet life of it, and devotes herself to her children. She has three — I have not even seen the two youngest."

"Are you fond of children?"

"I have no great experience of them to tell the truth, Lady Molly. I had none of my own, but I thought Henrietta's eldest a sweet child. However I have not seen him since he was two years old. Do you have children?"

"Alas, none of my own either, but you, at least, may yet be blessed. I have only my nephews. And my little dog." She caressed the spaniel's small round head. "I was very fond of all the boys as children. Am still."

"Oh indeed, I believe congratulations are in order. My father told me that your eldest nephew had just been promoted to the rank of Commodore. You must be very proud of him."

Lady Molly beamed. "I am! I am! His uncle, my late husband, would have been so proud too."

"All your nephews are in the service, ma'am?"

"I have four, and they are all serving, God bless them and keep them safe. Two are in the Navy, one in Spain, and the other in America. It is hard to know what to wish for them. Success and promotion, of course, but that seems only to come through peril and adversity. I could wish them safe at home, but I daresay none of them would care to be there." She glanced at Antonia. "You might have wished your husband safe at home, my dear, but I think you will find that however much he cared for you, he cared more for his duty, and he would have been unhappy to let others perform it for him. Oh, my dear child, have I blundered in again? Please forgive me. I *will* say things that were sometimes better left unsaid. I forget how long ago it is since you lost him."

Antonia blew her nose. "Longer than it seems, ma'am. Don't concern yourself. I have come to terms with the end of my marriage, I assure you. But every now and then – a word seems to hurt more that it should."

"In that case, my dear," Molly said, "I shall try to take care not to speak of that part of your life."

"That might be best," Antonia said gratefully. "For a while."

It might be wonderful, she thought, to tell Lady Spenlow about her marriage to Alvaro Cabral, and how she had come to be in the mountains in the heart of Portugal, about where he had died and how, and what Antonia herself had learned since his death. But not yet. Not yet.

The spaniel put his nose in her hand as if to express its sympathy, and Antonia smiled weakly. She stroked the soft head. "Why do you call him Samson, Lady Molly? He is such a small dog."

"Well, dear, it's my little joke I suppose. He is the very opposite of the biblical fellow, but he does have very long hair."

Molly was tactful enough to respect Antonia's reticence regarding her marriage, though Antonia had explained her injury to Molly more honestly than she had done to her father. It was not the whole truth, but Molly now understood that there had been a confrontation that had resulted in Senhor Cabral's death, Antonia's injuries, and her subsequent rescue by British officers. Now, as far as Antonia was concerned, it was almost as if that part of her life had never been, and no more was said of the Peninsula for some time, though at every street corner it seemed there was a cripple of some kind, in uniform, begging. It was clear that the casualties returning from the various conflicts were finding life at home almost more of a battle than the fighting in the front line.

CHAPTER TWENTY EIGHT

The early part of Antonia's visit to Yorkshire was a great success. Henrietta had matured into a loving mother of three gifted, charming children, and showed herself clearly able to manage, the large establishment into which she had married, but while she felt unable to offer Antonia a home without first asking the consent of her lord and master, who was of course absent - or even conceive that Antonia might consider an independent existence, she was delighted to see her younger sister and proceeded to take her about the estate and into York. She had done her duty by her husband, producing an heir together with his brother and the youngest child, a little girl of eighteen months who was the image of her mother. Antonia was glad to renew her acquaintance with the eldest boy, a solemn little lad with the sweetest of smiles, and she was soon a favourite playmate. For the time being, Antonia put her difficulties to the back of her mind, and gave herself up to the pleasure of the family's company. After five or six weeks, however, the whole atmosphere changed with the return of the master of the house.

Richard Hetherington was still an abrupt and an exacting man, and it soon became clear that the whole household went in fear of his displeasure. Henrietta had told Antonia that she loved her husband dearly, but it did not seem this feeling was reciprocated. Nothing Henrietta did ever seemed to be quite good enough for Richard Hetherington, and he seemed quite as dissatisfied with his offspring. He was studiously polite to his sister-in-law, which in view of the intemperate language he used to his wife made Antonia all the more uncomfortable, and she found herself no more able to confide in Henrietta than her father or Beatriz.

Until Hetherington's arrival, Antonia had almost begun to entertain vague hopes that she might find a home and prove useful to the family there, but she was not invited to prolong her stay and, hating to leave her sister but at the same time relieved to be away from the underlying tension at the Hall, Antonia realized that for a short while until she could find an alternative, she must return to London and her father's house.

She re-entered the house in Smith Square with a heavier heart than usual. Outside, as she had climbed down from the coach, the sight of a legless veteran leaning against the railings of a neighbouring house had been a shock. It seemed ex-soldiers, limbless and scarred, were now more numerous in the streets, tattered uniforms still proudly worn, but holding out to passers-by a box with crudely written details of their service. The soldier had saluted her gruffly as she gave him unlooked for largesse in the form of her last sovereign, and Antonia wondered if anyone were looking after this human debris of war, and was afraid to ask where and with whom he had served.

She paused in the hall while her boxes were brought in. Above her soared the dome of the house's central vestibule, and with her head tilted back, Antonia's eyes rose automatically to its furthest point, two floors above. She had never remarked upon it before, but the sight brought back childhood memories. She must have stood here many times. It had always made her think of the interior of a church: the high dome, the smooth marble floor underfoot, the hushed voices of the servants as they passed to and fro, the candles fluttering against the dark wall, the sense that she had somehow misbehaved . . .

It was foolish to pit herself against her father. Hadn't time taught her that? He had a way of wearing down all opposition to all his plans, ignoring any opinion but his own. Now what had seemed to her to be the only course of action upon leaving Portugal seemed as impossible a life as remaining at the Casa Cabral would have been. She should have remained at the convent.

What a haven that place seemed from this distance.

It should have been an unhappy spot. The nuns, save for their great veils of white, had gone about in mournful black, and their charges were the sick and the poor and the dying, yet it managed to be cheerful, purposeful. With its white walls and melon-coloured features, the convent of Nossa Senhora da Misericordia had an atmosphere that was at once soothing, calm, and uplifting. And Antonia's association with the nuns had tempered the hours of tedium as she slowly regained her strength. Antonia smiled with particular fondness as she thought of Sister Jerome, and hoped war would keep far away from the convent. And from London too – where she must decide if she could what she was to do with the rest of her life.

Her father greeted her return with a mixture of smugness and irritation, but continued to remind her that he did not intend to keep her indefinitely, and she must marry. "And if you do not make some shift, Miss, to do so, you had better remove yourself to Gloucestershire, where you can see how you will manage there on all the allowance I can spare you."

If her father was not wholly delighted to see her again, Molly Spenlow was. She called on Antonia the morning after her return from Yorkshire, and carried her back to Henrietta Place, where Antonia renewed her acquaintance with the little spaniel, and she and Molly reviewed their respective absences. Molly had been in London some weeks already, and took delight in giving her younger friend an account of all the recent comings and goings, the latest plays, the Court gossip, the progress of the war, and the machinations of the politicians. Lady Spenlow was far from being a blue-stocking but she enjoyed a lively debate. Her friends and acquaintances were an interesting mix of writers, politicians, musicians, scientists and courtiers. Antonia had, rather to her surprise, enjoyed the intimate dinner that had been given prior to Lady Spenlow's departure for her Hampshire home, and Molly spoke of that evening, when there had been eight other guests to dine.

"Lord Boscawen was much taken with you, Antonia. He asked if I thought he might call on you."

"Oh, Molly! Do not say *you* are matchmaking now?"

"Not at all." She smiled mischievously. "Though he is handsome and rich. I hope I did not do wrong in telling him that you were to leave almost immediately for Yorkshire, and that I was unsure of your return?"

"In that case, I thank you. He was perfectly charming, and I much enjoyed our conversation, but I had no idea - " She smiled ruefully. "Ah, well, I shall be safe in Gloucestershire soon."

"Do you leave again so soon? What is in Gloucestershire to tempt you away? Another sister, brother?"

"No family at all. My father has a house there, which is let at present. He never goes out of London himself, but he has told me that unless I fall in with his plans, I must take up residence in one of the cottages there."

"What!"

"I don't mind. It will give me a chance to think, and the country is perfectly lovely. Most of the year." She laughed. "And I shall have some peace, at last."

"But what will you do for Society? For conversation? Are you near a town of any size? A theatre?"

"I can read. There will be a piano."

"Your brain will turn to mush! No, Antonia, it cannot come to this. So, listen. I have been thinking. And I have been thinking that it would be a capital idea if you would consider moving from your father's house to take up residence here. For as long as you wish to do so."

"I beg your pardon?"

"I have been exercising my thoughts on this matter for some weeks now, and I am convinced we should both benefit from the move. Now more than ever."

"Oh, Molly, you don't have to feel sorry for me."

"My dear, I am not suggesting this move because I feel sorry for you. And do not worry. I do not intend you to be under any obligation. You shall not wait on me, nor be at my beck and call. You shall live just as you please."

"But Molly, I *know* why I want to change my circumstances. Why should you want to change yours?"

"I enjoy your company. I like to have younger people about me. I miss my nephews, and I fancy you could stand in their stead. I never had the pleasure of a niece, or do you fancy yourself an honorary god-daughter?"

"Molly, this is too much."

"I am serious, child. I only regret not having suggested it sooner. Do not reject the plan out of hand, I beg you."

"But this is too generous! I could not - "

"You could indeed, if you wished. Unless you think you should not like to live in a house that considers a small dog part of the household."

"That is of no consequence! But you have not known me long enough to be sure that I should not annoy you. I have a thousand and one irritating habits, I am sure."

"Well, I daresay we both may. You may find life in Henrietta Place even more unendurable than in Gloucestershire. But I think with good will on both sides we could rub along very well. Shall we not give it a try? Your father will be heartily glad to have you out of Smith Square."

Antonia gave a laugh of disbelief. "He will indeed. Are you quite sure about this, Lady Molly?"

"Quite, quite sure, Mrs Davenport. Here's my hand on it. Tell your father tonight, and I shall expect you within the week. Now come upstairs, and tell me which of the rooms you would like as your own. There is a very pleasant sitting room on the second floor, with another adjoining you might use for your bedroom, or one or two others but I leave you to make up your mind."

CHAPTER TWENTY NINE

Within a month, it was as if Antonia had never lived anywhere else.

Henry Davenport, taking the announcement of her relocation with astonishing bad grace, had barely spared her a civil word since, and had stopped her tiny allowance. Fortunately there was still the small income from her mother's legacy, but Molly would not allow Antonia to use any of it on household expenses. She had only to please herself, and since her tastes were simple and she had no extravagant style, the diminutive account at her bank began to look quite adequate, and she found she could still make as generous a contribution to the veterans' cause, one that had come to mean a great deal to her. This was a great relief, and her readiness to do all she could to please the sponsor to whom she felt so indebted was matched only by the pleasure Molly Spenlow and Samson seemed to take in her company.

They spent the rest of that winter of 1813 in a London gripped by fog and the worst frost within living memory, with the Thames frozen over at Blackfriars. Antonia's determination to do something for the wounded veterans and their families, found Molly just as sympathetic to their plight. They had collected warm clothing and blankets and were trying to organise a fund for the relief of the hardships suffered on every side. At first they were not as successful as they had hoped, for the general opinion was that such casualties were the inevitable consequence of war, and that the rank and file knew this when they took the King's Shilling. Antonia persisted, however, and in this found herself indebted to Molly's friend, Lord Boscawen, who was a frequent visitor to Henrietta Place, and soon proved a generous benefactor, with useful connections.

A little later they celebrated together the rout of Napoleon's army at Leipzig, and the news of the Allied sovereigns entering Frankfurt. Like the rest of the country, they were caught up in the completely unfounded rumours of a great victory won at the gates of Paris and Napoleon's death at the hands of Cossacks, but it did seem at last that the tide had turned. All England had begun to hope that there might soon be an end to the twenty-year struggle.

Towards the middle of March, Molly expressed a wish to go down to Hampshire, and to show Antonia her country house.

"You will love it as I do, I am sure. And we can be there in no more than three days from now."

"I long to see it. You have told me so much about Bridge House that I have imagined it already."

"I wish you may not be disappointed. But I think that would be impossible! Even my brother admitted that it matched our family's - his - estate, for charm."

"Where does your brother have his house, Molly? You rarely speak of him."

"We fell out, as you know, ten years or more ago. He was furious with me over – over a matter of upbringing, I suppose. I am not to know how to bring up a child as I never had one, you see. He hurt me badly, but I forgave him that long ago. He does not often correspond with me, though I do have hopes recently that we are coming at last to some sort of *rapprochement*. I have offered to let bygones be bygones, but I will not apologise for what I did for the boy. . and please God, if the war be over soon, as it soon may be, all our boys will be home once more - but I still think I was right, so Sir John keeps to Kent, though I was born there, and I keep to Hampshire, and perhaps the twain shall never meet. But Bridge House is the equal of Bartonhurst, even in Maytime when the orchards are in a froth of bloom!"

"I do not know Kent well," Antonia began, and sighed. "But it is wretched, is it not, when families fall out."

"It is, dear. And we can only hope that one day we may each be re-united with our families. You may look doubtful, but it is just as likely that you will be reconciled with yours as I with mine. Now, where did we decide the proceeds of the last Bazaar might most usefully go?"

Antonia was enchanted at first sight of the elegant mansion set in a small park overlooking water meadows. Built for Ralph Spenlow on the occasion of his marriage, Bridge House had every modern convenience implemented in its construction and a full complement of staff the year round, since Molly liked to come and go at will. Fish, game and meat were provided by the estate: pheasants and rabbits, much to Samson's delight, abounded in the twelve acres of meadow and woodland around the house, and the river flowing through the estate was home to speckled trout. After years in Portugal, an English Spring was a renewed delight to Antonia, and she took great pleasure in exploring her surroundings either with Molly and the little spaniel in the carriage, or alone on foot.

They had been in Hampshire barely a fortnight when they heard that Paris had finally surrendered. For an instant, Molly was tempted to fly back to London to join in the celebrations, but the war was not quite over; six hundred miles south of Paris the British army was still fighting, and casualties continued to return home. Still, they celebrated with their neighbours, and like houses all over England, Bridge House was soon decked out with laurels and lit with coloured candles in all the many windows.

April saw the last of the French resistance. Yet fighting in America continued, and Molly still did not know when the end might come and her nephews could come safely home.

"We have nobody to shoot or fish here now, sadly," she said one morning at breakfast, as she opened the morning post laid beside her on the silver tray. "Ralph used to fill our larder on a regular basis, but it is down to the gamekeeper now. I tell my neighbours to use what they can. This reminds me I must tell Evans that old Mr Kennedy is to bring us a fine buck that will need hanging. How my nephews used to love hunting here in the old days!   - Oh, My Lord!"

Antonia looked up from her coffee to see her friend clutching a page, her eyes wide and already spilling over with tears. She sprang to her feet. "Molly, what is it?" But her friend was beginning to laugh.

"Oh, my dear, such – such news!" Molly pressed her napkin to her lips as if she could say not another word and waved the letter at Antonia to indicate she should reseat herself.

"Good news?"

"After all this time!" Molly exclaimed when she felt able to speak at last. "My brother wishes a reconciliation."

"Oh, Molly. That's wonderful."

"It is, it is. He writes that his son - my dear nephew of course - is expected home before the end of the month, that the boy is once again promoted, oh my goodness me! and that in thanksgiving for his safe return and his success, he wishes me to join in their celebrations. Gracious! I cannot say what delights me the most, to have my brother write kindly after all this time, or to have my nephew return! The lad is no great correspondent, needless to say, and of course I hear little of him through his father. I've had no more than a letter in these last two years, and that was terse to a degree."

"Communications would have been difficult, but how thankful you will be to have him home. It will be wonderful for you to see them both again. I am so very pleased for you. How long has it been since your nephew was last in England?"

"He had a spell at home after his return from the West Indies, but since I was *persona non grata* at that time and not invited to Bartonhurst, the dear boy came here. I think that was in the year six or seven. Imagine! I have not seen him for six, seven years. How he will have changed. Boy, I call him. He must be close to his thirtieth birthday but then we always think of the young ones as children, do we not? Thank God he is well. He was badly hurt early in the campaign, I understand, but recovered well. Imagine, a Colonel, and he no more than an Ensign when I sent him off. That was the root and cause of the disagreement, of course, between my brother and me."

"The reason for your falling out? Does your brother refer to it at all?" She indicated the letter.

"He does not mention it, I am pleased to say. And I shall say no more on the subject either. My nephew is returned home safe from the war, and I shall dance with him at Bartonhurst! And with that stubborn brother of mine, too," she added with a laugh, "whether he will or no."

"And this is all to take place shortly? We had better bustle about, had we not, to get you ready for an expedition into Kent? There is the matter of the fund raising concert still to arrange, but that is some months yet. Would you want me to return to Town, Molly, or await you here? Shall I mind Samson while you are gone? I will fall in with whatever plans you wish to make."

"Oh, but my dear, you are to come with me, surely?"

"Surely not. This is a family celebration, the chance for you all to become reacquainted."

"It is to be no intimate gathering. Sir John writes that there is to be quite a party. He is opening up the Dower House in my honour, he says, but I fancy if the main house is to be packed out as he suggests with my nephew's comrades, we shall not be the only guests sleeping at the Dower House either. But Antonia, I should very much like my brother to meet you, and for you to make his acquaintance. And of course that of the blessed boy himself. You must come with me, dear Mrs Davenport, I insist. One more in that number will be as nothing, and you will enjoy it, I promise you."

"But there is no invitation for me, ma'am," Antonia replied, laughing. "I cannot descend upon your poor brother at your wish only! Especially when you are only recently reconciled. It might just cause a fresh rift between you. And then I should never forgive myself."

"Leave that, my dear," Molly Spenlow replied firmly, "to me."

Antonia found that she rather hoped she might make the acquaintance of Lady Molly's older brother. If he proved to be anything at all like her friend, she was sure she would like Sir John, even if sister and brother had once fallen out - though quite why they had done so she had not yet discovered. Rather as she was reluctant to speak of what had caused her own departure from Portugal, Molly seemed reluctant to speak of what had caused the rift in *her* family, and Antonia did not press her.

She also thought she might like to see Bartonhurst Manor, which Molly described as being set in the Garden of England amid hop fields and apple orchards, so that she was almost excited when, as Molly had promised it would, her invitation to join the party arrived some days later. Molly handed over the stiff card with a smug smile.

"Did I not say? And with only a day to spare."

"Is this the invitation?" Trying not to appear too eager, Antonia took it from her friend, and turned it over to read:

SIR JOHN HURST BEGS THAT MRS ANTONIA DAVENPORT WILL
JOIN A SMALL GATHERING AT BARTONHURST MANOR
TO CELEBRATE THE SAFE RETURN FROM THE PENINSULA
AND THE PROMOTION
OF HIS DEAR AND ONLY SON, WILLIAM ALEXANDER HURST
AT 6 o'clock ON .   .   .   .

There followed the date of the celebration and details of the Colonel's Regiment but Antonia did not see any more. There was a sudden roaring in her ears, and she could only stare in disbelief at the card in her hand. Sir John Hurst? William Alexander . . . Hurst?

"Is something the matter?"

"I - I did not know your family name was Hurst," Antonia gasped, when she could speak.

"I must have mentioned it a hundred times. But what of it, dear? What on earth has driven the colour from your face so very suddenly? Is there something I should know about my brother, his family? Antonia, speak!"

Antonia knew that she must confess, or confront untold awkwardness later. "'Tis nothing very grave, Molly, I assure you. Just the shock of seeing the name. I always thought your brother would be a Spenlow. Stupid of me. I never imagined . . Molly, the officer who came to my assistance in Portugal all those years ago was also called Hurst. Captain William Hurst. Can it possibly be one and the same?"

"Are you serious? You encountered my nephew in Portugal? How marvellous is that! It *must* be the same. He is tall, very fair. Very handsome too, I swear. You could never forget him if you saw him."

"I never have," Antonia agreed, breathlessly. She sat down, hand to her mouth, still staring at the card. Her thoughts flew back and forth like a bird flown into a room by mistake. William Hurst, a relative of Molly Spenlow, and all this time not to realise it? Had she not listened? Could it be the same? What must Molly think? How very - odd it would be to meet him again. After all this time, when they had parted under such circumstances. Would he have changed much? He had showed so many different sides to his character. Would he remember her at all? Would he remember Alvaro Cabral? What would he think to encounter her again? In England? Living with his aunt? Heaven forbid that he should think she had deliberately sought the connection! Oh, why had she not listened more carefully when Molly had spoken of her family?

"It was a considerable time ago - " she stammered, at last. "I daresay the gentleman may not even remember - " *Would he remember? Would he remember what had happened all those years before? That they had fought and argued, and that he had tricked her. He could hardly have forgotten that her husband was a traitor who had tried to kill them both? Would he have forgotten that he had saved her life? Would she ever forget his kindness, the words with which they had parted?* "He and I were thrown together when – He saw me to safety – at some difficulty to himself - " She hesitated again, then got it all out. "My husband was killed at about that time, and Captain Hurst came to be of the greatest service to me. But for his intervention, I might have died too." Her voice dropped, remembering. "He did save my life, Molly," she whispered. "I would have died if he had not got help for me, and brought me to safety."

"Oh my dear girl, that is the most romantic thing I have ever heard. And have you never seen him since then? Oh, just wait until I tell his father, he will be so proud."

"No!" Antonia sat up quickly. "Oh, no, no! Promise me, you will not speak of it. Imagine how your nephew will feel, to find that some poor woman he once helped years before is now in England, and has been taken in by his aunt, and that his father knows about it even before he has realised what is happening. It's not romantic in the least. Your nephew may not care to be reminded of it. No, please, please, do not mention it to another soul." Her thoughts were rioting now. She could not go to Kent; she could not join Molly in the celebrations. It would be too humiliating, too awkward for the Captain. "Oh, Molly, I cannot believe I could have – " She covered her face with her hands. "Molly, I cannot come with you to Kent."

"Not come? Because of this? Well, of course, you will come. Imagine your being acquainted so long ago and his being of such service to you. Is this not your chance to express your gratitude to my nephew once again?" She smiled, half teasing. "I should think you a very poor fish should you not come now. And Antonia, my love, I have been at such pains to secure the invitation. Sir John would think it very odd, I assure you." Molly took her hand. "Come, come, child, I cannot understand what all the fuss is, I really cannot. You must come to Bartonhurst with me on Thursday, I insist. She must come, mustn't she, Samson?" She added, in a softer tone: "Please."

I should tell her all, thought Antonia, but the words would not come, and Molly seemed to take her silence for assent.

"Well, we have only one day to get you ready. Do not shake your head at me, Miss. You are to come. Do not spoil this great treat for me. I long to present you to my brother – " and her lips broke into another smile, "and to reintroduce you to my clever, handsome, and brave nephew."

Antonia wondered what she could say. How could she refuse such pleas when Molly had been so good to her? Perhaps it *would* pass off more easily than she feared? It had all happened so many years before. Perhaps William Hurst would not recall that dreadful period as she did. Yet, even if in all his campaigning he had been through far worse, it was because of her that he had been imprisoned, and beaten, and confronted with cold-blooded murder. How could he have forgotten that? She had never forgotten it. Or him. And in spite of her fears, her heart quickened at the thought of meeting the man again.

If she said nothing more, perhaps it would pass off as Molly seemed to think it must: a heroic episode, and one in which she was greatly beholden to William Hurst.

It was only in the carriage on the final stage of the journey from Hampshire to Kent, with Molly Spenlow growing more and more excited at the thought of seeing her childhood home and her long-estranged brother once more, that Antonia's misgivings deepened. Suppose William Hurst had not forgotten the episode. Suppose he should suddenly blurt out questions about Duarte Cabral. In front of his family? In front of strangers? How could she answer?

Perhaps she should have written, when she first realised what was planned, explained her predicament, appealed to him to be discreet. She should have written, but it was too late now. Besides, if that nightmare episode had meant nothing, he would be puzzled now to hear from someone whom he had perhaps forgotten entirely. It would raise matters best left alone. Would Molly allow him to forget? She might tell Molly the whole story now, if only she could be convinced that it was necessary. She would only know when she met William Hurst again.

Antonia sat quiet in the corner of the carriage, and let Molly chatter on in such excitement that she barely noticed that her young friend was not her usual self.

The Dower House had remained Lady Spenlow's property though she had not occupied or visited it in more than ten years, and Molly, who had always liked the place, wondered aloud how it would appear after all this time. She told Antonia that Sir John had written that he had had it redecorated and refurbished for her. "He said some very unkind things at the time of our estrangement, so I suppose these efforts were to persuade me to come. He don't realise that I would have come if it had been filled with cobwebs! But at least you will see it in a good light, my dear. It's not as big as it sounds though. I hope we shan't have to share it."

In fact, the Dower House was a grand name for what was in reality quite a small building set among lawns and tall cedars, nearer to the road than the Manor itself but still perfectly charming.

As they swept in at the lodge gates, the keeper was seen to despatch a boy up to the main house, so that they had not been many minutes inside the Dower House before Sir John himself was announced.

Alighting from a little dogcart, he hobbled up the steps to the entrance, and surprised his sister and Antonia before they had taken off their bonnets and while they were still exclaiming over the stylish decoration. There was silence as brother and sister stood looking at each other across the hall, and then Molly Spenlow crossed the space between them with open arms, and they embraced. At this point Samson joined in, to leap around them barking, and Antonia, unable to hear what was said but understanding that the rift was finally healed, felt tears prick her eyes at the obvious warmth of the reunion. It was only right to leave brother and sister to converse in privacy, she thought, and was about to steal into a nearby room when Molly, smiling brilliantly, broke away from the murmured conversation.

"Antonia, you must come and be introduced to my brother, my dear brother. Mrs Davenport, may I name Sir John Hurst? Our host. John, this is my particular friend and companion, Mrs Davenport."

"Sir John." Antonia dropped a deep curtsey, as Sir John took her hand and bowed over it.

"Mrs Davenport. Charmed, quite charmed. How do you do, ma'am?"

His voice would have betrayed his age if his stooped shoulders and old-fashioned wig had not, and Antonia glanced at him with a fearful curiosity, wondering if there was anything of the son to be seen in his father. It was not obvious at first. John Hurst was smaller than Antonia, with a very slight build, and dressed in a black suit that made him seem slighter still. The elaborate long grey wig sat atop a thin, deeply lined face, but behind small round spectacles his eyes were very bright and very blue. They twinkled at her.

"Well we have a pretty addition to our company, sister! You are very welcome here, Mrs Davenport. I hope you will find everything to your liking."

"You are most kind, Sir John. It was very good of you to include me in your invitation."

"I am sorry it came so late. I had not realised Molly had found herself such a charming companion. On the other hand, I was not at all sure she would agree in the first place to come to see us here at Bartonhurst." He looked across at his sister and smiled rather ruefully. "She don't come for me, I daresay, anyway. Only for the boy. Well, sister, I am afraid you will have to wait a little longer to see him – He was only home three days before he was called away to Town yesterday on some business, and is not yet returned."

Antonia was astonished to experience what felt like a great pang of disappointment at the news, though it was quickly followed by a surge of relief. Molly, however, was horrified.

"Not yet back. For his own party? But when do you expect him?"

"He promises faithfully he will be in time for the reception tomorrow evening, and I think I can depend on that. Luckily for me - though not perhaps for our young ladies hereabouts - he took half his friends off with him. I'm sure I don't know what to do with the fellows. Great noisy creatures that they are."

In spite of herself Antonia could not help but smile at the tone of amused disgust in her host's exclamation, and seeing it, Sir John laughed.

"Ah, until you have experienced the company of these great hulks you cannot believe how they fill a room, Mrs Davenport. They will terrify your little dog, Molly! We lead a very quiet life here in the ordinary way, ma'am, and these fellows come as a great shock to me, I may tell you."

"Mrs Davenport may well know what it is to encounter our military, I think, brother -" Molly began and, suspecting with good reason what she was about to say, Antonia cut in hurriedly:

"Do you have a large party here to bother you, Sir John?"

"There is to be a great assembly in the West Field, my tenants and the villagers, you know, an ox roast, and dancing, and we shall all go down there later for they will want to congratulate my son, but in the house there are but five officers from my son's regiment, and two of them are away with my son today. My immediate neighbours are invited tomorrow night, ten or twelve couple that is, but they will not come till evening, being close enough for a carriage ride. I do what I can to give some pleasure by inviting the young maids of the neighbourhood, though that don't please my son too much, but with his friends in the house, the girls do not stay here either. You shall have the Dower House to yourselves during your stay. We shall be a merry enough party tomorrow, I trust. Enough to have several couple stand up for the dancing." His face clouded. "I am not sure that William will dance though. He limps, you know, Molly, more trouble with that hurt he took at Roliça, I understand, and I learned the boy was wounded again only a few months ago."

"Oh John, no."

"Aye, and that is part of the reason he's home again now, he tells me." As he spoke, Sir John's cheerful front cracked a little. He took off his spectacles to dash a hand across his eyes. "His promotion comes hard won, Molly."

"Oh, John, John, will you ever forgive me?" Molly laid a hand on his arm. "I thought it was a great career for the boy. It was all he ever wanted, you know it was, and he was so unhappy. I never imagined that it would cost him, cost you both, so dear."

"It's done, Molly. Over and done. I'm not blaming you any more. He was happy. I could see that. Anyone could. But I'm not so sure now."

Brother and sister seemed to have forgotten Antonia, and she felt she was overhearing a private conversation when Sir John added in a low voice: "He is greatly altered. Tired and short-tempered. He tries to hide it, but he is not the carefree lad that went off all those years ago."

"No one would be, John, not with all he must have seen and done in all that time."

"No," the old man sighed. "No." He suddenly became aware that Antonia — beginning to understand at last why brother and sister had fallen out so long before, and with concerns of her own to bother her - was standing awkwardly at the bottom of the stairs, holding Samson. "My dear Mrs Davenport. I have forgot my manners entirely. What can I be thinking? You must be exhausted after your journey." He crossed the hall and pulled at a bell rope. "Molly, won't you show Mrs Davenport where she is to sleep? You have your old room, of course, and I have taken the liberty of having the Yellow Room prepared for our young guest. A meal, if it suits you, is to be served here this evening — the house is in uproar tonight in spite of the absence of the young men. We dine at six o'clock. Country hours, Mrs Davenport, you see." He bowed to her, and patted his sister's shoulders. "Excuse me now, Molly. I have a great deal to organise still for tomorrow. I shall see you at supper. Perhaps."

"Only perhaps? Will you not dine with us, brother? Surely your housekeeper might manage all that is needful?"

"Well, perhaps, perhaps, but I like to keep an eye on things, you know. I want everything just so."

"Mm, you always did like to have things under your eye - And done your way."

"Well, if all this is not for William, then who else?" Sir John replied, with a sigh, and with a last bow to Antonia, he left them and returned to his near-empty home.

CHAPTER THIRTY

Supper was a rather subdued affair. Molly was obviously anxious about her nephew's health and his current absence, while Antonia was still coming to terms with what she had heard, and fretting over what she should do. She found the news that the Captain had been wounded again extraordinarily distressing. He had not deserved that. Was his ill temper worse because of this - or merely worse than his father remembered? Perhaps she might not be able to talk to him at all?

"Antonia, my dear," Molly said, rising from the sofa after supper and putting down her teacup, "I find I am quite worn out by all that has happened today, and will retire early. May I leave you to your own devices? Though you will be very dull, I fear, on your own. Tomorrow evening we shall be all sparkle, I promise, but just now my bedchamber calls." She crossed the room to the long windows and looked out at the lawns stretching into the distance in the peaceful evening sunshine. "Mind, it is still so light outside the birds are singing yet. I hope I shall be able to sleep. Don't let my brother's anxieties affect you. He is a pessimist by nature, you will find. Come along, Samson."

She patted Antonia's shoulder on her way to the door. "Goodnight, dear girl. I shall see you tomorrow, though you may be sure I shan't rise too early if we are to have a late night of it after. Why don't you take a walk about the garden and breathe in the good Kentish air? The roses and honeysuckles are very fine. No need to get your slippers wet, there is paving on all sides, you know, and you can make a tour in no time."

"It sounds very pleasant, Molly," Antonia murmured. "Goodnight, ma'am. I hope you wake feeling quite refreshed." She gazed after her friend as the older lady quitted the room, the little dog at her heels. It was hard to remember sometimes that Molly Spenlow was more than 30 years her senior, and the day's events would have been a drain on her physically as well as mentally. Heaven only knew she felt strained herself, and the encounter she rather dreaded had yet to take place. Antonia got up and walked across to the windows.

How peaceful it all seemed. Though it wanted two more hours to sunset the shadows were already long in the grass, and golden light bathed the tops of the trees. A stroll in the still warm air might do her good. And since there was no danger of meeting anyone there, she might walk across the park and quietly look at Bartonhurst Manor itself.

Pulling her new shawl about her shoulders, Antonia stepped over the sill onto the terrace.

Molly had not been quite accurate. Bridge House was lovely indeed, but it did not really compare with Bartonhurst Manor. The house here was older, and had a look that suggested it could have grown from the earth on which it stood. It was not a mansion. It was a home rather than the showpiece she had expected, but a place of great charm and serenity under the distant spur of green summer woods. The façade fronting the drive had been new a hundred years before and had weathered to a golden grey. Great creepers of some sort climbed roof-ward, and the great doors were hidden under a pillared porch, while the many-paned windows each reflected the setting sun as if candles had been lit behind them. There were no more than two floors, and the roof was low behind the low parapet, but as Antonia trod further across the park, it was obvious that the stone façade had been added to a much older building, for the sides and rear were brick and irregularly timbered, with the second storey jutting out some distance over the ground floor. It had been erected, Antonia suspected, when Elizabeth, if not her father Henry, occupied England's throne. There were Tudor chimneys to right and left with gables in this section of the roof so that the line of the ridge wavered up and down in a pleasantly random manner. It seemed to have a character all its own. Antonia smiled. Surrounded by parkland and peacefully grazing sheep, the house sat exactly as it should in its gentle valley, while the brothers of the centuries-old oaks and elms that dotted the pastures might even have given up their timbers to build Bartonhurst Manor.

This was Sir John's house. This was where his son had been born. This is what William Hurst had left behind when he had taken his commission and left England to fight overseas. She could see him now, proud in his scarlet coat, the gold of his tunic… She remembered him firing calmly at the wild boar, snatching Josefina from her horse, laughing with their landlady over the wonderful hot food . . .

Antonia shook her head. She thought of the Casa Cabral in summer: the tall pines that dotted the estate already wearing a tired, rusty look; the quiver of air hanging over the road seemingly the only movement in the dusty landscape; the formal beds and glaring gravel paths throwing sunlight back at the cream stucco walls. She saw herself, a slight figure limping across the deserted rooms on the second floor to creak open the shutters and look down into the sunlit garden.

It had been on such a day that she and Baltasar had found the letters, she recollected, and flinched at the memory . . .

The rustling leaves of the great oak above her brought her back to England, and Antonia shivered, and tightened the shawl about her. Time to return to the Dower House, and bed, she thought, and turned for one last look at the lovely old house behind her before striking out across the park towards what, for a few days, she must consider a sort of home.

Molly was not up at noon, and Antonia lunched alone. It seemed the son of the house had still not returned, and there was talk of a friend's marriage he had promised to attend. Antonia found herself wondering that he would choose to spend more time away from his father after all these years. She wondered if he knew that his aunt was here to celebrate with him, and after that, to wonder if he might even have heard that Antonia herself had been invited, which was why he had absented himself so long - then lectured herself for being so self-absorbed that she should wonder any such thing. In any case she was sure her name would mean nothing to him. Would it mean anything to him? She almost wanted him not to have forgotten her. Would he remember Duarte Cabral though, and humiliate her? Not in front of his aunt or his father, surely. Why should she imagine he would remember an incident that had happened five years before?

She would tell Molly everything - but not today, when there was so much else for her to think about.

The afternoon was filled with the servants' bustle. Additional staff had been drafted in to help with the guests, and from her bedroom Antonia watched the spectacle of carriages coming and going to and from the big house, while carts loaded with barrels and flowers and baskets made the same journey and came away empty. The labourers came out with their scythes, and mowed close-cropped lawns once again, and the air grew sweet with the scent of cut grass.

With each hour Antonia grew more tense. A maid came to help her dress before she was ready, and afterward she could not sit still. She knocked at Molly's door to be told that Lady Spenlow was still dressing, and would see her in a half hour, so she ran down to the drawing room, and then up again to her room for the book she wanted, not knowing what to do with herself. But she could not read either. She stood by the window as the shadows lengthened and the room grew shaded and she had just made up her mind to return to her room when the sound of laughter came from the hall. She opened the door, and heard someone say:

"Well, 'e's cutting it fine, that's all. Bless him, 'e said 'e wouldn't be late for his own party. And now 'e's here and the squire can stop worrittin'." The servant caught sight of Antonia and shot a quick curtsey. "Beg pardon, ma'am, didn't see you was there."

"Do I gather Captain Hurst has returned?" Antonia felt her voice shaking.

"That's right, ma'am," the girl answered eagerly. "Only quarter of an hour since. Rode up the drive like a fury, on account of 'im bein' so late, like."

"Of course."

In the drawing-room, Antonia stood with her back against the door, feeling overwhelmed by the need to speak to the man before they met again in company. Just in case. If it was the same William Hurst? Had she left it too late? If she hurried up to the big house now, perhaps he would see her. She could be there in a quarter of an hour. If she just put on boots and cloak over her slippers and gown. She could be back in no time.

Antonia ran breathlessly upstairs, snatched her cloak from the hook in the wardrobe, and forced her feet into kid boots. Not wanting to be seen leaving, she did not put on her cloak, but ran downstairs again and into the drawing room, and out through the long window she had used the day before, and across the dewy lawns and park, to Bartonhurst and the big house.

The front door stood open, lights blazing inside the hall though it was some hours before darkness fell, and Antonia slipped inside and stood uncertainly in the vestibule. A passing footman stopped at the sight of her. It was too early for guests but he knew his duty. "Ma'am?"

"I would like to speak briefly, very briefly, with Captain Hurst, if he will see me, please."

The man's face showed his astonishment. "The Captain – beg his pardon, the Colonel - has only just this minute come in, ma'am. Will I see if he is at home to visitors? Is he expecting you particularly?"

"I do not believe so. Please ask him," Antonia said, "Tell him it's Mrs Davenport." She flinched as the sound of hearty male laughter boomed out from behind a door nearby. "Mrs Antonia Davenport. Just a word."

"Oh, Mrs Davenport! With Lady Margaret, of course. Sir John is expecting you."

"But it's the Captain - the Colonel, I need to see. Please ask him to spare me a moment."

"Well, I will, ma'am," the footman said doubtfully, "But he will be dressing, getting ready - Yes, ma'am. Please to wait here a moment." He disappeared into the further reaches of the house, and Antonia drew into the shadows away from the lanterns.

In his room, William Hurst had just finished a hurried bath when the footman knocked. He was feeling guilty at returning so late and knew he had worried his father - and in a rush and with great difficulty he was trying to shave and get dressed at the same time. He had been in London that morning at the wedding of his best friend, for whom he had promised long ago to stand as best man, and it had proved difficult afterward to extricate himself. He was exhausted from his ride and though he was prepared to indulge his father, he was reluctant to be the centre of the proposed celebrations so that when he heard the knock, and cut himself, he swore at the same time as he answered.

"Colonel Hurst, Sir?" The footman stood in the doorway. "There's a lady just arrived in the hall, a Mrs Davenport. I know Sir John is expecting you in the Gallery shortly, but the lady says she must speak with you. Are you able to receive her just now?"

"Of course I cannot receive her just now!" William frowned. The name, though vaguely familiar, meant nothing to him, and it was hardly an hour to be calling. He dabbed at his face with a towel and winced.

"Mrs Antonia Davenport, she asked me to say particularly, sir."

In the act of putting on his shirt, William stopped short. "Antonia Davenport."

"That's right, sir."

Antonia Davenport? Antonia Cabral's father had been a Davenport, he remembered. Henry Davenport. How, he wondered, could this visitor possibly be Antonia Cabral? A great rush of something he did not understand swept over him in an uncomfortable mix of shock, pleasure, apprehension, disbelief, and still after all this time, an awful guilt. How could Antonia Cabral be in England? How could it be her? Yet would anyone else, he thought, announce herself in that particular way and in such a manner, or at such a time of day, "Antonia Davenport," he repeated stupidly.

"That's what she said, sir. Lady Margaret's companion, I expect you knew that. Shall I tell her you'll see her?"

"No! Yes – No, wait a minute." His mind was racing. His aunt's companion? Antonia Cabral was Mrs Davenport? Since when? And why should she want to see him? at this hour, after all this time? And why on earth would he want to see Antonia Cabral? Or Antonia Davenport?

Unless Molly was ill? "Has she come with my aunt?"

"Oh, no sir."

"But she is in good health?"

"The lady's a bit pale, like."

"Not her! My aunt!"

"Oh, yes, sir, far as we know, very well."

William stared at the servant, bewildered, until the man coughed politely behind his hand. "I'll tell her you're not at liberty just now, shall I then, sir?" he suggested, warily.

William did not answer, but walked up and down the carpet. "Tell her, tell her I - " he began, then: "Oh, dammit, show her into the library. I'll go down shortly." The servant disappeared, and William hurriedly finished dressing. Checking himself in the mirror, he tugged at his waistcoat and pulled irritably at his neck cloth, but staring at his reflection he saw nothing. All he could think was: "Antonia Cabral, here at Bartonhurst!" And he did not want to see her. Or did he?

Why, he thought wildly, has she chosen to come here and make herself known tonight? And why is she in England? How long has she been in England? With my aunt? Does she plan some mischief? Is she going to announce that I killed her husband? Is she after some sort of retribution? Blackmail? *Does my father know about her?* He felt a spurt of anger. Tonight was his father's celebration even more than his, and he would not have it spoiled by Antonia Cabral or Davenport, or whatever she chose to call herself now.

He limped down to the library. Several brother officers had moved into the hall, and gathered round laughing when they spied him descending the staircase.

"Not ready yet, Will?"

"Hurry up, sir, we're waiting!"

"Your guests are waiting, Colonel."

"We're two glasses ahead of you already, Will. What are you about?"

He pushed his way through them, forcing a smile. "Two minutes. I have some business I must attend." And, under his breath, he prayed they had seen nothing of Senhora Cabral being shown into the library, or the joshing might go beyond a joke. His father would not be amused. He opened the library door, stepped inside then took the precaution of locking the door behind him. He did not intend to be interrupted by his friends just yet.

The low, panelled room was illuminated by a cheerful fire in the hearth but there was only one great branch of candles lit so far, and for a moment William thought the room empty. Then a figure at the window turned with a rustle of silk and threw back the hood of her cloak.

William took a deep breath. "Senhora."

"Captain Hurst." She dropped a curtsey.

William started. This was not what he had expected. This was not Dona Cabral. "Your servant, ma'am, but I think there has been some mis - "

"I am obliged to you for agreeing to see me," the lady murmured. She took several halting steps further into the room, and as the firelight shone on gilded curls, he saw then that it was indeed Antonia Cabral, as beautiful as ever, standing taller and straighter than he had seen her for some long time. They were a continent and five years away from the events in the Portuguese Serra, but for a moment it was all crystal clear. William swallowed hard.

"Good God, I would never have believed it," he said in a low voice. He saw her flush at his tone, and as he took a step forward, she stood still and let him approach. "This is an unexpected pleasure, Dona Antonia," he said, fighting to keep his voice cool and dry.

"I see you remember me, Captain. I was not sure that you would. I was not even sure for a while that you were the William Hurst I once knew. You will be astonished to see me here, I think. I regret being obliged to call on you so soon after your return."

So formal! As if they had never endured days and danger together. He would have to be too. "I confess I am beyond astonished to see you here, Senhora, - and it is Captain no longer, ma'am, I am happy to say. Pray don't apologise. But to what do I owe this unexpected visit? Is my aunt -?"

"She does not know I am here. But I thought – I knew we should meet later, shortly in fact, in the company of others, rather against my will, - and before we come to be re-introduced formally I wanted to be sure – I needed to ask – to *beg* you, to make no great reference to our previous acquaintance."

"W -what? - "

"Hear me out. Please, do not mention the circumstances under which we first met, and please," she added, "do not call me Senhora – or Dona Antonia - Nobody knows me by that name here in England. I go by my family name now, Davenport, and I – I do not care to have it remembered that I was Senhora Cabral."

William stared at her, astonished at the breathless delivery of the request. "Does our previous acquaintance cause some difficulty then, ma'am?"

"You must be aware, sir, that I have no reason to be proud of my - my history. I had rather your Aunt, who has become very dear to me, does not learn the whole - story until I can find a way to tell her myself."

"My Aunt knows nothing of your past?" William marvelled. "I understood you to have been with her some time." She shook her head. He said more slowly: "My Aunt doesn't know? I cannot believe that after all this time you have told her nothing of your story."

"Tell her what? That I am the – widow - of a traitor, that the man I married betrayed his country, caused the death of so many - ?" She paused. "Believe me, Captain, until a few days ago I had no idea that you and Lady Molly were at all related. Since then, I have told her only," she hesitated, before adding, "somewhat inadvisably, that you saved my life."

"Saved your life?" he echoed, embarrassed. "Good God! What on earth possessed you to tell her that?"

"It is no more than the truth, Captain. If you had not returned for me . . ."

"If I had rather stopped you going into those damned mountains in the first place - " William halted, confused at the direction the conversation was taking. "Why mention that to my Aunt in the first place?"

"It – came out. I was taken by surprise to learn you and she were related. It was a very great shock." She bit her lip and fell silent.

"I can imagine it was. Nearly as great as mine to find you here tonight," William said, with a curt laugh.

"You won't say anything?"

"Is it so important after all this time?"

"The shame and the hurt remain," she said in a low voice.

"Evidently. But the shame was not yours, ma'am."

"Even so, I have not spoken of it to your aunt. Except that you were there and able to help me . . . "

William shook his head. "And if my Aunt greets me now, and says 'Dear boy, my companion informs me you've had occasion to save her life - you must tell me all about it' - what am I supposed to do?"

"You must say – say that you . . . " She faltered, and looked away.

"You do not appear to have thought this through very clearly, ma'am. And now it seems you want to involve me in the deception of an aunt of whom I am particularly fond."

"I am very fond of her too, sir, and it is not a complete deception," Antonia asserted. "She knows that we were searching for – for my husband in the mountains, as we were, and fell captive to partisans, as we were, and that you rescued me, but he was k - killed. As – as he was."

"Very dramatic," he said quietly. "You seem to be quite an accomplished accommodator of the truth, Dona Antonia."

Her chin came up. "Believe me," she retorted, "if you had had to live as I have these last years . . ." She broke off, turning her head. "Will you not do as I ask, Captain?"

"There is so much more I need to know." As he spoke, there was a knock on the door, the door handle turned against the lock, and William heard the voice of his valet.

"Excuse me, Sir, you really should be . . . "

"Damnation! Yes, yes, I'm coming," he promised. He turned back to Antonia, the key in his hand.

"I am going," she told him. "I realise there's no time now. I'll try to explain everything later but please, for now . . ."

"I make no promises. I will try to take my lead from you, but if it becomes impossible, well, on your own head be it." Under the cloak her shoulders slumped as if in relief, and William realised then what a burden of anxiety must have been pressing on her since she had realised they would meet again. Yet there were still all sorts of unanswered questions to be dealt with, if he could do it, as any gentleman would, without causing her any more awkwardness.

"Thank you," she murmured. "I will tell Lady Molly everything as soon as I can. I do not want to spoil this evening for her . . . "

"You don't mind spoiling it for me?" William raised an eyebrow, then relented. "For the two of us, I suppose. Spoiling it for you *and* me. You must have had a wretched time lately."

She glanced at him, but did not answer, and drawing the cloak about her, she went to the door. "Is there another way out?"

William indicated the French windows and the terrace outside. "But where have you left the carriage?" Again there was no reply, and as she slipped away William was aware of one last glance of reproach and entreaty directed at him over her shoulder.

CHAPTER THIRTY ONE

Breathless from hurrying across the park, Antonia regained the Dower House. In the gathering twilight the smooth lawns proved not quite even; she had stumbled more than once, and the hem of her gown was dew-soaked but she hardly regarded these mishaps. Such bother she could have saved herself, she told herself, if she had only told Molly everything from the start. Now she felt quite light-headed with relief, for despite the Captain's indeterminate response to her helter-skelter pleas she felt he did understand and might help if he could. She might have realized that earlier, but the expressions that had chased each other over his face had shaken her confidence; he had not even recognized her at first.

She would have known him anywhere though, she thought. He had always held himself well, but his shoulders seemed broader now, and his hair had bleached in the Spanish sun, so that the blue eyes seemed more vivid against the sunburned skin, even by candlelight. He was good to look at . . .

There was a great weariness though about him, the lines round his mouth were deeper. He looked older, but it was, after all, five years since she had last seen William Hurst, and he had endured much since then. As had all the army in Spain.

Had she altered so much that she was unrecognizable? Antonia studied herself in the clouded pier glass and shook her head. She *was* a different person. Her experiences had altered her as much as William Hurst's had altered him. She smoothed her hair - which had grown somewhat, she thought inconsequentially, since their last meeting – and fragments of the past flashed before her: the captain at her carriage window at their first meeting; the morning he had come hammering on her door, furious at her speaking to Pereira; the look on his face as he had fired at Duarte; his careful explanation that he was leaving to fetch help; his expression as he draped her shawl about her in the convent room and told her he was sorry. And now tonight . . .

"My dear girl, where have you been?" With Samson at her heels Molly Spenlow hurried into the drawing room, and Antonia's reflections fractured and went flying. "I thought you would be ready by now – Oh, you are ready. You even have your cloak on. You look a little flushed, dear. The excitement. I hope you did not eat too much bread and butter at tea. Oh, hark at my running on. I am in just as great a ferment! I hear William is only just returned himself. How I long to see him. I wonder if he will have changed."

"Older and rather browner, ma'am," Antonia replied without thinking, and added hastily, "So one might imagine."

Molly Spenlow laughed. "And more handsome than ever, no doubt. I can hardly wait for you to meet him again, my love."

And Antonia found she had to agree.

The carriage was prompt, for Molly was to stand beside her brother and nephew to welcome the guests, and the short ride to the Manor was accomplished in no time. They were greeted at the door by maids who relieved them of their cloaks and ushered them up the curving stone stairs to the long Gallery, which was prepared for dancing. At the top of the stairs they were met by Sir John, who kissed his sister, and shook Antonia's hand with great warmth.

"Our neighbourhood misses will be put out to find such beauty already arrived before them, I think, Mrs Davenport. Do you not think so, Molly?"

"She is not only a beauty, John, but the best of creatures," Molly smiled. "And I am daily thankful of our meeting as we did."

"You are too kind," Antonia murmured, lowering her gaze after finding that the son of the house had not yet made his appearance. Sir John beckoned a servant who approached bearing refreshment, and she and Molly each took a glass, and moved further along the Gallery, where Sir John pointed out various alterations and decorations. For an ancient chamber it looked wonderfully festive, and the musicians at the top of the room had just begun to tune their instruments.

"Oh, we shall have dancing tonight!" Sir John said, in a wry tone. "Those young men of William's are in high spirits. I only hope they remember their manners."

"You forget what experiences lie behind them, brother," Molly observed, and he nodded without much enthusiasm.

"I suppose you are right, Moll. Well, mind your feet, Mrs. Davenport, when the gentlemen take *you* up to the dance. Ah, here he is, at long last. William, you are late, sir. Though I am very glad to see you. Well, Molly, how do you find him?"

Molly choked, her intention not to weep apparently gone out of the window. "William! My dear, dear boy." Clasping his hands, she kissed him effusively, and Antonia, watching and tense, was touched to see the nephew return his aunt's greeting with equal affection. "So you are home at last. We have missed you so very much." For a few minutes the two of them murmured together, and it was clear there was a mutual fondness. Sir John seemed content to look on proudly, but at last he remembered Antonia and touched his son's sleeve. This was the moment Antonia had dreaded, and she hardly dared raise her eyes to the figure above her.

"Mrs. Davenport, may I introduce to you my dear, my only, son, newly home from the war, and promoted to Colonel. William, this is Mrs. Davenport, your Aunt's friend and companion."

"Why, Mrs. Davenport and I have already met, father."

Antonia swallowed, and the hand that she had extended to William Hurst tightened under his warm, strong grip. It had not been such a very great deal she had asked of him, she thought. Did he mislike her so much that he must embarrass her in front of Molly and the other guests? Her eyes flew to his face and, in his grave smile, saw just a suspicion of mischief.

"How do you do, ma'am. I am very glad to see you, in vastly better health than before. What a pleasure to find you here tonight."

"Captain Hurst," Antonia managed to say, breathlessly extricating her fingers. "It seems no time at all since we last encountered each other. I am - also very glad to see *you* again." She turned to her host. "We met many years ago in Portugal, Sir John, where I have to tell you your son was of the greatest service."

"Only think, brother," Molly intervened, bursting with pride and apparently quite missing the look of dismay that crossed her nephew's face, "William was the means of preserving this lady's life! Can you imagine? And is it not the greatest coincidence that they should meet again here tonight?"

"Extraordinary!" William's murmur was not lost on Antonia but before she could respond, the first guests were heard climbing the great stone stairs, and Sir John quickly excused himself to her, and took Molly away, calling for his son to accompany them.

"I look forward," William said, with a meaningful look, "to a longer conversation with you later, Mrs Davenport." He bowed again before joining his family at the top of the stairs.

Antonia's heart continued to thud as he walked away. She supposed it was anxiety. Her breath seemed to have just jolted to a stop the moment she placed her hand in his. For an instant she had been afraid that he would say something she would regret. How dare he give her cause for such alarm! She looked across the gallery. The Hursts appeared relaxed and happy as they greeted their guests, and she wondered what had happened to the Captain's ill humour. But then he had not always proved curt, nor short-tempered - and his father and aunt were so pleased to have him home. Her gaze went again to the group at the top of the stairs — and found the guest of honour's glance upon her. Shaken by a feeling she did not recognise, Antonia turned and walked away.

William's eyes followed her. Apart from the robe she had worn at the convent all those years before, he had never seen Dona Cabral other than in mourning, but she was clad now in a gown of oyster satin, a slim column of elegance that fell without frills or flounces to the ground. Around her slim neck was clasped a stranded pearl choker set off by a central cluster of diamonds, a matching bracelet circled the wrist of one of her long white gloves, and there were diamond drops twinkling at her ears. Her hair had been the only thing he'd been aware of in the library. Until now he had not remembered her elegance. Others had noticed it however. She was very shortly surrounded by his friends.

Soon all their guests had arrived. Sir John and Lady Margaret circulated to talk to their neighbours, with Sir John, before he left, giving his son a little push towards the nearest group of young ladies. William chatted awkwardly for a while before making his excuses. He had little small talk and was always more comfortable in masculine company, but he was now in no great hurry to spend the evening with his comrades either. There was a tension in him that he did not recognise. It was not unpleasant but not entirely comfortable either, and probably because he'd been made the centre of attention these last few days. He wondered what Antonia Cabral made of his family. How long had she been with Molly, he wondered. There was much he needed to have her make clear, and their earlier conversation had been necessarily rushed and confused.

Limping slightly, he wandered through the rooms, receiving compliments and congratulations with a pleasantly bemused air and mixing with the various groups as a good host should, to find her at last, in conversation with a group of seven or eight young men, his friends amongst them. He circled the group, not sure whether to intrude, but then she caught sight of him. Her flow of talk faltered, and in mid-sentence she excused herself to the company and came forward to meet him.

"Captain Hurst." Hesitantly she gave him her hand, and when she raised her eyes to his, he was reassured to find now in their depths the very faintest signs of pleasure as well as of apprehension.

"*Colonel* Hurst, ma'am." His lips twitched in the smallest of satisfied smiles at the correction.

"Colonel, of course. I have not yet offered my congratulations. I was – I was very pleased to hear of your promotion." Her voice dropped. "I am very glad to have this opportunity to speak with you again."

"And I you, ma'am." He took her by the arm, and moved her away, saying quietly, "I confess I should have been less surprised to have encountered you again in Lisbon than to find you here." He eyed her. "I trust you are quite well now?" She nodded. "I am relieved to hear it. Having said that however I don't doubt we shall now find ourselves in all sorts of difficulties. Are you surprised? You must see it was somewhat foolish to have made such a point of my part in your rescue. Had you not done so, we might have claimed a more casual acquaintance, but – Well, you cannot imagine we have heard the last of that episode? Between my aunt and my father, who will be told all, we shall have a hundred awkward questions to answer, such as 'why you were in the mountains? How did we meet? How exactly was I of assistance?' Even though all this was years ago." She bit her lip and said nothing. William looked about him at the throng, and went on: "We cannot talk here. Perhaps the library? I need to know what you plan to disclose."

"I hope to say the least possible that is commensurate with the truth," she said. "I have told your aunt only that when my husband was killed your intervention saved my life. But I will - admit if I must, that my husband shamed the name of Cabral in betraying his country."

"Is that why you call yourself Davenport?"

"Davenport is my father's name."

"I remembered that. What does your father think of this deception?"

"Like everyone else," she said, "he knows only that my husband was killed fighting in Portugal."

William halted. "So who exactly is it that you are trying to protect, Senhora?"

"I don't know," she sighed. "My family, myself, the Cabrals - "

"They are still ignorant? After all this time? Senhor Tavares doesn't know either?"

She glanced at him. "I'm glad to say Sergio never found out." Her voice wavered. "His chest was always weak, you may remember. He died a year ago."

"I am sorry to hear that." William was conscious of a sincere regret. "He was a splendid old gentleman. I liked him very much – "

"He had an equal regard for you, Captain."

He gave her a look, but said only: "Does no one know then?"

"Pedro knows the large part, of course – but he left." She paused. "Baltasar is the only one who knows everything."

"Baltasar?"

"My brother-in-law, sir. He married my husband's sister, Beatriz."

"And who is he that he should know what no one else does?" He did not mean to make the question sharp.

"We found some documents – " she faltered, and then "It doesn't signify, Captain. He will say nothing. He and Pedro, and Colonel Ashe, are the only ones who know the truth."

"Apart from you and I, Mrs Davenport."

"Apart from you and I, sir."

"Then I wonder if anything need to be said at all, ma'am…"

"You told me you loved to dance, Antonia!" Molly Spenlow appeared before them, beaming and breathless. "I'm sure my nephew would be delighted to partner you. Have you not asked her, William?"

He nodded rather stiffly. "Of course, aunt, if Mrs Davenport wishes." He never danced, had not danced for years, not since Roliça, and he did not feel like dancing now.

"Thank you, Captain, but I am not dancing, Lady Molly."

"Why ever not, my dear? The musicians excel, there is a wonderful card of dances, and your father is not here to chase you."

Antonia stammered: "I find it – awkward now, ma'am."

Molly was contrite. "Oh, my dear, I should have remembered – "

"Mrs Davenport was telling me," William intervened, "that she finds walking beneficial. We are just taking some exercise now, Aunt."

"Then I shan't detain you," his aunt said, looking delighted. "Walk! By all means, walk. But take his arm, Antonia."

He offered it at once, and his aunt beamed as she moved away.

"How long," he asked mildly, "do you suppose it will take you to remember I am promoted, Mrs Davenport?"

"It may be some time." She coloured. "I have thought of you so long as Captain Hurst."

She thought of him then? William sighed. "I still think of you as Dona Antonia. When did you arrive in England?"

"A year ago." They had reached the bottom of the staircase by this time. "How quickly the time has gone."

"Were you in danger in Lisbon? Has your husband's family joined you here?"

"They remain in Lisbon. I could not - I felt I could not stay after – after all that has happened."

William glanced at her averted face. "I had not intended to rake over unhappy memories." But she turned back to him, her fingers tight on his sleeve.

"Please let there be no awkwardness. Frankly I should be glad to speak of the past to someone who knows the truth. There has been no one who knew me in those days. I think I might welcome the chance to make some sense of what happened. I feel I have no - no need to pretend with you, for strange as it seems, it is almost as if we only parted a week ago. But then, Colonel," she forced a smile, "*you* may have no desire to relive the past. You have had a desperate few years. It is good to see you so successful and safe again in England."

"Madam," William interrupted, more gently now. "Believe me, I am more than willing to listen, if you feel you can speak of what has happened since we last met. Shall we walk on the terrace? My comrades are dear to my heart, but they are also very noisy, and rather merry."

"Thank you," she whispered. "I should be glad to do so."

He led her out of the hall, and across the orangery to the doors leading to the terrace. Light spilled out from the huge upstairs windows on to the smooth flagstones so that there was no danger now of an unwary step, but William was very conscious that she leaned very slightly on him, and that her perfume wafted towards him in the slight movement of air. Music from the dancing followed them out, but there was no other company on the terrace, and there they walked to and fro.

"Did you say Pedro had left your service?"

"In a manner of speaking. He was always Sergio's man, of course, and he married, a dear girl. They have two children -"

"Pedro a father?" William grimaced. "That is hard to imagine. I take it Maria Josefina is the lucky woman?"

"Oh no. They were never suited. She would not leave Guarda in the end and married an ostler at the inn. No, Pedro's wife is the maid I had from the convent in Josefina's place. Sergio insisted we engage someone, and her mother was known to Sister Jerome, so -"

"Ah, Sister Jerome." His mouth twisted. "There was a woman to put the fear of God into a man."

"You do her an injustice, Captain – Colonel."

He acknowledged the hasty correction with a nod. "You hear from them? Sister Jerome? Pedro?"

"From the convent nothing. Pedro rarely. When Sergio died, he went to his wife's family on the coast."

"He was a loyal servant, and I owe him much. He was devoted to you, I think."

"Dear Pedro. How could I have managed without him?" She looked away into the darkness beyond the lawns. "I miss him. And I miss Sergio."

"I am sure you must do so," William agreed quietly, and his eyes rested on her drawn face. Eventually he said: "Tell me about Pedro's wife? Is she pretty?"

She smiled then. "A sweet face, and a sweeter nature. I think it was love at first sight. For them both."

"Is there really such a thing then?" William wondered almost to himself, and added hurriedly, "So my old friend Pedro is a father now?"

She seemed not to have noticed his first remark. "Two little boys, the image of their father."

"Short, dark, and round?"

"Exactly so!"

"It is good to see you laugh. Was your recovery prolonged? Were you obliged to stay some time at the convent?"

"We left for Lisbon in the middle of March."

"So long? You must have been anxious to be away. With the French advancing?"

"Sergio was – though he tried not to show it. We heard the news of your army's progress, and of course there were frequent alarms. Sergio was very relieved when the sisters declared I might travel without ill consequence. He had the carriage at the door the day after."

"You were not the least bit worried yourself?"

She responded to his subdued grin. "I hated my inability to travel when he was so anxious about us, but with that contraption on my foot - " William could not help wincing at the memory of her damaged foot. - "There is no need for concern, Captain. I am completely recovered, apart from this slight limp." There was silence for a moment before she said: "But you have suffered far worse and far longer than I, and more recently too. There will be many experiences that you would rather forget."

He drew a deep breath and smiled. "It's nothing. Tell me how you came to know my aunt."

*

In the early hours, as he pulled his shirt over his head, and kicked off his shoes in preparation for bed, William realized he had spent much of the evening in the company of a woman and had hardly thought of her other than as some long lost acquaintance that he'd been happy to encounter once again. He supposed he might see Antonia Davenport at dinner that next day, and was surprised to find he hoped he would.

He wondered too if she would remember that he was no longer a lowly captain, but Lieutenant-Colonel Hurst.

CHAPTER THIRTY TWO

William slept well and woke just before noon to another warm day. His friends, already lunching, greeted him enthusiastically. Since Sir John had eaten earlier, there was no one to disturb them, so the previous evening was discussed with some delight and not a little ribaldry, though William felt he was standing outside the conversation somehow, in spite of the fact that he figured in most of it.

It was too late in the year for hunting and too early for shooting, but after a visit to the kennels his guests eagerly agreed to an afternoon's fishing and before William knew it the day had gone. He found, upon his return to the house, a message from his aunt begging the favour of some conversation. Much as he loved his aunt, and much as he enjoyed her conversation, he was somewhat disappointed, having walked down to the Dower House, to find no-one keeping her company except for a small dog but, since conversation was in the main about his finances, he soon persuaded himself that it was just as well. He was gratified to find himself richer by two hundred pounds, and after taking a dish of tea William kissed his aunt, patted Samson, and returned home, wondering if the guests at dinner might not now include his aunt's companion.

Dinner was not a large affair; there were his five fellow officers, four of whom were departing the next day, the Thorpes - neighbours and old friends with their two unmarried daughters - Sir John as host, William himself and his aunt, and, he was pleased to see, Antonia Davenport. They were granted however only the briefest speech together before dinner, and he was obliged to take in the eldest Miss Thorpe. He was seated not quite opposite Antonia at table, and conversation was not easy, but when the gentlemen joined the ladies for coffee, he took his cup over to her.

"Mrs Davenport. I began to wonder if we should ever have any conversation again."

"You've had a busy day, sir," Antonia replied, putting down her cup. She had been seated next to one of the young officers and had obviously heard about their activities. "I gather tonight's supper was in part due to today's sport – and also that your pack of hounds is to be augmented by several pups any day now."

"Indeed. Maria Thorpe has just made me promise to keep her one. Against my better judgment I shall do so, though I have to say that, unlike spaniels, they are not a woman's pet. They're pretty enough creatures to begin with, but they have some odd habits and their heads sometimes seem remarkably empty of any common sense."

"Is that dogs? Or women?"

He gave her a challenging look. "I meant the hounds, of course."

She smiled. "I'm glad to hear you say so. For myself, though I am truly fond of Samson, who is a dear little fellow and beautifully behaved, I have always preferred cats."

"You'll have seen the kittens then? In the stables? Four or five weeks old now, I think. They were born just before I returned home."

"I've not seen them. They will be adorable just now."

"Would you care -? May I show them to you, tomorrow, perhaps?"

"I should like that, thank you."

"You sound surprised, ma'am."

"I imagined you would have more important things to do, Captain."

William gave her a crooked smile. "Colonel, ma'am."

She flushed. "Colonel, of course, excuse me. I should find it easy to remember the altered rank when you – you seem quite different here."

"What do you mean by that?" But before she could answer Sir John interrupted.

"Mrs Davenport, my sister tells me you have a beautiful voice. Will you indulge us? I can vouch for the pianoforte. Had it tuned only recently."

"Oh!" And William caught the reproachful look directed at Molly. "This is a larger company than most. I quail at those who are not indulgent friends."

"You will not tell me you are nervous, Mrs Davenport," William said, taking her hand. "I cannot believe that you are ever nervous. Come." He led her towards the piano.

"Hardly ever, Captain – Colonel, but at this particular moment, I am."

"Shall I accompany you?"

"I think not. You must be sadly out of practice."

He grinned. "I'm afraid you are right. I was a fool to offer."

Her expression softened. "Not at all. It was kind of you to do so. But - perhaps you will be able to practice?"

"Is that a promise, Mrs Davenport?"

"You have not yet heard me sing," she returned, awkwardly.

She riffled through the sheets of music, found something to please her and played a little country air without words. She looked doubtfully at the rest of the music before laying it aside. As the company fell silent, she began quietly on 'Dido's Lament', and by the time she reached the line 'Remember me' there were more than a few moist eyes, and Molly was dabbing her face. When the music finally died, the silence grew briefly until there was an eruption of applause. This evidently startled the singer, and William saw there were tears in her eyes too. She bowed her head and made to rise, only to be immediately surrounded by her enthused audience. Pushed further away than he would have liked, William heard his Adjutant complimenting her choice of music.

"A glorious voice, ma'am, and somehow the song felt to me in the nature of a memorial," Yelland confided. "To fallen comrades, you know."

William heard her intake of breath and stepped closer. "Mrs Davenport. Allow me to rescue you from your admirers," he said in a tone that brooked no contradiction, and with a look of gratitude she gave him her hand. The crowd around her fell away to return to their seats, and he led her back to her place, talking gently all the while.

Across the room, his father and his aunt looked on.

"What do you make of this, Moll? I've never seen the boy so sure of himself around a woman. He seems very taken with your Mrs Davenport. What do you know of her?"

"Why should he not be sure of himself, brother? He is thirty-one and no longer the shy lad who went off all those years ago. He has lived in the world some good while now. As for Antonia Davenport, she is a sweet girl, John, and I cannot fault her, but I presume you mean 'what do I know of her family?' Well, her father is some kind of diplomat, though how he came to be so is a complete mystery, for he is a thorough boor and has no tact at all . . . Her mother I knew years ago. Oh, and she is god-daughter, one of many of course, to Lord Castlereagh. Antonia's sister is wife to Lord Hetherington, and her brother Charles - "

"Oh, Charles Davenport I believe I know. Don't like, but I know. Supercilious fellow. But I don't only mean her family. The girl's been married. It cannot be a good idea for William to involve himself with a married woman, widow or not. And she is no longer a maid just out of the schoolroom. Why cannot he find a nice wife from amongst our neighbours, one of the young girls he grew up with? The feller was a foreigner, you say? There were no children of the previous marriage, I take it? Fortunate in some respects, but it does not bode well for grandsons."

"He is not involving himself, brother. They are old acquaintances. Naturally they will be familiar with each other. Even William must find that after all this time he knows no one intimately among your neighbours. As for children, well, Antonia is still a relatively young woman. I think you are a little ahead of yourself, John."

"But look at him. He seems to have a care for no one else in the room just now, and I was hoping he might take a fancy for little Maria Thorpe. I want him to settle down, sister. Get married, have children. Before I'm gone."

"Before you're gone? You have a good many years before you yet I hope! But you had better not let William hear you say you want him to settle down. You remember how stubborn he can be. Remember when you told him you wanted him to learn how to manage the estate - "

"But he will not remain with his Regiment now that peace is here?"

"He has not said what he intends, not to me at any rate, and I was with him some couple of hours this afternoon."

"Did you ask him?"

"No, I did not, and I advise you not to do so yet awhile either. Let the lad find his feet back at home. Everything will seem very strange for some time, and he needs to get used to the idea of a life at peace, though it may be, of course, that he will be sent to Ireland or to America if his regiment is not to be disbanded."

Sir John groaned. "No, Moll, I cannot lose him again."

"I do not believe I have heard a performance bettered, ma'am. As well, I think, that I was *not* your accompanist?" As William had intended, Antonia Cabral smiled at that, and he could relax. "How did you enjoy the company of young Roley Cunningham at dinner?"

"Captain Cunningham? He - he was very diverting. He told me his brother had just got married in London, and that you and he had been at the wedding. Is that why you were late arriving home?"

"My good friend John Cunningham, yes. I made a promise long ago to stand as best man when he wed Fanny, if we were spared - but I did not imagine it would be quite so soon after our return. Husband and wife were to have left upon their honeymoon by now. I wish them joy of Europe."

"Do they venture there already? It is a charnel house!" She shuddered.

"Italy only for now, France later, perhaps. John will have seen for himself the conditions there."

They fell silent.

"My aunt tells me you take a charitable interest in those unfortunate fellows who find themselves casualties of war."

"It is nothing," Antonia replied, looking away. "Your aunt is good enough to agree that something must be done to alleviate the problems those poor fellows face. But there are so many, and we can only do so much. We try to raise funds for their relief and hope meanwhile to persuade the powers that be of the necessity to consider their plight."

"An admirable cause, nonetheless." There was another silence. "Will you ever go back to Portugal?"

"I think not," she replied. "Will you remain in England?"

"I do not know, frankly. There may be a posting overseas . . . " His voice trailed away as he remembered one blood-splattered foreign battlefield after another. "I shall be glad to spend some time at home. I had not realized till now how much I missed the green after all the brown and grey landscapes of the last few years - Perhaps you feel the same. But whether I can settle to the kind of life my father enjoys remains to be seen. Here comes my father now, by the way. Probably to drag me off to play whist with the Thorpes."

Antonia regarded his retreating figure with a curious sense of loss but was not left alone long enough to regret it. She was persuaded eventually to join the young officers in a card game of their own, and the laughter that rose from that part of the room soon reassured both Molly Spenlow and her nephew - though the latter, casting supervisory glances in that direction, felt he would have preferred to be at that table himself.

CHAPTER THIRTY THREE

The four officers who were leaving departed for London on the morning coach leaving only Captain Yelland behind. Military habits meant none of the gentlemen were late risers, but the adjutant had regimental affairs to see to, and if the Colonel would excuse him, he said, he would see him at luncheon.

Sir John was already busy with his agent and William, still restless after his customary gallop up on the nearby ridge, was at a loose end. He remembered as he re-entered the stables that he had offered to show Antonia Cabral the new kittens and went to inspect them as they tumbled about in the straw in one of the stalls: four small bundles of fur – three ginger, one grey. He was certain the Senhora would find them appealing and gave himself a lecture on the need to remember she was Mrs Davenport now. However, if she could not remember that he was now Colonel Hurst, it was perhaps not surprising that he still thought of her as Dona Antonia. He found himself wondering what she had meant by him seeming rather different since his return to England?

He walked across the lawns to the Dower House to ask if either his aunt or Mrs Davenport were yet down. Rather as he expected, his aunt was still abed. Mrs Davenport however had breakfasted and was in the morning room. She looked up when he was shown in, and William was pleased to see more pleasure than anxiety now in her expression.

"Good morning, ma'am, I hope you slept well after last evening's excitement? You won a guinea, I hear?"

"Have you spies everywhere, Captain?"

"Only those who tell me you are incapable of recalling my promotion," he grinned. "Dona Antonia."

She winced. "Forgive me, I *will* recall it shortly, I assure you."

"Meantime, I am come from the stables. Would you still care to see – ?"

"Oh, the kittens! Yes, indeed."

"Only if it is convenient."

"I am merely engaged with a letter to my sister in Yorkshire. I have only to fetch a shawl."

"It is warm and fine, but you should perhaps have a shawl. I have sent for the dog-cart for you, and I shall walk beside, if I may."

"Is it so very far then. Shall I not walk? I am quite capable of doing so."

"I suppose you must be, since I gather you made the journey on foot the other evening."

"The other evening." She flushed. "I wonder what you must have thought?"

William tried to recall that odd sensation of shock, pleasure, apprehension, disbelief, and guilt all in the span of a moment. "My thoughts were indescribable," he said, and smiled awkwardly. "Shall you send for your shawl?"

"I shall run up for it at once, Captain – Colonel! Excuse me."

Instead of taking the path, they walked across the park in the morning sunshine, William pointing out various landmarks: the tree he had planted when he was ten years old, the burial site of his old dogs, the fine view that could be had from that slope, the church where he had taken his first communion, and the ridge where he had ridden that morning."

"You must have missed this when you were away."

"Not at first," William admitted. "I did not know any better and was quite overjoyed to finally follow my dream. Home was the last thing on my mind, I'm afraid. But now . . . " He gazed out over the pleasant prospect of meadows, lawns and trees.

"Shall you be sorry to give up that dream if Peace means disbandment, and an end of your regimental duties?"

"I don't know." He stopped in the shade of a broad elm to consider the question, one that he had asked himself many times in the recent past. "I heard someone say once that fighting is one eighth furious bloody action and seven-eighths boredom. I don't know. It meant everything to me. I should miss the comradeship, that sense of worth, of belonging." He shrugged. "But - I don't know . . . "

"Your father is so glad to have you home," she murmured, as they moved on. "He is evidently immensely proud of you. As is your aunt."

"My dear aunt. To whom, of course, I owe my career. It was she, you know, who stood up for me when my father was set against it, and it was she who gave me the price of my first commission. Against my father's wishes, of course. But then, I might add, she could not resist telling him so, in spite of our agreement that she would not do so."

"She is very direct," Antonia said solemnly.

Equally solemnly, he agreed - before breaking into a slow grin.

"But you perhaps understand now your father's reluctance to have you 'go for a soldier'?"

"Now I can, believe me, now I can. But what did I know at seventeen?" He was silent for a moment, then smiled. "Had you been a man, Mrs Davenport, what career would you have chosen for yourself at seventeen?"

"Ten years ago?" She sighed. "Like you, what did I know at that age? But now I imagine I should be quite the expert at managing a farm or a vineyard, thanks to my Portuguese sister-in-law and her husband! You cannot imagine how much I had to learn about the estate eventually." She sighed again, and it did not seem a happy sound.

"What happened," William asked, "when you eventually returned to Lisbon? I should like to know - If you feel you can speak of it?"

She halted. "I sometimes think it would be the greatest relief in the world to tell all. And then I remember the pain, and the anger, and the lies." Her voice had grown harsher with each word.

"I beg your pardon, Dona Antonia. It is none of my business."

"Don't apologise." She shook her head. "It is all still so fresh - Sometimes I cannot help but feel - You know nothing of the letters of course."

"Letters?"

"The letters we found, Baltasar and I – a year ago." She stopped there, distracted. There was a fallen trunk, a great chestnut lying in the shaded grass nearby, and she walked towards it, head down. William saw her seated, and sat down himself, wondering what she might say.

After a long silence, Antonia said: "We left the convent in mid-March that year nine. Your troops had been taken back to England after Corunna, and there was only a small force left in Lisbon."

"I was with them," William murmured.

"Were you? Ah, I did not know." There was another silence, a moment as she wondered how best to continue, before Antonia related the tale of the return to Casa Cabral, her reception, her gratitude to the young couple who had made life bearable for her. "Of course I could not tell anyone the truth. It was impossible. The parents were already crazed with grief, and I could not add the burden of secrecy to either Beatriz or Baltasar." She had explained her brother-in-law's disability, and the situation in which they all found themselves. "The worst part was trying to keep the truth from Dona Isabel. She constantly pressed me for details and scolded me when I could not give them. How could I explain I was to blame for the death of her son?"

"You knew then?" He was staring at her. "All this time I have been thinking that you must blame me for his death, for firing that shot at him in the monastery . . . But – then when did you realise it was your shot that finished him?"

Antonia dropped her hands, and looked at him in horror. "My shot? What do you mean? *You* shot him at the monastery, and we escaped. He fell, beside the bed. I shot Silva – while you had gone for help!"

"No." William bit his lip. "I thought you meant . . . " He cursed, and put his head in his hands, and Antonia felt understanding dawn.

"I had only meant I felt *responsible* for his death," she gasped. "So then - Duarte was only wounded when we left the monastery? *He* came after us? It was *Duarte* who fired at me, Duarte I shot at - " She was aware that William was now crouched beside her. "Then – then I did kill him - But you let me believe that *you* had done so? You *knew* it was not Silva I had shot." Perhaps he had never intended her to learn the truth.

He took her hands in his. "I cannot tell you how much I regret that you should learn this now, like this. I never meant to mislead you - but how could I add to your grief? I thought it better you should blame me. I meant to kill him, Dona Antonia. God forgive me, I meant to, and I wish to God I had done so."

There was sorrow, and anger, in his eyes, and Antonia realised with a pang that all this time William Hurst had been protecting her from the knowledge of what she had done.

"How can I blame you for that?" she whispered. "He tried to kill us. He tried to kill me. But I did not know it was him that night. He just - loomed out of the dark into the firelight, I heard him coming, grunting like a wild thing. It was like some nightmare. I had the pistol ready. He fired, and so did I!"

"And you were the better shot, thank God." He tightened his grip on her hands. "Well, the nightmare is over, Dona Antonia. Over."

"Yes," she said, at last. "I begin to think it may be. I am glad I did not know before. Thank you for sparing me that. I might never have been able to face Dona Isabel, had I known."

They were both silent for some long moments. Antonia took another breath and tried to smile. She had still not told William Hurst of the letters. It might be easier now.

"And so afterward?" he prompted gently, and she gave a tired shrug. Now she could tell him.

"This state of affairs went on for two years or more. The French had been unable to break through the Lines to Lisbon but their retreat was even worse. You were there, of course, weren't you? That's when I learnt a great deal, from the da Fontes. Especially Baltasar."

"He sounds a remarkable gentleman."

"Oh, he is." And Antonia explained how Baltasar had dealt with the workers that hot afternoon.

"You kept your nerve then."

"That's what Baltasar said." She smiled faintly. "He can seem stern, but he was... is, the most amazingly gentle character. And, well, his legs may be useless, but there is no mental weakness in Baltasar. He runs his own estate every bit as capably as Dom Luis once ran his."

William began to feel he might not care for Baltasar da Fonte, but the man had obviously made an impression on Antonia Cabral. Was he the key to her distress? "He impressed you, evidently, but you mentioned letters," he reminded her, with an edge to his voice that she did not notice.

"The letters, yes." She paused. "We found this ancient desk, you see, with a secret compartment and gold hidden away. Almost a fairy tale. And then another just like it − in a study that my- my husband had used - this one stuffed with papers. We - we hoped to find some bills amongst them, but wrapped inside were - were letters − And − Well, it seemed almost every French general had corresponded with him!" She gave an incredulous laugh. "Do you know, after so long living with my mother-in-law's faith in her son's nobility and sacrifice, I had almost begun to wonder if she was not right, and I was wrong. He had *not* been a traitor, there had been some mistake, that I had misunderstood, that *you* had misunderstood somehow. That his death had been unnecessary. And now here in my hands . . . Here was the proof that he had sold himself to the French long ago! And do you know what else I discovered from the letters?" She uttered another bitter laugh. "I found that for some time he had had a mistress! The wife of one of Junot's staff officers, whom he had met in Lisbon only a month after we married. What a fool I was, so easily charmed by his manners and his looks, so easily pushed by my father into marriage. Was my father taken in too, or was he only thinking what a good match it was?"

William found he had taken her hands in his. "Who else knows of this?"

She looked at him then, and shook her head. "No-one. We burned the letters."

"We?"

"Baltasar was with me when we found them."

Baltasar again! William bit his lip. *He seems to have shared a good deal of her life.* He released her hand, wondering what Baltasar's wife had made of the relationship. "What did you do?"

"What could we do? I was only afraid that the next time Dona Isabel praised her sainted son, I would blurt everything out, but with Baltasar's help I managed to hold my tongue for the next half year, and then – then Sergio died, and we were plunged into mourning once again. The Cabrals refused to take Pedro into their employ, and created a scene when he came to Baltasar, at which point Pedro lost his temper and went off to his wife's family. Baltasar was deeply upset. And – then - to my horror – to my amazement - "

In the silence that ensued, William gritted his teeth, anticipating what would follow.

"I truly never intended anything other than friendship," Antonia said. "I loved Beatriz as my own sister and would have done anything for her. It was so stupid of me not to realise what she was feeling when she was always so calm and steady, but she – she imagined that Baltasar and I had - had become lovers."

"Imagined?" William repeated. "You – you were not - then – lovers?"

"No! Never!" Antonia looked at him aghast. "I loved him dearly, but only as a friend, who had been such a prop and a support always." She put her hands to her flaming cheeks. "I decided to leave, and then Beatriz would see she had no need to fear me, but when I said must go, Baltasar declared that if it had not been for me he would have left the Casa Cabral long before, and given it over to ruin. He – he said that much as he loved Beatriz, he cared for me, and that it would be hell if I went. I did not know what to do. I loved them both. I wanted to help, but I could not risk staying. I might have gone to Porto, but by then Sergio was dead and it was too late." She closed her eyes.

She had believed Baltasar when he promised he would remember his duty to Beatriz, that what he felt for Antonia must remain a secret spoken of only in the confessional.

"I decided then I had to return to England. Back to my father. Who did not want to see me either." She shuddered, and, catching her breath on a sob, said angrily, "So here I am. And now you know everything. What part of it do you want me to tell your aunt?"

"Antonia," William murmured.

"No, no," she said, dashing tears away. "I swore I would never weep again, particularly not in front of you, Captain."

"What? Why? Why should you ever promise such a thing?"

She looked at him almost fiercely. "Do you not remember when we fled from the monastery? I swear I could have wept forever then - but you - you are not one, I think, to tolerate tears. And besides you already seemed to hold me in such contempt. I could not bear you to think me as feeble-witted as I felt."

"But I had no idea," he protested.

"You seemed to dislike me so much. That was clear from the start."

William could not answer immediately.

"You are mistaken," he said. "It is true I disliked my duties as escort, but I did not – dislike you when I came to realise at last how much the search meant to you - how fearless you proved - "

"Fearless? You frightened me often enough."

"I did?" He shook his head.. "I never would have guessed. I thought you were frightened of nothing. When I bellowed, it only seemed to bring out the steel in you. That chin of yours would come up, so – like it did just now, and I believed you quite alarmingly fearless." He was relieved to see the faintest of smiles. "And what you have told me, ma'am, I swear will remain between the two of us. I feel - grateful that you have confided in me. I hope you might even feel that a burden is less heavy because it has been shared?"

She studied him, as if doubting his sincerity, and then apparently unable to speak, nodded.

At last he said softly, "You must be exhausted. This has been a morning of tragic memories and revelations. Shall we remain here till you feel quite recovered, and return to the Dower House? Or to the Manor, which is closer, and I will take you back in the trap?"

"I should like to see the kittens, if you please, Captain Hurst."

"Truly?" William was startled at the faint but determined statement, and he managed a grin. "It's Colonel Hurst, ma'am."

She smiled through the tears. "Colonel Hurst."

"Since we seem to have this small difficulty, Mrs Davenport," he said conversationally, "might I suggest, without impropriety, that you call me William? No rank. Easy to remember." His eyes were gentle. "If it is possible, that is, for you to regard me as a friend? It may help you forget those times when you thought of me as someone less than human."

Her lips formed the words. "I - I don't - think I can - "

"What? Regard me as a friend?" he asked gravely, "Or remember that I am human?"

"You make it difficult for me to respond," she replied in a voice that was not quite steady. "But I assure you, Captain – Colonel - "

"William?" he suggested softly.

She lowered her gaze. "William," she conceded finally. "I believe I can remember that."

It was a simple statement. Why did he suddenly feel almost light-headed?

In the stables, Antonia dropped to her knees beside the kittens. She felt almost dizzy with relief and something like gratitude. It was all out in the open at last; perhaps now the past would no longer torment her. "Where is their mother?"

"Catching mice for them to play with, I daresay. Do you like them?" He lifted one and cradled the ball of ginger fur in strong hands.

"They are all quite adorable." Looking up at him, Antonia found William brushing the kitten's silken fur absentmindedly against his face, and for a minute, before he stooped to release the little creature, experienced a flush of unexpected heat rising into her cheeks as she imagined the sensation.

The kitten had sprung at the tassel on William's boots, before tumbling back into the stall where the whole litter scuffled in the straw. He grinned, and scooping them all up, put them into a box.

"Do you suppose," he said, "that little dog of Molly's will eat them if it gets the chance? If you think not, perhaps you might like to take one with you when you return to Hampshire?"

"Oh but they will not be able to leave their mother for a week or two yet," she said slowly, "and we are to leave before then. Your aunt told me last night she has business in town, so I believe we shall go direct to Henrietta Place."

"Oh, I see." He cleared his throat. "I am sorry to hear that. They will be grown before you see them again, I think."

"But at least by then Samson may think twice before adding them to his diet."

*

"Antonia! I thought you would miss lunch!"

"Oh Molly, I'm sorry. I went to see the new kittens. In the stables. Had you wanted me?"

"Not especially. I have not long been downstairs myself, but I did wonder where you were. The servants said you had gone out hours ago. With William?" Molly frowned a little as she spoke and thought of her brother's concerned comments.

"He called for me, yes. We walked across the park. There are four of them, you know. Kittens. Quite adorable."

"Antonia, I do not mean to suggest anything at all by what I am going to say next, but it is perfectly clear that you have charmed my nephew. I don't hold that against you or him. A pretty girl - and you are a very pretty girl as well as being very charming – as I say, a pretty girl must be welcome company for any young officer just returned from the Peninsula, but he does seem to spend an unusual amount of time in your company, and it may occasion talk. Don't look so horrified, dear. I realize you and my nephew are not entire strangers, and you share an experience that draws you to each other, but William does sometimes seem to forget himself, and to treat you over-familiarly."

"Oh, he is not in the least ungentlemanly, Molly. It is true we find it easy to converse, because we have known each other before but . . ."

"But how well did you know each other in Portugal? Did he conduct himself differently there? I realise you must have every reason to be grateful to him - "

"Molly, please, this is not William's fault. If there is any familiarity it must be mine."

"Gracious, Antonia, do you call him William now? Surely not, dear?"

"No, no, I do not – I have not done so, yet, I think."

"And does he always address you as he should?"

"Indeed, I am always Mrs Davenport."

"It still seems strange that you should call yourself so. Doesn't it, Samson?" Molly shook her head, smiling. "Well, my love, I have said what I must. Forgive me. Let us hope Sir John will be satisfied with that."

"Sir John?" Antonia faltered. "Does he feel as you do – that his son and I are over-familiar? Oh, heavens, Molly, I am mortified." She covered her blushing cheeks. "I would not upset him for the world. Lord! How can I face him tonight?"

"Well, he worries, dear. He imagines William must settle down and engage himself to one of his young neighbours, you know. That his son seems to prefer the company of a young widow, a very pretty young widow, well - I suppose he sees you as a possible complication. Don't take it to heart, my love. We are to leave at the end of the week in any case."

"Yes, yes, of course you have business in town."

"Well, that is what I have told John. I do not want him to think I am acting on his needless suspicions. But I do not want him to blame me, or that we should fall out with each other once again."

"No, of course not," Antonia responded. "That would never do."

William dressed for dinner that evening, astonished at himself. He could not believe he had suggested that Antonia Cabral and that Portuguese brother-in-law of hers might be lovers. He had crossed the boundaries of courtesy in far too many ways, and then told her she should call him William . . .

But it did seem to him that he and Antonia Cabral were, had been for some time, more than acquaintances, bound by convention. For heaven's sake, he had nursed her, saved her life…

He studied his reflection in the mirror as he smoothed his hair, realising with an odd start that, since their farewell at the convent all those years before, he had almost regarded their coming together again as inevitable. He wondered what his father or Molly would say if they knew all the history between himself and the lady they knew as Mrs Davenport? Perhaps it was just as well Antonia was leaving at the end of the week. Antonia. He repeated the name, and then horrified at himself, tugged his cravat straight, pushed the mirror away and went down to a family dinner.

The formality between them now was so marked it was almost artificial: William's demeanour occasioned by a sense of shame, and Antonia's by embarrassment. Sir John studied them both, and with his earlier fears allayed, he was soon his charming, scholarly, absent-minded self, and conversation grew less stilted and more animated. He asked Antonia to sing after dinner, and soon, since despite long years of celibacy he was as susceptible as the next man to the charm of a pretty girl, he found his sister's young companion most congenial company, and quite regretted that his sister needed to take her away so soon.

CHAPTER THIRTY FOUR

Molly had not been back in London a fortnight before she had an unlooked-for visitor. It seemed William's regiment was to disband after all; his attendance was required at Horse Guards after which a last celebration with his fellow officers was planned. It was probably the last time he would be wearing his uniform, he said, and he thought his aunt would like to admire it. He had left Sir John well, he reported, confiding that his father seemed to have mellowed in the time he had been away; they had spent a good deal of time in each other's company since his return and he had found the experience more rewarding than he had imagined he might.

Molly was delighted to hear this and overjoyed to see her nephew - even if she suspected she was not the main attraction at Henrietta Place - and the scarlet coat did show off the new insignia to advantage. She admired the epaulettes, which had now added a star to the crown and buglehorn, and exclaimed over the silvery grey fur-trimmed and frogged pelisse slung over his shoulder.

"It has put you to some unnecessary expense, however," she commented dryly. "You will have worn it but three times, I think, since your promotion."

"I am to wear it again tomorrow, when we go to see the Czar and the Grand Duchess at the theatre, after which I shall lay it up in paper to get out on high days and holidays," he joked. "With all the other old soldiers reminiscing about how we trounced Napoleon. Though how long this fancy dress will fit me, I am not sure. My father keeps too good a table."

"Is it really over, William? Is the monster quite safe on his island?"

"Elba seems a deal too close to France, aunt, but he will be well-guarded. Is Mrs Davenport at home?"

"She is not, dear, no." Molly found it hard not to smile at the crestfallen expression. "She has this minute gone out with some books to the circulating library. Do you care to wait, and show yourself off to her?"

"I don't intend to do any such thing," he replied, "but in any case I am obliged to be at the Horse Guards in an hour, so I will not stay. Please give my compliments to Mrs Davenport. I shall hope to see her, see you both, next time I call."

"Which will be when, dear?"

"Later this week, perhaps."

"We shall look forward to it, I'm sure."

He called later in the week to say he was on his way back to Kent the following morning and did they have any messages for Bartonhurst, only to find himself in the middle of one of Molly's 'salons'. Feeling out of place in such an assembly, and unexpectedly irritated to find Antonia Davenport the centre of an animated group that included several noblemen amongst its company, William did not stay long before making his excuses.

He told himself he did not need an excuse to see his aunt and could visit when he pleased and be sure of a welcome, but he was not quite sure enough now to make the journey from Kent and call again. Several weeks slipped effortlessly away by which time Molly and Antonia had removed once more into Hampshire. In one respect Molly was encouraged by his absence and wrote to her brother remarking on it. Under the circumstances, she felt she could now invite William to Bridge House if he cared to come and bring a friend or two. She might organise a ball if there were sufficient girls and young men still in the neighbourhood, and if William were prompt in replying.

She did not hear from him promptly, and this too, she told herself, would reassure Sir John, but at the end of another week she had a note from her nephew, accepting her kind invitation to stay for a fortnight, and to say he would not bring anyone with him, but that three of his friends would come down if there was to be a ball and she needed men. He hoped, he said, that this would not prevent her arranging some kind of function and he looked forward to meeting such young people in her neighbourhood as she thought proper to invite, but to "remember, dear Molly," that he himself did not dance!

Molly however did dance, so arrangements went ahead to hold a supper party for about thirty at which there would be dancing and ices, and possibly fireworks, in belated celebration for the Victory of the spring. William arrived three days into September, and four days before the supper, and was soon bullied into organising the strategic siting of chairs, tables, torchères and the putting up of bunting and swags of ivy along the stairs, landings, porches and doors. The staff working under his direction found their task made lighter by his efforts, and Bridge House was soon ringing with good-humoured laughter as decorations went up and rooms took on a festive air. Even Samson became excited, and tore around with ribbons in his mouth, defying anyone to take them from him. Outside it was raining, but indoors no one except Molly seemed to notice.

William and Antonia had resumed a relationship in the easiest manner possible after the drama of her revelations and now, studying her as she worked on an arrangement of garden flowers for the vestibule, William wondered at the turmoil of emotions she had woken in him, first during those initial weeks following their flight from the monastery, and later upon seeing her again.

He had never before enjoyed a warm relationship with a woman; his mother had seen to that - and his aunt, involved with her own life when he was growing up had been, from force of circumstance, a distant benefactress, only fully appreciated now for herself and, now that he was ending his career, for her help in achieving his success. His several affairs - trivial, ships that passed in the night – had been cast off the minute they threatened his independence. But Antonia Cabral, Davenport - Antonia was not like any previous encounter. He felt relaxed in her company. They had had long conversations in the last few days.

It seemed her family life, like his, had not been a happy example, nor conducive to the desire to immerse oneself in the same situation. She spoke hesitantly of her family: her giddy mother, her older sister who had married well but was rarely able to leave her Yorkshire estates, her brother whom she saw even less often and whom she did not appear to like much, and her father, difficult, autocratic, an opportunist. Finding her a good listener, he felt drawn to relate his own history, his lonely childhood, his interests and his hopes for the future, and the antipathy he often felt for any relationship outside a military world where the life had given him many good friends. Conversation was easy. Antonia had a sense of humour that often accorded with his own, and they seemed to like, and dislike, the same things. Her wish for independence struck an answering chord in him, but he was equally delighted that she would occasionally accept his assistance. He liked to be of assistance, wanted to amuse her. He told himself that if he had had a sister, he would have wished for someone like Antonia and, for the first time in a long while, he was feeling younger rather than older than his thirty odd years. Could that all be accounted for simply by the end to the fighting?

Antonia seemed touched by his attention, but Molly was not sure that she herself wasn't disappointed by the absence of lover-like behaviour in her two favourite young people.

Everything that had to be made ready for the evening party had been made ready, and everything that needed to be done had very nearly been done. The sun finally came out from behind the clouds, and the evening looked as if it would go off splendidly when it was discovered that during the last downpour the old icehouse had finally let water and was awash.

"Disaster!" groaned Molly. "I have promised ices, which will be puddles, and the wine will be warm!"

"Does not your neighbour at Bourne Park have an icehouse?" Antonia suggested. "Mr Everett comes tonight. Perhaps, if he can spare some, he might send some over early, if it is well wrapped in straw and hessian?"

"I will ask him, Aunt, if you wish. Do you want me to take over a note?"

"One of the servants can go, William dear, when they are finished. Oh, but by then it will be much too late."

"I'll go, Aunt. I will charm the ice out of him by stressing the excellence of your iced cream, which might go to waste should he be unwilling. I daresay he does not care much for warm wine on a balmy evening either."

"Well, you are very obliging, and if you will go at once all may yet be saved. Antonia, go with William. You know the way across the park, and you will find the ford quicker than going round by the road."

"Captain – Colonel Hurst must know the way without *my* guidance surely, Molly?" Antonia wondered.

"Well - well, he has not been across the park to the Everett place for years, so with you there can be no mistaking the way. Hurry now! There is no time to lose."

They reached Bourne Park on foot, half wishing they had ridden, for the grass was long and damp, but Mr Everett was at home and very obliging. They should have as much ice as they wished, he said, and he would send it over directly. Did they want to stay and ride home with it on the cart? They looked at each other and declined. They would return the way they had come, wet shoes or no. The sun was shining and it was a lovely day to cross the park.

To their surprise however, a new stream now blocked the route home. It had been no more than a rivulet on their way there, shallow with broad stepping-stones, but now it rushed between its banks, and the stones were several inches below the surface. It was too deep to wade. William might have tried crossing, but Antonia had only kid boots, ankle high.

"The mill must have opened the race to let water through," Antonia said, eyeing the depth. "With all the rain the millpond must have been very full. It will go down shortly, I am sure."

"Meantime we must wait?"

"See those blocks downstream. They were part of this ancient route here," Antonia replied, "Look at them now."

Set in the rushing water several hundred yards away were great moss covered stones, hollowed from centuries of use, weed streaming in the current's flow. William had always taken them for ruins of an older bridge, for they normally stood well clear of the water, but now the water bubbled almost to their tops. The crossing looked wet and rather hazardous. He remembered his mother's reactions to escapades such as this, and sighed. He believed he might manage it without difficulty, but his legs were long and could manage the step from one great stone to the next; Antonia might find the stones slippery. "Let me try first," he suggested. "If it is too difficult, it must be the longer route home for us instead."

Leaving her on the bank he strode across without a problem. The rocks were wet, but only the one nearest the far side was uneven, rather weedier than the others. He could stand on the far bank ready with a helping hand. He crossed back to assure Antonia that it was indeed passable, then stepping ahead, made sure she was secure on each block before he moved to the next, relieved to find Antonia negotiating the jumps very neatly. She began to laugh as she felt the first dampness penetrate the soft boots and the raised hem of her gown grow wet. "I never expected to drown on our way home," she said merrily.

"Ah, you never know what excitement awaits you," William answered with a grin – And then "Have a care!"

On the last block Antonia missed her footing, her boot slid on weed, and with a smothered cry and arms flailing, she lurched towards the fast-flowing stream, only to be snatched to the bank by a strong arm just as Josefina had once been snatched from under a rock fall. Antonia found herself flung up against her rescuer, pressed to what seemed a solid wall of muscle from chest to thigh, gripped firmly in the crook of an elbow around her waist. The impact left her gasping. But instead of relaxing his grip William continued to hold her. For what like seemed eternity they stood locked together by his arm around her waist, their faces inches apart while they swayed from the impact and the uneven ground.

Antonia struggled to get her breath. A warm, familiar fragrance, the masculine smell of leather and tobacco and lemon, filled her nostrils, and in an instant she was back on the mountain, held just so, William's eyes, mouth, lips on a level with her own. Only . . .

William felt her strain away from him, her eyes wide with shock and alarm, and stepping back from the riverbank, he freed her. He could not think why he had not done so at once, and his apology was half-uttered before he realised her expression was more than just reaction to the affront.

"What?"

"Nothing," she gasped. "Only - " His concern seemed to steady her. She took a deep breath. "I was only remembering…"

William knew very well what she remembered; had he not been reminded of the self-same thing? The rocks, her white face, pages torn and fluttering in the breeze and floating into the valley below them, the thud of her heart against his, her breath against his face. Was that why he'd continued to hold her?

"I was unnecessarily harsh," he said, in a low voice. "That night on the mountain when I took that letter from you. I was rough, and I hurt and insulted you. I beg your pardon. I was tired, and not thinking straight, and I imagined you were trying to contact your husband's men." Her expression had barely changed, and he gripped her arms above her elbows, and shook her very gently. "Antonia, I am truly sorry."

She shook her head. "You were exhausted, and wounded, and worried to death for our safety. I was the stupid one, it was a stupid gesture, but I was not myself either. Just now it all came back to me, that insane chase down the mountain, not caring whether I lived or died . . . " She shuddered and closed her eyes.

There was a long anxious pause while he studied her, and then William shook himself back to the present. "Are you all right?" he said. "Did I hurt you when I seized you so fiercely just now?"

She shook her head. "Saved yet again, sir," she said, brushing down her skirts and trying to smile. "I hope it is for some useful purpose. You seem to be making a habit of rescuing me from misadventures of my own making."

"I cannot think of anything, ma'am," he responded gently, "more worthwhile."

CHAPTER THIRTY FIVE

The slow walk home afforded an opportunity to recover and regain a semblance of normality, for neither had appreciated quite how much the episode had affected the other. Antonia was subdued, conscious of breathlessness and a still racing pulse, and puzzled by its failure to steady once the danger was clearly over. She had been rescued once again though, and not made to feel a fool or a liability.

William, trying to appear calmer than he really felt, glanced sideways, and catching Antonia's eye, smiled reassurance.

"Nearly there," he said. "I believe we shall be the first ones to see Bridge House decked in all its finery."

They could not help but be impressed with their handiwork.

"The house looks lovely, Molly!"

"No small thanks to you, William dear. You have worked so hard – you both have, but should you not now be preparing yourselves, ready for tonight? Samson and I intend to take as long a nap as we are permitted, and I advise you to do the same."

Halfway through the evening, William appeared at Antonia's shoulder, murmuring into her ear. "Lay the King."

She laid the cards against her breast. "I will play my own game, thank you, sir."

"Leave them anyway, and meet two particular friends who have only just arrived."

"When this hand is over, I will." But he stayed at her shoulder, joking and generally distracting her until Antonia lost her concentration and subsequently the game. Laughing now, she excused herself, and accompanied William to the other end of the room where two young men in uniform were studying the room through wineglasses.

"Mrs Davenport, may I introduce you to two of my reprobate friends, come hotfoot from Winchester, Major John Cunningham – You met his younger brother at Bartonhurst in the spring? – and Major Edward Fairburn?" he said. "Gentlemen, Mrs Davenport."

Antonia curtseyed to their stiff bows, relieved to see their cheerful smiles did not match their ramrod bearing.

"I remember your brother, Major Cunningham, I hope he is well?" she said, "You will have met your hostess, Lady Spenlow?" They all nodded, grinning. "But have you only just this minute arrived? If you have come direct from Winchester you will be hungry."

"We had a bite to eat on the way, ma'am, thank you - "

" – but our appetites, sharpened as they are on the field of battle, mean we can always manage more, ma'am, if there is anything available."

"You do not mean a recent field, I hope?"

"I am sorry to say I do. Fairburn here has just come from Ireland where they love to fight, and they eat nothing but potatoes, you know."

"Then you had better have some ham and chicken at once. Lady Margaret has some very fine pies made which I am sure will satisfy you." Antonia led them through to the dining room where food was laid out, and William took the younger officer to a table decorated with ivy and pyramids of fruit, where he heaped two plates.

"You were married earlier in the year, I recollect, Major Cunningham." Antonia looked about her. "Is your wife here?"

"She is not, ma'am. Her sister is lying-in, and Fanny insisted on being there, but she did not know we had received an invitation for tonight. I was not to come myself at first, being Duty Officer, but found myself at liberty to do so at almost the last minute. William said to come if I could."

"I'm sure we are very glad to see you, sir. I know that Will – that Colonel Hurst is delighted you've come. There will be dancing very soon, but there are card tables - or conversation - as you wish?"

Edward Fairburn was eyeing a trio of young ladies chattering on the other side of the room and had sighed rather melodramatically.

"Conversation then." Antonia smiled. "I cannot presume to introduce you, but you might feel you can do so, Colonel?"

With a sigh of his own, William took the young Major to the other side of the room, and John Cunningham and Antonia continued her conversation. After a few pleasantries, he asked: "Have you known the Colonel long, ma'am?"

Antonia hesitated. "Some little time, I suppose. I am companion to his aunt, Lady Margaret, you know, and he visits when he can. Have you been friends a long while?"

"Since we were in Spain together, ma'am." He said it proudly.

"Your family must be as relieved and thankful for the safe return of both their sons as William's family is for his homecoming."

"My third brother unfortunately does not return. He was killed at Talavera. Our return must be coloured with sadness at his loss."

"I am so sorry." Antonia laid a hand on the young man's sleeve, and he smiled at her.

"Are you dancing, John?" William had reappeared. "Shall I find you a partner? My aunt has invited every eligible female in the neighbourhood, and I understand from my father I am to marry one of them or else! I daresay I can spare you one. Not too pretty, mind. You have a pretty one of your own at home!"

"You're very obliging, sir, but I believe there is beauty closer to hand. If Mrs Davenport would do me the honour?"

"You are very kind, Major Cunningham. But I – I do not dance."

"Never, ma'am?"

"Not for some time now."

"I am sorry to hear it. The Colonel does not dance either, but he uses his wound as an excuse. The truth is he has forgotten how."

"I believe the same applies to the pianoforte, sir."

"Thank you, Mrs Davenport," William retorted. "And that will be all from you, John. A shameful lack of respect for your superiors! Go and find yourself another partner, sir. My aunt will be glad to have a few more in the set."

The dancing had begun, and with a grin for William and a bow for Antonia, Major Cunningham went to find a partner. William offered Antonia his arm, and they moved from the supper table into the hall, stopping to watch the sets forming and to listen to the musicians. Molly was leading the dance with her friend, Lord Boscawen, and Antonia, foot tapping in time to the music, watched her with a wistful expression. "Your aunt is very light on her feet," she remarked after a while. "Do you suppose she will waltz? It is so new I am surprised that she should agree to its being included, especially in this company. I mean, of course, that we are in the Shires and not in Town."

"I think she will. She loves to dance. You loved to dance too, I think."

"I believe I liked it as well as any girl might. Well, perhaps a little more."

"And do you never dance now? Too painful?"

"Not so much pain as weakness. I had a lesson or two but I am very clumsy."

William wondered if Antonia Cabral could ever be clumsy, but said: "I have the same problem, though you sound as if you have tried to practise at least. As for my cursed leg - My limp cannot make me a figure of elegance on the floor." His expression made Antonia smile.

"What a pair of crocks we are to be sure, Captain - Colonel - "

"William," he finished.

"William," she assented. "But I may not call you that in front of just anyone, you know. Not your aunt, nor your father, nor your friends and acquaintances either. So perhaps I should concentrate on recalling your exalted rank."

The music changed. "They are playing a waltz, Mrs Davenport."

She turned to listen. "And Molly is dancing," she observed.

"It seems a pity you should not be doing so." They looked at each other. "If not in public where we can make ourselves figures of fun, then why not here on the terrace?"

"You do not dance, sir," Antonia reminded him breathlessly.

"We might prop each other up, do you think?" He held out his arms. And after a moment's hesitation, Antonia stepped into them. He held her very lightly but firmly enough to make her feel secure, and they took a few steps together.

"I think we shall do very well, Mrs Davenport," he murmured, essaying a gentle whirl with every appearance of elegance, but Antonia, conscious of the arm encircling her, and the lemon scented and close-shaven jaw on a level with her eyes, could hardly speak. The bliss of moving to the delicious rhythm of the music was intoxicating, and it had been so long since she had been able to dance, or been held just so . . .

"You will not tell me you have not been practising," she stammered.

"Just a little, ma'am," he smiled. "Just as I have been at the piano."

She looked up at him. "Wonders will never cease," she said, and tried to stop the banging of her heart.

CHAPTER THIRTY SIX

In no time the supper party was over, the visit was over, the summer was over, and it was time to return to Henrietta Place and the task of fund raising. William's visits to his aunt now became an almost weekly occurrence, and though she was under no illusions as to the attraction her nephew seemed to find in town, Molly was delighted.

Sir John did not do much travelling. He never had, he said, and he would not start now, so people must come to him at Bartonhurst. Molly made return visits to Kent, and though Antonia did not always accompany her, she was treated when she did very much like family – much to her alarm. She was very conscious now of an attraction to Molly's nephew and found it confusing given the circumstances of their previous relationship. She could hardly believe sometimes that she was that same person. After unburdening herself of the past to him, the ease and freedom of their conversation had become one of her greatest pleasures, and though she would never have described herself as William Hurst's equal she often felt regarded as such. This was something quite new in her experience, neither the sentimental emotion nor the submissive deference of all those years before when she had been persuaded to marry Duarte Cabral. She found her heart jumped whenever the sound of his voice was heard in the hall, and when he did not call, she found she longed for him to come. Sudden glimpses of him made her breath catch in her throat and her heart begin to hammer, and when he sat beside her to talk, she sometimes thought happiness might burst out of her.

She even began to suspect that William felt some reciprocal attraction. There was a thrill of energy that seemed to leap between them when he brushed by her, or took her hand briefly in his, or when his eyes met hers in the candlelight - and this alarmed her even more. She was not a child. And she remembered Baltasar. Antonia knew when a man and a woman were thrown in each other's company a good deal, an attraction might not be wholly unexpected. She was all too aware of Sir John's concern for his son's future, and William's own stated opinions, and as deeply uncertain of her own feelings as she was, she knew she must keep the atmosphere between them on the lightest footing, doubting that there could ever be a satisfactory ending. There must be no more waltzing, no more being held in his arms, no more private conversations to stir past memories and emotions. Remembering how close they had so recently been, she must put a little distance between them.

William was vaguely aware that Antonia had withdrawn slightly from his company, but he did not question it. Her company pleased him, and he sought her out, his manner settled into a delightful and comfortable habit, not over familiar, nor too formal. He was always glad to see her, and missed her when she was not of the company, but he did not care to analyse his feelings too deeply. Nor did he confide in his father, aware that Sir John wanted him to settle down at Bartonhurst, while he himself still hoped vaguely that there were more adventures still to come overseas.

Meanwhile Sir John had begun in despair to introduce him to every single young female of his acquaintance, but it seemed he was wasting his time, and he began to look at Antonia Davenport with fresh eyes.

"If you are not fully engaged over the Festive Season, Moll, will you share our celebrations in Kent? As you know, I ask my neighbours to dine always at the New Year, but we shall be very quiet otherwise, and I fear William will find it rather dull this year. Of course, you will regret giving up your festivities and all your good works in town . . ."

"My dear John! Do you realise how long it is since I was at Bartonhurst for Christmas? Of course I shall come!"

"And bring the pretty widow with you, too, of course."

"I'm very glad to hear you say so. If Antonia does not care to go to her sister in Yorkshire, I would not dream of coming without her."

Antonia who had already considered a further visit to Yorkshire, remembered the long journey, and Richard Hetherington's exacting standards, and did not want to go. In Kent she knew she would not have to listen to raised voices except in music and laughter, and in Kent she would be welcome, and useful. In Kent, she might see William Hurst every day . . .

In the week before Christmas, Sir John, with his son on the steps behind him, welcomed their arrival at the porticoed entrance to Bartonhurst Manor, and bustled them into the warm parlour, where a great log fire was keeping the cold at bay, and the servants were ready with hot punch to revive them after the carriage ride. William saluted his aunt with a kiss, gave Antonia a warm smile and bowed over her hand before returning to the hall to oversee the unloading of parcels and boxes. His father greeted Antonia very affably.

"Delighted to have you here once again, Mrs Davenport. My sister took you away far too soon after your last visit! Well, well, so here you are for our country celebrations. I don't entertain a great deal, except at New Year, but I shall hope to make you known to the nearest of our neighbours. You will remember them, I daresay, from that affair we had to welcome my son home in the spring. I rarely entertain in fact, being fonder of my company than anyone else's, but there, two occasions this year already! I know my duty, you see." He looked in his son's direction, and Antonia was surprised to see a wistful expression fill the old man's face. Her own face must have indicated as much for when her host turned back to her he gave an awkward cough. "It's quiet here. Don't see nearly enough of the boy," he explained gruffly. "And it's time he was settling down and making plans for the estate after I'm gone. He's almost a stranger in his own home. Shan't be surprised if he don't recognise half the folk hereabouts."

Antonia thought of the hours William Hurst had spent at Henrietta Place and the days in Hampshire and felt guilty. "Your son speaks often of Bartonhurst, Sir John, and always in terms of the greatest affection."

"Hmm. Well, that don't signify unless he means to spend more time here," the old man replied, but it was clear he took comfort from Antonia's remark and, with a brisk exclamation, held out his arm for her to take, and they went out into the hall. "I look forward to having some more music from you, Mrs Davenport," he said. "If it don't fatigue you too much. I do like my music, and my own fingers are far too stiff to afford me or an audience any pleasure."

Since Molly had expressed a wish to stay in the Manor rather than the Dower House on this, for her, momentous occasion, there was an opportunity for Antonia to see more of it in all its eccentric glory: the passages that went up and down stairs and ended nowhere particularly, and the little rooms with tiny latticed windows tucked away in corners, as well as the splendid rooms that she had already encountered. It was a warm, friendly house, with a soul. Antonia felt comfortable there.

It was true that, apart from walking or riding, there was not much outdoor activity possible for the two ladies, but during the brief holiday they were dined at neighbouring houses and there were afternoon calls, while indoors there was music, and the library, and good food and interesting and easy conversation. The time passed quickly. Christmas Day was spent quietly. To the peal of bells they walked to the village church for the two services, and from the comfort of the leather lined family pew listened to the rector and parish clerk intoning the liturgy, with Antonia's clear soprano and William's resonant baritone making harmony of the hymns.

After dinner they congregated in the library to exchange gifts. For William, Antonia had parcelled a new riding crop, and had embroidered a tapestry footstool for Sir John. She had got Molly a pretty fan, and received in return a handsome pair of gloves, but William had found new music sheets, copies of her favourite pieces, and tied them up in tissue paper and a ribbon. He insisted on a performance.

Antonia was examining the music in astonishment.

"I have been practising as instructed," he told her. "And am now ready to accompany you, though even the best musician in the world might not do you justice." He looked at her from under dark lashes. "And I am nowhere near the best, Antonia. Dare you trust me with a performance?"

"How – where have you been practising?" demanded his father. "I have never seen you at the piano."

"I had an instrument delivered at the Lodge, father, a small one. Did you never wonder at the length of time I was out of the house?" He sat down at the piano.

"These are wonderful, William!" Antonia held out the sheets. "It was so kind of you to take the trouble. Which pieces do you know?"

"I will not dissemble," he grinned. "I have tried only Mr Mozart's 'Un Moto di Gioja' and Mr Handel's 'Lascia ch'io Pianga', neither of which befits the season, but I hope you will trust me with one of them at least."

"I have trusted you with a great deal more before now," she said with a look of great sincerity, and went to stand beside him at the keyboard.

Sir John flashed a look at his sister. "D'you see, Moll?" he murmured. "They use first names already."

"Antonia is almost family, John. She's like a daughter to me, at least. William hears me call her by her name every day." They both looked at the two at the piano discussing the music, Antonia bending to the music stand, William studying her, two fair heads close together in the light from the candles on the instrument's glossy surface.

"They make a pretty pair," John Hurst said slowly.

"They do," agreed his sister. And they smiled at each other.

The day after Christmas was given over to the servants, assembled after luncheon to receive their Christmas Boxes, the gift from the family to the household for their services during the year. Now more cheerful than ever, the staff were free until evening when they would have a celebration of their own, leaving the family to look after itself and smile at the sounds of music and sense of jollity that reached the library from below stairs.

The weather had been crisp but clear all week and plans for the New Year dinner went ahead. Sir John's neighbours, the Thorpes and the Mountjoys, together with the rector and his wife, were invited, but at the end of the second to last day of December the sky clouded and grew still. Just after supper the first few flakes of snow began to fall, and the weather now became a topic of conversation. Snow at that time of year was hardly unexpected, and everyone thought how festive it would make the park look, but Sir John began to fret for their expected guests, and when everyone went into the hall for candlesticks to take upstairs, he opened the hall door, and peered out, to return with a frown and a dusting of snow.

The snow continued to fall overnight, and in the late morning a servant, his cape thick with flakes, came from the Hall to make his master's apologies. Mrs Mountjoy was suffering a chill, and under the circumstances, her husband could not think of driving the four miles to the Manor with the possibility of finding the carriage in difficulties. He hoped Sir John would understand, and excuse them at such short notice. He enclosed an invitation for the following week, if the weather should have improved, and wished them a Happy New Year.

By the end of the afternoon, other apologies had arrived and Antonia found Sir John in the hall regarding them dolefully.

"It seems we shall be making our celebrations in solitary style, my dear. I hope you won't be disappointed." He evidently was. "I should have liked you to have had some diversion and a little fresh conversation. I don't doubt you are heartily sick of old folk by now." He was transparently obvious, and Antonia smiled.

"How can you think so, Sir John?"

"You're very obliging, child. I call you child, because you seem so to me, especially at my great age. I hope you will forgive my fancies. Dear me, we shall have an excess of food at dinner. I hope you will all bring a good appetite to table. You never eat much, I notice."

It was a delightful meal, bright with laughter, though insufficient justice was done – to the turtle soup, the turbot with lobster sauce, the ducks and the great joint of beef and saddle of mutton, followed by apple pies, blancmanges, and plum pudding – to satisfy Sir John. Finally the cheeses were set on the table, together with oranges and nuts, port, marsala and Madeira.

Molly rose from the table at this point, and the two men got to their feet. "I simply cannot manage another bite, John, I have eaten far too much. I shall take tea upstairs, I think, and return to see in the New Year with you all later. Send one of the maids to fetch me in an hour or two. No, don't bother to come, Antonia dear. I shall take Samson. Take coffee in the library with these gluttons. Come along, Samson."

"I have hardly touched a morsel," William protested, justifiably since he had not eaten much more than had Antonia, who was always abstemious. But Molly, anxious for the privacy of her bedchamber where she might loosen her stays, ignored him and, with the little dog tucked under her arm, left the oak-panelled dining parlour and went upstairs.

"I will also leave you, gentlemen," Antonia said cheerfully, while they were still standing. "And when you return to the library, coffee will be ready." They protested at her going, for the custom of retiring at the end of the meal was not always followed when the family dined alone, but she smiled and left them to their port and their tobacco, Sir John's in a long white clay pipe, and for William, his favourite cigarillos.

In the library a tray waited on a side table.

Antonia had always considered this room one of the most charming at Bartonhurst, especially after dark when a fire burned in the enormous hearth, and the candles threw pools of light on the polished wood floors. Three tall windows set in deep embrasures flanked the long room, and as yet the heavy curtains had not been pulled so that light from a full moon flooded in. It must have stopped snowing, Antonia thought, and went to look.

The moon's cold brightness offset the warmth and comfort of the room, but the view - across snow covered lawns with the shadows of the trees lying blackly on its whiteness, and down across the park to the hills beyond - was so unexpectedly beautiful that Antonia caught her breath. She stepped into the alcove, and pulled the heavy drapes behind her, so that the candles were no longer reflected in the glass. Now the scene was quite perfect, she thought, and as she watched, a small deer stepped delicately out from the shelter of trees and picked its way across the lawn. Antonia held her breath.

William left his father finishing his pipe and crossed into the library expecting to see Antonia. He saw the coffee cups untouched.

"Antonia?"

Her voice came muffled. "I'm behind the curtain, William. The snow has stopped. It looks wonderful. There's a deer on the lawn."

William crossed the room and drew the curtain aside. His smile faded. His hand fell to his side.

Drenched in moonlight, Antonia stood gazing out at the snow-covered garden, and William was stunned into silence. From the top of her glossy head to her pretty slippers Antonia had never looked quite as lovely, the sparkling gown seeming to outshine the stars burning in the night sky beyond the trees. He went on staring at her, dimly conscious of a pounding in his head, and a difficulty in breathing.

Sensing his presence Antonia turned, but at the expression in his eyes her smile, too, faded, and she was at once exultant and afraid, understanding that at this moment their relationship had changed, perhaps forever. She feared to move or speak and break the spell.

They regarded each other in silence.

Wonderingly, he reached out to touch her hair, "Antonia." His fingers caressed her cheek. "Antonia -"

She drew an uneven breath and brought up her hand to cover his. Never taking his eyes from hers, he said again as if he had just discovered her name: "Antonia - " and he took her face in both his hands, and bent his head to kiss her mouth, once as if he was tasting sweet wine, and then again, deeper and with great longing. The silence in the room deepened. Antonia melted against him, dazed, disbelieving, and dizzy with joy and desire - and hardly heard Sir John's voice from the hall. But William heard. He gasped, jerked away, leaving Antonia, eyes closed, swaying where she stood.

"William? Mrs Davenport?"

The spell was broken. William gave Antonia a startled glance before stepping back into the room. "We're admiring the view, father. Moonlight on the snow." He looked back at Antonia uncertainly as she came through the curtains and, with shaking hands she began to pour coffee as if nothing had just occurred.

The old man seated himself next to the fire. He had missed nothing, and when with an unsteady smile that almost broke his heart, Antonia gave him his cup, he patted the seat beside him. "Sit here, child," he said. "Let me look at you."

"Your son has not yet had his coffee," she murmured.

"Then let him get his own and bring yours too."

William laughed, an odd sound. "Sit down, Antonia, and let him charm you. He's barely civil to most people so you are greatly honoured." Avoiding her glance, he brought her the cup, and retired with his own to the far end of the room where the pianoforte stood. His father flashed him a look of reproof.

"My son has no respect for me, as you see," he remarked, but he looked at Antonia very kindly. "Well, my dear, have you enjoyed your stay with us?"

"Thank you, Sir John," she answered. "You have been most kind, and the – the house is completely charming."

"I know you are used to Town, but you've not found the country too tedious, I hope? The snow cuts us off from company, of course."

"I do believe I prefer the country, and with all there is to occupy oneself here, one could hardly be bored." Regaining her composure by the minute, Antonia could almost manage a proper smile now, and turning to glance at William, added, "Your son makes sure I get enough exercise with all the riding and walking we do." She turned back to Sir John. "And in the evenings there is music, and the pleasure of your conversation."

Sir John looked across the room to his son. "This house is far too big for me now," he said loudly. "It needs a young family in it, filling up the rooms." William looked up from the piano keys, a warning look in his eyes.

The old man ignored him. "My son refuses to marry, and provide me with grandchildren, you know, Mrs Davenport," he continued. "I do not believe he cares that I could die before I see my grandson."

"Father," William said in a low voice. "Please. Do not begin on that subject again."

Antonia was confused now, and embarrassed. She knew Sir John had spoken deliberately to provoke his son, and that the subject was an unwelcome one. She felt she was being used, but not knowing what was intended she stirred her coffee with greater concentration.

The old man abruptly changed the subject. "Will you give us the pleasure of a song tonight?" and caught the uneasy glance that she flashed at his son, before she answered with a shake of her head.

"Not tonight, if you please." She looked now as if she could not trust her voice in a song, and it seemed too as though William, wearing the look of a thundercloud, was in no mood for music either.

"Now, I see in 'The Register' - " Sir John began again, reaching for the paper on a nearby table, but having pulled it towards him, he stopped speaking and began to pat his pockets. "That's odd," he said, presently. "I was sure of having my spectacles to hand. What have I done with them?"

William answered from the other end of the room where he had been paying close attention to the conversation. "Did you not have them at dinner, when you read that note that Lewiston sent in?"

"I did. You're right. Just ring the bell for Lottie, if you will, sir."

But before William had crossed half the room Antonia had put down her cup and was at the door. "I believe I know where your spectacles may be, Sir John," she murmured. "Excuse me." And she slipped out of the room.

The old man pointed. "Now, you've embarrassed that young lady, sir. Do you see how anxious she was to leave the room?"

"*I've* embarrassed her?" William echoed. "I rather think it was your outburst, father."

Sir John huffed at that. "Well, don't think you can disregard what I was saying, young man. It's more than time you stopped racketing about the world and began to think of settling down. Here. I meant what I said. The place needs a family in it again."

"Then perhaps *you* should re-marry?"

"I am serious, sir! I've no wish to be maudlin, but I am not going to be here forever - " He held up his hand against William's protest. "And I want to see a grandson of mine, growing up in this house." He studied his son, and his voice altered. "You do – care for the place, don't you, William?"

"Father, you know I do. And for you," his son replied. "But - I am not ready to settle down, in Kent or anywhere else. I would still be serving if I could. Yes, in spite of your efforts! And I suppose I have enjoyed 'racketing about the world' as you put it, but having only just returned to civilian life I find I am not quite yet ready give it all up to take on the duties of a landlord and shut myself away in the country, like you."

"Then when?" protested his father. "William, you are thirty-one years old. With all your experience, you must know by now what it is you are looking for in a wife."

"Father, please! I really do not want to have to discuss this every time we see each other." His face grim, William returned to the piano and began to sort music.

Antonia had been glad to escape, and regain her composure, but Sir John's spectacles were only lying on the marble table at the bottom of the staircase, so she had not needed to go far to find them. Now, as she steeled herself to return she heard the raised voices and realised that the argument she had hoped to avoid hearing was still in progress. At the library doors she hesitated, unsure whether to enter. The tapestry screen inside blocked her view of the speakers, but she had just heard William declare he was not yet ready to give up thoughts of soldiering to settle for a country life. She could sympathize with Sir John, who would quite naturally want to pass on his name and inheritance to his son and his son's children, but the fact that she herself sometimes ached to bear those children must not stop her from understanding how William must feel.

She had made up her mind to tiptoe quietly away when she heard Sir John say suddenly, "Then what about Mrs Davenport?"

"What about Mrs Davenport?" William sounded astonished.

"Does *she* know you have no intention of marrying and settling down just yet?"

"Good God!" replied his son. "It is not a subject that has ever arisen between us. Mrs Davenport knows that my career continues to lie with the Army if possible."

Antonia shrank against the door, holding her breath. Eavesdroppers never hear good of themselves, she told herself. She ought to go, but she could not.

"So you're leading that lovely girl up the garden path? You've no intention of marrying her?"

"The idea of marrying Mrs Davenport has never crossed my mind!" Well, perhaps it had, once or twice, warned a voice in his head, and William dismissed it, almost angrily. "See here, father. There is nothing of that nature in our relationship. The lady has beauty, accomplishments, and as you are aware, I enjoy her company, but - but that is as far as it goes, and I do not intend to discuss her further with you. We are simply good friends."

Behind the screen, Antonia flinched at the statement. Until this evening she had told herself repeatedly that she could expect nothing from William Hurst, but hope had suddenly flowered in the moonlight and she had been almost giddy with wonder and anticipation. It was clear she was mistaken. And she was surprised to find the discovery hurt her more than she would have imagined. How she wished now that she had slipped away at once, as she should have done.

"Good friends?" retorted Sir John, "And when you were behind the curtain a short while ago you felt you were just good friends?"

Sounding embarrassed now, William snapped back, "We are good friends. The - the moment took me by surprise! I behaved very – unwisely. I admit it. I did not mean to insult Mrs Davenport either, but that doesn't alter the fact that I have never considered her other than as a friend." His words had a final ring to them, and Sir John fell silent.

Feeling more dejected than ever but fearing his father's arguments might cool William's avowed friendship for her even further, Antonia knew she must go in now and bring the discussion to an end. Lifting her chin, and straightening her shoulders, Antonia skirted the edge of the screen, and held out Sir John's spectacles.

He did not see her at first. He sat hunched up, looking into the fire, his bowed shoulders making him look suddenly defeated, and much, much older, and Antonia's heart went out to him. William was wrong to be so harsh, whatever he felt. The unhappy atmosphere in the room could not be ignored.

Impulsively Antonia knelt beside the old man and laid a hand on his knee.

He looked into her face, lit by the glow of the fire, and sighed, wondering why, when he and Molly could do so, his son could not see that she was the one for him.

Antonia glanced at William, and in her clear soft voice, said calmly: "I heard your voices from the corridor. It is such a pity when two people, who have not always seen as much as they wanted of each other in the last few years, argue when they meet again." Father and son both shot a look at her, then at each other. Had she any idea what they had been arguing over? Nothing in her gaze gave them a hint. "Please," she continued, "Won't you shake hands, and try not to let whatever you disagree on come between you?"

To her relief, William responded at once. "Father, I'm sorry. I don't mean to upset you. I'll bear what you say in mind."

The old man softened. "My boy, I don't mean to be a nag. You're only young once, I know. I'll try not to mention it again."

They shook hands and turned to Antonia as she scrambled up from the floor. Almost before they were aware of it, she had kissed them both quickly on the cheek.

"Thank you," she whispered, her heart full. "That was nicely done."

Confused, William put a hand to his cheek, but his father was full of smiles now, his whole manner brighter. "Not long to midnight now. I suppose we had better have Molly join us."

"Then I'll fetch her," Antonia said hurriedly, and fled.

Outside the door, she stopped to lean against the wall for an instant, then furiously dashing away tears she ran up the stairs to Molly's room.

"My dear, good girl! Whatever is the matter?" Molly sat up on her bed and looked at Antonia who had just appeared at her bedside. "Have you been crying?"

Samson, tail wagging, bounced over the quilt and put his cold nose into Antonia's hand. She patted him automatically.

"It's my head, Molly." It was almost the truth. "I have such a pain that I really do not think I can see in the New Year with you. I came to tell you it is nearly midnight, and they are expecting you downstairs, but, please, make my apologies. I think I had better go to bed at once."

"We all ate far too much of Sir John's feast, dear. I was so uncomfortable when I rose from the table, and *they* were still eating! But Antonia, is it only a bilious headache? I have some powdered ginger root in my travelling case, and if you take some in some hot water, like tea, you know, you may find relief. It would be a pity not to see in the New Year."

"But – Well, I will take your ginger tea, and come down if I feel any better, but I really do not think I shall, at least not for a while. Please excuse me to your brother, and to – and to William. But I feel really quite abysmal at present." She did look quite wretched.

"Here is the ginger, dear," Molly said, holding up a paper packet, "and I will send a maid to your room with some hot water directly. If you should not come down again, my love, perhaps I may wish you a Happy New Year now? You poor soul.! What a way to begin it!"

Antonia could only think, as she and Molly exchanged celebratory kisses, that the overheard conversation downstairs was an even worse way to end the old one.

CHAPTER THIRTY SEVEN

Next morning, New Year's Day, William took himself off to the stables before breakfast, having slept badly, and wanting to clear his head. Feeling battered and alarmed by the intensity of emotions he did not fully understand, he was well aware he had behaved badly on the previous evening, had then said things he did not mean to his father, and now was not sure how to put matters right with either him or Antonia. He was astonished to hear his aunt's voice as he was saddling his horse.

"Your father tells me," Molly said without preamble, walking into the stall, "that you have no intention at all of marrying Antonia Davenport."

Shocked to the core, William checked in the act of adjusting the stirrups, and it was a moment before he could manage to speak. "A Happy New Year to you too, Aunt. Does my father intend to broadcast what was a private conversation to anyone else now? The gardener? the lodge keeper perhaps?"

"You are annoyed, nephew, but don't take that tone, if you please, with me. Your father has made me privy to your conversation last night only because he has been badly upset by it."

"I beg your pardon, ma'am," William said tightly, "but I wasn't aware that it was anyone's business but my own."

"Nonsense, boy!" Molly returned. "Any marriage you make must concern your father – and me – and you must know we have nothing but your best interests at heart."

"My father, I believe, has only his own interests at heart. He had better accustom himself to the idea that I am unlikely ever to marry."

"Never? Don't be ridiculous!"

"Not at the wish of my father at any rate," William declared, "and certainly not unless I also wish it, and feel it is the right and inevitable step."

"And do you not feel," Molly said unwisely, "that marriage to Antonia Davenport is the best thing you could ever propose? Surely you have feelings for her now?"

William drew a deep breath, hardly knowing how to respond. Of course he was fond of Antonia but he never intended to find himself in love with any woman. "Mrs Davenport, aunt, is everything that is good, and beautiful and accomplished. I do not, however, intend to propose marriage to her, or to anyone else, merely to oblige you or my father, nor do I imagine that she would care to know of a discussion of her plans, or mine, at this point!"

"Come William," Molly said more gently. "Do you mean to tell me you have no interest in the dear creature?" She bit her lip. "Lord knows she has become very dear to me." Laying a hand on her nephew's arm, she looked up into his face. "It would do my heart so much good to see the two of you wed."

"Molly, that's enough."

"You cannot be surprised at my expecting some joy of your friendship?"

"I'm sorry that you are likely to be disappointed then," William said through clenched teeth, "but I have no more to say. Please, let it drop." Impatiently he made adjustments to straps and reins and prepared to lead the horse out into the yard. His aunt followed him.

"But you evidently prefer her to any other. The wonder is that there is not more talk of your attachment. If such has reached Antonia's ears, it will be a marvel if she herself has not come to expect a proposal."

William paled. He turned to face his aunt. "I cannot imagine what you mean."

"My dear, you have been more sociable in these last few months than anyone can remember. You are constantly in her company, which you evidently enjoy. You stand up with her whenever you can - when you have given us all to understand you do not dance. Do you imagine this has all gone unnoticed?"

"Enough!" William swung himself up into the saddle, his face white and furious, and with an exasperated sigh Molly turned away.

"This is not the end of it, nephew," she called after him as he rode off.

William took the horse into the lane, his heart pounding, unpleasantly aware that he had behaved with great impropriety. He had wanted to kiss Antonia and so he had kissed her and then pretended it had never happened. Had his earlier conduct too, been so blatantly indiscreet? Had his father merely imagined he knew what had happened, and spoken of it to Molly? Had Antonia spoken to Molly? She was no innocent child after all. She had made no protest when he took her in his arms . . . But how could he not have taken in his arms? Was it only the moonlight?

William had never before felt so out of his depth. Was this more than a simple affection, he wondered? Love? He did not want to even consider that. He was a soldier, he told himself, and a soldier's wife was no life for a young woman, forced as she would be to trail behind the army or to remain behind in England, alone. He reminded himself that his parents' marriage had been a disaster, as had her parents' marriage, by all accounts, and then there was her own. She had been married – how could he ever forget *that!*

Could Antonia have feelings for him? She always seemed delighted to see him. Was that just his vanity? He was, indeed, truly fond of her. They were good friends, the best. He honestly enjoyed her company, but there was none of the obsession such as his friends spoke of or exhibited when they declared themselves in love. He admired her – more than admired her, perhaps: her spirit, her accomplishments, her beauty. And there were alternatives to marriage surely. . .

In spite of himself William was conscious that his heart always lifted when he caught sight of her, the way she held her head, that lift of her chin. Her smile made him want to smile . . . What had he been thinking of? But he could not pretend it had never happened. He should not *be* pretending it had never happened.

He must speak to her as soon as he returned. Apologise. Explain. Antonia's friendship was not something he should trample on. No, he would speak to her now if she would hear him. He reined in, dismounted and led the horse back to the stable.

He finally found her in the morning room. There was a book open on the table in front of her, but with a frown and far away expression, she was looking instead out of the window. William hesitated at the open door. He studied her, unobserved, and catching sight of her profile now against the morning light he remembered the evening before and the snowy starlight, and found he wanted to kiss her again, imagining what it would be like to hold the slight figure against him once more . . .

Good God! This wouldn't do! He stepped into the room, and pushed the door shut behind him. "Good morning."

She turned. "William. Good morning. A Happy and Prosperous New Year to you." Silence followed, broken only by the silvery chime from a distant clock.

William forced himself to speak.

"Antonia, I must talk to you," he began, and saw from her expression that she was not sure how to interpret this abrupt statement, but she seemed to gather her composure and picking up her book, she moved to one of the upholstered chairs, indicating its twin. Perhaps she imagined he had come to declare himself. Must he do so? he wondered, with a stab of panic. But he would not be forced into this because it was something his father or his aunt or other people thought should happen.

"Will you sit then?"

Avoiding her glance, he took the chair, and Antonia sat, with her hands folded in her lap, waiting.

He did not keep her waiting long. "Our acquaintance, Antonia, - our - friendship – did not have a good beginning, but we - we are good friends now, are we not?"

He did not look at her, and his manner suggested that he had rehearsed a speech and was intent on delivering it. It would therefore be something he did not want to say, and worse, something she would not want to hear. Conscious of a rush of fear and pity, Antonia gripped the book. "Of course."

"I overstepped the bounds of friendship last night," he said, almost as if she had not spoken. "It was reprehensible."

"It was - " - *Heaven, breath-taking, unbelievable, magical, everything she had ever longed for-* "- it was very pleasant. Though probably - " She gave him a steady smile, "something we ought not to repeat."

His head jerked up - and his expression of obvious relief and gratitude stabbed her to the heart.

He said, with some awkwardness: "I don't mean to mislead you, Antonia. I allowed my instincts . . . "

"William, I'm no innocent maiden," she reminded him. "I have been married." Perhaps that was not the best thing to have said, remembering what that marriage had been, and how it had affected them both.

"Nevertheless," William continued, "I would - If - if you were to feel that I - I would of course propose that we marry."

Antonia swallowed. "Would you marry without love, then, William?" she wondered. "I do not think I would wish to do so now."

He stared at her uncertainly. "Few marriages are made on that basis, I believe," he said at last. "But if the truth were known," he added, "I have no great desire to marry at all."

Antonia flinched, but having been forced to school her emotions well at the Casa Cabral she could answer calmly: "I always understood those were your feelings on the matter. Though," she added in a low voice, "I fear your father might be deeply disappointed to hear you say so."

"I don't believe I need marry to please my father," he declared for the second time that morning. "But - nor would I want you to be hurt, Antonia."

"Are we now talking about me, William?"

"We have been a great deal in each other's company these last few months. People may have assumed our friendship more than it is. We may have raised an expectation that we should marry. I don't want you to get hurt." His voice dropped. "And it might be unwise if you were ever to fall in love with me, Antonia."

Too late, too late, Antonia wanted to cry, but she could hardly breathe, wondering how she was to answer. Finally she managed: "Everyone who knows you must feel an affection for you," she said steadily. "You would not have us all reject you out of hand, I hope?" But the smile she put in her voice nearly vanished as he lifted his eyes to hers.

"Then you would not -?" He hesitated. "I wondered if you had spoken to Molly - I was afraid that last evening - "

"I think perhaps the magic of the scene worked upon us too well, William. I think we were both carried away a little." Antonia lifted her chin. "I have not spoken to Molly, but she and your father must have mistaken the case. I place great value on your friendship," she said and the fingers gripped around her book were white to the knuckles, "and I expect nothing more from you."

"Thank you," he murmured, nonplussed but grateful. "I - I should have known I might rely on your complete understanding. I consider myself fortunate - in my friends, Antonia, if - if you are amongst them. We are friends still, are we not?"

"Friends." She nodded.

It was a dreadful and difficult few days to the end of the visit. Antonia was now forced to pretend that she had no deeper feelings than friendship for the man she had at last realized she loved, to pretend that she had not noticed that Molly and Sir John were following with expectation and frustration every move she and William made, together and apart, to pretend that she did not notice that William had lost his customary good humour, and his sense of what was due in the way of politeness and attention to his family. He was out now nearly all day long every day, with the excuse of having something to attend to elsewhere, and would come in chilled and raw, and make excuses not to join the party at dinner. Molly and Sir John made excuses for him too. They imagined he was ashamed of his recent behaviour and embarrassed at having to face Antonia every day, and so he was, but even more keenly William felt that in spite of saying otherwise, he had lost the capability of retaining the friendship of the one person whose company he preferred - and he did not know what to put in friendship's place. Antonia's response to his explanations, and her behaviour since, seemed to indicate that she had, as she had said, no deeper feelings for him - but instead of feeling relieved he felt oddly lost.

It was hard to know who was more grateful when the visit finally came to an end: Antonia, or Molly, or William - and Antonia had already foreseen the consequences of her own personal disaster, as it must affect Molly. She could keep away from Bartonhurst and Kent, but if William was still intent on avoiding her, he was unlikely to be seen in Henrietta Place as often as before and that would distress Molly.

She might not be able to stay.

Feeling more wretched than ever at the thought, and as heartsick and depressed as she had been at the Casa Cabral, Antonia began to realize that there was now nowhere else left to go.

CHAPTER THIRTY EIGHT

Molly Spenlow had been very forbearing in those first few days of the New Year at Bartonhurst. Previously forthright, she now behaved with enormous tact. She did not pester Antonia for explanations and details, nor did she commiserate with her, nor ask for sympathy herself. She knew something was badly wrong. Between them, she and her brother had precipitated a situation, and now neither William nor Antonia were as they had been. Molly suspected that without their interference the happy result she hoped for would have been achieved, but just now it seemed it never would. And she was not sure how to help. Antonia had lost her ease of manner, and was as tense as she had ever been, and William, ever since their confrontation in the stables, was behaving even more oddly. "Perhaps it *was* all my fault then, Samson." Molly addressed her little dog. "When I spoke to William that morning. I wish I had not done so."

"Molly, I believe I must leave London."

"Must you, dear?" Molly said, startled. They had only been back from Kent a week or two, and Molly had imagined Antonia would be glad to be in town once more. "Very well. I shall write to Bridge House and tell them to expect us."

"No, Molly, I mean I must leave. Leave you. In London."

"Do you want to go down to Hampshire on your own?"

"I shan't be going to Hampshire. I have had a letter from Henrietta. She says I may go up as soon as I like - "

"Go to Henrietta? Antonia! You hate it at Hetherington, you said. What can you be thinking of? It will be even more dismal at this time of the year."

"Nevertheless - "

"Nevertheless, fiddlesticks!" Molly exclaimed, startling her little dog off his cushion. "Antonia, my love," she said more slowly, "I have been very patient. You cannot deny I have been remarkably patient, and for me, you must admit, that is rather unusual. But my dear girl, you must tell me what it is that is causing you — and William - to act so out of character. Has he proposed after all and you turned him down? Is that what has caused this awkwardness between you?"

"No," Antonia replied steadily, "that is not the problem. And Molly I am truly sorry that this distance between your nephew and me affects you - "

"My brother knows something of its cause, of that I'm certain. Did he lecture William while you were present, and embarrass the boy? I gave him a lecture myself, you know, in the stable on New Year's morn. John told me that he'd tackled him just the night before on making a match and William had refused point blank to consider it. I had hoped, my dear, you know, that perhaps you and he might − Well, up until then it had been very clear that William very much preferred your company to any other."

Antonia's heart sank. She could not tell Molly what had happened if her friend was quite likely, if she thought it a good idea, to go straight to William and repeat her confidences. Antonia herself hardly knew what it was she wanted to happen as a result. "Your nephew has himself been charming company," she said lightly.

"But I did hope − It would make me so very happy if he were to have offered, you know, and Sir John is already quite captivated. The match -"

"Please, Molly. Don't think of it for a minute, I beg you. I assure you nothing is further from your nephew's thoughts. He is a very independent man who has just lost the career he cared for so much, and the last thing he wants is to settle down." Breathlessly, she added, trying to laugh: "And you would not wish another marriage on me." As soon as she had spoken the words, she regretted them.

"You make it sound as if your marriage was something you remember with less than pleasure, Antonia," Molly said. "Is that what it is? Has the fact that you were married made a difference to William? I realize your husband's death must be a source of sorrowful memories but -"

"Oh, Molly, my marriage was not all that I've led you to believe." One lie at a time was hard enough to manage, and it would be a relief not to pretend to Molly that she was a grieving widow.

"Few marriages are what they seem, dear."

"And my husband's death was not as you imagine."

"He was not killed in the Peninsula? But he served in Portugal? I know you never speak of it - "

"He did die in Portugal. I saw him die. But he was not fighting the French."

"I do not understand, dear."

Tersely, Antonia recounted the search for her husband, and the discovery at the monastery. "I learned that my husband was quite prepared to murder both my servant Pedro, and the English officer who was my escort – your nephew, William, you see, in order to conceal his treachery." She was aware that Molly, clutching Samson to her chest, was gaping in horrified disbelief. "Furthermore," she continued, "for the same reason, my husband attempted to kill me, not once but twice! Luckily his plans were thwarted, and he – he was killed before he could do further harm." She took a deep breath. "I killed him, Molly."

She felt Molly recoil. "What! You did what?" She sank into the nearest chair. "I cannot – I cannot *believe* -that you - *you* – Does William know any of this? Is this why . . . ?"

"He knows it all, Molly. He was there. I told you once before. He saved my life."

"But *you killed* your husband?"

"Yes," Antonia said flatly. "I did not know that it was him. He came after us in the dark, William had left me a pistol and gone for help. I was alone, and he fired at me, and wounded me, and I - I fired back."

"Then it couldn't have been helped."

"Perhaps not," Antonia said dully.

"I think I understand now why you have never spoken of it before. But what – what did William do then?"

"Your nephew, I'm afraid, had previously regarded me as an encumbrance. But once he learned the truth, he was quite prepared to kill my husband in order to protect me. He took care of me, and nursed me when I was hurt, and then cursed me when I let the horses run off leaving us stranded on the mountain, and then he went for help and made sure I was taken to safety, and all the time he was hurt and wounded himself, and – And I know now that I am in love with him, Molly."

"Yes," Molly said gently, after a long pause, "my poor girl, I can see that you are. You have kept this secret all the time?"

"I didn't love him then, I promise you. I thought he hated me for the longest time, and believe me, Molly, I never thought to ever see him again. And then when I met him again, and he was so kind, and not frightening any more, and so pleasant, and ready to talk, and he made me see that what had happened in Portugal had been – almost unavoidable, and I saw how he was with you, and with his father . . ."

"Oh, his father, Antonia. John doesn't know any of this?"

"Oh no, I am sure he does not. What would he think? I believe it would kill him!"

"John is more resilient than he likes us to think, but never fear, I shan't say a word about any of this. He shan't hear it from me. It's too shocking for words, but my dear, it's all in the past now."

"Thank you, Molly. And please, dear Molly, do not say a word to William. Nothing about Portugal, and not that − that − Don't you see, it's hard enough knowing that he does not care for me in that way, but if he knew I had some feelings for him I should never be able to - I could never face him again."

"No, Antonia, I'm sure - "

"Molly, swear to me that you will never tell William what I have told you tonight. Swear it!"

"But Antonia - ! Oh, very well, I swear. But you have no need now to go to Hetherington?"

"I will return in a month or two. I just need some time away for the present. In a month or two, all this will have blown over, and perhaps I will come back. But Molly, I couldn't bear it if you tell William what I have said tonight. Please, remember."

CHAPTER THIRTY NINE

William, in London to visit to John and Fanny Cunningham in their new house, had talked himself into calling on his aunt. It had been three weeks since he'd last seen her and he was conscious that his previous visits had been much more frequent. His aunt after all should not suffer for his idiocy, and it was just possible that she might be alone.

Furthermore, John Cunningham had already asked to accompany him back to Henrietta Place, and though William's heart sank at the thought that his friend might witness a first awkward encounter with Antonia Davenport and pass some misplaced comment, common courtesy made it necessary to agree.

They had only just turned into Henrietta Place when they became aware of two or three carriages pulled up outside Molly's house. A string of maids came out with packages, one with heavy blocks wrapped in steaming cloth which she laid on the carriage floor.

"Foot warmers? Is my aunt planning to leave today for Hampshire? She doesn't usually go down for another month. We shall be lucky to catch her, John. It will be a short visit if her mind is on getting out of London early. Look smart!"

Quickening their pace, they ran up the front steps and into the hall, to hear the buzz of voices in the drawing room on the first floor. They went up, without waiting for Rigsby to announce them.

"William, dear boy! What a wonderful surpr - Oh, Lord, this is unexpected." Molly looked anxiously across the room to where Antonia, in a plain coat and fur-trimmed cape and bonnet, was sitting in conversation with two gentlemen, looking as if she had just come in or was ready to leave. She seemed very pale but was endeavouring to attend to Molly's guests. George Boscawen was holding forth on a local election, his words audible to the group at the door.

William had followed her glance, and when Antonia looked in his direction, he bowed and turned back to his aunt. Pleasantries were being exchanged between Molly and Major Cunningham. "It seems you are about to leave for Bridge House, Aunt?" he said. "When do you go?"

"Er – not yet awhile, nephew."

"I don't mean to keep you." He glanced again at the group at the other end of the room. "Molly, what is that fellow doing paying such marked attention to Mrs Davenport?"

"That's Lord Boscawen, dear, you remember him. He has been such a help with our cause."

"I know who it is. I just wonder that you allow him to come here and monopolise the conversation?"

"William!" Molly gave a startled laugh. "I'm surprised at you. Go and monopolise it yourself if you wish to have him stop." She looked at him with a puzzled expression, then shook her head. "Well, I must speak to Benson. I shall be back shortly. Don't let Antonia be overwhelmed by the gentlemen now, please, William." But instead of joining the group, as his aunt had rather hoped he would, William withdrew instead to the bow window with John Cunningham, and tried to pretend he was looking out at the street. There was silence for a while apart from the conversation from the other end of the room.

Eventually Cunningham, who had been observing his friend quite as intently as Hurst himself had been studying Antonia and George Boscawen, spoke. "I should say, friend William," he observed very quietly, "that you have almost certainly fallen in love."

William stared at him. "Don't be ridiculous," he said, taken aback to find himself the object of his friend's scrutiny. He was even more annoyed to feel himself flushing. "Why would you say such a thing?"

"If you had observed yourself as I have had the opportunity to do these long minutes past you would not ask," Cunningham replied calmly. "You haven't taken your eyes off the lady. I don't wonder at that – Mrs Davenport looks enchanting in fur, but you have been in the fidgets since we came in to find her with Lord Boscawen and his friend. You have been scowling like a fiend, drumming your fingers on the windowsill, and looking daggers every time he makes her smile. Depend upon it, Will, you have a bad case of jealousy."

"What *utter* nonsense!" William's glance had already gone back to the group in the corner.

"Nonsense, is it? I tell you, you've a bad case. But you cannot be a dog in a manger."

Dog in a manger! William was stung. "Boscawen may look like a Greek god, but his charm is slick and easy, and Antonia has more sense than to be taken in by a man like that."

"He's rich."

"That will not affect her judgment." He thought of the Cabral fortunes, reduced but renounced.

"The fact is," Cunningham continued as if Hurst had not spoken, "you deceive yourself if you imagine you are impartial."

"Who employs you as Matchmaker?" William muttered furiously.

"I'm sorry to have left you for so long, my dears." Molly had returned. "What are you doing there in the window? I meant you should join the others. Antonia will be glad to see you."

"Mrs Cunningham is expecting us, Aunt. We should be leaving, John, don't you think?" But his friend put up his hands as if to warn William not to involve him in any pretence.

"But if you go now – " Molly looked across at her young friend. She bit her lip.

William followed her glance again. "Antonia's going somewhere? I thought she might just have come in. Where is she going?"

"Um – Out of town for a while, dear."

"To Bridge House?"

"Um, no, not to Bridge House."

"Then where?" His voice had risen a little, and the two men across the room turned their heads.

"Well, Antonia's sister - "

"Yorkshire? I don't believe it. She doesn't like it above half at that place - "

"Nevertheless, dear, and please keep your voice down, that is where she intends to go, as soon as our guests have gone."

"Antonia," William said, crossing the room and interrupting the conversation with no more than a bow, and an 'Excuse me.' "Molly tells me you are planning to leave shortly for Yorkshire?"

"Aha!" Boscawen laughed. "The secret's out, Mrs Davenport. Yorkshire is the destination."

"Excuse me," William repeated, and taking Antonia's elbow, he said in a low voice: "Mrs Davenport, if I may have a word?"

Mortified, and too startled to protest, Antonia was drawn away from the table to a quiet corner. "What are you doing, William?" she asked quietly. "That was very rude."

"Yorkshire, Antonia? Now? You said you had not enjoyed your last stay."

"I am going to Yorkshire, yes. And today, yes, as soon as my things are stowed in the carriage. I assure you I am looking forward to my stay."

"But - how long will you be away?" He was still holding her arm.

Antonia tilted her chin. "That – that has not been decided. The children have not been well . . . " She was lying and she hated it.

"I'll ride with you part of the way."

She was startled, frightened for a minute. "I'd rather you didn't."

"But - but must you go, Antonia?"

"To tell the truth, William," she said, flatly, "I do not care to be here at present."

He let his hands drop, silent, helpless, finally understanding.

"I - I wish I had not spoken."

She tried to smile. "*I* wish you had not spoken."

"Everything's changed."

"Nothing has changed, William."

"But you are going?"

"Yes."

"For how long?"

"I cannot say."

He took her hand again, and held it in his without speaking. "Yes, yes, of course," he said, finally, "Of course you must go. I wish you safe journey." He bowed and excused himself, leaving John Cunningham looking after him in astonishment.

CHAPTER FORTY
Spring 1815

Molly was caught in a cleft stick. On her honour not to disclose what Antonia had told her, she had seen how shaken her nephew had been to discover Antonia was leaving London for some indefinite period, and now did not know what to do for the best. She could not even give William directions for any letter he cared to write. He continued to call at Henrietta Place, but seemed unable to settle when he was there. Molly found him often, with Samson lying at his feet, seated at the piano, fingering the keys in a desultory fashion, discarding one melody after another. He told her he hated the inaction of his life away from his regiment.

She corresponded with her brother, but was constrained by her promise to Antonia so that her letters were no more than comments on her social engagements, the progress and dispensations of the relief fund, and queries over his health. She had also felt she must excuse her nephew's impulsive behaviour during Lord Boscawen's visit - but that was easily over and done. Luckily. Duels had been fought for less reason.

As the days went by Molly received letters from Yorkshire that sounded cheerful enough to reassure her. She trusted Antonia would find enough to occupy and distract herself there, but given that her young friend had described her earlier visit as 'occasionally stultifying', was not over hopeful. Days turned into weeks, and Antonia did not write of returning. Molly missed her badly, and told her so, but January turned into February and February became March.

On the evening of March 7th a courier arrived in Vienna with despatches from Genoa. Napoleon had escaped his island exile, and events began to move with terrible speed.

William appeared at Henrietta Place at 2 o'clock one afternoon towards the end of the month wearing uniform once more. The wind ruffled his cloak around him, and Samson barked at this stranger on the doorstep in his scarlet coat; it had been so long since William had called. He did not intend to wait for orders, he said, but, with several other officers of his old regiment, was sailing for Flanders that night, and had come to bid his aunt farewell. Up in the pretty drawing room on the first floor, he hurriedly explained what had happened.

He had left his father well, he said, but in some distress, convinced now that he would not see his son again, which was probably ridiculous. William hoped Molly would go down and comfort him if she could.

In some distress herself, she assured him she would but he did not seem able to make his farewells, pacing up and down, Samson at his heels. Curtains flapped at the open windows, and added to the sense of disquiet in the room.

"Aunt, I am desperate to have some word of Antonia. Do you have any news? I cannot leave without knowing something of her. I'd hoped she might have returned to London by now."

"I had a letter two days ago, William. She says she is well, but I do not think she is happy. Do you want to read the letter? I have it here." Molly held out the page, crossed and re-crossed with Antonia's attempts to save postage. William seized it gratefully, and read it in haste, but it was clear it did not made him feel any less agitated.

"I should have followed her there," he said, re-reading it with a sense of despair, "and now it is too late. I must be in Colchester before midnight. Molly, what am I to do?"

"Do about what?" Molly demanded. "The fact that you should have told Antonia that you loved her before she felt driven to leave? Done as I suggested last New Year's morning, and proposed?"

"You speak without knowing the facts, Molly. I told her – we discussed – our futures. She said – she said she understood that I cannot make any plans to marry. She said she herself would not marry unless it was for love, and I thought she had no other feeling for me but that of friendship."

"And you did not tell her you loved her? She understood you did not love her."

"I did not - think I - loved – her."

"And now you do?"

"I don't know, Molly, I don't know! All I know is that my life seems somehow emptier. I miss her terribly, and I just wish she was here, to talk to - and now when I may not return, to bid me farewell."

"Oh, William, William." Tears sprang to Molly's eyes. She wanted to tell him what Antonia had forbidden her to say. Her nephew had survived five earlier years of war – his luck might desert him at any time now. He might be going to his death. Was it fair that he should never know that Antonia loved him? But Molly Spenlow tried to keep her promises to her friends, and she would keep this one too.

"I will tell her you called, William," she promised. "She can write to you in Brussels, I expect? If she cares to write, that is."

"But *I* can write. Molly, I can write – leave a letter with you? You'll see she gets it, won't you?"

"You know I will, my dear."

"It's only now," he said with a tight smile, "when I look upon an uncertain future that I realise that I do not much care to face a life without her in it. And if I *should* die, I need her to know I regret my failure to understand sooner -"

"Hush, William, hush. You will return. You will. You are not to think otherwise. Write then. Here is a quill, and - " – pulling out drawers hastily in a search for a sheet of paper – "you must sit down, and think carefully what it is you need to say to persuade her."

An hour later, and he was gone.

Clutching the letter, and wondering if she would ever see her nephew again, Molly went on sobbing for an hour or more at her desk, with Samson circling disconsolately, unable to understand what was happening. At last, she pulled herself together, remembering that Antonia would want to have William's letter as soon as she could get it to her. She laid the folded sheets aside, and drawing another piece of paper towards her, began to write a note of explanation.

It was done. The window beside her rattled violently in a gust of wind as she sanded the sheet, and Molly sighed and leaning over the desk, got up to close the sash. William and his friends would have a rough crossing later if the wind did not drop, she thought, and did not notice that she had dislodged her nephew's letter. It caught in the breeze and fluttered towards the opening. She clutched at it in a panic and it moved out of her reach.

"No!" She stretched for it, but in another instant it was gone, floating out of the window, the pages caught in a sudden rush of wind and whirled away into the street. "No!" she cried again, and rushed for the door. Samson had begun to bark at his mistress's distress, but she disregarded him and flew out of the drawing room, calling for her housekeeper and the servants. Samson rushed after her, circling her feet excitedly. Molly reached the top of the stairs, crying, and the servants came up from the kitchen and the rooms below at the commotion. "The letter," she sobbed, "the letter's gone! Somebody catch it quickly – No, Samson! Mind . . . !"

It was too late. The little dog was under her feet. She tried to avoid him, stumbled on the top step, put out her hand to the banister, missed, screamed, and fell, hitting her head on almost every wrought baluster in the descent. She lay at the bottom, immobile, surrounded by her horrified staff. At the top of the flight, Samson regarded her in silence.

CHAPTER FORTY ONE

Mail coaches thundering out of inn yards had spread the news of Napoleon's progress northwards, but the first Antonia heard of it was from her brother-in-law at dinner one afternoon on his return from estate business in York.

The sisters exchanged horrified glances. Antonia jumped to her feet.

"Most of our regiments are elsewhere than England," she said. "And with so many discharged last year, the Army must be woefully depleted."

"How has this been allowed to happen?" Henrietta wondered. "How can Napoleon be resisted now?"

"They will raise all the troops they can." Richard Hetherington tried reassurance. "Russia, Austria, Prussia — Our allies have vast numbers of men but of course it will take some time to mobilise them. Meanwhile Wellington commands the advance guard. Every man that can be mustered will, I think, be sent to Flanders."

Antonia felt a chill settle round her heart. William would go. His regiment might reform but even if it did not, he would put on his new, barely worn uniform and rejoin his men, and they would follow the flags to Flanders. He would go back to the battle, and this time he might not return.

"Lord Hetherington, I must go back to London. Would you assist me?"

"Return to London? Whatever for, sister?" He stared at Antonia. "What brings this on? You are far safer here, let me tell you. In London there will be panic, and shortages and the Lord knows what else. You must see that arrangements for a journey of that distance are not to be accomplished in a moment. I cannot consent to your leaving yet awhile."

"Then I must go without your consent." She appealed for understanding across the table. "I am sorry, Henrietta, but I have to go as soon as I can."

"Of course you do. My lord, you must send my sister in one of our carriages some part of the way at least. She is bound in all honour to return to Lady Spenlow who will need Antonia when her nephew leaves with the Army for the Continent."

Her husband looked taken aback at his wife's support for her sister.

"Well, I really do not think . . . ! "

"Richard, you must *help*!" Henrietta had never insisted on anything before, and her husband was stunned into agreeing. He went to summon his groom, still astonished.

"Het, I cannot pretend. It is not only Molly I need to see. If William has joined the Army leaving for Flanders I may never see him again. I cannot let him go without a word when we parted on such terms. He must not leave without knowing that I am thinking of him, and praying for his safe return."

"But 'Tonia," her sister said, with her more usual timidity, "you said you had come to terms with the situation – that you knew you must live without hope of being any more than a friend."

"Then I lied, Het," Antonia confessed, with a bitter laugh. "William did tell me once that I was a great accommodator of the truth. The truth is that there is not an hour gone by when I have not thought of him. Perhaps I'm fooling myself even yet, and it is not for *his* sake that I need to see and speak to him once more, only mine. But truly, I cannot bear that he should think I care so little that I would not at least wish him well and safe again at home. And a letter may not reach him in time. Oh Het, he has fought in so many battles. How much more luck will he need to survive unscathed when he has been through so much already?"

"I had no idea you felt so, 'Tonia. All this time, and you never said . . . "

"I thought I would get over these feelings away from London, but it doesn't seem to have been so. I've been hoping and hoping there would be some word from him, Het, even in friendship. Every time there was a letter brought to the hall – did you not guess at my state? But," she rested her head in her hands, "only Molly wrote, and she being tactful for the first time in her life never spoke of the one person that means so much to us both. I must go, Hetty. I have to see him before he leaves for the Continent."

"Of course you do. I understand. I only wish you may get there in time."

After days of travelling, the chaise turned into Henrietta Place and slackened speed. Antonia who had been on the edge of her seat for the last mile now leaned forward with her hand on the window to look for the first glimpse of the house, and was surprised to see the road thickly strewn with straw, muffling the clop of hooves and the clang of the iron bound wheels bowling along. *Someone is ill,* was her first thought, and then, *I hope it is not Molly!* There were black wreaths on the railings in the street – and then a black wreath on Molly's door! *Dear God! Not William! Not William, so soon!* This was too cruel a homecoming.

The carriage came to a halt.

"Is this the house, lady?"

Antonia was staring at the door, and could not speak. The groom jumped down and ran up the three white steps to ring at the front door, but even before the peal of echoes had died away Benson, the housekeeper, had swung open the door, and hurried out in floods of tears.

"Oh Miss Antonia, thank goodness you've come. They wrote but we didn't think to see you for another week yet! It's the most awful thing; we just can't - " She continued to sob.

Antonia was numb, unable to move or speak. She gazed up at the house, at the crepe-shrouded windows, the mournful laurels.

"When - When did it happen?" she managed at last, her heart breaking. "Does his father know? How did his aunt take the news?"

Benson seemed confused now as well as distressed. "It happened two days ago. That – that silly little dog of hers was to blame, you know, running about - and what we are to do with the creature, I don't know. I can't abide the sight of it now." The housekeeper wiped her eyes. "But what news, Miss? Was there some other bad news? Whose father do you mean?"

"Why, the Colonel's father, of course. Sir John. I don't quite understand. Presumably he heard the news first?"

"Oh yes, Madam. We wrote to him first of all, and then to you, but this was only Tuesday. Did you get our letter?"

"No, no, I had no letter. I left York on Monday afternoon, hoping to see – Hoping– How could I know . . . ?" She covered her mouth with her hand.

"No one could know, Madam. It was the awfullest thing. Lady Molly came out of the drawing room, crying and taking on, something about a letter, and that little dog was rushing about under her feet, barking, and she couldn't have seen him, and she tripped and fell. Every stair, and us all there in the hall watching and not able to do a thing about it. And the Colonel only just left the house a half hour before!" Benson broke out sobbing yet again.

"She fell? Is she hurt? Oh, let us go into the house," Antonia urged, not knowing what to make of what she was hearing. She hurried into the hall. The housekeeper flew after her.

"Miss Antonia, you don't understand! Lady Molly is dead! She fell; she tripped over that silly dog, and fell. She died here in the hall, at the bottom of the stairs there!"

"Molly, dead? Ah no! No!" Antonia grasped the back of a chair, swaying, as she comprehended what she was being told. Tears spilled over, as a very real grief struggled with a jolt of heartfelt and joyous relief. "But then - the Colonel . . . ?"

" . . . is on his way to Flanders. He left on Monday, just before the accident. He doesn't know yet. He'll be heartbroken."

Once again Antonia's hand went to her mouth. "But not Molly! Not Molly! Oh, Benson, it can't be true!" She put her arms round the sobbing housekeeper, aware that in spite of the loss of her dearest friend, she must remain in tight control of her emotions. It would be simply too much to bear if she did not do so. But inwardly she wept. *Why Molly? Why now? She was always so full of life! What are we to do without her?*

At length, Antonia heard the whole story, but what was the letter that had fussed Molly to her death, and where was it now? There was half a letter on Molly's desk and Antonia picked it up listlessly, but it made no real sense. It was certainly nothing William might have penned.

'This may be what you have been waiting for all this time, my dear,' the note ran, in Molly's handwriting. *'Be patient a little longer.'*

It was not patently addressed to Antonia and made no sense even if it had been. What might have been awaited so long? Only William to reconsider what he wanted from his life, and the hope it would include her. Was that what Molly had meant? But it was not a letter, more a note. And William had been in the house only a short while before. To make his farewells, Antonia guessed, though there were none for her. Not a letter, not a word. Her heart ached for him, but he was safe, for a while at least. His father would break the news of his aunt's death. Should she write too? When he had left without a word for her? How did one write such a letter?

Sir John arrived from Kent the following day, looking more aged than ever. His beloved son had returned to duty, and his long-estranged sister had been killed in a stupid fall. He was sick with worry for William, and full of regrets for the years that had been lost. He seemed glad to see Antonia and spoke to her of William's departure.

"I once cherished the hope that you and he . . . You must forgive me if I speak plainly, my dear, I am too old to dissemble . . . that you and he might make some kind of life together, you know. It would have made me very happy. But he wouldn't have it, said his independence was too precious! His life is more precious. I hope it may be spared him!"

Speechless, Antonia took his dry, thin hand in hers, and remembered Sergio Tavares. Sir John seemed so much frailer since they had last met, and feeling ringed round with tragedy, she prayed he would see his son return.

The funeral was held at Bartonhurst. The service was attended by Molly's many friends and admirers, but Antonia was the only female present, and she did not accompany the hearse to the interment in the family plot, waiting instead in the hall for the gentlemen's return, and thankful that the library had not been considered appropriate for such a gathering. She was so sick at heart she could hardly function, and speech was almost beyond her. Those who knew her as Molly's companion were very kind, George Boscawen was particularly attentive, and somehow Antonia got through the day by doing what she could to ease the burden on Molly's beloved brother, imagining how much worse he must be feeling.

She was surprised late in the afternoon to be called into the study after many of the mourners had departed, and found Sir John there with one or two other gentlemen and Molly's lawyer. Molly's will had just been read, and it appeared that while the Hampshire estate was to go to the eldest of her naval nephews, the house in London had been left in entirety to her, with sufficient income for its upkeep. Antonia was stunned. Molly had never mentioned such likelihood, and Antonia had never imagined such a thing could happen. She had already steeled herself to return to Yorkshire if her brother in law would have her back, at least until she could find some position or employment where she might be accommodated. The alternative had been her father's house, but now there was Henrietta Place. It was too much.

"Molly wanted you to have some peace," Sir John said, smiling bravely, "but you know you will always have a place here if you are tired of living alone."

Antonia hardly knew how to express her gratitude. But she reminded herself that this dear man was William's father, and now Molly was dead and if William did not choose to continue their friendship, the connection was almost severed. "Perhaps you will visit London more often," she told him through lips that were almost numb. "The house will always be at your disposal."

"I'm afraid, my dear, I am likely to visit even less than before," he said sadly. "This terrible business has taken it out of me more than I would have believed. And not to know what is become of my son . . . "

"We have only to wait, Sir John, and hope for the best."

CHAPTER FORTY TWO

Slowly the days passed. Initial numbness was replaced by a sense of unreality. Antonia had suffered grief before, but she had had the support of sympathetic allies, first Sister Jerome and the nuns at the convent, and then Beatriz and Baltasar. Her heart ached for her friend. Molly was a terrible loss, and Antonia had never felt so alone. She had even had to send away the little spaniel. The servants blamed him for their mistress's death and cursed him at every turn, and the sight of his confused, miserable face as he hid from them all was almost more than Antonia could bear. She sent him down to Bridge House where she thought he might be happier, and the house was even lonelier without him.

No news came from the Continent to Henrietta Place. Sir John told her he had had a brief unhappy note from his son in Brussels following the news of Molly's accident, but did not expect to hear again - and Antonia did not write. William had far more serious matters to concern him now; he had shut her out of his life. That he had not made any effort to contact her before or since leaving for Flanders was the hardest reality to face and seemed to give the lie to his desire to remain friends. She tried to harden her heart against any more pain and grew frail and brittle. She threw herself now into her efforts to alleviate the suffering of those veterans who could not be recalled to service, telling herself that every one helped was one less on her conscience. Lord Boscawen continued to be an energetic and loyal ally to her cause, providing funds, useful contacts and advice. He would have liked to have been more, and tried to engage Antonia's interest, suggesting outings and visits. She was grateful for his help, but remained polite and indifferent. He assumed it was grief over Molly's death, and was undeterred.

"Whatever happened to that nephew of Molly's?" he asked once. "In the military, wasn't he? Always got the impression he didn't like me much. A bit over-familiar that last occasion, ma'am, didn't you think? What happened to him? He's off, fighting Boney with the Duke, isn't he?" Antonia murmured some non-committal reply. "Thought he was rather struck at the time," he went on. "Admire the feller though. Not many would care to be in his shoes just now. They have to make a better go of thrashing Napoleon this time.

Can't let him win! Disaster! But then I hear the danger may have passed. Brussels and the Low Countries are well guarded now."

The young, under-strength battalions that had been hurriedly dispatched from England were being joined every week by the veteran regiments that had driven the French from Spain and Portugal and were now returning from America. More than half a million men mobilised by the sovereigns of Europe were also on the march, closing in on the frontiers of France. No official state of war existed as yet. The French might even throw Napoleon out themselves and avoid the threat of invasion.

Antonia took some comfort in the fact that so far in the past few weeks there had been no fighting. If stories were to be believed Brussels was as gay as London and just as secure. Perhaps it was a false alarm and the battalions would soon be home again. She steeled herself against any further news, and went on with her half-hearted, half-dead existence.

By the end of June, it was all over. The battle to end all battles had been fought, and barely won. Wellington was victorious and Napoleon had fled. The trampled cornfields of Waterloo were soaked in blood, Brussels stank of gangrene, and the British Army entered Paris for the first time since Agincourt. Slowly, slowly the troops came home.

For a week or more Antonia lived on a knife-edge, aware that the battle had been won at a terrible cost. Fifteen thousand of Wellington's army were lying dead, dying or wounded, and she had no idea where William Hurst came in that list. Sir John had made enquiries but had no news for her either.

At last a letter came.

William wrote in mid July to let his father know that he was well, and hoped to be returning within three months. Antonia could scarcely contain her joy and relief. If William was spared, nothing else mattered. He was safe and would be coming home.

This new lightening in her spirits prompted George Boscawen to press her once more to attend the theatre with him. Surprised, she agreed and found it mildly entertaining, and in his Lordship's undemanding company she managed to forget for a while the hours of grief and worry. He invited her again, and together they attended one of the victory balls – though Antonia would not dance – and she found she could function on a different level if she steeled herself to be gay and inconsequential. She tried not to notice that his Lordship was becoming increasingly attached to her. When he suggested attending another such Ball, she lightly agreed to accompany him, but was taken aback when, halfway through the evening, Boscawen drew her into a quiet corner, dropped to one knee, and solemnly proposed marriage.

"I think we should suit each other very well, Antonia. You must know how fond I have become of you. You'd want for nothing, you know."

Antonia looked down into his earnest, handsome face, and was suddenly overcome with guilt. He had been the most tremendous help to her in all sorts of ways, but how wrong she had been to let matters come to this pass. Was it possible that she could accept him? He would be an amiable husband. A kind, good man.

But one for whom she felt nothing. So now she must hurt and offend him, for had she not once declared she could not think of marrying without love.

He took her gentle refusal like the gentleman he was, but it was obvious that he was deeply disappointed. Rising to his feet, and brushing his knees, he said he hoped that one day she might reconsider; would always remain her devoted servant. By mutual consent however, they agreed that they would not now stay on to supper and that he would escort her back to Henrietta Place.

On their way through the ballroom Antonia, all too conscious that she had behaved very badly, became slowly aware that there was a ripple of anticipation in the air. People were murmuring in excitement.

"The Regiments are nearly all returned," she heard someone say. "Some of the officers are here in London. They may attend tonight."

Antonia fought to remain calm, but even as she passed steadily through the crowd she struggled with the desire to rush away, to return to Henrietta Place to see if there was further news; to hear that William was home, safe, unwounded. But that desire was inappropriate, she reminded herself, and should be suppressed, especially since she was in another gentleman's company. A gentleman she had just refused.

In due course she would hear from Sir John. In due course, she would call. It would be impolite to do otherwise. What else could she do? She could not imagine what she might say if she ever saw

William Hurst again. 'He is only someone I used to know,' she told herself desperately. 'I can, I must, be sensible.'

And so she endured the glittering scene, and the conversation of those who gathered now round Boscawen on the first floor landing to discuss the war, and tried to avoid all reference to those officers she knew.

It was not long before there was a buzz through the rooms, and at once most of the ladies and many of the gentlemen hurried away to overlook the hall below. People were drawn downstairs to greet and congratulate the new arrivals. It was impossible, Antonia realised, to ignore the interest. She would not join the others in craning to see them, but her heart thudded in anticipation. William might be amongst them. If not tonight, then soon. Most regiments would be home soon. At some point she must see him again.

"Will you not welcome them back, Mrs Davenport? Daresay the sight of you will make 'em feel it was all worth fighting for."

Antonia tried to smile at the gallant compliment from her disappointed suitor, but against her will was drawn to the vast lobby. Against her will, she took in the flashes of scarlet and green and blue and gold amongst the satins, and brocades. William's regiment. Antonia turned away. Her hands were clammy, her breath rapid. She was shaking. Against her will, Antonia turned to look over her shoulder, and caught her breath.

He was there! In dress uniform, tall, and upright, fair hair gleaming brighter than the gold of his braided shoulders, William Hurst made his way into the lobby with his fellow officers, at his side a young, pretty woman in a pink gown. It had been almost a year since Antonia had last seen him, and her heart was turning somersaults. She did not realise she was holding her breath until dizziness overtook her. She put out a hand to the nearby balustrade while her eyes feasted on the sight of him, safe and sound. "William," she whispered. "Thank God."

He seemed to catch sight of her, but as he started forward the girl beside him laid a little hand on his sleeve, reached up and whispered in his ear. He halted, startled at first, then Antonia saw him pat her hand, the ring finger of which bore a gleaming band of gold.

Antonia stood frozen as the crowd around her surged and flowed down the staircase. He was safe. She could leave now.

CHAPTER FORTY THREE

Appalled, William watched Antonia vanish into the crowd. For a minute he could not speak, and he did not hear the plaintive voice of the young lady beside him. Eventually she pulled at his sleeve.

"William, dear, where is John? You said we should meet here, and I do not see him anywhere."

"Fanny, something has happened. I have to leave you." He gazed around him distractedly. "John will be here directly, I am sure."

"But - but I do not know anyone here but you and John. Please don't leave me, William."

"But - Oh, thank God, there he is! He is here, Fanny. Forgive me, I must go." William left Frances Cunningham to her husband and hurried towards the stairs, impeded by people he did not know, wanting to congratulate him on the outcome of the battle they had taken no part in. He struggled up the stairs and through the rooms, growing increasingly distressed.

He had not come intending to search her out. He had been warned that the lovely Mrs Davenport seemed to have become quite *distrait*, but when he'd learned that it was likely she would be present, he could not keep away. So he had come, hoping to see her but not knowing what sort of reception he might receive at her hands. He had been crushed by the fact that, while he had laid open his heart in his letter Antonia had never replied, and while he told himself he deserved no better, he had hoped she might realise how his feelings had changed. He'd found it impossible to keep her from his thoughts, though he had tried, and in spite of all the events of the last few months. It seemed she had quite forgotten him.

He had felt his heart leap at the sight of her face, suddenly illuminated with joy and pleasure, but before he knew it she had turned to the man beside her, said a few words, and moved away. Had that been George Boscawen with her?

Now he didn't know what to think. Had Antonia come to the Ball with George Boscawen? Why had she left? Had she misinterpreted his own appearance with Frances Cunningham? Did she care enough to mind?

All he wanted was to talk to her again and explain himself. But she was nowhere to be found.

*

William hardly slept that night, and next morning was pacing the pavement in Henrietta Place, for he'd been told the house was now Antonia's and he might find her there. He remembered she was an early riser, and wanted to be sure of being admitted as soon as the household had come properly to life, so on the dot of nine he rang the bell, repeating over and over to himself what he would say when he was admitted.

It was a relief when the door swung open at last to the impassive face of Molly's old butler, Rigsby. Just for a moment there was a flash of expression in the servant's face before he spoke.

"Colonel, good day to you. May I say how very – how exceedingly thankful we all are to have you home again."

"Thank you, Rigsby. I have come . . . "

"I – I regret Madame is not at home this morning, Colonel . . . "

For one terrible moment, William thought that perhaps Antonia had spent the night elsewhere. "She didn't come home?"

"She is not *at* home," Rigsby corrected him.

Then she was in the house, William thought, with relief and shame for having thought otherwise. "But I am particularly anxious to see her, Rigsby." He detained the servant with a hand. "Please," he said, earnestly, "Please ask her to spare me a few moments."

The man looked troubled. "She said no one, Colonel." But he opened the door all the same, and gestured for William to step inside.

It was obvious something was astir. There were two large boxes, banded, standing in the hall, and the urgent sound of voices above stairs. Rigsby however did not mount the staircase but went into one of ground floor rooms. A maid came out as he went in, a basket of books in her arms, and bobbed an awkward curtsey to William before setting the basket next to the boxes and running on up the stairs. Puzzled and apprehensive, William looked around him. Rigsby reappeared, his expression resigned and regretful, and William knew at once what message he had been told to deliver. He forestalled the speech.

"What's happening, Rigsby? Is Mrs Davenport travelling again?"

The butler was plainly uncomfortable now and seemed not to know how to answer. Taking a deep breath, William strode towards the drawing room. "I will see her," he insisted over his shoulder, as Rigsby came hurrying after him, and he threw open the double doors and went in.

By the fireplace, on a small stepladder, stood Antonia, pale and strained, half-turned to the door. She had several slim volumes from the bookshelf in her hands, but at William's challenging look, dropped them abruptly into a basket at her feet. If it had ever occurred to her that she might have fallen out of love with William Hurst, she knew in that moment how wrong she was.

"Antonia, where are you going?"

She struggled to keep her composure. "I am not at home, Colonel. Rigsby?" But her man had already thought better of following the Colonel and was not to be seen.

"Antonia." His voice was low but firm. "What is this? I know we have not seen each other for some long months now, and terrible things have happened in the meantime, but last night when I hoped I might speak with you at long last, you had suddenly disappeared. I know you saw me. Now you tell Rigsby you won't receive me. What is happening? Are you planning to go somewhere? Why? Where? *Where* are you going? And will you come down from that ladder!"

Shocked by his appearance in the rooms that had once been Molly's, this flurry of questions was too much for Antonia. She did not even know William had seen her the previous evening, and she half fell down the steps at the commanding tone. "Away. Abroad!" she answered in a rush, fending off his approach. "I don't know. Back to Portugal. I don't know! Away." Her voice trembled and died.

"Back to Portugal? Is that why – is that why you never responded to my letter?" His expression altered. "You're not going back to da Fonte?"

"Baltasar?" Antonia's face must have mirrored her astonishment. She felt herself colour violently. "Of course not! How you could you think so?"

"How?" William raked fingers through his hair. "I don't know. I hardly know what to think any more." More calmly he asked: "Then where?"

"I- I – don't – the convent perhaps . . . "

"The convent!" he repeated in disbelief "But why? Antonia, you cannot return. The war is only just over. Why go? Why must you leave England at all?"

She faced him. "There is nothing to keep me here."

"Nothing?" he faltered. "I know you must miss Molly terribly, Antonia. I shall miss her too. I cared for her as you did - but even so you have many friends . . . "

"I - I have no friends in England," she got out, "for whom I care so greatly that I would wish to remain."

He seemed to find it as hard to speak. "None? You don't consider me then?" He swallowed. "You don't care enough to remain even for my sake?"

Unsteadily, Antonia managed to reply, "To tell the truth, sir, I - I have found it better to have no feelings with regard to you."

William felt his heart sink. *Oh Antonia, don't. Don't say that.* "If this should have anything to do with last night," he began, "I can explain if you will let me."

She lifted her chin. "Please don't feel any need to do so," she murmured.

"I owe you an explanation if what I do causes you distress. If you are unhappy, then I must be concerned."

"I - I am happy to know you are s-safely returned," she began, then fixed her glance upon the carpet, and would not meet his eyes again.

"The lady with me was John Cunningham's wife, Fanny. You remember John, Antonia? You remember we talked of his marriage before. He was not free until midnight, and he asked me to escort Fanny. We came together. I came with her as a favour to them both."

She looked up at last into his face, uncertain. "To tell the truth, I was hardly aware that you were in company, sir, so there is no nothing to explain," she repeated.

"But there is!" His strong, warm hands captured her pale, cold ones, and he made her look at him.

There was utter silence. Had there been, just for a moment then - a gleam of something like hope in her eyes? William saw with a sense of despair that it had died to a shadow almost at once, as Antonia turned her face away.

"We have not met in almost a year, William. In all that time there has been no word from you, not even after Molly died, although you wrote to your father." The quiet words grew fainter. "I do not recall that you even bade me farewell."

His grip on her fingers tightened. "I might say the same, Antonia. And I have been to hell and back. But I hoped you would understand what I was trying to say in my letter." He stooped to look into her face. "I am here now. Are you not in the least glad to see me?"

"Of course I am glad!" she answered passionately. "Glad to see you returned at last, safe and whole! Thankful that you survived, and are able to return to your father who was sick with anxiety for you. All your friends are glad to see you!"

"Nothing more than that? Is that why you made no response to my letter?" he wondered. "It was brief, I know, but I had hoped – Did Molly never explain how I felt, how loth I was to leave without a word of farewell? But the letter, I hoped would make it plain . . . "

"You keep speaking of a note, a letter? What . . . ?"

"Why, the letter I left in Molly's hands for you when I left, of course. We were called away so suddenly. I knew she would see you first. I had no time to do more than scribble those few words at her desk, and entrust them to her. They were miserably few, I confess, and I made a very poor job of it, evidently. I hoped they expressed what I was feeling but – But evidently not."

" Y -you wrote? You wrote to me before you left England?"

"Why yes, as I said. A few lines. "

"I had no letter from Molly."

"I entrusted it to her the night I left for Flanders. You had disappeared. I didn't know where you were. Molly said you were still in Yorkshire . . . "

Antonia remembered. Had she not rushed back to London only to find him gone? And Molly dead.

"B-but Molly's accident," she faltered, "happened before my return. She never spoke again. I know nothing of any letter, none was left." *Benson crying. Molly flying out of her room, distraught. 'The letter. Catch the letter!' But there was only a line or two from Molly on the desk. What had happened to the letter?* Antonia looked out of the window, where the wind rustled the branches beyond the open sash. "There was no letter," she whispered. She freed her hands and walked some steps apart.

"You believed I had deserted you without a word? And I misunderstood, and when you did not respond I thought my letter unwelcome."

"M- might the window have been open that day?" Antonia had laced her fingers, was pressing them to her breast.

"The window? What . . . ?" William frowned. "I believe it was open, though I expect Molly would soon have closed it. There was a March wind. I nearly lost my hat as I left, but . . . " He suddenly seemed to understand what the question meant. "Antonia . . . "

"What did your letter say, William?"

She felt him step after her, felt his hands on her shoulders as he turned her to him. The early sunlight pouring into the room laid bare the emotion in his grave blue eyes. Quietly, he answered, "That I had been a fool long enough. That it had taken me until then to realise how necessary you are to my happiness."

Giddy with apprehension and longing, Antonia felt his fingers gentle on her hair as he smoothed it back from her upturned face. "I said I could hardly bear to leave England knowing that I might not return, might never voice my feelings for you." He took a deep breath. "But I am here as you see. Fate has been kind - and I can tell you now, face to face, Antonia. I love you. Perhaps I have always done so."

She let out her breath in a little shuddering sigh, felt his hand curve down over her cheek till it held her chin. He tilted her face to him.

"Have you nothing to say?" He sounded unsure of himself, anxious.

"I thought you cared nothing for me. I thought you had gone away without a word, never knowing I loved you so. Oh, William!" She pressed her cheek to his chest. Her present happiness, and the so-near-loss of it, gave the words the edge of a sob.

He pulled her closer. "Then you do care for me?" he said, huskily. "God, I hardly dared hope after all that has occurred between us." He released her briefly only to take her face once again in his hands, his fingers deep in the gold of her hair. "Antonia, dearest love."

She lifted her mouth to his, and he bent his head and kissed her.

His lips were as warm and as sweet as ever and for a few minutes they were oblivious to everything, locked together, the months of misunderstanding and heartache melting away as if they had never been. When they broke apart it was with a sigh.

"I love you so very much, Antonia," he said, seeming to revel in the confession. "All this time I've been such an idiot. My father said as much. I thought I knew better. I thought there was no place in my life for this, for love, and told him so." He searched her face. "I feared you had overheard what I said to him. That New Year, you remember, at Bartonhurst? You smoothed over an argument on that very subject. I don't suppose you remember." He sighed. "And then we spoke. You seemed so cool for so long afterwards. I think it was then that I began to realise what I might lose."

"I do remember," Antonia admitted. "And I did overhear that conversation with your father William. I did not intend it . . ." She shook her head at his horrified expression. "I heard what you had been discussing - it was almost unavoidable. You remember I had gone to fetch the spectacles your father mislaid. I heard my name, and almost at once your words, and though I wanted to retreat I could not move. I confess I felt so wounded and awkward, aware I had misinterpreted your attentions, but I saw that you had your reasons, and I thought then that you could never love me except as a friend, so - I determined to be no more than a friend." She buried her forehead in his coat. "I never could manage it," she whispered, "so I thought it would be simpler if I went away for a while. When I heard news of the mobilisation I flew back to London but you had gone. And Molly was dead. I thought," she added quietly, "I should die of grief."

"Oh, sweet, I did not mean to make life more distressing. I will do everything I can to ensure you are never again made unhappy." William bent his head to kiss her lips again. "I love you, Antonia. Forgive me for taking so long to realise it."

Wonderingly, she reached out to caress his cheek, and he seized her hand and raised it to his lips. "What a fist I made of that proposal I made you at New Year. No wonder you wanted nothing more to do with me!" He had caught both her hands in his. "But you'll marry me now? Say you will, Antonia?"

"Yes. I will marry you."

He gave a great sigh of satisfaction and pressed a kiss into her curls. "Then you have made me — and my father — very happy!" he joked, his voice soft.

Antonia smiled tremulously back at him. "I am very fond of your father. But William, will you leave him again? Am I to be a soldier's wife?"

"I shan't ask that of you, darling girl. You know the Navy, and the Army, will be first to be pared, now success is assured. Those that fought with me are unlikely to get either pension or medal, and I expect to be discharged any day now, together with the finest army England has ever had. But it will not come as hard to me now as it did before. I have seen enough fighting to last me the rest of my life."

"Yes," she said quietly.

"Shall we be staid lords of the Manor at Bartonhurst then?" he wondered, a little later, half-smiling, his heart half melted with desire. "You won't miss my red coat? Shall I be a farmer, managing my estate, and acting Justice of the Peace? Can you really be happy, Antonia, as the Squire's wife, content to visit the parish, and manage his house?" Shakily, his fingers traced the outlines of her lips, unsteady with wanting her. She caught his hand.

"Yes," she said again. "Yes."

"But would you still want to continue helping those unfortunate and forgotten casualties of war as you have been doing? Oh, don't look so alarmed, my love. Because I can help you now. I would like to help you now. But I shall need practice, 'Tonia," he admitted. "This will be a new beginning for me."

"For us both. A new life for us both," she promised.

"The Peace is hard won. We have been at war a long time now."

"If we two have made peace, *Captain* Hurst, perhaps there is hope for us all?" She smiled, but her eyes were dark and serious.

"I think with you beside me anything is possible, Antonia," he said softly, and took her in his arms once more.

THE END